ALSO BY ELLEN COONEY

A Private Hotel for Gentle Ladies

Gun Ball Hill

Small Town Girl

All the Way Home

The Old Ballerina

The White Palazzo

Lambrusco

Lambrusco

BY

Ellen Cooney

PANTHEON BOOKS • NEW YORK

This is a work of fiction. Names, characters, places, and incidents either are the product of the author's imagination or are used fictitiously. Any resemblance to actual persons, living or dead, events, or locales is entirely coincidental.

 Published in the United States by Pantheon Books, a division of Random House, Inc., New York, and in Canada by Random House of Canada Limited, Toronto.

Pantheon Books and colophon are registered trademarks of Random House, Inc.

Library of Congress Cataloging-in-Publication Data
Cooney, Ellen.
Lambrusco / Ellen Cooney.
p. cm.
ISBN-13: 978-0-375-42496-0
1. World War, 1939–1945—Underground movements—Fiction.
2. Intelligence officers—Fiction. I. Title.
PS3553.O5788G86 2004
813'.54—dc22 2007015270

www.pantheonbooks.com

Printed in the United States of America

First Edition

2 4 6 8 9 7 5 3 1

To my son, Michael

with thanks and appreciation to my mother,
Viola Garofoli Cooney

and to Gabriella Ambrosioni and Antonio Selvatici
who believed in this book before
I ever wrote a word of it.

Glittering air, the sun so clear
you seek flowering apricot trees
and hawthorn, for that bitter scent of the heart.

But the trees are dry, and the stiff plants
undercut calmness. The sky is empty.
Under your pounding feet, it seems the land is hollow.

A hush, all around.
Only, in the rising wind, faraway songs . . .

—Giovanni Pascoli

Every love is a shield against sadness,
a silent step in the dark.

—Salvatore Quasimodo

Cast of Characters

Lucia Fantini, soprano
Aldo Fantini, her late husband, founder of Aldo's Restaurant
Giuseppe (Beppi, Beppino) Fantini, their son, manager of Aldo's, founder of partisan squad
Marcellina Galeffi, their housekeeper
Ugo Fantini, physician, Aldo's cousin
Annmarie Malone, professional golfer, member of U.S. Army Intelligence

Vito Nizarro, headwaiter at Aldo's, partisan
Mauro Pattuelli, waiter, partisan
Carmella Pattuelli, partisan radio operator, his wife
Marco, Francesca, Mario, Sandro, Rudino, Antonella, Alda, Lucianna, Giuseppina, their children
Cesare Morigi, waiter, amateur baritone, partisan
Ermanno Vizioli (Zoli), waiter, partisan
Cenzo Ballardini, waiter, partisan
Assunta Ballardini, egg dealer, his wife
Pia Ballardini, their daughter, a deaf-mute
Lido (Cherubino, Bino) Linari, waiter, partisan
Geppo Ravaglia, waiter, amateur archaeologist, partisan
Tito Roncuzzi, butcher, partisan
Tom Tully (Tullio Tomasini), Annmarie's fiancé, U.S. Army Intelligence officer
Etto Renzetti, factory owner, partisan
Frank Lamb, American soldier, truck driver

Peewee Wilkins, American soldier, jockey
Annunziata Galimberti, eldest member of the Galimberti family
Pippo & Giorgio, her great-nephews, thieves, partisans
Ignazio Innamorato (Polpo), fisherman
Giuseppe Verdi, composer
Giacomo Puccini, composer
Gioacchino Rossini, composer
Enrico Caruso, tenor

Eliana Fantini, Ugo's wife; Don Enzo Malfada, priest; Franco Calderoni (Nomad), waiter, partisan; Galto Saponi, Carmella's father, fisherman, partisan; Mariano Minzoni, head of the kitchen at Aldo's; Gigi Solferino, Fausto Fabbi, Romano Buffardi, cooks; Ferro Pincelli, waiter, former soldier, partisan; Rico, his brother, apprentice cook; Teo Batarra, pharmacist, partisan; Emilio, his brother, tobacco shop owner, partisan; Berto Venturoli, his son Adriano, Nico, Lolo, Fusi, Toto, Braccini & Cardella, farmers, partisans; Valentina Roncuzzi, the butcher's teenage daughter; Brunella Vizioli, Zoli's mother, enemy of Marcellina

Lambrusco

1

ON THE TRAIN the whole world was the train.

No noise from the corridor. The other passengers had settled in. The door of my compartment was closed. The conductor had already been through. I was only traveling locally, going home, but nothing was normal; every journey was complicated.

No police, no soldiers. It was almost easy to forget that if it weren't for soldiers and police, the trains would not be running.

My papers were in order. Lucia Fantini of Mengo. Age fifty-five. Born a Sicilian. The lady with the voice at Aldo's. Widow of Aldo, mother of Beppi.

No problems: just a couple of brief confrontations. The usual. I knew how to raise my guard graciously, so the barriers didn't show. To make it seem I'd said yes, when saying no.

"Excuse me, Signora Fantini, it's a great piece of luck we've run into you. As hurried as you are, could you pause two minutes to sing something complimentary? Tomorrow's our wedding anniversary, ten years. My husband was with the army in Africa. He doesn't like to talk about it, in fact he doesn't talk at all. It's the same as if they cut out his tongue. But look, his ears are wide open. Just one short song, something lively?"

"Signora, pardon me, one night I heard you sing at your husband's place which became your son's, I'm sorry the Fascists took it, the bastards. In the company of my in-laws who were paying, as I'd never afford it myself, I thought only of an expensive dinner. No one warned me that Aldo's had singing from the operas of our country. Sitting there unaware, I was destroyed for any voice except your own, and don't bother thanking me for a compliment. It's a fact. May the soul of your husband rest in peace, although truthfully, one doubts that it can, if he knows what's going on. But I trust that one day soon, your splendid restaurant will come back to your family."

The anxiety of departure was over. No mechanical trouble, no schedule changes, no last-minute boardings, no unexplained delay.

My two shopping bags were from a fashionable dress shop in Bologna, but they were heavy; they contained two sacks of flour. There was still black market flour to be bought. Buried inside, one to each sack, were German guns—Lugers, which my son called "useful, no-fuss bang-bangs, courtesy of our invaders."

I minded the strain of making it seem that all I carried were tissue-wrapped dresses. In my purse were sturdy little cardboard boxes from a well-known confectioner's, as if I planned to stuff myself with candy. The boxes were packed with ammunition.

I was too hot in my good wool coat. I should have worn something lighter, but the wool had the biggest pockets, for a pair of Berettas, as simple and small as two toys. One was wrapped in my blue and orange silk scarf, an end of which streamed from the pocket elegantly, like a fashion statement. The other was covered by a pair of gloves and some balled-up handkerchiefs.

Our bank accounts were frozen. I had paid the gun-and-flour merchant with a pair of Aldo's gold cuff links. We were running out of jewelry. I no longer wore my wedding ring, but refused to give it up.

I wore no makeup. Sweat, and the possibility of tears, would have ruined it. I hated going out of the house like this, in this particular nakedness, and I was careful to avoid all mirrors. My throat was dry, and so were my lips and mouth, but not because I was thirsty. It was stage fright, the same old symptoms. Sometimes in the spotlight at Aldo's, I'd feel I had swallowed a handful of sand.

But here I was, doing this again, pulling it off again: a lady out shopping, oh, there's nowhere to go to dress up for, and I shouldn't be spending what little money I have, but it came to me this morning that I should spit in the eyes of the war and buy myself something nice—and anyway, I was fed up with how the only other women going into good shops were women of *nazifascisti*.

The curtain on the compartment window, tattered and grimy, had been lifted, tucked back by some other passenger. I left it that way.

The train progressed slowly past narrow country roads, wide fields, closed-up houses, trees, Nazi trucks, Nazi tanks, Nazi soldiers in casual groups, smoking cigarettes, their helmets tipped back as if they were working on suntans.

It had rained heavily the day before, but now it was dry and shiny and clear. A perfect November morning, 1943. Every few miles, a small, fluffy pillow of a cloud came into view, framed by the window like a painting.

I thought only of home. This was Aldo's birthday, his seventy-fifth. Just because he wasn't alive was no reason not to acknowledge it.

Three-fourths of a century. A milestone.

I'd made up my mind to be festive about it, and not to let it bother me that Beppi's reason for sneaking to the house later on would be simply to pick up the guns. There was no electricity—it had gone off a month ago. We were nearly out of candles. There wasn't any meat, fish, or bread.

But tonight there'd be a real meal, although the pasta wouldn't take the form of *tagliatelle,* the egg-and-flour noodles Aldo had loved, like all Romagnans. There weren't eggs.

Marcellina Galeffi, our live-in housekeeper, had already cut up leeks for soup. There were tomatoes, chestnuts, artichokes, mushrooms, a few ends of cheese, a little oil, wine, basil, rosemary, and garlic.

Marcellina would do most of the cooking. She was right now at daily Mass in the village, safe with the priest, Don Enzo. "One of the good ones," she called him. She was crazy about him: a bookish, mild-tempered man, the same age as Beppi—they'd been at school together—but his opposite in every way.

Enzo would come for the dinner. His family, the Malfadas, were cheese people; they'd supplied the restaurant almost exclusively. Aldo, then Beppi, let Enzo eat for free whenever he wanted, which had been pretty much daily. He had a private table near the back. He used it as an extension of the little stone rectory where he lived, and the church as well.

Just yesterday he'd told Marcellina, as a matter of faith, it was reasonable to expect that, any day now, someone would stick a pin in the German Army, and also all the *fascisti,* plus Mussolini himself, and also Hitler. Pop-pop-pop-pop, and this nightmare would end, with four deflations, and finally his stomach would operate again at full steam.

God bless him, he'd touched Marcellina, no easy thing at her age; she was seventy-one. It was all she'd talk about: balloons, Enzo's belly, poppings. He'd made her feel tender, even though it only lasted one second.

I imagined the dinner preparations. I pictured my smooth old wood table.

In the center, a high mound of flour, volcano-shaped. At the top of the mound, an opening, exactly where lava would erupt.

It was always like this. I was born in a house facing Etna. I'd had plenty of time for my eyes to make imprints of the smooth Romagna hills, which never moved and never would, but still, if something was available to be formed in a mound—laundry, nuts, bittersweet greens from the garden, sticks for a fire, clams from the beach we couldn't go to anymore because of the war—my hands made that shape, sometimes pointed, and sometimes with the top leveled off. Even those fleshy spots at Aldo's hips were this way, another lifetime ago, the little mountains he called "the places where you like to hold on to me, not that either of them is where something important could burst from, heh heh heh."

As if that were the reason he'd grown so stout. To give me something to hold on to. He had died nearly four years ago, at home.

Not a surprise. His cousin Ugo, the only physician he'd let anywhere near him, had been saying for ages that if Aldo's chest were the hood of a car, he'd open it up to let everyone see that the engine was cracked and decrepit; the hoses were clogged beyond repair, and the whole thing was so dysfunctional, the only place it was headed was a junk heap. That was how he had put it. "Good thing you're not a car, Aldo."

At the moment of his heart attack, the fourth, the one that killed him, he was sitting at the table for lunch, drawing breath to blow on his soup, a fish broth made by Marcellina. He often had his midday meal at home before leaving for the restaurant. The soup was too hot; he'd been running late.

When the bowl crashed to the floor, it took Marcellina a

moment to turn around from the stove to see what had happened. She thought he'd thrown it down on purpose. She was waiting for him to shout at her.

Now every time the wind blew hard against the kitchen shutters, she announced with a sigh, "There's Aldo again, blowing. I'll go out and tell him to be quiet. He knows what the Blackshirts have done, but he's got to be patient, which maybe he'll manage in death, having failed at it in life."

Would Marcellina find milk in the village, to be mixed with water for the dough? She had taken some black market salt to be traded. There would have to be milk. Water into flour without eggs could be done, but water without milk?

I pictured a jug of milk and a saucepan of water heating up. Lacing the water with the milk. Not letting it come to a boil. Taking the pan off the stove. Bringing it to the flour. Tipping it over the mound, dead center. Pouring slowly: an eruption in reverse.

Marcellina would step in for the rough work: bending over the table, mixing and kneading, grunting from the effort, cursing. Until the last of the dough had been cut, she'd raise her creaky old voice—huge and a little raspy—against God, the Fantini family, her lot as a servant, her age, the hills, the farms, flour itself, Mengo, all Romagna, the Adriatic coast, and all of doomed, hapless, incompetent Italy. Against Germans and Fascists, she never spoke a word in the kitchen. She believed that if she did, the food would be poisoned.

Sunlight. Flour dust. A faint smell in the air of the sea. Mushrooms by the sink, waiting to be washed, with stems in the shape of bullets. Artichokes on the counter like a hill of spiny grenades.

A party to look forward to. No one in Aldo's chair. No one else ever sat there.

Beppi hadn't said what time he'd arrive, but surely he'd wait until evening. What if he showed up with the whole squad? There would not be enough food. They'd get five or six noodles apiece and start squabbling like children. Would Beppi be that impulsive, slinking down from the hills past the Germans with all of them?

They'd made up a song, a merry little tune, easy to whistle or hum. *Oh you ask me.*

The group didn't have a proper name. They called themselves "the Mengo squad, mostly composed of waiters."

Oh you ask me why I closed up my shop, why I brought up my boat to dry land, why I walked away from that restaurant . . .

Deep within the rhythm of locomotion, that song was with me.

Beppi had a version of his own, which he felt he deserved; he was the leader of the squad. He used to pace around the house in a frenzy, muttering his own lines roughly.

It wasn't really singing; he had no voice. He tapped out the rhythm on the back of his father's chair, or on the top of his own head where, to his horror, at thirty-four, he was balding: I'm a partisan because I want my lights back on, I want fish from my beach, I want gas for my car, I want them out of my restaurant. I want to be back there myself, doing what I learned from my father, which is overcharging my customers, making money, chasing women whom I don't want to marry, hearing my mother sing, and exploiting my lazy waiters and cooks with all my heart.

There were many more lines, some of which he cut short if I entered the room, but I didn't have to hear them to know what they were: I'm a partisan the way two good ears would put up a fight to not be deaf, because the sound of my mother not singing is like looking up at a tower, waiting for the ring of the bell, waiting and waiting, although they told me the clapper was muffled, it was useless, it was wrapped in some kind of shroud.

"I'm going on strike." I'd announced it like a vow. No discussion.

One day early last spring a young Fascist showed up. He was barely twenty; his chubby cheeks were as smooth as apples. I knew him. His father, a longtime widower, not a Fascist, was with the railway. His mother had died of pneumonia when he was small. An aunt of his—the mother's sister-in-law, whom he kept no ties to—used to be a work-at-home baker for Aldo's: a cake woman.

A couple of high-ranked officers had paid the aunt a call, demanding her services, as in, "Here is a list of the types of cakes you will make for us, starting immediately." She showed them the scars and blisters all over her hands—ugly things, beet-red and almost leprous. She couldn't wrap them in bandages for fear of gangrene, and it wasn't from burning herself. It was worse; it was a horrible disease, perhaps contagious. The officers hurried away.

I was the one to apply the makeup to those hands. After all my years in the spotlight, I knew a few things about cosmetics.

The young Fascist wasn't in uniform. He wore an ordinary jersey, as if he were headed for a game of soccer. But he also had his boots on, newly polished. A revolver was on his hip. He kept touching it nervously, as if it itched, and he couldn't not scratch it.

An invitation. A banquet, with guests of the German Army.

Respectful. Earnest. He was a fan. He had a speech in his head, delivered like a recitation at school.

"Signora Fantini, I once heard you sing in your late husband's *trattoria* by the shore, as long ago as that, before he moved up in the world to have a grand, well-known restaurant, named Aldo for himself, which your son made twice as successful, as young as he is. I'm sorry that, due to needs of our government, he's no longer in charge of it, not that I've had the pleasure of a meal there, as it's a mess hall for officers only. When I heard you sing, although I don't recall what the tunes were, I said to my mother and father, because we'd just got a power line to our house, 'I feel that this beautiful lady is singing to us like electricity, but without any wires or plugs.' "

"My voice, unfortunately," I answered, "is not what it was. It's full of static these days."

"I'm told it has aged like the best of wines."

"You were misinformed."

"Signora, please, I'm not insensitive to the personal struggle you may feel, because of the location of where they want you to come. It would be wise of you not to refuse them. I've been instructed to ask you, how is your son? It's been said he's not well."

Beppi was living at home then, pretending to be a lunatic. The squad was just beginning to be formed.

All through the visit, Beppi walked around in the nut orchard, briskly. Now and then, as if some inner peasant self of his had kicked in, he pulled at weeds or tall grasses; he swung his arm like someone who held a machete. He was out of breath in five minutes, but he put up a good front.

Marcellina stepped forward to answer the young Fascist's question, and the others he came up with. There was never only one.

Look, out the window. Look at poor Beppino in the orchard—we let him out for exercise. You can see for yourself what sort of state he's in since the change in command of the restaurant, not that I'm bringing up that subject. No work. No women to pay lavish attention to. He's taking it personally, what else could one expect? He's nonpolitical; his whole existence is his work. He has become unbalanced. Soldiers everywhere; he can't remember why. We give him medications; he has to be treated like an *anziano,* like he's ninety. He goes around like his bones are as heavy as metal—we keep remarking on it inside the family; it's almost a prophecy come true. He sits in a chair with a shoe in one hand, six hours at a time. If you want the shoe on his foot, you have to do it for him. All day he asks the same crazy things, over and over: why are my waiters, whom I loathe, coming to see me at home, talking cheerfully about absolutely nothing, like I'm a patient in bed, and why am I home all the time anyway, did my restaurant fall into the sea? The doctor's here twice a day, Ugo Fantini, yes, the cousin, the same one who looked after poor Aldo. He's tearing his hair out trying to find a cure. For Beppi, anything. Also, the priest comes daily, yes, Don Enzo Malfada, of the cheese family. There's always solace in prayer.

"What was that about a prophecy coming true?" asked the Fascist, stricken with curiosity.

Marcellina had managed to fully engage him, so he didn't know that I'd gone into the kitchen to gather up the guns we'd been cleaning at the table. I got them into the broom closet as Marcellina talked and talked.

"Don't you know about Beppino Strepponi? You poor boy, you were deprived! He's a legend! I could swear he's better known than even Pinocchio!"

"What's the legend about?" For an instant, the soldier's voice was the voice of a boy.

"Beppino Strepponi," said Marcellina, "whom our Beppi was named for, lived to be two hundred years old, not that he ever died."

"Wait a minute. Beppi Fantini was baptized Giuseppe," said

the Fascist. "I looked it up, which I had to do because I'm investigating him."

"That's right. Giuseppe, for Verdi. A formality only. Let me enlighten you. The bones of Beppino Strepponi, which were made of iron, had ended up rusting. It's all this sea air. He was a giant and as rich as the Pope. He knew everyone, he was fantastic. In fact, he was a direct descendant of Adam, on the Italian side. Do you know the big rock hill by the sea, near the pier called Crab Point? Of course you do, you grew up here. If you don't know the legends, you at least know geography. Those rocks were once a mountain of dangerous cliffs, against which boats kept crashing. As his last act of life, Beppino Strepponi slammed his fists at that mountain and battered it to pieces, most of which fell into the water. It's said that if you move the rocks of Crab Point, you'll find a bunch of rusty old pipes. But they're not pipes at all. They are a hero's bones."

"I used to swim there."

"The original Beppino protected you from drowning," said Marcellina.

Good for her for changing details to make the story local. She'd never made up anything before; she hadn't thought she had it in her.

In the original story, invented by Aldo for an operetta that was never written down, the iron-boned giant was a Sicilian pirate. The part about rusting was true. The hero's remains were buttressing a fishermen's pier, but he came to life every couple of years to rob banks, private vaults, and even the Vatican, which was not, he'd point out, like robbing an actual church. It was more like robbing a *palazzo* in which the king, or maybe a duke, was so awash in riches, he'd never notice that anything was missing. Beppino Strepponi, always mindful of his roots, brought all the loot south, off the mainland, to his people.

Aldo had planned an intricate theatrical production for the restaurant, with guitars, tambourines, accordions, drums. He talked about it all through Beppi's childhood. I'd play the pirate's mother.

"It's Raining Gold Coins In Palermo" was the only song he had actually composed. It was Beppi's favorite lullaby.

It's raining gold coins in Palermo,
It's raining gold coins in Palermo,
So thank you, Beppino Strepponi.
Go to sleep now, you deserve it.
Sleep well. Tonight we love you even more.

I was now back in place beside Marcellina. "I apologize if you've been bored with old legends no one knows about anymore," I said to the Fascist.

"I enjoyed it."

Then came the presentation of a gift. The boy was all business again. "For you, Signora. A fine, dry Lambrusco, your wine of choice, and the specialty of your adopted region. It's distressing to see your son unwell. I'm sure you agree with me that it's imperative he come to no harm, especially due to an incorrect decision you might make, at this moment."

I accepted the bottle, but it was never opened. Later that night Beppi shattered it on rocks behind the house.

Suddenly the train slowed down, with a huge metallic shudder and a hissing of brakes. An unscheduled stop? For military reasons?

When I was on it last month for a flour-and-gun run, it came to a halt nowhere near a station; the *nazifascisti* who came aboard were prowling for partisans. When they reached my compartment they merely peered inside, and one of the soldiers grinned at me. He pointed to my bags—from a hat shop that time. He told me in bad Italian he was sure my new purchases would look spectacular on me, and if he weren't so busy, he'd love to have me open the bags and model them for him, as there was always a place in his heart for pretty hats.

It was all right. This was not a forced stop, just a regular one: civilian comings and goings. I'd miscalculated the length of time between stations.

Four more to go. The train was running on schedule. At this time of the morning, the soldiers on Mengo station duty went inside to tell a clerk to make them coffee. If there wasn't any, they headed across the street to a bar.

I had to steel myself up for the long walk home from the station. It would take at least an hour, involving footpaths and old wagon lanes.

On the main road it was twenty minutes, but the main road was full of Germans. There was no gasoline for the car. My bicycle was at home in the yard, untouched since the notices went up in the village with the curfew alerts—in German, but you got the idea. Bicycle riding by Italian people *verboten*. How many Germans had entered Italy in the last few weeks? A hundred thousand. Two. Hard to tell.

I didn't hear the sound of the compartment door being opened. It was a current of cool air from the passageway that made me turn and look up.

A nun. A very tall, slender nun, ducking low in the doorway as if bowing. Coming in.

I nodded at her, said nothing. The nun took a seat by the door, leaned back, and adjusted the long rosary hanging down from her belt, so that the big black beads on the silver chain lay smoothly, not all bunched up. She reached into a pocket—nuns always had deep pockets—and took out what appeared to be a small Bible. She placed it on her lap and folded her hands on top of it.

She was almost six feet tall. If I weren't so weary and worried, I would have enjoyed the pleasure of finding this astonishing. Her age was close to Beppi's. She had a long, smooth oval of a face: attractive without being pretty, with a high forehead, high-set cheekbones, a narrow nose, thin lips, and not a spot or blemish. She made me think of the word "rugged." Her skin looked as weather-exposed as a farmer's. Her eyes were wide and slightly squinty, like eyes that gaze very often into sunlight.

The main garment of her habit—the long dress—was dark gray, and made of a light wool or flannel. It didn't belong to a local order. Over the dress was a black, surplice-type second layer: a sort of jumper, ankle-length like the dress, but without side seams; it was held in place by her belt.

The headdress was a gray veil, edged with a semicircular, narrow white band. Not a hair of her head was exposed, but her eyebrows were brown-blond, the color of dry beach sand. The veil went down her back to well below her shoulders, lightly. At the top of the dress, covering most of her neck, was another white band, cuff-like.

Not Italian. Absolutely not German. French, maybe, but probably not; the habit was too simple. French nuns dressed elaborately, like white-winged, exotic birds, always about to fly away. American? English? Did England have nuns? Weren't nuns supposed to travel with their orders, or at least in pairs?

What did it matter what the rules were? All rules were off in wartime.

I moved closer to the window, pretending that everything out there fascinated me, as if looking out the window were the reason I rode this train. The bags were on the floor between my feet. The weight against my ankles was comforting, like a pair of sandbags.

We chugged on, rocking in a jittery way. Soon the sea would appear. I looked forward to the sight of the coastline above Rimini. So far, there were no encampments in the area. I loved the names of the towns: Cervia, Cesenatico, San Mauro, Bellaria, all tucked in with their colorful cottages and gaudy hotels, autumn-lazy and placid, staring out at the sea as though nothing could ever go wrong.

The night I came home from singing to the *nazifascisti* at Aldo's was when I committed myself to the strike.

What did I sing to them? I kept trying to remember. There were requests from the audience. I'd been handed a typed list of song titles with instructions at the top, in Italian, saying, "Members of tonight's audience will make requests from the list below, allowing the beautiful singer to concentrate on her performance by sparing her the trouble of putting her own program together."

I was driven to the restaurant by a German soldier who talked to me in German and never seemed to notice I didn't answer. I'd walked into the restaurant the back way, at the kitchen entrance. Talking to the cooks was forbidden.

The head chef, Mariano Minzoni, was there, along with the four other cooks. Not by choice. They were not getting paid. In two chairs near the main prep table were two Germans. Kitchen guards.

In the old days, everyone used to call sharp-faced, leathery old Mariano a tyrant, as if the worst thing that could happen to them was abuse from a bullying chef. Even Aldo had been afraid of him.

He was flanked by soldiers, in his apron, a knife in his hand, getting ready to carve the roast that smelled so good. When he looked at me, his eyes welled up and he grabbed for an onion, leaning in close to it to chop it. He made a point of tipping his head in a particular way, then turning, as if he'd cramped his neck and had to loosen it. He did this several times, until he got it across to me that he wanted me to notice his ears.

He had stuffed them with cotton. Was he telling me he had a head cold or infection? Did he want me to get the message to Ugo Fantini that he needed a doctor? Everyone knew that Ugo's house, with his office on the ground floor, was being watched. Fascists followed him on house calls, sometimes in their own cars, sometimes in his. They suspected there was a squad; they figured its leader was Ugo. But if Mariano needed him, he would come.

I was about to say, with my eyes and a tilt of my head, "You have earaches, Mariano, I understand, I'll fix it up with Ugo," when I realized that the others had paused in their labors and were showing off their ears, too: little Rico Pincelli, the pimply apprentice, whose brother was a waiter on the squad, and who had to be watched so he wouldn't run off and try to join them; shy, blond Fausto Fabbi, the seafood specialist, whose hands were always red, always cold; Romano Buffardi, pasta and vegetables, who was beginning to form a paunch; and sullen Gigi Solferino, the sauces and soup man, who was next in line to be *capo della cucina* if Mariano ever retired, which was highly unlikely. Gigi was older than Mariano by several years, and suffered from a palsy that made his hands shake; he couldn't be allowed to use a knife.

All their ears were plugged with cotton, same as their boss's. The guards had no idea. "Sing as badly tonight as you can, and we won't know, as we've made the effort to restrict ourselves to your best," they were saying to me. Or simply, "We won't join the bastards in hearing you."

Black shirts at the tables. Leather, regalia, boots. I had not experienced stage fright, because it didn't count as real singing.

Waves of applause. Compliments in German, translated by Fascists: I was a songbird, an angel. When the war was over they'd arrange for me to sing in great houses all over the world—in their Paris, their Vienna, their London, their Milan, their everywhere. I had not eaten the food placed in front of me, as hungry as I was.

The cooks. Stuck in the kitchen like prisoners. I imagined them with me, crowded together, finding fault with the train, the seats, the view, each other. They resented it so much that they weren't with the squad. I could smell the kitchen, as if it were imbued in their clothes and skin and hair: garlic, onions, roasting meats, tomatoes, and complicated scents of the sea, salty and fishy and marvelous. *Oh you ask me.* I imagined them singing our partisans' song, with the train wheels beating time.

Oh you ask me why I closed up my shop,
Why I brought up my boat to dry land,
Why I walked away from that restaurant,
Why I gave up all pleasure, worse than a penance in Lent.
Do you want me to say I went into the hills with guns
Because of love in my heart for liberty,
With the fight in my blood for the freedom of my country?
I will tell you, please, put your fancy explanations up your ass.
I came into the hills so I can run my shop,
I can fish in my boat,
I can make love in peace like there's no tomorrow,
And go seven days a week to that restaurant,
To suffer complaints and insults,
And bust my balls in servitude,
Which no one cares about,
Because no one ever worries about men who work with food.

2

A DISTURBANCE. A clearing of the throat of my compartment companion. A little cough. It startled me. I'd been so wrapped up in my thoughts, I'd forgotten all about her. It was the type of noise one makes when one hasn't spoken for a while, and is getting ready to say something important.

"Excuse me, Signora Fantini," she said. "Please don't mind this intrusion on your privacy, but I've been trying to get your attention. I really must speak with you."

It was the voice of an alto, measured, discreet. Foreigner-Italian: a little hesitant, a little too careful. But perfectly understandable.

Barriers. Graciousness. Nuns had often patronized the restaurant. Aldo—then Beppi—never charged them full price.

"You know me?" I said.

"I don't mean to startle you. I've been sent by your friends to offer help."

The nun picked up the book in her lap. She lifted it so the cover was showing. It was not a Bible, and I recognized it: Beppi's mysterious, fell-from-the-plane book. It was some sort of diary. We knew it was American because stamped inside were the words "Made in U.S.A." There was no name. All the pages were blank except for the first two, on which someone had written carefully, in black ink, what appeared to be a poem, without a title. In English.

Six days ago Beppi had turned up at home to take a bath. He spotted the book in the nut orchard, in the crook of a tree, as if it had grown there. He had to use the ladder to take it down. The book was unharmed except for a chipped-off, tattered corner.

He concluded that it had fallen from a reconnaissance plane, which I'd refused to believe. Why would a pilot throw out a handsome book? It was obviously worth some money. The leather was luxurious.

There were more than twenty lines. If the thing was a poem, was it obscene? Had the pilot written it, like a literary version of pictures of busty, cleavage-showing movie stars, which American pilots were said to tape to their consoles, like icons, where an Italian would keep his pictures under his mattress, and have Mary Queen of Heaven in his cockpit?

The lines seemed to be some sort of American dialect. The crucial word was "surrey," which had a "fringe."

Beppi became fixated on it. Was a surrey a woman? Why didn't we have dictionaries in the house? Why were we so provincial? Why were we so illiterate?

He felt sure the whole thing was a code. He deciphered a few words from having heard English in the restaurant. I helped with the little I knew from songs. We understood wheels, dashboard, take, drive, bright, shiny, and high, as well as the pronouns and three edible fowls—chicks, which we assumed were chickens, and ducks and geese. Marcellina helped, too, remembering that someone had told her that Englishwomen called the bangs on their foreheads a fringe.

Beppi rushed off with the book in great excitement. What he wanted to do was speak quickly to the one Mengo partisan who knew the language: a waiter named Nomad, who had worked for six years in a London hotel.

But all that week Nomad was out of touch in a village near Urbino, helping to train a new squad of farmers; he was teaching them English expressions. Everyone thought it would be useful to know a few phrases in case it really did happen that they looked out their windows one day at the American Army, shooting their way up from the south like cowboys. Hello, GI, how are you? Good to see you. Has anyone killed Mussolini yet? Can you spare some ammunition, rifles, anything?

And here it was, the fallen book, with its injured corner.

"Are you American?" I said to the nun.

"I am."

"Where did you get this?"

"From your son, although not directly. I only saw Beppi for a moment, in passing. We didn't speak. It was given to me by Vito Nizarro."

"Prove it."

"He asked me to give you his greetings. He said to tell you, the glasses in Aldo's at the moment are so filthy, one could get venereal disease just by looking at them. And it's always a good idea to have the spaghetti with mussels."

Nizarro was our headwaiter. He'd created a code for the Mengo squad that was based on expressions they used with each other in the restaurant. The partisans who came from other lines of work—Emilio Batarra, the tobacconist; his brother Teo from the pharmacy; Tito Roncuzzi, the butcher, and Galto Saponi, the fisherman—had been forced to play catch-up, which they'd all complained about. But the system was working. A filthy glass that gave you diseases meant all *nazifascisti*. Mussels and spaghetti meant "a German supply truck, which we could hijack."

It was odd to hear a nun talking about venereal disease, even as part of a code.

"No one," I said, "told me anything about you."

"That's what I was told you would say."

Was this some sort of trap? Just because someone was a nun didn't mean they sympathized with partisans. An American *fascista* in a habit? Anything was possible.

It wasn't out of the question to think that an outsider might have found out about the waiters' code. The nun might have stolen the book, having been trusted to read it for Beppi and look for clues.

"Tell me," I said, "what my son looks like."

"He looks like someone who would succeed at American football, especially in the position of a guy on defense, who has to knock down opponents. *Tackle,* it's called. Tacklers get everyone out of the way, so their own team keeps the ball. Basically, he looks like a barrel with arms and legs and a head."

Well, that was accurate. "And Nizarro?" I was convinced, but I was also curious.

"Nizarro is a bigger barrel, but not as good-looking, which I say in the most objective way possible. He looks like, if he knocked you down, you might die. Look, he'd wanted to write you a proper letter, but there wasn't any paper."

The nun opened the book to a page near the back. Someone had penciled in a message. It was Vito Nizarro's penmanship: squat, block-like letters, very muscular. I'd know it anywhere. His writing was just like his body.

He'd written, "The bank account, Lucia, has been checked, and I'm sure you understand my meaning here. The customer, in this case a female *grattacielo,* as you can see for yourself, is good for the whole table's bill. No problem. She's with us. Don't worry that I'm marking up someone else's notebook, as our friend will erase this. By the way, Beppi's really looking forward to Aldo's birthday, which I know because he just told me. But in case he doesn't show up, don't hold it against him, as we've got our hands full with a couple of minor details. I hope your shopping expedition was everything you hoped for. If we can't see your new dresses at the scheduled time, we'll arrange another."

The nun closed the book and put it back into her pocket.

"Nizarro has a sense of humor," she said. "A female skyscraper. I like that."

"It's interesting that he doesn't refer to you as a Sister."

"He was in a hurry."

"But he would have said Sister."

The nun sighed. "Perhaps he was telling you something indirectly."

"You're not a nun?"

"It's a long story."

"You're not! You fooled me!"

"I wasn't about to for much longer. I'll tell you—"

"No, I'll tell *you.*" I kept my voice low, almost whispery, holding back my temper. This was not a good time for a flare-up.

"I never know what's going on," I said. "They send me on errands like this and tell me nothing. Not long ago outside the station I was accosted by a filthy, bad-smelling man selling chestnuts. He turned out to be a partisan, but he was truly selling chestnuts. And he was Italian. What's the meaning of the poem in that book?"

"It's not a poem, but I can see where you'd think so. It's a love song about a wagon."

"A wagon?"

"A fancy carriage, the type that horses pull. A *surrey.*"

"Is this an American way to say a type of woman?"

"No, it's just a wagon. A man sings the song, and he wants to take his girlfriend for a ride. It's from an American musical play, *Oklahoma*. In case you never heard of it, it's a state. It's western."

"Like cowboys and Indians?"

"Sort of, but without the Indians. In the title of the musical, instead of just having the state's name, there's an exclamation point, for special effect. It's been a very big hit since last spring."

In another part of the world, people were going to plays? Were hearing songs? I tried to imagine this.

"Funny it landed in your own particular territory," said the nun who was not a nun. "But I'm sure it's a coincidence."

"Where did it land from?"

"A parachute drop. The box it was in had been shot at, and everything was scattered. There've been problems with radio communications. But it may be the key to messages, or orders. Americans in fighter planes are very resourceful, almost as much as partisans."

"I'm sick of your planes. Who are you? Where have you been? Where did you come from? What are you really?"

"My name is Annmarie Malone." She said it in five syllables instead of eight, and I offered her a correction, as a question.

"Annamaria?"

"Yes."

"Mah-lo?"

"Mal-lo-*nay,* if you like. Or, Mal-*lo*-nay. I'm from the state of Connecticut, and don't even try pronouncing it. It's in the East, near New York. Right now, as it happens, I'm with the army. There's a special branch involving secret operations, and I'm part of it. But what I really do is play golf. That is, before this shitty war, I used to."

"Golf? With a tiny white ball and a stick?"

"A club, not a stick, actually. In fact, for a while back home, in certain circles, I was famous."

Well, so was I. How much did she know about me? About my singing, my strike, my favorite songs? What about my special one?

"Lambrusco," I said, and she looked at me with confusion.

"Isn't that a wine?"

"Never mind. I just felt like saying the word."

Beppi hadn't told her about that. The shattered gift bottle.

He'd never appreciated the taste of it. He felt that the buoyant little fizz that sparkles so wonderfully in the mouth and throat does not belong in a wine, and never mind he was the only one he knew who thought so. He claimed to hate my song about it, but he loved it.

The tune was from the glorious song of Rosina—not the betrayed, unhappy countess of Austrian Mozart, but the real one, the Italian one: the Rossini Rosina, gutsy and alarming, the star of the show, a woman with some steel up her back, *una voce poco fa, qui nel cor mi risuono.* A little while ago, a voice echoed inside my heart.

Every time I sang it, I'd enter a place without fright, and feel as dizzy as if I stood on the edge of a roof, which I'd want to jump off of—a roof, a cliff, anything high, *l'ingegno aguzzerò,* I'll sharpen my wits, *se mi toccano dov'è il mio debole,* if they touch me in my weak spot . . .

Instead of those words at home, what did I sing instead?

Lambrusco. Every way you can arrange those syllables, I'd do it, lam-bru-*sco,* lam-*bru*-sco-*lam.* I'd start out comical, a clown, but the song would find its own way, lightly, airily, importantly, *lam-brus-co, o-o-o, o-o-o.*

I'd cut off vowels, draw them out. In the act of ascending, I'd look at the three of them—or four if Ugo Fantini showed up, or five if Enzo showed up, too—all of them in front of me, listening with the faces of people bewitched: my son, my husband, his cousin, the priest, Marcellina with her mouth wide open, with the five or six teeth she still had turning pearly, translucent.

We were coming into Mengo. The American stood up, swaying and ducking her head; the ceiling of the compartment wasn't high. She picked up the two bags effortlessly, as if they weighed almost nothing.

"I'll take charge of these, Signora Fantini. I won't mind if you take out the guns and keep them with you, in case you haven't decided to completely trust me."

"The guns," I said, "aren't loaded."

"You look at me as if you wish they were."

"I am annoyed, not violent."

"That's good to know."

The American didn't move toward the compartment door. She sat down in the window seat opposite me and placed the bags on the seat beside her.

"Go away from the window at once," she said softly. "Please don't be alarmed. It's not possible to get off here."

"You're mistaken. I've a dinner to prepare, which I suppose I'll have to invite you to, as you seem to have decided to come home with me."

The train was grinding to a halt. Outside the window, no soldiers in sight. Just people. Just the plain old Mengo station and the fields and trees all around it, and the ordinary Italian fall sunlight, yellow and crisp and luminous. No trucks, no tanks. Not a plane in the sky. All was quiet, as if the war were taking a nap.

But as I started to get up, planning to make a grab for my

bags, my angle of vision shifted, and I saw, at the far end of the platform, some half-dozen German soldiers, standing there like a welcoming committee.

A few of them were officers. They were not the usual station guards. Annmarie reached up and closed the curtain.

"Move," she said. An order.

I did as I was told. And for the first time that day, I was aware of no aches and pains, no dampness and dryness, no annoyances. I felt I'd taken some sort of medication, without knowing it, and it was now beginning to work, making me numb.

I thought, Nizarro. His writing. His note. He'd gone out of his way to say that Beppi was eager for his father's birthday party. He really looked forward to it, *which I know because he just told me.*

The part of my mind that had ignored those words on the page was now prepared to face them, with a sharp and glittering clarity. Nizarro wouldn't have known this, because Beppi never talked with his waiters about fights at home, but he didn't want a birthday party for his father. We'd discussed it, fought about it, Beppi and I and Marcellina, but in a one-sided way. It was useless to argue with Beppi when he ranted and stomped.

"I will feel like burning down the house if you say another word about a birthday! We're not having parties till we get Aldo's back from those bastards! You want a party? Have it in your imaginations and don't tell me about it!

"Also," he'd added, more calmly, "I'm sick of your superstitions, so don't tell me anymore about Papa being the wind at the kitchen shutters."

Marcellina had shrugged it off. She told me later it was a pity we couldn't spare flour for a cake for Aldo. "The poor man will be disappointed. He was always so happy for a cake, especially on his birthday, when he'd never want to share it. Don't you feel sorry for Beppi? He thinks we cower at his commands. Imagine calling us superstitious! I think being squad leader has really gone to his head."

Beppi would not have changed his mind. I found myself making small, cough-like sounds in my throat, as the other woman had done, as if we'd begun to develop our own code.

"Tell me what has happened to my son."

Annmarie did not look away from me, but gave me a look of surprise, unguardedly. Then a look of distress, then resignation, and a tight little nod of her head, as if saying to herself, well, I should have expected this; she's his mother.

"Beppi is alive."

"Alive where, please?"

The nun-like facade was gone, in spite of the habit. It was a voice of military terseness that answered me, as if speaking the lines of a telegram. "No one knows where he is. He's hiding. There was an incident with a German truck, a brand-new Opel, wildly expensive, which was parked in the road not far from—"

"The restaurant," I said. I did not apologize for interrupting her. "That truck's been there all week. Everyone said they planned to mount one of their cannons on it."

"They mounted it. Beppi blew it up. The cannon stayed pretty much together, but they won't be using it soon. The truck was a good target because it was far enough away from the building. But some of the windows were shattered."

"Was anyone killed?"

"No. There were injuries, but they weren't severe. I'm sure he's sorry about the windows."

"Was it the whole squad, or just my son?"

"Just your son."

The only thing Beppi had ever blown up before was his temper. Surely something went wrong.

"You're not telling me something," I said. "I can see it in your face."

"You're seeing incorrectly. He wouldn't be able to go back to the squad. They know they have to lie low for a while."

"He was hurt?"

"I know this is a shock."

"Tell me if he was hurt."

"I don't think so. We're going to find him, you know."

Marcellina, what about Marcellina?

"I have a woman who takes care of my house," I said. "I've got to get to her."

"I know about her. I was told your priest will keep her with him."

"Where are you taking me?"

The voice softened. "To tell you the truth, I'm not sure. No one knew how quickly they'd be looking for you, but we'd suspected it. We're to wait for a signal farther down the line."

"Today is Beppi's father's birthday."

"It was a very successful explosion."

The Mengo stop was over. The train hissed out some smoke and gave a lurch and started moving again.

Annmarie had lifted an edge of the curtain. "We're lucky. The soldiers didn't board," she said.

"They were waiting for me."

"That's a good conclusion."

Last week, the news had come to Mengo, through Enzo, that the wife of the leader of a brand-new partisan squad in Forli had been kidnapped by Blackshirts while she was hanging out laundry to dry; they had swaddled her in a wet sheet; they'd lifted her as if she were a dead woman already. A neighbor witnessed them putting her into the backseat of a car—the last that was seen of her. A handwritten notice had been placed on the front wall of her house by the door, addressed to her husband. His name was Budino. "Budino, be sensible. Your wife is a nice, pretty lady. We will not harm a hair of her head. We'll set her free when you turn yourself in." So far, according to the latest reports, he had not turned himself in.

But Forli was Mussolini's hometown. Partisans there, I'd reasoned, had it harder.

We're going to find him. She had said that. It wasn't even her country. What was she doing here anyway?

We're going to find him, you know. A golfer, an American lady golfer. Maybe she thought of Beppi as one of her little white balls, obscured in a bush somewhere. Weren't golfers always hitting balls into bushes?

"I don't know much about golf," I said.

"Almost no one in Italy does. That's all right. I don't know much about . . ." Her voice faltered, stopped. Maybe she'd been about to say, "singing."

"Being anyone's mother," she said. "This would be a good time for you to close your eyes and get some rest."

"Do you honestly think I can *rest*?"

"No, but you should close your eyes. Now that we're moving faster, I'm going to open the window and get rid of all this flour. We can't have it weighing us down, and I believe it's not something you'll want to watch. Don't worry, I won't throw out the guns."

"I won't look."

"They told me that you're a woman of astonishing strength. I can see they understated it."

I made an attempt at a smile. "No one my son associates with would say a thing like astonishing strength, not even our priest, as eloquent as he is."

"I admit, it was put to me more colloquially."

But I didn't feel strong. I didn't feel I could even pretend it.

Sometimes when I was about to enter the spotlight at Aldo's with an especially vicious fright, I'd pick up some object from a table, as if seizing a prop, whether or not it suited the song I was finding it impossible to sing. A spoon, a napkin, a salt cellar. Nothing easily breakable. It didn't matter what it was. I'd grip it intensely: a good-luck charm. I'd think of my voice as something to speak to. Maybe it was a little like praying. "Please, don't let this be the day you leave me." At the end of the evening, I presented the object to a patron at the table I'd taken it from: a little ceremony. A souvenir. A waiter rushed over to put it in a white paper bag, embossed with a silver A, which Aldo's had crates of, for favors at wedding banquets and free sweets to children who behaved through an entire meal. "Good children get candy. Bad children drool while watching them eat it," was Nizarro's rule of what to say, discreetly, while seating them.

Something to hold.

I remembered the Italian pistols. I put my hands in my pockets. I wasn't so numb that I couldn't feel how good it was to touch them, even though they weren't loaded, yet.

"Beppino," I said to myself, as if my son were with me and I'd reached for him, patting him lightly. "What kind of a partisan are you, blowing something up without telling your mother? You'd better not be hurt in any way. You're a good boy, although I'm sick of all these surprises."

3

THE VILLAGE OF SAN GUARINO had been built in the early nineteen hundreds because of a furniture factory. It consisted of a long, broad avenue lined on both sides with trees, front yards, and boxy, tidy brick houses. There was no town square, no *trattoria,* no church, no school, no café. It looked as if someone had taken it from Ravenna or Bologna—a whole residential block—and plunked it at the edge of a marsh, far enough from the sea to be uninteresting to tourists, but close enough to call itself coastal.

In spite of its well-kept appearance, it looked like a misfit in that countryside. The one avenue began at the train station. Like the long line of the letter T, it stretched out to the gates of the factory, which formed its top line.

Adriatic Fine Furniture for Home and Commerce. The building was four stories high, and as gloomy and imposing as a prison. It had its own little grocery and dry-goods shop, its own kitchen, cafeteria and gardens.

I detested San Guarino, which the train would soon approach.

I'd only been there once, years ago, when Beppi was eleven or twelve. A family outing. The factory was where Aldo, and then Beppi, bought tables and chairs, which forever needed repairs and replacements.

An armload of flowers had been presented to me. The carpenters wanted me to sing to them, but it was out of the question. I had to save my voice for the restaurant, I told them.

Then Beppi got away from me and Aldo, and went missing for a couple of awful hours, when that visit should have lasted five minutes. The only reason it took place at all was that the owner of the factory, that son of a bitch Etto Renzetti, had offered Aldo a line of credit, with one small thing to be given in return.

Aldo was expanding then, moving up from our first to our second *trattoria,* which was double the size, and ten times more expensive. Privately, he'd been operating on bluff and optimism. He'd had little by way of capital.

The one thing Etto Renzetti asked for was that I accompany Aldo on his next visit to the factory. He was a fan. He was also a Sicilian.

There was nothing improper about it. It had happened before that I'd gone with Aldo to meetings with bankers, bureaucrats, suppliers. I didn't mind being looked at as collateral. But I'd never had to speak.

Aldo had helped me prepare what to say. He'd thought it would be nice of me to speak Sicilian. Thank you, Mr. Renzetti, for allowing my husband to pay you in the future, without interest, for one hundred chairs and forty-six tables, half of them square and half round.

He had fat fingers and oily skin. Aldo had been standing beside me, but at the sound of my voice in dialect, so alien to him—all those z's and choppy oo's; the cadence that sounded to his ears like growling—he'd tuned me out. He didn't know that Etto had quietly said to me, "I've heard you sing at least a dozen times. Your voice is always in my ears, and yet, why do I have the feeling that truly, of everyone you know, and everyone who has ever laid eyes on you, the only one who doesn't know you are beautiful is yourself? What's the matter with you?"

A hot flush had spread over my neck, my face, as if I'd stood too close to a fire, as if that man had burned me. I was polite about it. I did not let him know the degree to which he'd rattled me. "Aldo," I said later, "if you were paying attention, you'd know he was speaking to me about how happy he feels to help you, and he wishes you a beautiful success."

San Guarino. That odious man, and then we couldn't find Beppi.

We thought he'd only gone to the car, having had his fill of that environment, full of wood, sawdust, banging. He was crazy about the car, a brand-new Fiat, bought on credit. He was always begging Aldo to let him get behind the wheel.

He wasn't in the car. The whole factory came to a halt to search for him. They even went out to the well to see if he'd fallen in.

We found him at last in a hollow by the back gates, in the shade of some high bushes, flat on his back, fast asleep, clutching a smooth piece of wood a laborer had given him. "Mama, Papa, I like it here very much," he said when we woke him up. "I looked at everything, and I was just now dreaming about it. I want us to move here, because I want to be a carpenter."

"He sounds like Jesus, at the very same age," Renzetti pointed out, which made Beppi *glow.* All the way home, and for days afterward, all we heard was, "I'm like Jesus! Jesus! I'm like Jesus!" Marcellina made Aldo let him drive the car in our lane, to shut him up.

The one good thing you could say about Etto Renzetti was that he wasn't a Fascist. Did awful San Guarino have a squad? I hadn't heard of one. The top floor of the factory served as housing for the workers who came from other places and could not afford houses on the avenue: Sardinians, Calabrians, Sicilians, Africans, Greeks. Maybe because of the war, they'd all gone home.

Maybe the factory had been shut down. Maybe the San Guarino station was closed. We might chug right through without pausing, and I could say to the American, "The village we're passing through—not that it's really a village, as it only has one street—is the biggest eyesore in Italy."

The fact was, I had the crazy idea that Etto Renzetti would be standing on the platform, watching for me, shouting to be heard above the train. Your voice is in my ears! Why don't you know what you're like? What's the matter with you?

The American was watching me. "You didn't get flour on yourself when you threw it out," I said.

"I was careful. What's the next station?"

"I don't know. But it might have been closed."

My throat was beginning to feel uncomfortably dry. Sand-dry. I could feel the edges of a fright creeping up on me.

"Tell me, Annamaria, where you learned to speak Italian. I'm curious."

"It's a long story."

"That's the second time you've said that to me."

"I'm not very good at conversation, not when it's about explaining things I've done."

"Then I'll ask you something simple. Why are you in the army?"

"I didn't have a choice. I'd got into some trouble. The army was the best way out of it. If you don't mind, I'd rather not—"

"*Va bene,* of course, I understand. I won't press you, as we haven't known each other for long. But why are you in disguise?"

"I was ordered to."

"Are you Catholic?"

"I went to a convent school, yes."

"Is your habit from the order at your school?"

"Yes. The Sisters of Mary of the Rosary."

"Ah, the rosary. I suppose they made you pray one every day."

"Only on Monday mornings."

"In Sicily, where I lived before I married, nuns didn't teach school. They were in hospitals, or they were cloistered."

"Cloistered. You said that as if it's something you admire."

"I don't always like the world very much, it's true."

"Is your home in Mengo like a cloister?"

I didn't know how to answer that. Maybe. I didn't want to talk about home. I said, "You have a ring. It looks religious. Are you married?"

"The ring is part of my disguise, and I'm engaged. Sort of. It's a long—I mean, it's complicated."

"He must be Italian."

"Basically. He grew up American."

"Like an immigrant?"

"Yes."

"When my son was fourteen years old, his father wanted for us to move to your New York. A friend of his was opening a restaurant. Beppi had no intention of having this happen, so he began a hunger strike, and kept it up till we agreed to stay home, which was impressive of him. But he wasn't so pudgy back then."

"You could have sung in New York. That would have been wonderful."

"I didn't want to go. I wouldn't have. I wanted to only sing here. What's his name, this maybe *fidanzato* of yours?"

"Tom Tully, in American. But really, Tullio Tomasini."

"How is he? Is he handsome?"

"You would think so if you got to know him."

"Is he shorter than you?"

"Oh, yes. But I never held that against him."

"Does he play golf?"

"He doesn't, but he used to work at a course. In the clubhouse."

"In the state you said I'd never pronounce? Con-eh-tah-kit?"

"Yes, Connecticut, and you said it almost perfectly. It was at the golf course where I first learned to play, secretly. It seems ridiculous to mention it, but the whole business of taking lessons was a secret. I was only sixteen."

"Secret because your family disapproved?"

"My family didn't know until later. It wasn't them. American golf clubs don't let in Catholics."

"I didn't know that. Surely this boy Tullio, if he worked there . . ."

"People at the club thought he was a Protestant from the north of Ireland, but don't get the idea they were fond of the Irish. They weren't, but they were much less fond of Italians. At least the Irish spoke their language."

"How was his English?"

"Perfect. No accent."

"He was like an actor."

"I suppose so. Good jobs were hard to come by. He was good at concealing himself."

"Who were the people this club was fond of?"

"Oh, themselves. Is this too much talking? It must be tiring for you."

"It's not. You fell in love. He's the one who taught you Italian?"

"That's right."

"He's older than you?"

"A little. But young as he was, he was already married."

"I should have guessed it. Don't tell me his wife died."

"She's alive."

"Is he a soldier?"

"He is. He's an officer, in fact. I haven't seen him for a while."

"But you must know where he is."

"He's in Washington, D.C., at a desk, safely, thank God. It seemed that working at a golf club gave him practice for helping to plan invasions and things."

I didn't know why, but I found myself pleased to know that this Tullio was far away, and would not turn up suddenly at some station, greeting his possible future bride in his perfect English. I seemed to feel resentful to know he existed.

"Look," said Annmarie. "I think we're coming to a village. I think—my God, what's *that*?"

There was a wide, low hump of a hill, barren and weedy, about a mile before the San Guarino station. The train had to slow to a crawl to negotiate the curve. The hill and its occupants were in full view.

"Do you recognize those children?" said Annmarie.

I was tempted to answer no, as if I'd never seen them before, even though it appeared that they were on that hill to send a signal regarding what to do next, the very thing the American had been hoping for.

"They belong to a waiter, all nine of them," I said.

"Which one?"

"Maurizio Pattuelli."

"The one called Mauro? The cheerful one?"

"Are you being sarcastic?"

"I am."

"Then, yes. His village isn't far from here. It hasn't got a station."

The children were solemn and wide-eyed, clustered together like a partisan squad of their own, which they no doubt imagined themselves to be. They were waving at the train innocently, as if watching a parade go by, as if this were the joy of their lives. In their hands were what seemed to be ordinary squares of white cloth—just something to flutter in the air, like handkerchiefs or little flags—but they were linen napkins, heavily soiled.

The squad's code phrase for "you're in danger where you are, exit your situation at once" was "dirty napkin." As far as I knew, it had only ever been used theoretically.

Those napkins had probably come from the restaurant. Each one had been spotted all over with mud.

The children themselves were freshly groomed and impeccably clean, although their clothes were ragged and worn. The five younger ones were wearing white—the boys in shorts and the girls in dresses—like children at church for First Communion, and I recognized the material. Tablecloths from Aldo's.

"I believe they're telling us to get off at the next stop," said Annmarie. "Are they reliable?"

They were, but I didn't want to say so. "They might be playing a prank," I said.

"It doesn't look like a prank."

Mauro and his wife, Carmella, had named the three youngest—three girls—in honor of me, Aldo, and Beppi, and it was only fair to have learned all nine of their names: Marco; Francesca; the first set of twins, Mario and Sandro; Rudino; Antonella; the second set of twins, Alda and Lucianna; and the baby, Giuseppina, who was called Beppina. Their ages were between fourteen and five.

Carmella Pattuelli wasn't with them on the hill, but of course she was with them in spirit. When the squad was being formed, she got hold of a couple of radios, and set herself up at home as the squad's civilian operator. She'd learned the basics in her days as a Fascist Youth. Beppi complained that she abused protocol by contacting the squad to send personal messages to her husband: a child had broken a tooth; it was lonely in the house without him; good morning, good night, I love you, what did you have for lunch, if anything?

Carmella was a Saponi, from a long line of fishermen. Her father, Galto, had been the first nonwaiter to join the squad. She'd contact him, too. "Papa, if anything happens to my husband, I won't forgive you, and if anything happens to you, I won't forgive him, but if anything happens to both of you, I will personally, with my own two hands, wring the neck of your leader, and I swear that I mean it, Beppi Fantini, in case you're listening."

She was a slight, small-boned, curly-haired blond woman who should have looked, and felt, terrible, after birthing nine children in less than a dozen years, never mind raising them on the salary of a waiter. But the opposite had happened.

There was a light in her eyes. A sureness. She was a woman who believed herself to be beautiful, regardless of what anyone else had to say about it. And she believed herself to be brave. That shine of hers rubbed off on anyone who was near her. "We're naming this new girl, the ninth one, and we swear, the last, for your Beppino."

The children had inherited their mother's personality, and every one of them had Mauro's big, droopy dark eyes and hang-dog expression, as if they'd been born middle-aged and a little saggy, looking out at the world with such a deep, quiet sadness, you'd think their lives were full of misery and deprivation that could not, by any effort, be concealed.

Mauro Pattuelli was the most popular-with-customers waiter Aldo's had ever had, even though he was clumsy, slow, and inept. To have as your waiter a man who looked as woeful as Mauro was to feel that all the worries of the world were off your shoulders, having been placed onto his, and you could really sit back and enjoy yourself.

All he had to do was walk over to unhappy customers and listen and nod his head, looking at them as if he felt their grievance so keenly, he was ready to cry; he was struggling to hold back the tears—their predicament reminded him of things in his own experience, all tragic—and the complainers would change their tune, would feel uplifted, would even make an effort to get the sad clown to smile, which was different from what happened when Beppi was involved. Beppi would stand there with his arms across his chest, as staunch as a plow, saying, "If you have anything bad to say about my restaurant, go to hell."

The train had come to a stop. San Guarino. No one was in sight, not even a stationmaster or an assistant.

"I have the feeling," said Annmarie, "you're reluctant to leave, but please, let's go."

"I want to find Beppi."

"That's what we're trying to do."

"I want to stay on until the end of the line."

"That's not possible. We've had a signal. Look, this is the first station we've come to without Germans. I have the feeling we've been told to get off here because the stations down the line might not be safe."

"I don't care. Leave without me."

"Oh, for crying out loud, come *on.*"

It should not have been surprising that a woman who was a golfer and also a soldier should have powerful arms, a powerful grip. But I had not been expecting this course of action, and I gave a little cry as I was yanked from my seat—*yanked!*

The son of a bitch American! Was I supposed to be afraid of her? Was I supposed to be intimidated? Was I supposed to believe that if I didn't obey her, she'd throw me out the window like the flour?

"It looks like it's snowing in your Romagna." That was what she'd said when she got rid of it. What a smug, self-centered, unfeeling thing to say! What did she care about wasting the dough for Aldo's party? That flour had been so hard to get! Falling flour was not like snow! It wasn't snowing!

The arrogance! Pretending to confide in me, like a normal woman, in a real conversation, like a couple of friends! To the point of telling secrets! A sham to gain trust! There wasn't any trust!

Thrusting my purse at me! Pulling me out of the compartment, dragging me out the door! Not letting go of me! Yanking me harder! Like an enemy! If she were really a nun, she would still be a son of a bitch!

"ARE YOU ALL RIGHT?"

No answer. I believed the American didn't deserve one. I was off the train and on the platform, catching my breath, getting ready to describe out loud how I felt. Carmella Pattuelli never would have put up with this. She would have found a way to be strong.

I imagined Carmella as the heroine of an opera, strong, indomitable, small in size but huge in spirit: a secret, at-home radio operator to partisans, mother of a gang of children who did what they were told to, wife of a sad-sack, adored waiter, daughter of a tough old Adriatic fisherman. How I envied her!

A role. When was the last time I'd enjoyed studying a new part?

The train pulled slowly away. Before me was the small, trim box of a station house. The door was locked with an enormous outside bolt. The windows were covered with dust, which made the darkness and stillness inside unbearable.

"Looks like no one's been here for a while," the American said.

"Don't speak to me. Everything you said to me on the train,

believe me, I forgot. Already in my mind, I've erased every word."

"I'm sorry I had to use a little force."

"You *assaulted* me."

"I apologize. I wonder what the name of this village is. It's only got one road."

"Did you hear what I said? Don't speak to me."

"But I have to. I've been assigned to you, and I don't know where I am."

"That doesn't concern me."

There was a smooth old wooden bench against the station house. I moved it away from the wall, so I could sit down—I was still very shaky—and not have to look at San Guarino. You couldn't give it one glance without filling your eyes with Etto Renzetti's factory.

It was a village with a curse on it, I remembered. An actual curse.

"I wonder if those extraordinary children are on their way to us," said the American. "Even better, their parents, with a car that's got some gas. Or maybe we should start walking. Do you think so? Is that some sort of a factory, straight ahead?"

"Shut *up.*"

The bench was filthy but I sat on it anyway. *La Cenerentola.* Rossini's Cinderella. That was the last new part I had purely, simply loved.

All those years ago. How old was Beppi when I first sang those songs?

He'd seen a puppet show in the village, the usual thing, a castle, a king, a queen, a prince, a princess, and the minute he came home he went to work on us with demands that we produce a baby sister. He cried his eyes out when Aldo explained that Papa was too old for babies and Mama didn't want one, as I was satisfied, most of the time, with the one I had. Beppi felt that we'd plotted together to break his heart. "I need a princess! I need a princess!"

"You already have one, and it's Mama," Aldo had said. "Come and listen to the new songs. She learned them only for you. There's a girl named Cinderella. She's in a wretched situation, which we hope will improve."

Early-primary-school age. Beppi had been six or seven, around the age of Carmella and Mauro's second set of twins. The American, who'd been quiet, was scanning the area hopefully. She must have been waiting for those kids to appear at the station like a rescue party.

It wasn't going to happen. The Pattuelli family had been banished some years ago from San Guarino: the hill outside the village was the closest they'd go.

Mauro was the son of a carpenter, but he'd not followed in his father's footsteps. He'd been working in the factory kitchen, and met Aldo and Beppi on one of their buying visits. Having taken one look at his long, sad-clown face, which even then was heavy with feeling, they saw the potential; they talked him into coming to the restaurant.

Mauro had inherited his family's house in the middle of the one street. The Pattuelli Eight, as they were called—Beppina was only a toddler then—would only play among themselves. They did not attend school in the next village like the rest of the San Guarino children, but instead took the train to Mengo to be in classrooms with other waiters' children. This was something San Guarino objected to, having objected in the first place to their numbers, as if Mauro and Carmella were two rabbits in a hutch in their midst, breeding like crazy.

And their house and everything they owned smelled like fish. There was just simply too much fish.

One evening, after hours, the crew boss of the came-from-away laborers who lived on the factory's top floor discovered the Pattuelli Eight with the workmen in their private quarters—jumping on cots like trampolines, climbing on bureaus, being chased about by homesick Sardinians, and talking in dialects they'd picked up, probably filled with profanities.

If they had been anyone else's children, the crew boss would not have decided to have them officially charged with trespassing. And the older boys had slingshots made from materials they'd taken from the scrap heap on the side of the building, which made them thieves.

The village had never been suitable for that family anyway. Banishment was what everyone had agreed upon, instead of a very large fine, or consignment in a permanent way to a Fascist school, which had been threatened.

I knew all this because Beppi had told me about it, the whole story, including the part about the curse.

The fisherman grandfather of the children, Galto Saponi—"This is what happens to people who complain that my family is fishy"—had commissioned one for San Guarino from a fortuneteller who was another fisherman's wife, and a genuine witch, people said, who had once cursed French archaeologists for raiding a burial site near San Marino. On the way back to France, their ship sank. They were stranded on a raft for a week and would never recover their health, but their plunders were safe, at the bottom of the sea.

"Banishment or not, never go past the little hill before the train station, or you'll step on cursed land, and nothing can protect you," Galto had instructed the children, by order of the witch. It was said that the current, carpenter-family owners of the old Pattuelli home were plagued by problems, which were never there before: mice kept appearing in cupboards, and the cats who tried to catch them died; the roof started falling apart; the walls had an unnatural dampness, which often smelled outhouse-type foul.

Oh, but the children had been lovely on that hill, somber and sweet in a huddle, especially the second twins, Alda and Lucianna.

And the baby, too. Of every child and every grandchild belonging to Aldo's waiters and cooks—and there had to be more than fifty of them—Beppina Pattuelli, with her big, sparkly eyes, was by far the most indulged, the most cherished. Beppi adored her. He didn't care if anyone accused him of playing favorites. He called her the Italian Shirley Temple, although her hair was dark like a chestnut, and as straight as a poker.

Why hadn't Beppi married?

What happened to that girl from Forli who came to Mengo with her family because they didn't want to live in Mussolini's town? They were all Communists, and they lacked a sense of humor, but still, she'd been nice. Beppi had courted her for nearly a year. "She bored me, Mama." What about that pale, pretty art student from somewhere north of Milan, who sat in front of the church and drew pictures of it, which were not especially good, but weren't terrible? Beppi had been so serious about her, he'd looked at property for a house of his own, but the plans had popped like a bubble. "She bored me even worse than the Communist." And Enzo's cousin Donata, with the Malfada cheese industry behind her, a perfectly suitable girl, if on the plain side? "She's too pious, Mama. She gets along better with cows than with people." And Mariano Minzoni's niece from Verona, coming often for visits when she couldn't stand Mariano? "Mama, I'd be someone with a death wish if I wanted a Minzoni bride. She'll henpeck me. She'll chase me around the kitchen with a knife."

Nothing. Why hadn't he given me grandchildren? He was the son of a widow. You'd think with all the women he'd been involved with, there'd have been a *bastardo* or two.

Not even that! Selfish boy! What was he blowing up trucks for? Why did he have to make a squad? Why didn't he stay in the restaurant with Mariano and the cooks, and so what if it was loaded with the enemy? I'd know where he was!

Tackle. Beppi would have been good at football if he lived in America. That's what the American had said. Why hadn't we moved to New York when Aldo wanted to? There weren't any Nazis in Manhattan.

"Lucia, are you listening to me?"

Annmarie stood close by the bench, but at least she'd had the sense to keep her distance and not sit down.

A tackler. Just like Beppi. They must have recognized each other as kindred spirits when they'd met.

"Lucia, please don't tell me again not to speak to you."

No apology. No remorse for having acted to me like a thug. I realized that she had stopped calling me Signora Fantini. I didn't correct her for using my first name.

"It's a good thing I didn't throw out this shopping bag," she said. "I've got the guns in it, wrapped up nicely. Would you happen to have a hairbrush, not that I have a lot that needs brushing?"

I turned around. The American had changed her clothes.

Well, she discarded her upper layers. In the place of the towering nun was a towering woman, short-haired, broad-shouldered, in a tailored, light-gray flannel shirtwaist dress with a round, dark-gray collar.

"You took off your habit!"

"It's here in the bag."

"And your ring!"

"It's in one of the pockets, with a Luger."

She looked at me in a new way, with a pained bashfulness, as if saying, apologetically, "This is what I really look like. I won't blame you if you think I looked better as a nun."

Her hair was the color of wheat grain and did not need brushing. It had been cut almost as short as a man's, but there was enough for curls and waves. In spite of having been flattened by the veil, it was light and springy.

So was my heart, suddenly. "You look nice as a woman," I said.

"Thanks for saying so. It's kind of you. I planned to make the switch on the train, in case I'd been spotted, but then we received the signal. By the way, if anyone wants to know, I'm a professional translator, employed by the American government. That's my other cover. I happen to be with you because you've decided to put songs in English into your repertoire. I'm helping."

"Like the surrey song, for example?"

"That's a good point. We've got the words. I hadn't thought of that."

"Is your name the same?"

"It is."

"Ahn-ma-ree."

"I like it better when you say Annamaria."

The gray dress was not Italian or European, but it was stylish, and even elegant, in its own American way, and fit her perfectly. The hem went exactly to the bottom of her knees. She did not wear stockings. The parts of her legs that were visible were evenly tan.

It did not appear that any part of her body wasn't finely tuned and well aligned. She was an athlete, all right.

"Your son looks like a barrel," she had said. What was the opposite of a barrel? A rainspout?

"She's a rainspout," I said to myself.

And a light went on in my mind, and illuminated a scattered mess of different pieces of things, gathering them together into a clear, whole picture.

Beppi. The American.

Maybe this was what highly religious people—and witches, too—meant when they claimed to have been touched, or inspired, by strong, mysterious outside forces, not that I believed in forces. Was I having a vision?

It certainly seemed so, even though it was only of commonplace things: a barrel, a rainspout. A wagon called a surrey, which was not a type of woman.

I imagined Beppi and Annmarie side by side on the seat of a horse-drawn wagon. The countryside I pictured was Italian.

What about the American boyfriend, married to another woman?

"You have a funny look," said Annmarie cautiously, standing there in all those inches of her new self. "Do you think this dress is awful on me?"

"It's fine. Do you ever wear anything colorful? I only ask because I think you'd look nice in blue."

Blue was Beppi's favorite, all his life, even when he was a teenager and felt that boys shouldn't think about things like colors. The walls of his bedroom at home were a dark, manly blue, and so were many of his shirts and jerseys. He owned three or four blue sweaters and at least half a dozen blue linen handkerchiefs, and neckties, too; there was some shade of blue in nearly every one of them. He also had a dark-blue jacket for fall afternoons, like this one.

Beppi believed I sang at my best when I wore blue. I wore blue for one composer: Mozart.

I had coded my costumes a long time ago. It was superstitious of me, but I'd held on faithfully to my system, with the feeling that, if something's not broken, don't fix it. Technically, they couldn't be called costumes, those gowns of mine. It wasn't as if I sang on a stage, in an actual theater.

Green was for Puccini. Yellow, red, orange, and gold were for Rossini. White and silver were for Verdi. Multicolored prints and stripes were for occasional Sunday afternoons of folk songs, mostly Sicilian, but also the old songs of Naples, which made tourists feel lavish about tipping the waiters. Black, brown, and beige were for Bellini and Donizetti, and the wildly popular program I put on in the spring, around Easter, of songs from *Cavalleria rusticana.*

Aldo had claimed not to favor one color or composer. But all the same, when I showed up at the restaurant in blue, his face lit up. He'd loved my Mozart, especially my countess, but also Susanna. And my Donna Elvira, Zerlinda—all of them.

It used to worry Beppi that I sang songs by a non-Italian, but I told him that Mozart's first name was Wolf, and his middle name was Amadeo. He was God's Beloved Wolf, and you couldn't get any more Italian-sounding than that: Romulus and Remus, say, combined with a Catholic God. It had appeased Beppi. He grew up in a Fascist world, *patria,* Mussolini, children around him being drilled, being taught to handle guns almost as soon as they could handle a pencil. Beppi had skipped the summer camps and youth groups because Aldo said he needed him too much in the *trattoria,* where he could do his part by serving good food to Fascists who had the money and the palate to appreciate it.

There was a certain hush in the restaurant when I finished singing from *Figaro,* first with pragmatic, perky Susanna, the most famous about-to-be-married maid in the world. Sometimes—this was rare—I added a bit of Figaro himself. No one ever said they minded hearing him in a soprano's voice.

Customers loved it when I mimed Susanna at the start of Act One, posing before a mirror: "Figaro, look at me, do you like my new hat?"

Her *fidanzato* doesn't give a damn about the hat. He's too busy. I'd pace out those steps of Figaro's as he measures the space for their bed, counting off the numbers in lustful, proud joy, *cinque . . . dieci . . . venti . . . trenta . . . quarantatre!*

After a pause, the time would arrive for the Countess Almaviva, Mozart's Rosina: beautiful, complicated, brave, heartbroken, wise, kind, forgiving, heroic, luminescent. It was all right that her composer wasn't Italian. It was enough that her words were. "Mozart has no nationality," Aldo once said, "the way an angel doesn't." I sang every one of her lines on Mozart nights, sometimes in the order of the opera, sometimes not.

For the countess, always, that same hush.

"Mama, you sing best when you wear a blue dress, so please don't waste it on an Austrian," Beppi would say. "I don't care what his name means. Please put on blue for our Rossini, the greatest of all, who'd be hurt if he knew how you slight him."

For Rossini I could feel that I sparkled, I climbed heights, I wanted to leap into air, I was dazzled. But for Mozart, I could feel that I possessed a soul, because I had to turn myself inside out to reach into it, like trying to become, with all of myself, pure air.

And Aldo's face would take on that particular light, and

Beppi would pull a chair away from a table, positioning himself near me, with his head tipped back, looking up at me, bright-eyed, solemn, with that soft little private smile of his—insider's knowledge. He'd never say so, but he understood a lot about that hush, even at a very young age. "It's quieter in the restaurant, Mama, than it ever is in church. After you sing those songs, it's quiet like when it's raining, and then all of a sudden the sun comes out, and the sky's all blue again."

And the waiters and the cooks would line up at the back to hear me. "Look, she's wearing blue tonight!"

"Actually," Annmarie was saying, "back in America, when I put on exhibitions, I wore very bright skirts, and dresses, too. Designers used to give me clothes for free, to show them off."

"Exhibitions?" I said. "Of your golf game?"

"Yes, but without the game. It's when people come to see technique. I got paid, more or less, to show off."

"People paid money to watch you?"

"Oh, yes."

"Are you rich?"

"Not exactly."

"Do you have a house?"

"I do. In fact, I have two, but they're nothing fancy. They're very small. One's in Connecticut, my real home, and the other one's in Arizona. I play at a club there. Arizona's another state. In the West."

"Like Oklahoma?"

"Sort of, but it's mostly a desert."

"Golf is in a desert?"

"It sure is."

"It must be hot."

"You get used to it."

"It's hot here, too," I pointed out. "All the time, I hear people talking about how Italy needs to have golf. I'm certain that after the war, there'll be plenty of people building clubs and courses. You can put on exhibitions here."

"I'm not sure that's part of my future, but it's an interesting idea."

"It can be part of your future!"

I went back to thinking about barrels and rainspouts. Annmarie had said she didn't care if a man was shorter than she was, which proved she was sensible and not vain. And she had said she'd found Beppi to be handsome, objectively.

"I don't care if she's a virgin, which she very most likely is not," I said to myself. "She and Beppi don't have to mention to each other what their pasts are. That *fidanzato* of hers will have to find himself another golfer."

Baby hips. It was a good sign that, lean as she was, her hips were curvy, ample. Women with narrow hips, I'd always heard, have a terrible time in childbirth.

For the first time in I didn't know how long—in spite of the war, in spite of that cursed, unlookable-at, Etto-Renzetti-tainted village—I felt at peace with all the world. I wasn't thinking about danger, guns, Germans, Blackshirts, trucks, explosions. "Beppi has a future, which I know because I just saw it," I thought. "I'll keep quiet about it, but obviously, he'll be very much staying alive."

Suddenly there was a movement at the far end of the platform: a shadow. I became aware of it as if it made a sound of its own. One second later, Marcellina came bustling around the corner of the station in her good, go-to-church tweed coat, replacing the shadow dramatically.

"Please tell me you know this woman. Please tell me she can help us," Annmarie said quietly.

"That's my housekeeper. That's Marcellina," I said. "She's

probably got our priest nearby. I can't imagine how they got here. Neither of them drives. But I suppose we're being rescued."

"You say that as if you wish we weren't."

"Only because it means that now, we have to go back to the war."

"Did you feel we left it?"

"I did."

"So did I. I'm sorry I assaulted you. I promise it will never happen again."

"I forgive you."

"Thanks."

"You're welcome."

Everything was all right. Marcellina was rushing toward me. I felt the same as if I were back in the spotlight at Aldo's, holding on to a salt cellar, or a spoon, or a napkin.

I HELD OUT my arms to receive the embrace Marcellina was bound to give me, but there was no embrace. She sizzled with agitation, and came to a stop in front of me, punching the air with a fist.

"Lucia! Who is this flagpole of a woman? They told me they sent you a nun! Tell me what is happening! Beppi threw bombs at that fancy truck with the cannon! By himself! He could have blown himself up in the process! No one knows where he is! Enzo's with Eliana! In a hiding place! Everyone says there's going to be bombing! We have sandwiches! Enzo's holding them! He'll eat them all, if you don't hurry! Where is the nun? What have you done with her? I'm going to learn to shoot! I'm going to kill someone! If Beppi hurt himself, I'll shoot him! The stupid boy! Five hundred Germans are looking for him! I sneaked out the vestry with Enzo! Enzo's a hero! Eliana was with us! She lit every candle before we left! Germans came into the church! Ugo drove us out of Mengo! We left the other two at the hideout so we could fit you in the car! We're just like refugees! Refugees in our own country! Did you hear me say I'm with Ugo? He's not seeing patients today! He's got gas! We had another bunch of sandwiches, for Carmella's children! We passed them on the way! One of them fell down and had scrapes on his knees, but Ugo had his medical bag in the car! Carmella's on the radio all the time, but no one is answering! Ugo smuggled the sandwiches from the restaurant! The cooks are going crazy in there! The restaurant is their prison! Lucia! There's no one in San Guarino! It's empty! Everyone's hiding! Even Renzetti with the tables and chairs! The Germans said they want his factory! But Germans aren't here! Maybe there won't be bombing! I don't know! Poor Aldo! I left the soup for his birthday on the stove! He won't know where we are! I want to go home! Lucia! Why aren't you talking to me? Why aren't you telling me about the nun?"

Pausing for breath, she teetered a bit, as if she'd just run too fast up a flight of stairs. Then she tipped back her head and looked up at the tall, tall stranger, and whispered to me, "I don't want this woman near me, Lucia. She looks like a flagpole, but even more, a giraffe. Is she a Fascist?"

"She's American, she's the nun, and she understands everything you've said," I said calmly.

"Parlo italiano," said Annmarie. "Excuse me for being uninformed, but who is Ugo? Who is Eliana? What bombing?"

"She means the rumor we've heard of bombing by your countrymen. I am Ugo. Eliana is my wife."

He'd come up silently behind Marcellina, who immediately seized his arm and clasped hands with him, allowing him to help her hold herself up; she was exhausted.

Here he was, Ugo, standing there, with his same old warm, tired eyes, and his same old never-looked-rumpled suit. His same old elegant, paper-white silk shirt. His same old narrow dark tie. His same old quietness.

Why was Annmarie giving me that narrow-eyed, scrutinizing look? Was this how she appeared when she was about to take a shot at a golf ball? Squinting fiercely like this, studying the situation?

I could feel my face pinkening.

Ugo should not have been roaming the countryside. He was a watched man. By now, he must have known the first names, and probably the ailments, of every Fascist and German who trailed him. Sometimes when he went to his patients' homes, people brought refreshments, if they had some, to the black cars or trucks parked nearby, especially when Ugo was there for a long childbirth, or a deathwatch.

Ugo. His same old high forehead with its deep-set creases, his same old warm, tired eyes.

"*Ciao,* Lucia. I've given my followers the day off."

"*Ciao,* Ugo."

"Lucia!" cried Marcellina, restored. "Introduce this stranger! Nun or not, where are your manners? Just because there's a war doesn't mean you should act like a peasant!"

Ugo stepped forward to take care of it himself.

He held out his hand to clasp Annmarie's, not mine. Of course not.

His same old mild voice. "You must be Signorina Mal-*lo*-nah. Forgive me if I've said it wrong. It's fortunate that the Americans assigned an officer to our part of Romagna. I've heard that your collaboration with our squad is going well."

"She's an officer?" cried Marcellina. "Ugo Fantini, what are you saying? She's a woman!"

"I can see that."

"You pronounced my name perfectly acceptably," said Annmarie. "Are you a physician?"

"He certainly is!" said Marcellina. "He's ours, but not Lucia's! She insists on going to another one, across two villages, just because he's Sicilian!"

"They tell me you play golf," said Ugo.

"Golf!"said Marcellina. "Everyone's talking in riddles! Signorina *Americana,* or Sister, how should I know what to call you? You have a nun's hair! I am Marcellina Galeffi, which no one has mentioned! No one makes introductions of a housekeeper! Let's go to the car, not that I look forward to being stuck in a cave!"

Marcellina stamped her foot like an impatient nanny. "Lucia, you're not saying anything!"

"My throat feels a little dry. A little scratchy."

"You're ill on top of everything else! You sound hoarse! Ugo, do something!"

"We have some wine in the car," said Ugo.

His same old calm manner. His same old echoes of Aldo: a resemblance in the narrow lines of his nose, the curve of his quick, soft smile, the slight hollows under the cheekbones, which had stayed with Aldo even after he'd got so overweight.

His same old bushy eyebrows, so at odds with the rest of his face, not having grayed at the tempo of his hair: two tweedy, black-and-silver, woolly-looking caterpillars. "Ugo's awful caterpillars," Beppi used to call them, running to a mirror, licking his fingers, reaching up to smooth down his own.

His same old way of not looking at me directly. His same old stoop. He was almost as tall as Annmarie, but they had opposite methods of coping with their height. Where Annmarie was straight-backed and full of ease, poor Ugo acted as if he hated it. He always seemed to be ducking down low, as if worried about hitting his head on a doorframe.

His same old imperfections. The eyebrows, the stains on his teeth from smoking, the wrinkles; the hollows, the narrow chin with its tiny scar, just off-center, about the size and shape of a thorn, where a patient had once attacked him, with his own scalpel.

A voice inside me rose up, like a warning. Always it was this way. Don't do it. Don't go near him.

To go near him would be breaking a rule. Where had I heard the rules about being a widow? What song was it?

It was an old one, a folk song, about someone giving a new widow advice. An old woman talking to a younger one. A litany of proper etiquette. Hymn-like, but it wasn't a hymn.

I remembered. The proper title was "The Apparition To Mary Of Jesus' Grandmother, Following Joseph's Death." But everyone called it "Mary, Mary, Don't Do It."

Mary, a new widow, is walking away from her husband's grave, bent low in mourning. Her mother, dead for many years, steps down from a cloud to have a talk with her.

It was no surprise to me that I was thinking of it now, in a village of carpenters, all of whom were likely to have Joseph as their personal occupational saint.

Follow my simple widow's rules.
Soon, you may want to look at men,
You're human.
You may want to look at men a certain way.
You're not a saint yet.
It's well before the Assumption.
You may want to look at men,
But they're married, all of them.
If a certain someone flutters your heart,
Keep your distance!
Mary, Mary, don't do it!
Don't go near him!

Spring, 1924. Almost twenty years ago. That was when I knew about Ugo.

It was a Saturday evening at the *trattoria*. This was the second one, the bigger one. There were six long tables seating eight apiece, or even a dozen if people were willing to be squashed together, which they usually were. The smaller tables—prime seating—were by the windows.

Mariano Minzoni, stolen by Aldo from the Grand Hotel in Rimini, was already head of the kitchen, and even then, still youthful, he was cocky and arrogant, terrorizing everyone. Poor Gigi Solferino, having hoped for the position, was overwhelmed with depression, realizing that Mariano had it all over him; he'd been relegated to a life of second place. It never occurred to him, or to any of them, to quit working for Aldo. "Aldo Fantini," they'd say, "is the devil himself in many ways, but no one pays better, and no one else shuts his eyes when you're squirreling from the larder for your family."

Gigi was the one cook I felt sorry for. When he came to me, bashfully, to ask me to sing something special on the last Saturday of April, I agreed, even though I wasn't thrilled about the choice.

A certain woman, Gigi told me, would dine at Aldo's that Saturday, and he planned to ask her, at the end of his shift, to marry him. Her name was Bianca. She was originally from Turin, and worked as a seamstress in San Marino.

The piece he requested was *"Una furtiva lagrima"* from *L'Elisir d'amore,* in my opinion the worst, most drippingly sentimental song ever put into an opera by an Italian. The opening lines, with the "one secret tear," always made me imagine that the young woman being sung about was a bizarre, Cyclops-like creature, with a giant, wet eye in the middle of her forehead. It was maudlin. Who ever cried just one tear in one eye?

Gigi, however, was within his rights to have made the request. Waiters and cooks were entitled to petition me for songs: for birthdays, anniversaries, births of children, confirmations, baptisms, deaths, all sorts of things. That winter, I'd done an all-Verdi evening for Franco Calderoni, who was leaving the next day for his new job in London; that was when everyone started calling him Nomad. The name stuck, although after he returned, six years later, he never went anywhere again.

And Nizarro had wanted some *Rigoletto* for his teenage daughter, who was mooning around for a handsome, son-of-corrupt-old-aristocrats boy, and was, Nizarro felt, on the road to a personal disaster. He'd thought it would be a good idea to bring her in for dinner and let her see what happened to girls like Rigoletto's daughter, Gilda. Seduced by a prince, thinking yourself in love with him, you end up dead in a big burlap bag, on your way to being heaved into a river.

It was always something. Sing this, sing that. I honored them all as a matter of course. The one-eye song was my first request from Gigi, as well as my own first performance for a marriage proposal. So I took it seriously.

The air was unusually chilly. It was fizzy with a cold rain. Fog had rolled in from the sea—not the gentle, wispy-white fog of most spring evenings, softening everything, but a gray, harsh cloud, as if the shoreline were burning.

People waiting for tables were supposed to stay outside in a queue, along with villagers who turned up to hear the singing. Around nine in the evening, just before I went on, they decided to come inside, some twenty of them, damp and shivering.

Aldo eyed the newcomers warily. Standees made him nervous, especially the ones who weren't spending any money. He sent me a signal: a smile, then an uplift of his right hand, with his thumb and index finger measuring about an inch of space, which meant, "Darling, keep it brief."

My gown was beige silk, for a Leoncavallo-Donizetti program.

I hadn't sung from *Pagliacci* for a while, and it always went over big. I planned to open with Nedda-Columbina's dramatic *ballatella* from the first act, describing loud, cawing flocks of birds, shooting off into the sky like so many arrows, chased by wind and storms—a song about portents, dreams, and mysterious powers. Next would come the *"Vesti la giubba"* of Nedda's miserable actor-husband. Well, a soprano version of it.

Singing his song made me feel I wore clothes that belonged to someone else, in a fashion I'd never choose, but I was forced to make the best of it. I knew how to play it so that it seemed I'd stepped outside of myself, as though, personally, I was incapable of emotions such as malice, spite, possessiveness. Ha ha ha ha! Laugh and everyone will applaud! Laugh, Pagliaccio, about your shattered-to-pieces love! Laugh at the poisonous pain in your heart!

It was the only non-Rossini song that Beppi liked, but he was a teenager then.

L'Elisir d'amore would follow it, with two brief parts-of-songs, preceding Gigi's special one. Where was Beppi anyway?

I hadn't spotted him. I saw Gigi by the kitchen door, beside Mariano, who must have found out about the girlfriend and the song. Mariano disliked it as much as I did, and he sent me a signal of his own. He put on an exaggerated frown and held a finger to the side of his face, languidly tracing the line of one tear down one cheek.

Which female diner was Bianca? It wasn't my custom to look around at the tables, but tonight was different. Was she the long-nosed girl with a group of other girls, all of them apparently single, looking merry and hopeful and a little bit tipsy? The one in a bright flowered dress nearby, seated with a family but very much alone, with pale skin and tired eyes, and hair pulled back so severely, it seemed that the tightness pained her?

Then there was Beppi at last, at the height of that phase: half boy, one-quarter man, one-quarter God knew what kind of creature, prickly and scowling and restless, at odds with himself and the world. He was coming out of the kitchen to stand at the back with the cooks. I was able to meet his eyes—our old habit—before positioning myself to start singing.

Then I saw Ugo Fantini.

There were often Fascists among the diners. That night there were three officers at a window-side table. They weren't local men. The standing crowd had gone nowhere near them, in the same way standees in a theater wouldn't approach the high-priced seats.

Their waiter was Nizarro. He didn't often wait tables, but he preferred to handle the big-time Blackshirts himself. He'd placed himself near the oldest-looking Fascist, as if he'd taken on the role of a soldier standing guard.

It seemed the fourth chair at that table was unoccupied. Nizarro wouldn't have been blocking it like that if someone were in it. But something had distracted him, had made him turn, just for an instant.

Why was Ugo sitting in that chair? Why was Nizarro concealing him?

Why was Ugo here in the first place? He was a temporary bachelor. Eliana had gone home to the Abruzzi, to the grim little mountaintop, perched-on-a-cliff village that was her home. I knew from photographs that the village looked like a raptor's nest. I knew from Marcellina that Eliana planned to visit a shrine on the mountain that was said to be helpful for women with her problem: she was almost forty, and still, to her sorrow, barren, not that anyone was using that word.

Ugo had a habit of staying at home when his wife was away. On Thursday, Marcellina had wanted to go to his house. She'd made a batch of *piadine*—which Ugo never could get enough of. No one, he felt, made it half as well as she did. And she'd bought cheese from the Malfadas to go with it, his favorite: the creamy, custardy, almost-sweet Emilia specialty called *squacquerone.*

A simple thing like flatbread and cheese could send him into raptures, even when he knew Marcellina was trying to bribe him. In this case, the time had been drawing near for her annual checkup. She believed that if she buttered up Ugo in advance, she'd be much more likely to be told that nothing was wrong with her or, better, he'd tell her to skip the appointment altogether.

But Aldo had said not to bother. He and Beppi ate the bread and cheese themselves. Ugo, he explained, had decided to take advantage of his wife's absence. He'd gone to Bologna for a seminar at the medical institute, and to catch up with old friends of his. Political friends? No, no, Aldo said, not that; Ugo's not a Socialist anymore; he thinks of nothing but medicine, his patients. He was simply taking an impulsive, working vacation.

Which was something he'd never done before. When was the last time Ugo left Mengo overnight? No one could remember, but Aldo had sounded convincing.

Ugo at that table!

Nizarro resumed his secretive guard stance, and the room grew quieter, with that same old pre-performance background noise of throats being cleared, little coughs, tinkling silver, whispers, shufflings, chairs being turned this way or that, scraping against the floor.

The main lights dimmed. When the spotlight came on, I wouldn't be able to see anything—or anyone. Nizarro only needed to keep Ugo hidden in normal light.

I had seen the way he wasn't sitting up straight in that chair. I'd seen him sideways, slumped a little, his head low, as if he were staring at his own chest. I had the sense that his eyes weren't completely open, or he was struggling to stay alert, like a man who'd had too much to drink. Was he drunk?

No, of course not. He had a sensitive stomach: anything more, or stronger, than a couple of glasses of wine would only have made him sick. He'd have gone off by himself to the toilet. Then he'd go home. He wouldn't have chosen to let anyone see him weak or out of control.

The spotlight: pale silver-white, an expensive luxury. Aldo had had it rigged up from the ceiling, so it would look like I was standing in moonlight, the only one in the room the moon would choose to shine on. The trick was to not flinch or even blink when it came on, and I didn't.

The suit Ugo wore was his dark-brown one. The only brown suit he owned.

He'd been wearing it four days ago, in the middle of the

morning, when he stopped by the house on his way to some patient. Aldo had asked him to listen to his heart. He'd felt an irregularity. He'd been scared. Beppi had been at school.

We were in the kitchen: me, Marcellina, Aldo, Ugo. The heart was listened to.

"If you were a car," Ugo told him, "you'd have a couple thousand miles or so before you need an overhaul, so don't worry. You're rattling, but you're far from conking out."

And that was that, and Marcellina started bustling around, and there'd been coffee and biscuits. Sitting at the table. Aldo in his chair, handing Ugo an ashtray. Marcellina telling Ugo he shouldn't smoke in front of me, as it was bad for my throat.

Ugo not lighting the cigarette in his hand. Putting the cigarette back into the flat silver case he carried everywhere—a gift from Aldo. Slipping the case into the pocket of the brown jacket. Picking up his cup of coffee. Looking at me. Yes, looking at me.

That look in his eyes. Quick, so quick. He was careful about it. He made it seem that all he cared about was the condition of my vocal cords. I hadn't imagined it.

"I'm only rattling! Hey! I've got miles and miles!" Aldo had been happy.

Now the light. Everyone had said that Mussolini's Fascists wouldn't pose any actual danger, not here. Why should they care about a place like Mengo? Wasn't it possible that when Blackshirts showed up, they were only instructors at the new youth camps? With their make-believe guns? Or they came for the sea air, just like anyone else?

In places like Rome and Milan they were going after journalists, intellectuals, professionals. Everyone had heard stories. A man here, a man there. A body turning up on the side of a road, another one on the steps of a newspaper office, another in the center of a square.

Terrible, alarming stories. But still, they seemed to have come from far away, from a different country—from another Italy, remote, unfamiliar, unreal. There was only one man in Mengo who'd fit a description of someone a Fascist would be nervous about.

I went shaky all over, as if a fright were coming. But the symptoms were different. Prickles all over my skin. A sense that a wet, chilly air had blown in. A bothersome irritation at the back of my mouth, as though a sob or a gasp were trying to get out, and could not.

Simple, physical things. All manageable. Anyone else in my situation would have felt the same anxiety, the same sensations. But this time it wasn't about singing. It wasn't a throatful of sand.

"It's real life," I said to myself. "Fascists took Ugo four days ago, and no one told me and he hasn't been home to change his clothes, and Aldo lied to me so I wouldn't worry, and Beppi lied to me, too, by not telling me, and Aldo made Nizarro hide him, and everyone's bent on concealing real life from me, even Marcellina!"

These facts entered into my brain like the story of an opera I had just started learning. Aldo would have known I wouldn't sing if I were distracted. There must have been interrogations. What was Ugo up to? Why didn't I know what he'd been doing?

They had hurt him. I saw that. They were forcing him to be with them as part of the audience. His cousin's restaurant. His cousin's wife as the entertainment. The bastards.

I had never changed a program before. I'd never dared for spontaneity in the spotlight. But I could not go through with my planned songs. This was not a time for portents and mysteries and cawing, sky-wheeling birds, or the *Pagliacci*. How could I have sung the song of a malicious, murderous clown, full of bile and hate and cruelty, as a prelude to a love song—when the real-life stuff was right in front of me?

It would have been inhumane of me. It would have been Fascist of me.

"Please give me an elixir of love." Gigi had as much as said so outright. Maybe his chances with Bianca were slim. Maybe it was useful to think that love deserved all the help it could get.

Nemorino of *L'Elisir d'amore* is a poor man, in love with a better-off woman, Adina. Gigi had said Bianca was a seamstress. Maybe her earnings were higher than his? That was doubtful. Maybe she'd been born to a prosperous family.

Just in time, Nemorino inherits a fortune and he's a prize catch. Every woman for miles around wants to marry him.

The one secret tear is in Adina's one eye because—why? I took a moment to remember. I often forgot the backgrounds of songs, like looking up at a foggy night sky, where only four or five stars are shining. You can forget that they belong to constellations; they're all involved in systems. They're not just hanging up there on their own. So many plots. So many details.

Jealousy! Sadness! All those women clamoring for the now-rich Nemorino! Adina had been worried that she didn't have a chance. She loves him, all right. He can see it. He says so.

"Here, Ugo, take some coffee," Marcellina had said, handing him a cup. "Consider this a celebration for telling us Aldo's heart is not a piece of junk, not fully. Now I don't have to go out of my way to be nice to him."

"*Grazie,* Marcellina. Your coffee is always excellent."

"I'm going to make you some bread!"

"Superb!"

Taking the coffee cup. A sunny morning in the kitchen. Peace.

The brown sleeve of his suit jacket. The smell of the shaving lotion he wore—slightly medicinal, not male-perfumey like Aldo's. The way he had looked at me.

"I know you're sick of hearing this from me, but you're too political, Ugo," Aldo had told him. This was just before the listening-to of his heart. "You talk too much to people you shouldn't be talking to. You should be more like me. Mussolini isn't going to last, so you'd be better off ignoring everything he's saying."

The little tremor in Ugo's hand, holding the coffee cup. He almost spilled some. Ugo's hands never shook. It wasn't because of Mussolini. Aldo said things like this every time they were together.

The way he didn't look at me again.

Time to sing. I could feel the growing tension through the tables, the unstated questions of all those diners. Was something wrong with the singer? Had she forgotten her lines? Was she ill, was she panicky? Is she going to walk away in silence?

I opened my mouth and started singing *"Una furtiva lagrima,"* patiently, carefully. Not sentimentally, but simply, as if stating a fact.

I changed the pronoun from "she" to "you." And when I reached the last lines, about sighing and dying for love, I made the decision to eliminate them. I had never altered a song before. It seemed all right.

What more do I seek?
That you love me,
Yes, you love me.
I see it.

Then I paused, and the hush all around me came into me deeply, like something to hold on to with every part of myself. I turned away from the light, looked back, and burst out with some *Barber.*

Act One, second scene: Figaro himself, rascally, boastful, on top of the world, unstoppable, un-Fascist—how marvelous life is, how pleasing, for a high-quality barber! Here I am! Figaro! There was never such an illustrious life as mine!

I sang the whole of that long song in what felt like one breath. I was running with it, running faster, and it seemed that a wind had come up at my back, lifting me. I felt that I'd turned into someone you have to tip back your head to see; I was flying; I was air. *Ah, bravo Figaro! Bravo, bravissimo, fortunatissimo per verita! Son qua, son qua . . . Figaro! Figaro! Ah, bravo Figaro! Bravo, bravissimo!*

Under any other circumstances, it would have been unthinkable for an audience at Aldo's to be satisfied with just one song of Rossini's. He was one of their own—Rossini from Pesaro, composer-son of the Adriatic, their own star.

This was different. No one asked for more. They recognized flying when they heard it.

Thunder. Much more than the usual applause. Silverware being clinked against glasses, feet thumping the floor, tables being pounded with fists.

"You'd better be sitting up straight now, Ugo," I was thinking. "You'd better have really, really heard me." Then I went home, by myself. I never spoke of what I knew.

Ugo came out of it all right. Around dusk on the following Monday, he was back in our kitchen, with a fading bruise on the side of his forehead, which no one mentioned. He'd come to pick up a fresh batch of bread and take a look at some eczema on the back of Aldo's neck.

"I feel like I'm coming down with leprosy, Ugo," said Aldo. "So how was your trip to Bologna?"

"Oh, it was good to be back in the city again, talking shop, comparing patients, picking up new procedures for minor surgeries, things like that. It was very successful."

Everyone maintained the charade. "You wouldn't believe what you missed out on, Ugo," said Beppi. "Mama sang a Donizetti on Saturday night for Gigi Solferino and now he's engaged."

"Lucky man!" said Ugo.

"She was magnificent," said Aldo. "Two songs only, but I'd told her to keep it short. We had people waiting for tables all over the place."

A balm for Aldo's rash. Ugo taking a tube of ointment from his medical bag. Handing it not to Aldo, but to me.

The one time.

All those years, the one time he spoke privately to me. It could not have taken place if the others, that moment, had not been suddenly occupied with other things.

Marcellina wrapping up the *piadine,* still warm and flour-fragrant. Beppi and Aldo at the same time rushing over to grab some for themselves. There was too much, they cried, for just Ugo.

Marcellina slapping their hands. Ugo bending toward me. "Put this on Aldo's neck twice a day. It smells bad, but it may prove to be effective."

Aldo and Beppi and Marcellina squabbling loudly over the bread.

Ugo's mouth at my ear, as if he needed to give me further instructions, all medical, and couldn't otherwise be heard. Whispering.

"I know that you saw me, Lucia. I'm fine. I was lucky. They had talked about exile. They were going to send me somewhere inland, to some town. Inland and south. Some awful, dusty, desolate little town. I would not have been able to bear it. I believe that, neither would you."

"You're right. Put this on his neck twice a day," I said. "I should ignore the bad smell."

"I will never forget that Donizetti. As another favor to me, please, will you never sing it that way again? Not for anyone else?"

"I'll do as you ask, Ugo."

"Thank you for making me feel like Figaro."

"It wasn't hard."

"We'll never speak of this again."

"I understand."

Always after that, formality. *Ciao,* Lucia, how are you? *Ciao,* Ugo, I am well, how are you? I am also well, Lucia, thank you for asking.

In the autumn of one of those years—maybe it was the same one—Marcellina came rushing home from the village in great agitation because Eliana Fantini had just told her she was pregnant. "That Abruzzi mountain shrine of hers must have worked, at her age! It's just like Elizabeth, old and doddering as she was, conceiving John the Baptist, which I'm sure Eliana thought of herself, she's so religious."

Marcellina was deeply fond of Ugo's wife. Everyone was. Good-natured, always-acts-kindly, never-raises-her voice, sweet, mild Eliana, with clear eyes as shiny and green as a cat's, with her ink-black hair always pulled back in a braid, knotted up and pinned in place, exactly in the center of the back of her head, like an ancient burl on a tree.

She ran the business part of Ugo's practice and, since she'd had some elementary training as a nurse, she took care of patients with mild, or imagined, symptoms, or injuries that required only basic first aid.

Her touch was gentle, people said. She never made a mistake. She knew of, and used, remedies involving plants and herbs taken out of her garden and carried about in the old basket she'd brought from her mountain home. That basket was always on her arm. She never made anyone feel intimidated, stupid, or guilty, as if their sickness or wound were a fault of their own, like Ugo did, with his fancy education, looking down his nose in an imperial way at the very people he'd grown up with. He'd say things like, "A fishhook is stuck in your skin and you waited all these days before coming to me—are you crazy? I believe the infection you've given yourself may be fatal." Or, "What do you mean, you fell off a ladder? That homemade piece of junk, made from sticks which were rotting to begin with, is not a ladder. Even a sparrow would know to not step on it. I believe all the bones in your legs, which are broken, will never be right. You'll have to reuse those sticks to make crutches."

Eliana would say that the fishhook was embedded in the fisherman because Satan had chosen that day to journey out of hell, from an exit at the bottom of the sea; having happened upon that particular boat, the devil animated the hook, or something, so that it leaped from a wave like an evil fish, with unavoidable, terrible teeth. And she would praise the ladder, and warmly describe how the bones were already healing; she'd pray by the bedside and put roots and leaves in the victim's wine.

Ugo had married her in Bologna. They'd met at a hospital there. They'd already been married, and were settled in Mengo, when I arrived with Aldo. But what if they weren't? What if there were no Eliana?

I refused to allow myself to think about it. Eliana and Ugo were Beppi's godparents. There were birthdays, holidays, parties.

Sometimes, too, there were confidences from Eliana, unexpected and never encouraged. "Lucia," she'd say, "I'd give the world to have a voice I could sing with. You're so blessed!" And, "I'm homesick. The sea makes me unhappy, but don't tell anyone I said so." And, "I pray every morning and every night for a child."

It wasn't only the news of the pregnancy that had excited Marcellina. Eliana had made a request for a song at the restaurant. She wanted a window table to celebrate her condition with her husband, and a meal with lots of meat.

Marcellina said Eliana was convinced it would be a boy. The song she wanted was, in her words, *"Mio bambino."* She wanted to surprise Ugo with it.

Marcellina didn't know what to do. "Lucia! *Gianni Schicchi*! The *babbino caro*! Eliana got it wrong! She thinks *babbino* is *bambino! Bamb,* not *babb*! She only ever heard of the title! She thinks it's about a baby, not a girl who talks to her father about, if her boyfriend doesn't love her, she'll go to a bridge and throw herself into a river! I didn't have the heart to tell the truth! She'll feel ignorant! She'll feel like a hick! She'll never get over it! You know how mountain people are! Think of something!"

"I'll change the words to suit her circumstances," I said.

In fact, I had a song about Eliana I'd put together long before—a song no one would ever hear me sing.

I hate your basket.
It's tattered and ugly and dirty.
I hate how it swings on your arm.
I hate that braid on your head, like a giant wart.
I don't care if I'm damned forever
For thinking badly of a woman who's a saint.

There was no celebration dinner. The pregnancy was short-lived, and Eliana didn't come to the house or the restaurant for a long while.

I had already begun adapting the *babbino caro* when I learned there would not be a child. I could feel Eliana's heartbreak like a black cloud in front of the sun. I cried for her. Although I often wished she'd go home to the cliff and never return, I had never wished her ill, especially not in that way.

The furthest I got with her request was this:

O my dearest baby,
I love him, he's handsome, handsome.

I sang those words over and over, as if I could send to Eliana some sort of balm, even though she couldn't hear me. If Beppi was home, he'd come over and stand behind me, ducking his head at the back of my shoulders, nuzzling his forehead against me. He'd believed I was singing about him: my own, big baby, alive, strong, well, fully and absolutely himself.

Now here was Marcellina's voice, cutting into me.

"Lucia! Why are you standing there? Are you suddenly a statue? Come at once! We're getting into the car! We're getting out of San Guarino! We're going to a cave!"

Ugo and Annmarie had gone ahead. I heard the sound of a car engine starting up. It was Ugo's, smooth, reliable, gentle.

"Beppino!" cried Marcellina. "Think of your son! He might have gone to the very same cave! He may be there already! Waiting for us! Worrying! Stop being a statue! You're scaring me!"

What cave? Beppi would never go into a cave. He was afraid of the dark. He grew up in a restaurant, in light, heat, noise, abundance, smells of cooking, people all around him all the time. He was afraid of bats, of insects, of close, tight spaces. Dampness made him ill. Any time he'd been near a rocky surface, he'd scraped himself. He hated anything rocky.

A distant sound of thunder made me look up. It seemed that a storm was brewing, far out at sea, and might be moving toward us.

"Marcellina, it's going to rain. I think we're about to have a thunderstorm. We should stay here until it passes."

I'd never been in Ugo's car before.

"Lucia Fantini!" cried Marcellina. "There's no storm! I have a bad feeling! Ugo may drive away without us! If you don't start moving your feet, I'll pull you! Like a cow at the end of a rope! I'm stronger than you are, old as I am! I'll pull you so hard, your arm might come out of its socket!"

Then we saw planes. Two of them. Not German.

"Lucia!" cried Marcellina. "The Americans! They'll bomb us!"

She threw herself into my arms. "It's all right," I said. "They're not our enemies. We're on the same side now. You know that."

"I want Beppi."

"I know, I know."

"The Americans are still mad at us for Mussolini joining Hitler. They don't forget things like that."

"You're wrong. They only bomb Germans. There aren't any Germans here."

"I don't want to die."

"I won't let you. Don't think about such things."

Marcellina was trembling, and I held on to her more tightly. "I didn't tell you this before, Lucia. You left the house so early. I dreamed about Aldo last night, and he said to me, 'Marcellina, everything feels wrong. Why aren't you making a cake for my birthday?' I lied to him and said the only reason was, it was the middle of the night. I had no intention of getting up in the dark to do baking. I didn't tell him we couldn't spare the flour for a cake, because we'd have to save it for noodles. Did you buy it? Where is it?"

"It's a long story. I'll tell you later."

"We have to *leave.*"

She was right. I couldn't put it off any longer. "We'll go and hide now, even though I don't see the point," I said. "We'll have a nice lunch and believe me, I'm starving. When we get to the car, I'll let you ride in front with Ugo. Don't argue with me about it. After what you've been through, you deserve the special treatment. And please, try to be nice to the golfer, as I think she's someone you ought to get to know."

"She's too tall. It hurts my neck to look at her."

"Try."

"I can sit in the front?"

"Absolutely. Look, it's all right with the planes. They saw there aren't Germans here. You were smart to think about Aldo. He's up in the sky, right now, and he's going to make sure they do their job the way they're supposed to. He'll make them go to places where there are Germans."

"Poor Aldo. All that huffing and blowing."

"He'll be fine."

The planes had come from the north, a matching pair. It seemed they'd followed the road from Ravenna.

I knew they were American because they were similar to the reconnaissance planes. They let out the same throbbing whir, the same deafening racket. They were blunt-nosed and faster, in spite of their larger size, and as deep and wide as a fisherman's rowboat, with a long tail that looked something like a whale's fluke, and a stick-up-high fin in the center that was just like a shark's.

Newer-model reconnaissances, looking for Germans. When they tipped their wings and glinted in the light, one closely behind the other, it seemed they were up in the air for pleasure only, as if playing a game of tag. Maybe one of the pilots was the owner of the leather diary, as unbelievable as that seemed. Maybe he was looking for his book.

Marcellina clung to my arm as we made our way down the platform toward the dusty little yard on the other side of the station. Up ahead was Ugo's black Fiat; he was behind the wheel, turning to say something to Annmarie in the back.

Just beyond the car was a small, semicircular grove of cypress trees, thick and high and deeply, sunlit green—was the grove still a shrine?

There used to be a box, like an open-front birdhouse, attached to a tree where low branches had been stripped away. In the box was a small, rough, wooden statue of the village's saint, Guarino Guarini, the mathematician theologist who came from Modena, in the middle of the seventeenth century. He was a prototypical Jesuit, all brain and ascetics. He wandered the countryside, solving problems in geometry, certain that his shapes and equations would lead to, if not a direct encounter with God, some sort of approximation.

I knew about the shrine because Aldo and Beppi and I had stopped there all those years ago, on the day we went to Etto Renzetti's factory. We'd stopped because Beppi had to pee. The three of us went into the grove—this was Aldo's idea—to say a prayer to Guarino for Beppi's progress with arithmetic at school.

It was cool and serene in the grove, I remembered. Guarino was said to have gone there one summer to wait out the harsh midday heat, and he'd worked a miracle. Some farmers came by, shuffling in the dusty road, bent low with despair. There'd been a drought; crops were failing; everyone was hungry.

But they stopped to see who the stranger was and what he was up to. They looked at his parchments filled with figures and took him for a madman, although his education and his gentle, monkish austerity impressed them. They described their situation in great detail. As if he minded being bothered, and was having a tantrum, Guarino lifted the page he'd been writing on and threw it into the air. As it fell, it changed to a rabbit. When it reached the soft grass, it changed to two, then half a dozen, then twenty, thirty. The grove turned into a breeding hutch, and the rabbits just sat there twitching their noses, waiting to be scooped up and put into the farmers' bags. When the last one was secured, it started raining; the fields were instantly brought back to life.

"See, Beppi?" Aldo had said. "Good things come from doing well in school."

"Marcellina, do you know if the saint's shrine is still in those trees?" I said.

She looked at me in a scowling, worried way. She didn't care about a shrine. "What if Brunella is in the hiding place? This is the village she came from. Her dead father was a carpenter and I don't know what I'll do if I find out she's there."

Brunella was the mother of a waiter, Ermanno Vizioli. Zoli, he was called. Was Ugo blowing the car horn? Were they calling? It was hard to make out sounds with the planes.

Marcellina leaned in closely to be heard. "Don't you remember? At Aldo's funeral she said it was wrong how I was treated like family. She said I should have sat with the help at church. The help! You'll have to go into the cave ahead of me, and come out and tell me if she's there. Zoli is a treasure, he's always been my favorite waiter, but she doesn't deserve him for a son. I haven't said a word to her in four years. If she's in there, tell me the spot where she is, so I can go to the opposite side. In case you don't remember what she looks like, she's ugly. She's all dried up, like a prune. You'll pick her out right away, even if it's dark in there."

The sound of the planes grew louder. Why were they circling?

"Lucia! Promise me you'll go in first and check!"

"Stop shouting at me."

Then the bombs began falling.

7

I WAS UPSIDE DOWN, more or less. I took stock of my situation in what I felt was a rational way, and the slant of my body, I decided, was like the figure of an inclined plane in one of Beppi's science books, or maybe the subject was mathematics. Sometimes at Aldo's I threatened to go home without singing unless Beppi put some effort into his studies.

I'd hover over him in Aldo's office while everyone waited for me, Aldo in a fury, the waiters impatient, the customers getting worried, the spotlight in the rafters like a big blind eye.

Stubborn boy! He'd hold his pencil like a dagger, aiming it at his chest. "Mama, I'd rather stab myself than do these lessons."

I had wanted him to go to university in Bologna. I'd daydream of taking the train to visit him, then strolling beside him down narrow old streets and under splendid vaulted arches, nodding pleasantly as he greeted fellow students in bright scarves and loose jackets in need of repair, like the male characters of *La Bohème.*

It wasn't written in stone that Beppi had to grow up to run a restaurant. I imagined him reading philosophy, literature, history. I pictured him at medical lectures, in a laboratory, in the white coat of a scientist—or a future physician, like Ugo.

All those wishes. I'd pester him until he wrote the required composition, worked out the necessary equations, translated Latin verses of some poet he only felt sorry for, for being so pompous and dull.

Maybe I should have listened to him when he told us he wanted to be a carpenter. He was good with his hands. The first thing he ever got excited about learning was a sentence in a science or maybe mathematics book that said, "The four basic tools of humanity are the lever, the pulley, the wedge, and the inclined plane."

"Mama, look at these beautiful drawings. Look at the little wheels on the pulley. Look at how the shapes are." He'd been awestruck.

The inclined plane is a close relation to the wedge, I remembered. The secret of the inclined plane is in the path of least resistance.

"Lucia, talk to us. Even if you can't see us, we're here. We're all right. So are you. It's very, very important that you stay calm, until we figure out a way to free you."

Voices. I could understand the words, but the voices calling to me sounded far off and muffled, with strange reverberations. I felt I heard them underwater. One male, two female. Whose voices they were, I didn't know.

"Lucia, I hate to say it but I told you so! I *told* you what would happen! What were we standing around talking for? Why did you make me keep talking? We should have been safe in the cave, and now you're partially buried alive! I'm going out of my mind!"

"Lucia Fantini, please listen to me. Say you can hear me. I will kill myself if anything is wrong with you that can't be easily repaired, and I mean what I say, as I've been thinking about it anyway, now that they've blown up my factory."

Four voices, not three. Two male, two female.

I made no effort to answer. I had no memory of what had happened to me, but I didn't care. I felt no curiosity. A childish feeling of guilty pleasure had taken hold of me, as if I'd done something wrong on purpose.

I wasn't sorry for it, whatever it was. But it might have had something to do with this position of mine. Surely there'd be consequences for hanging about with my feet against a ceiling of air, and my head resting so very comfortably like this, so very gently.

The voices stopped.

I shut my eyes, and when I opened them a moment later the sky was over my head, gray and empty and still. It appeared to be the dusty sky of twilight.

Time to go to work?

"Roosters crow at sunrise, and Mama sings at the end of the day," Beppi would say, like a law, like the fact of the tools of humanity. "Roosters are the opposite of Mama."

I was looking up at the sky, it seemed, from a window. The restaurant?

Yes. Aldo's office. Everyone waiting for me, as if my body were a kettle of water on the stove, and they knew how long it took to reach a boil. That was how casual they were about it. Steam rose up from boiling water; the singer's voice rose up from her throat.

Time to go on, Lucia. Four, sometimes five, sometimes six times a week, plus Sunday afternoons.

How lucky I was! How marvelous it must be to be gifted! People said this to me all the time, as if I'd been born with the privilege of breezing through life in an effortless way, when most of humanity had to trudge through endless mud, with a bag full of bricks on their backs.

But getting ready to go out and sing could feel like getting ready to be born all over again.

No Beppi in sight. He wasn't at his father's desk. No schoolbooks this evening, no fighting. Where was he?

Oh, it was a Saturday evening; that explained it. It was the one time of the week he was allowed to be free from books. He was up to his usual Saturday habits, of course, following his father at his heels, arguing with the cooks, monitoring the cash box, greeting customers at the door, bothering the waiters, and all the while, walking about like a prince, beloved and indulged, in a safe, completely unassailable castle.

There was a window seat, like a church pew without a back, cushioned. Aldo had brought in carpenters from Etto Renzetti's factory to build it for me to sit and rest, pre-performance.

As if I could rest, with everyone waiting for me.

But this evening, I felt no agitation. The window seat was where I was, half sitting, half lying back. When I turned my head, I saw that I wasn't alone.

Verdi and Puccini were here, side by side, in chairs they must have dragged over from the other end of the office. They were just to my right.

Verdi was stiff with dignity. His dark beard was perfectly trimmed. His chin was tucked deeply in his high-rise collar, and he looked like a giant bird, all face and no neck: an owl. Puccini's clothes were badly rumpled; it seemed he hadn't had a bath in weeks. He started humming from the first act of *Tosca*.

Verdi was silent, pretending not to hear—pretending, I felt, not to be jealous.

Then directly opposite me appeared plump, sparkly-eyed Rossini, with his ink-black hair slicked down, as if he'd stuck his head in a bucket of oil. He reminded me of Etto Renzetti.

He'd pulled up the chair from behind Aldo's desk. I felt the need to address him.

"My dear maestro," I said, gently but firmly, "as much as your arrival doesn't bother me, I'm afraid you don't belong here with these two."

"These two? These *two*?" This from Verdi. "I mean no offense, because, my dear lady, where you come from, it's possible you weren't educated properly. As every Italian should know, in music there is only myself. There is only one *sommo,* at the highest of heights, as there is only one summit of a mountain."

Puccini showed his disagreement. He made motions in the air to indicate not a mountain but a woman's two breasts.

"Your son sent me," said Rossini. "You know I'm Beppino's favorite."

Puccini, raising his eyebrows, hummed louder.

"Change your tune, please," said Rossini to Puccini. "Enough with your Tosca. I'm sure people are correct when they call her heroic, but it's also correct that she's somewhat overly hysterical. Don't take that the wrong way. This is a time for calmness. Don't forget, Tosca's doomed."

Puccini ignored him. He'd just begun the menacing, boomy part of his opera where Tosca's enemy expresses his desire to have her followed, to have her found, to have her delivered to him, so that he—Scarpia, chief of the secret police, that black-shirted fiend, that sadist—can act out his fantasy of lording it over her. If he can't get her to be his lover, he'll go ahead and destroy her.

"For the second time, enough with the tragedy. Cut it out," said Rossini. "We need something optimistic. We've got to keep up this lady's spirits. We must fill her with lightness, yes, lightness, even lighter than air itself, which, if you ask me, is the point of all music. It's a sort of buoyancy, I suppose."

"No, no, no. The point of music," said Verdi, "is beauty."

"The same thing, exactly," said Rossini. "And then everyone goes home at the end of the show with an interest in making love. If they're sleeping alone, at least they'll have pleasant dreams. Pure and simple, and don't look at me like you want to kick my teeth in. What I mean is, this lady must have nothing to worry about."

Puccini surrendered, but not completely. He covered his mouth with his hands, muffling himself. His humming became a low sound of moaning, as if Scarpia had a toothache.

"How about a few lines from one of my big choral numbers?" suggested Verdi. "Something rousing and patriotic seems in order."

"I'm sorry to tell you this, but only Fascists are singing those types of things these days," I said.

Verdi took that calmly, with a sad shake of his head. He must have known already that Blackshirts hummed him all the time.

"Fascists," said Rossini. "Just what I was thinking about. Tell me, Signora Fantini, about the business I've heard of with the dogs in your village being trained to piss on their boots. I might like to do something with that—in a chorus, perhaps—unless I can think of a way to put a pack of mongrels on a stage."

Verdi couldn't hide his disgust. "You're so vulgar."

"You're so smug," said Rossini, in a friendly, cheerful way. It was astonishing how much he reminded me of Etto. Same hair, same smooth skin, same brightly shiny dark eyes, same plumpness. And Rossini had the air of someone who considers himself purely unique—just like Etto Renzetti.

"As long as we're speaking along these lines," Rossini was saying, "I must tell you, your compositions lack the simple touch of an ordinary human heartbeat. The plots of your operas, for the most part, are outlandish. I suppose it comes from thinking of music as a mountain. And I also suppose, any mountain of yours would not be volcanic, like the one this lady comes from."

Puccini had finished Act One. He uncovered his mouth and said, "I love volcanoes with all my heart. In my heart, I am Sicilian."

"So am I," said Rossini. "Sicily is the root of all Italy."

Verdi didn't care about Sicily. He wondered out loud if "outlandish" was an insult. A rhetorical question, he decided. He was uninsultable.

"I'm uninsultable, like Dante," he pointed out.

"No one's insulting you. I only wanted to identify your problem. You got addicted to lofty grandeur," said Rossini. "All that magnificence, and no heat. That's not beauty. Why do you think this lady sings your songs just seven or eight times a year, and only when people have begged for them?"

"She sings where people eat," said Verdi. "You can't have a *sommo* with spaghetti."

Rossini looked at him with an indulging little sigh. "They put down their forks the minute she opens her mouth. Remember, on the peak of a mountain, it's cold." He turned to Puccini. "Listen, Giacomo. I know you agree with me. Say something. Back me up."

"I can't," said Puccini. "Sorry, but I'm storing up breath for my second act, doomed or not. By the way, I'm honored you called my Tosca hysterical. She is an artist."

"I have heat!" cried Verdi. "What about my *Traviata,* for example? What about my Violetta?"

"She's dying of tuberculosis, like half the women in Italian operas not written by me," said Rossini. "Maybe there's a spark there, I'll grant you that. But she has no backbone."

This could get ugly. "Don't fight," I said, mother-like. "We've got enough of that as it is. They say in my village it wasn't difficult for dogs to learn that particular trick, as only the Fascists have boots. It was a butcher who taught them. But they have to be untrained, because too many of them have been shot. I don't think it's a good idea for an opera, to tell you the truth."

"I surrender to your judgment," agreed Rossini. "But listen to this! "

A moment later, into my head, full orchestra, with a great, wondrous burst, came the opening sounds of *Cenerentola*.

"Beppino's old favorite of his favorite," said Rossini proudly. "I figured you'd benefit from it, right about now."

I could hear the overture, fizzy and shiny, pulsing with sparks and eruptions . . .

"What's that irritating noise?" said Verdi.

"It's beautiful music," said Rossini. "I'm not saying so merely because it's mine. It's the music of shooting stars, a couple of waterfalls, plus waves full of bubbles, all over the whole, wide sea. And also, in terms of the listener, a great deal of pleasure, mental stimulation, and intensive pumping of the blood, so that the veins are nearly bursting. This is lightness! This is buoyancy! I am the best in the world when it comes to an overture, don't deny it."

Verdi's face grew pinched with a whole new level of disapproval. "But it's only a fairy tale. Don't you know there's a war on? It's inappropriate for a war. Stop it at once."

"A fairy tale? No, no, no, no," said Rossini. "It's solidly grounded in real life. My Cinderella is a girl of astonishing dimensions. Most importantly, she's not doomed. I pity your narrow-mindedness and lack of imagination."

Verdi looked ready to explode. "No one pities Verdi!" he cried.

"I'll stop humming now," said Puccini. "My throat's a wreck. I just want to say to you, Signora Fantini, I was disappointed when you didn't play the role of Tosca for those *nazifascisti,* on that terrible night when you were called on to serenade them. All the same, you were very Sicilian about it. You were resilient, and you did what you had to, and you were highly successful with that last song, even though it wasn't mine."

"It was mine," said Rossini. "It couldn't be otherwise. And it wasn't on the list they gave her."

Rosina, I remembered.

All those soldiers. The cooks with their ears stuffed up.

Uniforms, leather, boots, guns, the smells of scented colognes and shaving lotions. And a poster of Mussolini's face on the wall, bigger than life size, all doughy and jowly in a tight-fitting black helmet, as though the helmet had taken the place of his skull. I had promised myself when I first walked in that I wouldn't look at it carefully, but then I did. You won't win in the end, I'd thought. You big coward. Under that stupid iron hat of yours, your bones are as weak as a sparrow's.

The Barber of Seville.

I'd felt Rosina take possession of me. I'd felt that her lines were advice, which I'd decided to follow. If you touch me in my weak spot . . .

I'll sharpen my wits.
I'll be a viper.
I'll devise a hundred snares.
I'll never give up.

"I sang badly that night," I said. "I sang like an amateur. I sang with less than half of my strength."

"Badly on purpose doesn't count. They didn't know. That is

the essence of a Fascist." Saying this, Rossini leaned in more closely to me, taking hold of both my hands. Puccini came over to the window seat and touched me lightly on the side of my face.

Poor Verdi. He seemed to be feeling left out. He looked like he needed some sympathy.

"I wear white when I sing you," I told him. "Or silver. It's a sign of my respect. Customers tip generously when it's you—that's a fact. When I sing the dying song of Violetta, everyone weeps, even our head cook, who, believe me, is tougher than nails."

"Excuse me for changing the subject, but I wish I could hear you sing right now, Signora Fantini," whispered Rossini.

"I'm sorry, but I'm very far away from my voice."

"Perhaps another time. However, I don't know when we'll meet again, so I must tell you something. It breaks my heart to think that of everyone you know, the only person who doesn't know that you are beautiful is yourself. What's the matter with you?"

"Oh, be quiet," I said. "You embarrass me."

"Tips and weeping in a restaurant!" cried Verdi. "On top of being the favorite of Fascists! I've got to do something about this! *Bella, ciao,* I must hurry! I have things to do! I am Verdi!"

He was incredibly loud. His big, deep voice set off echoes that seemed to come at me from all directions.

Now I was alone. The slant of my body was shifting. The earth was moving. What had happened to the music?

The new sound in my ears alarmed me. Was this a landslide?

It was raining rocks and pebbles and loose bits of gravelly earth. In the distance was the sound of thunder, and it seemed that Verdi must have left me to go up to the top of a mountain, white with clouds and snow, where he was flinging his bolts at the earth, just like Zeus.

The grayness in the sky wasn't twilight. It was smoke.

Then suddenly those voices again. Closer.

"Lucia, I've got your hand. Hold on."

"Careful, careful."

"Lucia, you're a mess and your clothes are ruined, but at least you're not dead, not that I thought so. It's a good thing we're near the shrine to the saint here, because he's the one who protected us. Etto Renzetti's all right. He's right here. He came looking for us from the cave when we didn't turn up like we were supposed to. All of San Guarino is hiding in that cave! Had I told you that? Before the bombing, they had a feeling it was coming! Who knew carpenters could be fortunetellers? Etto's factory exploded, which I think he told you already. It exploded along with most of this town! I'm not speaking to your American golfer. I refuse to even look at her, because *Americans were the ones who did it.*"

"Signora Fantini, can you hear me? It is I, Etto Renzetti! I lost everything I had, but your ordeal is over! Here we are to set you free!"

8

Talking and talking and talking, the three waiters began laying out supper on the grassy floor of the grove.

The cypress trees were still standing. The grove was intact. It was still called the Saint's Grove, and it was still the special province of Guarino Guarini, even though, as Etto Renzetti explained, the shrine had been moved to the church in a nearby village some fourteen or fifteen years ago, when the station was being built. The people of San Guarino had felt that the racket of trains would be unsuitable to the memory of such a quiet, contemplative man.

But the nearby village had been bombed, too. The people of San Guarino who'd gone into hiding felt too afraid to come home. The roads were a mess—debris, fallen trees, household objects everywhere, battered, unrecognizable.

A stillness was in the air. Not the slightest breath of wind was stirring.

The three waiters had come on bicycles: Cesare Morigi, Cenzo Ballardini, Ermanno Vizioli. They carried guns. They'd put it out of their minds that Italians on bicycles were *verboten*. They had not met Germans along the way.

Talking, talking, talking. They didn't know where Beppi was.

They hadn't been told about blowing up the German truck ahead of time. Who knew that Beppi could keep anything to himself? All his life, he'd never been able to keep a secret. A secret to him was like accidentally picking up a piece of charcoal you thought was cold, then you felt a sensation of red-hot burning.

He'd given no warning of his plan, no hint. It was a totally covert operation, and they didn't give a damn if Beppi had meant it as a birthday present for Aldo.

When they found him, honest to God, they and all the rest of the squad planned to break his goddamn neck for leaving them out of it. If there happened to be a barrel of water at hand, or better, a barrel of piss—sorry to sound offensive—they were going to put his head in it, his whole head.

Nizarro had ordered the squad to separate. The three of them were sticking together, just as they'd always done in the restaurant.

They didn't know where anyone was, not counting Nizarro, who had the radio; they'd left him about an hour ago. Nizarro was on his way to Mengo to my house, no, not for the supper that wasn't going to happen, but merely to check it, from a safe distance, to see what was what. No one thought Beppi would have been stupid enough to try to hide at home, but it was reasonable to suppose that Germans had gone there. It was not a good idea to dwell on worries of what they might have been doing.

Nizarro had been in radio contact with Carmella Pattuelli. She'd given instructions on what to do with us in San Guarino. She knew what had happened. "I think this might be a good time for a picnic, especially if the grove, which I always loved, is still there," she had said. It wasn't a coded phrase, but it sounded like one.

A picnic in the trees, the pretty grove, a good time for it, yes indeed . . .

I tried hard to imagine those words as part of a song. It didn't work.

The three waiters didn't know if Carmella would join us, with or without Mauro. But it was probable, seeing as how their children had arrived already. The younger ones had somehow managed to keep those white clothes clean.

They were safe, they were fine, all nine: Marco, fourteen, their *capo,* head and shoulders above the rest of them and obviously thinking himself a man already; Francesca, a year younger, a real tomboy, and with her sharp eyes and quick tongue, she was the brains of that particular squad; the first twins Mario and Sandro, twelve and roly-poly, who not only were identical, but resembled their father so much, you could call them two more Mauros; Rudino, eleven, skinny and agile, with a slingshot in his hand and a homemade bow on his shoulder, along with sticks for arrows poking out of his belt; Antonella, eight, the graceful one, who wore her hair in two long braids and liked to walk on tiptoe, as if she fancied herself a ballerina; the second twins, Alda and Lucianna, seven, the honorary Fantinis, full of hell and in trouble every minute, but also a little aloof, a little formal, and it was true they had a special sort of brightness in their eyes, and a lustrous, unusual shine to their skin, like two apples scooped up from a dusty pile and polished; and then of course there was the baby, Giuseppina, five, a cherub, in spite of the way she had her father's sad-clown face.

Oh, that Beppina! She was a joy, a princess, a good-luck charm—but all the same, God help her if she grew up to be anything like the pain in the ass she'd been named for, no offense intended.

"You're not telling me anything I don't already know." Those were the first words I'd said since I entered the grove.

I lay on my side, with my knees bent up, on the backseat of Ugo's car, against the tree trunk where the statue of the saint used to be. The seat was the only part of the car that survived in one piece, although some of the leather had been charred, and reeked of burning. For a blanket, I had the long dress of Annmarie's habit. Etto Renzetti's jacket, smelling of wood and the factory, had been fashioned into a pillow.

Etto Renzetti. I *knew* he'd show up, as crazy as it seemed. The one non-Fascist Italian I'd wished never to lay eyes on again.

There were bird's-feet wrinkles around his eyes, his hair was thinner and less greased-down, and he had two gold teeth now—business must have been good. Other than that, he looked the same as he had all those years ago.

"Here, Lucia, let me fix my coat for you to rest your head on."

His face close to mine. Speaking to me gently, softly. Not making me feel that he burned me, like before. Making me feel that he wanted to warm me.

"You're injured, I know. I'll be brief. Do you remember the day Beppino was lost and we even looked in the well for him? I know you must remember. I know your distress, not knowing where he is, although you're being so careful not to show it. Distress is too mild of a description, I know. Myself, a bachelor, childless, being married to my factory, I can only imagine your state of mind. He might be lost at the moment, but the outcome will be the same, I swear to you, although I can't guarantee he'll be found on his back in some bushes, happy as anything, dreaming about becoming a carpenter, like Jesus. Let me say also, when they dropped their bombs on my factory, I shed no tears. The moment tears poured from my eyes—tears of *joy*—was when we pulled you out from those stones, and saw that you were very much alive."

I hadn't been pretending not to hear him when I didn't answer. I had not been able to speak.

But it felt good to hear Sicilian. It felt good to turn my face into that pillow.

And the waiters kept talking, soothingly, professionally, expertly.

Remarkable children! They'd decided on their own that the curse on San Guarino had come to an end, and the Pattuelli banishment was over, seeing as how, more or less, San Guarino wasn't here any longer. There was plenty of food for them, if they ever came indoors from their first-ever golf lesson.

Indoors. As if this were a house we'd all moved into.

Don't worry! They were safe out there, swinging sticks at rocks where the train station used to be. Wasn't that a great thing about the aftermath of bombardments? A peacefulness sets in.

Yes, the golfer was out there teaching them golf. There were plenty of holes in the ground now, to hit their little stones into. And they were learning new words: *putt, bogey, birdie.* The waiters didn't know what the first two meant, but the third was *uccellino,* little bird. Whether or not it was a good thing to have in golf, they didn't know.

But really, it didn't make sense to resent Annmarie Malone for what her countrymen had done. She was a good one. She was a soldier, not a pilot, and—not to be vulgar about it—she had balls.

And what about that dinner at Aldo's not even a week ago, part of the *nazifascisti* program of inviting nuns and priests to eat with them? Not that they included Enzo, of course.

Wasn't it something that the golfer, as a nun, had made

friends with a secretly partisan convent in Riccione, right near Mussolini's summer villa? It was the reason she came to Romagna in the first place!

So they all went to Aldo's on a Fascist bus, that whole convent, and the golfer came away with the thing she'd gone there to steal: a map of German mines on the shore from Rimini to Bellaria. Well, with the Americans getting interested in taking hold of the beaches, naturally, it would help out a lot to know where, and where not, to put down one's feet.

But surely the American had described all of that to me?

I didn't answer. I was listening carefully, though.

From within the grove the outside world could not be seen. The trees were like a wall without windows, and the open part of the semicircle faced a pale, shadowy hayfield, undamaged.

The three waiters went about their business as though they were back in the restaurant laying out a table. The Triumvirate, Beppi called them. To everyone but Beppi, they were Cesare, Zoli, and Cenzo.

Beppi was partial to Cenzo, whom he loved as a relative—an uncle, perhaps. But to cover it up and not seem to play favorites, he'd combined their names into one, and used it for each of them: *Cesarezolicenzo.*

They weren't related by blood, but they were pretty much the same age, in their early fifties. They had formed their own subgroup a long time ago.

Zoli, the son of Marcellina's now-despised old friend who'd spoken so awfully to her at Aldo's funeral, was a round-faced, sunny-natured man, and he knew how to make customers feel that the only reason he ever got out of bed in the morning was to serve them, charmingly and gracefully.

Cesare, white-haired and lion-like, had a strong, lovely voice—he was an amateur baritone. He sang at church and sometimes at wedding receptions, accompanied by his wife, if a piano was there.

Cenzo Ballardini was stocky, muscular, gruff, and growly, and the husband of the egg dealer Assunta. Before the war, she'd never slaughtered her chickens, but treated them as if they contained in their feathers a soul and a personality. She gave them pet names, let them die of old age or their own diseases, and buried them in the back of her yard. "My ladies," she called them.

I tried to look kindly on Cenzo because of Beppi's affection for him. Maybe he had a reason to be rough with the world, and so did Assunta—who in fact was shy and gentle, his very opposite.

They never complained about this, or seemed to feel sorry for themselves, but they only had one child, a daughter, Pia, close to thirty, who'd never been to school, but had always stayed at home, and was likely to stay there forever. The poor girl was sweet and pretty, but she'd been born as deaf as a nail, and mute as well. She might have been—no one knew for sure—a little feeble in the mind.

"Cesare-zoli-cenzo," I said to myself, hoping I'd hear it echo in my head, song-like. It didn't.

I tried to enter into the spirit of the picnic, but that didn't happen, either. The provisions came from the Pattuelli pantry. I had the feeling the three waiters must have emptied it. They had filled their bicycle baskets and their pockets: salami, ham, *mortadella,* cheese, biscuits, bread, cakes of roasted polenta, jars of olives and pickled artichokes, tins of anchovies, wine, water, and two of Aldo's large-table tablecloths, which, they pointed out, had been confiscated by Carmella Pattuelli.

They'd spread the tablecloths side by side on the grass, covering nearly every inch of it, as if the point of a picnic was to make sure that no part of the earth came in contact directly with one's body.

All along, Ugo sat alone by the opening of the grove. He looked like someone who'd been praying on his knees but had given up the position and sat back on his heels. His expression was perfectly blank, as if he were asleep with wide-open eyes.

"*Dottore,* please," the waiters implored him. They took turns addressing him. "Talk to us. Tell us what sort of car you'll buy next. Tell us how you knew to get out of it before the bombs hit."

"The American commanded me to jump out, and I obeyed her." Ugo seemed to answer the question only because he knew they'd keep asking it. His voice was flat, not like his own at all.

He'd feel better, Marcellina had told me, if he were reunited with his medical bag, which had been within reach his entire life as an adult. She'd been so upset about that. She'd felt that it might have been the same to Ugo as if he'd lost a part of his hand.

She and Etto had gone outdoors to search for it. Marcellina believed they'd find the bag in perfect condition in a pile of rubble or car parts, for certainly God, through the intercession of Guarino Guarini, would have spared it. And while they were at it, they'd look for my purse, and the guns that were no longer in my coat pockets.

The Lugers, saved in the shopping bag with the nun's habit, were in the possession of Annmarie, which had appalled Marcellina. "How are we supposed to know she won't use them on us? I don't care if she insists they're not loaded. I'll never trust an American again."

I tried to lift my head to look at Ugo. An astonishing tremor of pain went through me, as if I'd just been hit hard in the face, but I was able to not cry out.

How still Ugo was, sitting there like that! He reminded me of the time Buddhist monks had appeared one evening at the second *trattoria*—four or five of them, Asian-faced and nearly bald, in colorful, sunset-colored robes, like an old Roman senator's. They spoke no Italian. They had wooden bowls in their hands and chopsticks in pouches that hung from their belts. They'd been going about the countryside, looking at things, requesting food along the way. When they knocked at the kitchen door, the one who answered was Beppi.

He was thrilled with them. He made Aldo invite them inside, to be seated at one of the best tables, which they'd refused. So Aldo and Beppi set up a table for them in the yard.

It was the first time, maybe the only time, I sang without Beppi in front of my eyes. Where was Beppi, where was Beppi? The spotlight was about to go on, where *was* he?

One of the Triumvirate—Cenzo—had come to my rescue. He knew what I was feeling. He maneuvered himself to the front of the room and whispered to me, "Your son is with monks. That's not a joke, or wishful thinking. Those Buddhist monks are on the patio. They are eating with chopsticks. Your son's eyes are popping out of his head. He's overjoyed, and Aldo says leave him out there, because this is the first time he did actual work around here. He's waiting on them. I'm sorry to tell you, your performance tonight, as far as he's concerned, has been trumped."

To annoy Beppi, I sang from *Cenerentola,* in spite of an all-Puccini program. And afterward, it was all we heard about. He wanted to study meditation, he wanted a crimson robe, a pouch, a bowl, his head shaved. "I'll still use a fork when I eat, though," he'd said. "I'm too Italian not to."

At home, he plunked himself down on the floor in the front

hall every morning, sometimes cross-legged, sometimes sitting back, half kneeling. He'd be absolutely still for as much as half an hour at a time. Marcellina had worried about it a great deal. "He's turning himself into a doorstop! He's going to convert, and leave us! He'll run away to the Orient!" At work, the cooks and waiters told him if he wanted to sit around underfoot, like a fresh head of cabbage, they'd pick him up and throw him into the soup.

That was what Ugo reminded me of. I'd had to lie back again—the pain wouldn't let me do anything else—and I knew I had better keep quiet. Keep quiet, and hide all feeling.

My heart, my heart, under the sand like a clam.

Nothing. That wasn't a song, either. On the day of Aldo's funeral, Beppi had said to Ugo, "You have to be my substitute father now, and don't tell me I'm too old to need one."

Another, lesser man might have shuffled in his shoes with anxiety and discomfort, or made a joke of it, thinking Beppi too sentimental, a big baby. Ugo had held out his hand to seal the deal, solemnly.

"Please give her something to drink. God help me for having nothing else to suggest." It was Ugo who'd spoken, but if my eyes were closed, I never would have guessed it. What was the matter with him? He sounded too flat and despairing to blame it on his lost, blown-up car, or his missing medical kit.

Zoli crouched down beside me. He had a canteen of water. "I'm sorry we haven't got any glasses," he said.

I could not lift my head; it was simply too heavy. When he pressed the spout to my lips, I couldn't bear it.

"Where's your mother, Zoli?" I said. "Marcellina thought she'd be hiding in the cave with everyone else, because San Guarino is her hometown."

"Mama," he said, "is at home with my wife and the kids. They're probably hiding in the cellar."

"Marcellina's not speaking to her. Her old best friend."

"I know. It's all right. It gives them more pleasure to hate each other than to behave with any affection."

"How many children do you have, Zoli? It's so hard to keep track."

"Seven, but I'm still working on it. I want to beat out Mauro, even without the advantage of all those twins. I want to have ten altogether. Please, will you drink a little water?"

"I can't."

Poor Zoli, he looked as if I'd made him want to cry. At the restaurant he was the second most popular waiter, after Mauro. He was a born coaxer, a real artist at it. Whenever the cooks ran short of one type of provision, invariably with a surplus of something else, they prevailed upon Zoli to go out and sell the something else to Aldo's customers. Often he went through a whole shift without waiting on tables of his own. He'd take on the role of kitchen spokesman and hobnob with the diners, suavely and effectively.

He'd inquire how everything was. He'd make suggestions, in an insider's way. "You should consider changing your order for the veal. Confidentially, I tasted it myself. It pains me to say this, at the risk of my job, but for me, all that matters is the satisfaction of my customers. The veal may have come from an inferior breeding line, or an unscrupulous dealer, who, believe me, if that's the case, we will never use again," he'd say silkily, on an evening when the veal had run out. "But the calamari's spectacular tonight, and so is the grilled *sogliola,* not to mention the heights they've risen to with the crabs, which, if that's what you want to order, I'll have to rush to the kitchen to make sure there's any left. You know how it is when a cook has spontaneously created a masterpiece. Word gets out and there's a rush on it, because everyone wants to talk the next day about how they were among the lucky few to have had it."

There wouldn't be squid; there wouldn't be grilled sole. There'd only be crabs, dozens of them, scrambling and fighting in the sinks, and in buckets all over the kitchen.

"She doesn't want water," said that not-Ugo's voice. He didn't even sound like a doctor prescribing something. He just sounded so terribly *flat*.

"Get out my way, Zoli, before I trip on you. The doctor's right. I've got something better."

Cesare's silver-white head came level with mine. He was a large, tall man; it must have taken a lot of effort for him to get down on the ground. I felt as if a big shaggy creature—a tame, oddly colored lion—had decided to lie down beside me.

I felt a special tenderness for him.

One morning, Aldo sat up beside me in our bed, tapped my shoulder, and told me he didn't feel well. His face had an ashen pallor; his eyes looked terrified. It turned out to be the first of his heart attacks, and I refused to leave him, even though Ugo had come and promised to stay. I didn't care that a large English tour group from Oxford University, or maybe it was Cambridge, had booked the restaurant for a private party, paying extra to hear the singing.

Aldo did that. He never let tour groups know it was free.

We decided to enlist Cesare to take my place. "We're giving you a splendid baritone, who so far is only famous in Italy, but the whole world is panting to receive him," the waiters said. "Wait until you hear his Verdi! He will heat you so deeply, you'll retain the warmth, long after you're home, in spite of your damp and frigid climate. You'll hear some of your Shakespeare as well. We feel you can't possibly appreciate him until you've heard him in Italian, the language of his soul."

Aldo had been hoping anyway to get Cesare to expand his horizons as a singer, and not just give his voice to people he already knew, and to God. He'd never sung in a professional capacity, but Aldo had felt that, given the chance, he would soar, he'd be a sensation. This had not happened.

Around nine on the evening of his performance, when the spotlight should have been just turned on, with Cesare in it, I looked up from my chair at Aldo's side to see Nizarro in the doorway—not coming to see how Aldo was, or to speak to Ugo about his prognosis, which was, "Don't worry, the engine only stalled, and he's a long way from dead."

Nizarro had come to beg me to get dressed and rush to the restaurant and sing some *Otello* and *Aida,* because Aldo wasn't the only one who'd had an attack. Cesare had panicked. It was completely hysterical, with no basis in anything physical, but all the same, his throat closed up like a fist.

It had not been possible for me to leave that room, not with Aldo so frightened, not with Ugo right there.

There'd nearly been an English riot of protest in the restaurant, but Beppi refunded their money and gave them free wine. He ordered Nomad into the spotlight, after lathering him up with *grappa,* to tell jokes in English and sing the drinking songs he'd learned as a waiter in his London hotel. The professors and their wives had enjoyed it.

And then Beppi came home to cheer up his father with an enthusiastic bellowing of a song he'd memorized immediately, about the interest of famous philosophers in getting drunk. "Aristotle, Aristotle, was a lover of the bottle," it went. And, "I drink, therefore I am."

When Aldo was on his feet again, I went to Cesare's house, a thing I'd never done before with a waiter. I grasped his hands. I told him I knew how he felt. I told him that if he wanted to stick to weddings and hymns, he should do so. I told him that if he attempted to stop singing because of one small misstep—that was what I called it, a misstep, not a failure—I'd stop as well, I'd never sing another note, and Aldo would hold it against him, and fire him, and make sure no other restaurant would have him, end of discussion. He'd wanted to know if I had ever walked out on an audience without performing, and I told him the truth. "Almost, but there's no comparison, because you're not the one who has to go home with Aldo."

Cesare trusted me. He deserved the same in return.

He didn't ask me to try to move any part of myself. It occurred to me to wonder what I looked like. "Cesare," I whispered, "what do I look like?"

"Like yourself."

"I think I have bruises. My face—how is my face?"

"As lovely as always, Lucia."

He had removed the hard crust from a small piece of bread. He'd soaked it with wine. "Look, Lucia, pink bread. Taste it. I think it will go down easy."

I didn't want to taste anything. "What's the matter with Ugo, Cesare?"

"He's despondent because he hasn't got his instruments and medicines, and also—much worse—he's got it into his head that, any second now, you are going to die. I'm begging you to help me cheer him up."

"Die from what?"

"From starvation, thirst, and a very big headache, Lucia. So we're taking care of everything at once."

I allowed Cesare to feed me a bit of the pinkened bread, then more of it, then all of it.

Lambrusco! I'd never had it in this manner before, but the taste was the same, light and slightly fruity, but minus the little fizzy sparkle, which the bread had absorbed.

"It was Cenzo's idea to fix it like this for you," said Zoli, who was just behind Cesare.

And there was Cenzo, peering down at me from over Zoli's shoulder, narrow-eyed, worried, without his usual, I'm-about-to-start-growling expression.

I'd often wondered if Cenzo's wife's chickens were terrified of him, as if, in their eyes, he looked like a fuming, enormous, mythological god who might raise his foot and kick them at any moment or crush them to feathery bits. But with his daughter, Pia, he was said to be angelic, doting on her, never letting on to her how rotten he felt about her condition. A deaf-mute for a child! It was unimaginable to me.

There had never been requests for special songs from him. Unlike all the other waiters and cooks, he'd never spoken to me about the way my singing made him feel. He'd never congratulated me for a successful program. Maybe he'd taken a psychological stance against music and all beautiful sounds in general, in alliance with Pia, in much the same way that Cesare would not eat nuts; one of his children was allergic to them.

Cenzo's specialty at the restaurant was to spare his bosses from direct interaction with troublemakers.

Every night it was something, some problem. He'd taken over as cop because Nizarro, lording it up as headwaiter, turned out to be, as Aldo had put it, overly energetic in his tactics. One night Nizarro broke an expensive Etto Renzetti chair by rushing out to the parking lot and slamming it against the hood of a car that was about to be driven away by a man who had not paid his bill. When the man flew to Aldo to insist that the restaurant foot the bill for repairs to his car, Nizarro took a swing at him with the part of the chair he still had left in his hand, and they'd had to call in Ugo to stop the blood, and everyone heard about it; it was a full-blown scandal, and the only thing Nizarro would say by way of accounting for his behavior was, "At least I took the time to make sure that he wasn't a high-placed Fascist, or some political bigwig, before I sprang into action."

Cenzo had some subtlety, which took customers by surprise. He'd unnerve a problem maker by not acting like the thug he seemed to be. Valuing discretion, he'd be thoughtful and sparing of words, which might have come from his experience as a father. He'd created a hand-signal system so he could talk to his daughter at home, like a one-of-a-kind, daily-life mime show, which had delighted Beppi so much when he found out about it, he'd had to learn some signals himself.

It was just like what had happened with the Buddhists—that same fascination. He drove the staff wild by screaming at them with his mouth shut tight. He'd frantically wiggle his fingers and wave his arms, and let his hands flop about in the air, as if he suffered from fits, which he'd found absolutely delightful.

Cenzo's face looked softer than I'd ever seen it before. The cypress trees seemed to have moved their shadowy branches a bit closer together. I had the sense of being safe, in the protection of a soft, dark-green wall.

"How does it taste, the Lambrusco?" said Zoli.

"Doughy, but perfect," I said.

The three of them. Beaming at me, proud of me. The Triumvirate. I couldn't see Ugo beyond them, but I knew he was there.

"My father was a fisherman," Cesare said. "He used to tell me that a bottle of wine, preferably a good Lambrusco, is the best thing to have at sea, if your boat is about to start sinking. Drinking it will keep you safe in the water, better than any life jacket, while you're waiting to be rescued."

"I believe it," I said. I was now sitting fully upright on Ugo's car seat, with Annmarie's habit tucked around me like a lap rug.

"I wish Assunta would feed this stuff to the chickens," said Cenzo. "It might make them get up and fly away, and I'd have some peace for a change, although I'd mind the loss of income from the egg sales."

"Lambrusco is famous for its curative powers," said Zoli.

I nodded in agreement. "I would like some more, please," I said, "but this time without the bread."

"Certainly! Supper's ready!" they cried. It seemed that their voices had combined into one, rising high, leaping up toward the tops of the cypresses, leaping over them. "Renzetti! Marcellina! Signorina Golfer! Come indoors! You kids, if you don't come at once, we'll take away your clubs! We'll break them, stick by stick! We'll complain to your parents, and they'll take our side against you! Come indoors! Come indoors!"

I HAD NEVER SPENT a night before without a roof over my head. Sleeping bodies were all around me. Someone was snoring, probably Cenzo. He often had sinus trouble, no doubt the result of an allergy to his wife's chickens.

Marcellina was flat on her back with Pattuelli children packed in closely; the youngest ones had their heads at her breasts, her hips. The older two were slightly off to the side, curled up against each other, back to back.

A throbbing pain came down in waves from my forehead to my neck, then stopped and started over again, over and over and over.

"One thing I know as a physician is, if you think of the worst pain you've experienced," Ugo used to say, "and compare it to the pain you have now, the pain you have now will be lessened, as the body—and this is an axiom—has a memory of its own. This trick works every time, unless the pain of the moment is honestly greater than what was formerly worst, in which case, at least you know you've set a new standard." Ugo had said this to Aldo at the time of each of the first three heart attacks.

"The worst pain I ever experienced," Aldo would answer, "was the pain of my blood stopped cold in my veins when I asked Lucia to marry me and she told me to go to hell because I was too old for her. The second worst was one week later when I asked her to change her mind, and I expected she would say the same thing. The third, since things always come in threes, was when I told her I'd live with her in Sicily for the rest of my life, and I was afraid she'd take me up on it, even though she knew I'd only gone there in the first place to track down a supplier—not a Sicilian, by the way—who had cheated me, and whom I never found, and I was sure that my blood would never be pumped the right way, so far from Mengo and Romagna."

The worst for me, before this, was giving birth. The labor had lasted two days. Beppi had been astonishingly big and heavy, and worse, he had wanted to stay where he was. He'd put up resistance with everything he had. Right from the start he'd been stubborn.

Nine pounds, three ounces. "Our iron-boned baby giant. His muscles are probably stronger than mine," Aldo had said, in awe, the first time he saw him.

"Lucia," a voice whispered. "I know you're awake. Give me your purse. I need the bullets."

There'd been no luck finding Ugo's kit, but Etto had found my purse, on the not-ruined ticket counter of what used to be the train station, as if a hasty traveler had forgotten it. I'd fallen asleep with it in my arms, the way I used to bunch up Aldo's shirts and sweaters and take them to bed with me, which I'd only stopped doing when they stopped smelling like Aldo.

Annmarie. As commanding as ever. She was by my side.

"Is it true you went to the restaurant with Italian nuns and stole a map of the beach mines?"

"Never mind about that now."

"You should have told me about it on the train, when I met

you. I'm upset with you that you didn't. You didn't have to be so mysterious."

"Tell me about your feelings later. I want you to know what's been happening since you fell asleep, and then I want to load these guns."

"Did anyone find the Berettas that fell out of my pockets?"

"No. The Lugers are all we have."

"I didn't fall asleep, by the way. I passed out. I remember it. I've been fully unconscious, not that I'm complaining."

"You had a lot of wine."

"Well, the alcohol content of Lambrusco isn't high."

"It isn't low, either. I'm not arguing with you."

"I'm not expecting you to. I'm only trying to delay you from telling me something I feel will be bad. I was getting myself ready."

"Are you in much pain, Lucia?"

"Thank you for getting around to asking me. It's nothing I can't manage. Do I look injured?"

"It's too dark to tell. Are you ready now?"

"Yes. No. Go ahead, and then I've got to get up to relieve myself."

I had never peed outdoors before, not even as a child. It seemed like something important to look forward to: a normal adventure of life, a little risky, a little complicated. Something to plan. I'd have to step carefully in the darkness, but surely, if snakes were out there, or scorpions or rats, they'd leave me alone, as they'd all be hiding, terrorized from the bombs, and too much in shock to come out and bother with me.

"Carmella and Mauro were here," Annmarie whispered.

"Mauro went home to his wife?"

"No, they met just over there, in the field. They'd come separately, from opposite directions, at the same time. They only stayed a couple of minutes. They left with Doctor Fantini on the bicycles, and the waiters went on foot to help out. Their village was hit, I think badly. The church seems to have taken the worst of it, and it was filled with people when the bombs came. The children don't know about it yet, but when they wake up, we'll have to tell them. We'll have to keep an eye on them, especially the oldest two. They might try to run home to see how their friends are. There's been no word of Beppi, and nothing further from Nizarro on the radio, but Carmella's been away from it."

So it wasn't Cenzo who was snoring. It was Etto, the only man left.

"Excuse me, we're not stupid. We know what happened," said a child's shape on the ground. A boy. The voice was coming from the huddle of three of them at Marcellina's feet.

"Marco and I won't go home on our own, don't worry," said the girl with her back to her brother. "If you knew us better, you'd know that we never split up."

"Oh, Christ," said Annmarie. "Are all of you awake?"

"Only five of us." I recognized that one: Marco, the eldest. What was the girl's name? Francesca. I felt proud of myself for remembering this.

"I'm awake, too," chirped one of the small ones, a head lifting from Marcellina's hip.

"Alda, *ciao*. That's six," said Marco.

"Me too."

"Lucianna, *ciao,*" said Marco. "Seven."

Marcellina kept sleeping. I made out Etto by the open side of the grove, near the spot where Ugo had been. He was snoring away, lying on his side in his shirtsleeves. He'd slid under the edge of the picnic tablecloth, unlike Marcellina and the children, who were sprawled on top of it. The cloth covered him to the waist, in a normal way, like a bedsheet.

He'd found my purse! Etto Renzetti! The worst day of his life and he'd gone looking for it!

"You kids, you've got problems to deal with, very large ones, which we're not saying anything else about, at least not tonight. So be quiet and get some sleep," said Annmarie. "No one's allowed to have nightmares. I'm forbidding all nightmares, as you have more than enough in real life. Those are *orders.*"

"I want Mama."

"Beppina, *ciao.* Mama will be here in the morning. She wants you to be brave," said Marco. "That's eight of us."

"Americans can't give orders to Italians. We're co-equals." That was Francesca again.

Annmarie sighed. "You're right. Americans can't order you around, but nuns can. I am still, officially, let me remind you, a nun. I'm also your golf teacher, so when it comes to obeying me, you haven't got a choice."

"Can I ask you a question?" said another child in the huddle.

"Which one are you?"

"Sandro."

"All right, but only one."

"Do you want the bullets from Signora Fantini so you can shoot your own planes with the Lugers, if they come back?"

"She'd need a cannon," said the boy beside him, who must have been Mario, his twin. Their voices were more or less identical.

"I want Mama, too."

"Antonella, *ciao.* It's all right, she'll be coming. Nothing bad will happen to you, I promise," said Marco. "That's all of us and, in my opinion, if the planes are low enough to drop bombs, the way to get them is with howitzers, not cannons. Cannonballs are too heavy to go that high."

"Another plane would be best," said the boy who'd spoken up first. He had obviously given the matter some thought. "Not a bomber, and not a reconnaissance plane. What she needs is a fighter, a fast one. As fast as a shark in the air, with machine guns."

"I can't fly planes, and I'm not allowed to shoot them," said Annmarie patiently. "If I did, I'd get court-martialed. I'd languish in a military jail, wearing shackles day and night. By the time they released me, if ever, I'd be too worn down to go out on a golf course. I would never play again, never mind win myself more trophies."

"Doctor Fantini told us you already won everything there is. You've won more prizes than any other lady golfer in America," said a boy twin.

"But not in the whole world, not yet," said Annmarie. "To answer the question, I want the bullets because I'm on guard duty outdoors, and I have to be able to protect you. To tell you the truth, out in the dark by myself, I was a little afraid."

It gave me satisfaction to know that Annmarie was willing to admit to fear. I felt I'd been right to have decided before that she'd make a good mother for my grandchildren. "She's good with children," I said to myself.

"I'm never afraid," said the boy called Rudino. "Does the army teach you to load a gun in the dark, even if you're a noncombatant?"

"Spying in wartime is a form of combat," said Marco, the voice of authority.

"It is, and they do," said Annmarie. "They teach you all sorts of things."

"Did you ever kill anyone?" said Francesca.

"Go to *sleep.*"

It grew quiet within the grove. I gave Annmarie my purse and slowly, shakily, went about the business of trying to stand up. My wool coat was still on me, torn and gritty, but still in one piece. I was not wearing shoes.

"I want my shoes," I said to Annmarie.

"I'm sorry. We never found them. I'd lend you mine but you'd trip on them. Your two feet would fit in one of them."

"I'd give you mine, but the same thing would happen."

The sound of Etto's voice was startling. I hadn't realized that the snoring had stopped. It was as if a bassoon had started playing, in the wake of flutes and panpipes and clarinets.

Etto was a bassoon. "I'll go out with you, Signora Fantini. There's glass everywhere, a million things to watch out for. My job here is to offer protection. Every inch of this village, not that there was a lot of it, I know with my eyes closed."

"Etto, I'm going to the toilet."

"I won't look. I'll keep my distance."

"Stop calling me Signora. I have a first name like a normal person, and you should use it. Please keep your voice down. I don't want you waking Marcellina."

"He already did," said Marcellina gruffly. "Don't listen to him. Keep his distance, my foot! I'd go with you myself, but I feel like hell. I feel like I'm ninety, and I'm buried alive in Pattuellis."

"She wasn't trying to insult you, Etto," I said.

"Yes, I was, if that's what you call it when you're stating the obvious," said Marcellina haughtily.

"I'm not insulted, Lucia. Thank you for worrying about it."

"Thank you for finding my purse, Etto."

"You're more than welcome. It brought me almost as much joy as knowing you weren't killed when you were buried."

"Are you loading the guns now?"

"I just finished, Mario," said Annmarie. "They're all set."

"Can we touch them?"

"No, Sandro, you can't. If I catch any of you with a gun, by the way, I'll make sure you never pick one up again. Don't forget, I belong to the United States Army. You would not believe the things I learned to do to people who make trouble, and that includes children."

"How many trophies do you have?"

"Are you Lucianna?" said Annmarie.

"No, Alda."

"Forty-six," said Annmarie.

"How many would it take to have the most in all the world?"

"Forty-seven, Lucianna."

"Did you ever play golf against men?" said Francesca.

"Lots of times."

"Did you beat them?"

"Sometimes."

"How many times? More than half?"

"I didn't keep count."

"I bet it was more like seventy percent," said Rudino. "Probably thirty percent of American men are taller than she is."

"In Italy it would be ten," said a boy twin.

"It would be closer to three, actually," said Rudino. "Or maybe even two."

"Does it matter if you're tall in golf?"

"It's a factor, Marco," said Annmarie.

"Are you giving us a lesson in the morning, before Mama comes?"

"Are you Alda?"

"Yes."

"I'm planning to, but I'm finished talking. If there's one more sound out of any of you, I'll forget about it. That isn't an order. It's a vow. Since you're Catholic, like I am, I think you understand the difference."

There was instant silence. I could tell from the sound of Marcellina's breathing that she'd gone back to sleep. Good.

"I'll wait just outside for you, Lucia," said Etto. "I'll walk around and make sure it's safe. I wanted to stretch my legs anyway. The last time I slept on the ground, I swear to God, was never. It doesn't agree with me."

"It's very kind of you," I answered. "Seeing as how you won't allow me to stop you."

"A principle is involved. I'm a principled man, in case you didn't know that."

"You must be longing for your bed."

"I don't have one anymore. They blew it up."

"I'm sorry to hear that," I said. "It's no consolation, but it's possible that the same thing happened to mine. Who knows what I'll find when I go home? But in my case, the culprits would be *nazifascisti.*"

"We should hope for the best, even when it's insane of us," said Etto.

"I'll try to agree with you."

I was finally up on my feet, having taken what felt like an hour to get the sense that my blood was circulating correctly and that my legs could be trusted to hold me. I refused the arm Annmarie held out to me, but one second later, swaying back and forth, with an uneasy feeling in my stomach, like seasickness—I'd never felt all right on boats—I took hold of it, as if seizing a rail.

That was when the smell of my own body assailed me: the

unmistakable, shameful smell, then the sticky dampness, then the realization that, sometime earlier, I had soiled myself. Why hadn't I noticed before that the grove smelled like pee? It was overwhelming, especially in that heavy air.

"Are you all right?" whispered Annmarie.

"I don't know."

I considered allowing myself to sink back down on the car seat and let my bladder release itself again, like an infant's. And why not, when I was sleepy, weak, and aching, and the pain in my face was growing worse—the waves were faster now, without pause—and my clothes were already stinking wet? Yes, I'd lost my shoes, but if I hadn't, they'd be stinking wet as well.

"My will is gone and it doesn't matter to me. All I want to do is lie down again on Ugo's seat," I almost said.

I really came close to it. Certainly I had the right to that particular type of surrender. Sink down, let go, and stay put. Even now, the edges of sleep were closing in on me, pulling at me like a tide. I had never in my life been so tired.

But there was Annmarie, holding on to me. "Come on, start walking. If I told you the number of times soldiers piss themselves in bombings, you would never believe me. Or golfers before a tournament, sometimes even an exhibition, when there's not all that much at stake. Do you know what we call golfers who never wet their pants? We call them people who aren't actually golfers."

It worked.

"Stop trying to cheer me up. It's not working. And let go of me. I can get along without you."

"That's terrific. We haven't got water for you to bathe in, but when you get outdoors, you can change your clothes. You can wear my habit—well, the dress part, which smells all right, considering what it's been through, and it's dry. It'll be a mile too long for you, but you can bunch it up at the waist, and wear the belt."

"You want me to be a *Sister*?"

And there was Etto's voice, calling to me from outdoors. "Lucia! I've made you a path for your toilet! Come and see the moonlight!"

"Just wear it like a dress," said Annmarie. She already had the garment in her hand, and held it out to me, all the yards and yards of it, like a gift. Then she handed me the belt. "Do you want me to come with you and guard you from Etto?"

"You stay here."

"Watch your step," said Annmarie.

"Stop fussing."

"Excuse me," whispered a boy. It was unmistakably the somber, brainy Rudino. "May I have permission to be exempt from the vow, to say just one more thing?"

"No exemptions," said Annmarie.

"But I don't want to say it to you. I want to say it to Signora Fantini."

"Go ahead, dear," I said. "I'm on my way out, in a hurry, but I'm actually the one in charge here. If Annamaria is a nun, I promise you, I'm her abbess."

"That's what I thought," said Rudino. "I just wanted to say, as worried as I am about Mama and Papa and my village, I'm glad you didn't die when the station fell on you, and have a good walk."

"*Grazie, buona notte.* You can still have your golf lesson."

"Have a good walk outdoors, Signora Fantini. Can I still have a lesson, too?" Beppina's sweet voice rose up from the ground like a trill: the little namesake, clinging to Marcellina.

"*Ciao, carina.* You can have anything you ask for, but go to sleep now."

Etto called to me again, more impatiently. "Hurry, Lucia! I'm not kidding about the moon! I thought for a minute the Americans bombed it! But there it is! It's almost full! I never saw it so big! It's almost as good as the spotlight at Aldo's, but not quite!"

10

THERE WAS NO NEED to make him feel like a country bumpkin, Etto pointed out, a real provincial hick, when all he'd done was ask if I sang from operas of the famous Venetian clergyman-composer Antonio Vivaldi, often called the Red-Headed Priest—not that, after his ordination, he had practiced priestly duties. Plenty of people thought him inferior to someone like Verdi, but what was the use of the comparison? It was like saying that a man is inferior to a god. Italians couldn't all be god-like, or there wouldn't be a country of people.

I didn't think Verdi was a god? Just a very great composer? Ha! He agreed! He'd only said so because he'd thought it was expected of him!

He knew Beppi had been named Giuseppe in honor of Verdi. So it was actually Aldo who picked the name! Hoping Beppi would grow up to be a composer! Which became apparent at an early age would never happen! Ha ha! All those years knowing Aldo—he'd never mentioned that!

No one called him by his given name of Ettore, but he felt it was thoughtful of me to inquire. He was Etto, pure and simple. At the factory, he'd been Signore, *capo,* or just *cap.* Sardinians, Sicilians like ourselves, Greeks, North Africans, and mainland

Italians as well, had all sorts of names for him in their dialects. He didn't have to put two and two together to know that, even if they sounded nice, they were not always compliments. It was just as well that he never understood what anyone was saying. The people who worked for him had made fun of him, taunted him, and insulted him, but they'd done it only privately, among their own kind. He found that a sign of respect.

He didn't suit everyone's taste, Vivaldi, with all that baroque high-mindedness. But his life was purely musical and worthy of envy, as was, in point of historical fact, his lustrous red hair, which he'd been vain about. It must have been difficult for him to have undergone the natural process of entering into old age, when vanity can truly be a problem.

He, Etto, wasn't like so many people who thought the aging process was horrifying. In the furniture business, you know that when you age a piece of lumber, remove the layers of junk, and plane it down carefully until it's smooth, bare wood—well, maybe it's not music, but it's art, and it's going to be a lot more valuable, that piece of wood, than it ever was before, in its younger days, as part of a rough, uninteresting tree.

"I don't think you're a bumpkin," I said.

We walked down the avenue in moonlight toward a house that belonged, Etto said, to a family named Sabatucci: the master carpenter Corrado; his wife, Paolina; Paolina's old mother, who was also Paolina; and two sons, grown-ups, no longer part of the household, who had started out life with so much promise—two decent, handsome boys, wanting for nothing. But the Adriatic youth camps and little-boy squads, and toy guns and fancy parades, and all those banners had really had an effect on them. They were Fascists.

"Were they involved in banishing the Pattuelli family?"

"Lucia, no. Myself, I wasn't part of that, which you're probably wondering. I could have done more to try to stop it, I know. I admit to some culpability, indirectly, but I swear, as much as this is—as this *was*—a factory town, my authority never extended past my gates. By the way, those children who look so angelic were no angels when they lived here. And their parents did well on the sale of that house, especially when you consider that it was not in good shape to begin with, and now it's all gone. There's no need for hard feelings. I believe that very strongly."

"I don't hold anything against you, now that you've been wiped out, Etto."

"That's a relief to me. It's strange that the Sabatucci place was the only one more or less spared. It might have been divine intervention, with God feeling bad for the parents and grandmother, for how those boys turned out."

"I don't believe," I said, "that God, who is likely not to exist, cares one way or another about anything that goes on around here."

"I agree with you completely, when you come right down to it!"

The Sabatucci house was located about three-quarters of the way down the avenue from where the train station used to be. Etto had said it looked like a good place to change one's dress and perhaps find water and food; nothing had been saved for tomorrow from the three waiters' picnic.

Annmarie's habit was around my shoulders like a cape, which had seemed to be the best way to carry it. I was beginning to look forward to putting it on.

What the moonlight revealed was the fact that San Guarino was almost fully a village of rubble. But to me, it was a wondrous, rare thing, as if we'd stumbled on a site of ancient ruins, unlisted in the directories, and never seen before by modern eyes.

The waves of pain had lessened to the point where I was barely aware of them. Maybe the walk was good for me.

All was still. The eerie, strangely beautiful silhouettes of still-standing walls, or parts of them, cast shadows here and there along the avenue.

"Granted, my life has been fully occupied with making furniture," Etto was saying. "But in a time like this I see no reason for withholding a confidence. What I've longed to do is to take up the hobby of my late father and join forces with a composer and write libretti of operas, beginning with, if possible, simple things, then working my way specifically, and I say this with all humility, to the *Orlando furioso* of the great Ludovico Ariosto. Vivaldi himself made an opera of it, which was the only reason I brought up Vivaldi. It's not, in my opinion, very good."

"I don't know of it."

"You're not missing anything. Naturally, Vivaldi had nothing to do with the words, but neither he nor his librettist did justice to Ariosto, who was unquestionably a genius and the greatest poet this country has ever produced."

"What about Dante?"

A shrug of the shoulders from Etto, but then he took a moment to think of a way to explain himself. "He was too stern, and everyone he wrote about was dead," he said sadly. "This may seem like heresy to you, but I mistrust people who spend all their time obsessed with the afterlife. Where's the art in contemplating souls? I don't care how lofty it is, or how sublime or metaphorical. I would much rather hear about things you can touch with your hands, or feel beside you, living and breathing. And to further my argument, Dante was never bombed. He had problems, but he didn't know anything about hell. It's not a metaphor, if you've been bombed. Perhaps now, not that I'm offering apologies, you'd like to reconsider my hickness."

"Oh, I don't, but what about Virgil?"

"The Aeneid," said Etto, "great as it is, is second in my mind to Ariosto's *Orlando.* I'm not just saying so because he came from these parts. Reggio Emilia, in fact. His blood was pure Romagnan. There was a box in my house containing the attempts my father had made in his lifetime to put some of his cantos into songs. Unfortunately, along with my house, not to mention my factory, his work was bombed and destroyed. And let me say, speaking of bombs, I find it disturbing that I'm the only one wearing shoes. I can't stop thinking about that."

In the moonlit road were bricks, chunks of wood, heaps of linen from someone's bureau, a child's bicycle, a large kitchen sink, books, pots, broken roof tiles, parts of cars, rakes and hoes and spades and shovels. I soon stopped trying to put an identity to all the shapes.

"I'm all right, as long as we go slowly," I said.

"No trouble there. I've been slow, Lucia, all my life. I only wish there weren't so many obstacles. I wish it were smoother sailing for us."

"That's a funny way of putting it," I said. "Do you like to go out in boats?"

"Boats? Like a fisherman?"

"Any at all."

"Once, Lucia, when I was a child, I was sent west to some relatives. They lived on the other side of a lake from the train station I had arrived at, so they sent a boatman to fetch me and bring me over. The lake was perfectly tranquil, and the boat was a good one, very sturdy. The weather was excellent. The boatman was skilled and completely trustworthy, especially since he knew it was my first time on water. There was not one element of danger. However, from the instant the oars were lifted, and the boat began to move, I felt in so much peril, it seemed not only possible, but highly likely, I'd fall out, or the boat would spring a leak and sink slowly, with me in it, as if I'd been tied to it, which of course, I was not. At any rate it seemed certain to me that I was going to drown. The poor boatman had feared, by the look on my face, I might have been an epileptic, in the opening phases of a fit. He told me later that I wore grooves into the seat, like wormholes, but wider and deeper, in the shape of my fingers and thumbs, from gripping the edge so tightly. I'd really left imprints, he said. When it was time for me to leave my relatives and go home, they were thoughtful enough to send me to the station in a roundabout way, on the roads, in a mule-drawn wagon, which took three or four hours longer than the boat, but was, to me, worth it. With all my heart, and I'm sorry if this is not the answer you hoped for, and I'm sorry that it took me so long to tell it, I hate boats."

"Are you in shock, Etto?"

"Do I seem it?"

"You do."

"I apologize. Did you know I'm a partisan? I've been trying to form a squad. If we had someone like you to broker guns for us, we'd take a big step forward. I don't think we'll accomplish much as we are, with just saws and hammers, not that we've even got those anymore."

Etto had rolled up his shirtsleeves. The skin of his arms, from just below the elbows to the wrists, looked cool and pale.

"But, oh, you know," he said, "the Ariosto is simply magnificent. My favorite part, somewhat near the end, is when the wits of the poor, demented hero—Orlando, that is—must be rescued from the moon. Yes, the moon. He's gone mad. It's very dramatic. His sanity is returned to him in an urn."

"Why did he go mad?"

"It was a case of unrequited love. Look, here's the house. I'm sure it's all right to enter it, as no one's home, and there's no front door. I wonder where it is. It's chestnut. Corrado Sabatucci built it at my factory to replace the original, which had rotted. His two boys carried it down the avenue with a great deal of ceremony, but they weren't completely Fascists yet, and that had been a good day."

It was a wide, modest, two-story brick villa. The empty space where the door had been was in the middle of two long shuttered-up windows, perfectly intact. An overhanging section of the roof had collapsed, and so had the chimney. Two shutters upstairs were slightly askew.

Etto seemed confident. "I've been in here a thousand times. Every weekend for I don't know how many years, I've had a meal here. Being a bachelor, I appreciate the hospitality of my friends. I know where everything is. In case there's any danger, which I'm sure there isn't, I'll go in first."

Cautiously, he put one foot forward into the doorway, as if he were standing at the edge of the sea, barefoot, sticking in a toe to test the water's temperature.

As if the two of us had just finished a discussion about a moonlit swim.

Not once in our married life did Aldo have the time for a late-night stroll—not on the beach, not along the village roads, not even in the lane or orchard at home. A beach to Aldo was a place to have your restaurant near. A stroll was what you wanted your patrons to go and take while waiting for a table, sometimes with a complimentary glass of wine in their hands, or one of the free bags of sweets the waiters gave out to good children.

I hadn't been resentful of Aldo. I'd never had the time for strolls, either.

"I found the door," Etto said, over his shoulder. "I just stepped on it. It was blown inside. It's lying here like a carpet at the entryway."

"I think you should pick it up and put it back," I said.

"Right now?"

"Well, with all those years in the carpentry business, I'm sure you know what to do with it."

"It's not a question of knowledge. I'm strong in normal circumstances, but at the moment—not that I'm complaining—I'm so tired that if you asked me to lift one piece of dust, never mind this chestnut door—which, let me tell you, is as heavy as can possibly be—I wouldn't be able to do it. If a flea started walking up my neck into my ear, I wouldn't have the strength to pick it off."

"Do you ever say anything simply, Etto?"

"What do you mean? What's the matter with how I talk?"

"I mean—" I said, but then I stopped myself. I didn't know what I meant. I had hurt him.

The air was a little brighter. The moon! It was across the road from the Sabatuccis' house, huge and almost full, and so shiny and bright that the craters and mountains, and all those plains of basalt, appeared only phantomly, like shadings of relief or attractive, white-gray decorations. Etto's face was lit up in a silver way. I saw an exhausted man of my own age, looking elderly, fragile. I hadn't wanted to hurt him.

"I meant," I said, "about the way you talk, the only thing wrong is that, when you stop, I find myself looking forward to whatever you might say next."

"Thank you for the compliment."

"You're welcome. Now, I want to hurry and change my clothes. If I spend one more minute as I am, I'll go out of my mind. Like your hero, I'll have to send to the moon to get it back."

He didn't ask if he could take my hand; he just did it. He led me down a short passageway that opened up into a big farmhouse-type kitchen, where a pair of windows had gauzy white curtains. The glass was unharmed. Moonlight was pouring in.

There were no pots on the stove or on the counters, and no sign of food, but the table had been set for four: four soup bowls on four plates, four wineglasses, four forks, four spoons. The Sabatuccis must have taken their dinner with them when they fled.

"Corrado, his wife, her mother," said Etto, pointing out the chairs they would have sat in. "If you're wondering about the fourth person, it was supposed to be me. They had invited me, but then it was time to go into hiding. You don't need to feel like a housebreaker, in case you do. I belonged here, and you're with me."

"I feel bad about San Guarino, Etto. I didn't always think of it in positive ways, in the past."

"That's only because you're not in carpentry. Plus, you're someone, I believe, who'd find it unappealing that a village has only one road."

"You don't sound so tired, suddenly."

"I'm getting my second wind. I'll show you where the bathroom is. You'll need some light in there."

He pulled out a cupboard drawer and took out two candles, a pair of small brass holders, and a box of matches, but instead of giving them to me or setting up the candles himself—the bathroom was just off the kitchen; its door was slightly ajar—he put everything down on the table, as if they belonged there, with the place settings.

"Etto, what's the matter?"

"I think I should go over to the sink and see if the water's running."

But he just stood there. He seemed to need some help in figuring out the sink's location. He looked like a very old man out in public on an errand, who'd started out so optimistically, full of confidence, but was now in the act of discovering that he couldn't remember what the errand was, or where he'd come from, or if he'd ever stood on that particular sidewalk before, in front of that particular shop.

"Forgive me, but I was being delusional when I told you I have a second wind," he said. And he covered his face with his hands, bent his head, and started weeping, almost silently at first, then more and more loudly, in heaving waves of sobs, with his shoulders shaking so hard, he could have been standing in an earthquake.

I wondered, should I reach for him, pat him, comfort him, as when Beppi had fallen as a child and hurt himself? Certainly, if there was ever a man who had the right to fall to pieces in a war, it was Etto.

Instead I went over to the sink, turned the tap.

"Etto! Water!"

He'd taken hold of the back of a chair. He must have worried that his tears would knock him over. Was this the first time in his life he'd ever cried? It certainly appeared so. He wasn't very good at it. His sobs had turned into hoarse little yelps, puppy-like—oh, he didn't need me to feel sorry for him, I thought; he was doing just fine on his own.

I picked up a bowl, filled it halfway with cold water, and carried it over to him. He was bent nearly double at the table. I said his name so he'd look up at me—which he did, yelping and snorting and shaking, and making me fear he'd cave in on himself and do something like convulse or stop breathing. I emptied the water in one big splash against his face.

His eyes opened wide; his mouth opened in a wide, amazed O.

I set the bowl down on the table. "That's quite enough of that, Etto. Please find something to dry yourself with. When I've finished changing my clothes, I'll expect you to stop behaving like you're three years old. And I'll appreciate it if, when I put on this garment, you hold back from making remarks about nuns, even if I resemble one, but without a veil."

He looked at me, sniffling, dripping, blinking hard, straightening himself up to his full height. The tears had stopped. I thought, at first, that the reason he held out his arms to me was merely to make a large, shrugging-type gesture, like the one in the road when he talked about Dante.

Had he known I'd step into them? I hadn't known myself, until I did it. But there were his arms, circling me, pulling me toward him. We were almost exactly the same height.

My face was instantly wet, touching his. The top of his shirt was soaked. "Oh!" he said softly. "Lucia! My goodness! *Ciao!*" He did not appear surprised that this was happening.

"I really have to change my clothes," I said, as casually as if embracing him, and then turning my head to kiss him, were the most natural things in the world—were things I'd done already, a thousand times. His mouth tasted salty like the sea.

"I'm sorry that I smell bad, Etto."

"You don't!"

"I do."

"Paolina Sabatucci," he whispered, "keeps the good soap in the second drawer of the little bureau, just below the toilet window. The bar at the sink in there is very harsh, and strictly for Corrado, whose hands are so rough, he could just as well clean them with sandpaper."

He reached both hands to my face, touching the tips of all his fingers to my cheeks, the sides of my forehead, my nose, my lips. He was taking his time about it.

"Does this hurt, Lucia?"

It didn't hurt. His touch was feathery, tender. My eyes were closed. I felt that he'd had the idea to examine me as if he'd just become blind.

Ugo had a gentle touch, Aldo had always said. Ugo was an artist when it came to poking around in sensitive places. Beppi thought so, too.

Oh, no. Just as I was feeling so light, so airy, without pain of any sort, the image of Ugo Fantini began to appear in my mind, as it used to, sometimes, when the man who was touching me was Aldo.

Ugo's face. His eyes, his thick eyebrows, the little scar on his chin. His eyebrows furrowing like they did when he was frowning at something. I'd never thought about him in this way before, but it occurred to me now that he was always frowning at something, always expressing disapproval: stern, stern Ugo.

If he were a composer, he'd be Verdi. Who'd want to imagine Verdi's fingertips against their skin?

I opened my eyes. "Etto, I have *got* to change my clothes."

"Can you do me a very small favor? Will you promise me, as I remember that there's a mirror on the toilet wall, which may or may not be broken, you won't look into it, not even one glance?"

Not looking into mirrors at certain times was something I was used to. It didn't seem surprising that he'd mentioned it, as if he already knew that about me.

Ceremoniously, as if we were dancing partners leaving the

floor, he slipped an arm around my waist and steered me toward the Sabatuccis' bathroom. The door was only open a few inches, and he reached for the handle to push it the rest of the way. Nothing happened. He leaned a shoulder against it, pushed again. Nothing. He gave a little grunt and tried harder.

"Excuse me," said a voice. A child had come up behind us.

Rudino Pattuelli. "With all respect," he said gravely, "if you had looked at that side of the house, which we just did ourselves, you would have seen that it's partly caved in. The problem with the door not opening is that there's a bathtub against it, along with lots of other things."

There were four of them: Rudino, the first set of twins, and the eldest, Marco. "The tub looks new. So does the plumbing. I wonder when they got it," said a twin.

"I bet it was that ugly old Moscone who did the job," said the other twin. "Remember him? He had pimples on his nose. He had hair as thick as a beard in his ears. When they threw us out of the village, he said if we ever returned, he'd come after us with the longest length of iron he had."

The devils! How long had they been standing there?

"What are you doing here?" cried Etto.

Marco stepped forward to respond, in an official-sounding way, which he must have picked up from Annmarie. "We were ordered to find you so we could tell you—in case you didn't hear the truck and the jeep, even though they've been blowing their horns, and everyone's been calling for you—it's time to go."

"I notice your head's all wet, Signor Renzetti," said Rudino. "If there's water left in the pipes here, I hope you didn't drink it. It's probably contaminated."

"We're being evacuated," said Marco. "By the American Army."

"They're very sorry about how everything's wrecked, but it

wasn't their fault," said a twin. "When the bombing happened, they were in it, not doing it."

"San Guarino looks like the moon," said Rudino. "If the moon had a village on it, this is what it would look like if a giant rock from outer space crashed into it."

"I had two black eyes once, when I fell off Grandpapa Galto's roof," said the other twin. "I landed on rocks."

"Are you Sandro?" said Etto.

"Mario."

"He's Sandro," said his twin.

"I don't care who you are. I don't care about your grandfather's roof. Stop talking about black eyes," said Etto. "No one here has black eyes! I can't imagine why you'd bring up that subject!"

"The army said to hurry," cut in Marco. "They're not happy about having to wait, but Annmarie told them, Signora Fantini, you're a famous opera star. If they ask for your autograph, please comply."

"I will," I said. "Now all of you go outdoors with Etto. I'll follow along in a moment. I have a few small things to care of, on my own, privately, before I'm able to get into a truck, or a jeep."

"Goddamn," muttered Etto. He gave me a long, sad look, as if he were about to start crying all over again. "God*damn*."

11

THE BLOND, blue-eyed, square-jawed, impeccably close-shaven medic was pleased to tell me his name: Frank Lamb.

Lamb like what's born from a sheep, *agnello.* Or like the first part of what he'd heard was a certain type of *booze* in this part of the world, an Italian sort of champagne, lam-boo-so, lam-boo-ski, who cared what you call it? He was looking forward to having some. It was only a matter of liberating whatever town had the best *package store,* and *bam,* he was going to be a happy guy, for a change. All he'd had so far in Italy by way of the national beverage was one sip from a bottle of something so thick and dark red, well, never mind what it looked like, or what it tasted like.

I was his first-ever opera singer, his first laywoman wearing (when I'd come in) the clothing of a nun, not counting a veil; his first survivor of a burial—sorry about the bombing; and, best of all, his first mother of a heroic partisan. But that was the thing about Italy. You think you know what to expect and all you get are surprises, at every turn.

I was not to call him a doctor. He was a long-distance truck driver, hailing out of Seattle in the state of Washington—not the Washington where the government was, but the other one, the big one, West Coast, the Pacific Ocean, a real state. When you said the one where the government was, you had to also say *District of Columbia.* It was complicated. Even Americans didn't fully understand it.

He'd been all over America. He'd haul anything—lumber, hardware, food, iceboxes, you name it. He preferred cargo that was not alive, but he couldn't afford to be picky. He'd driven pigs, chickens, circus animals, rabbits, goats, lambs like his name, and once, for a zoo, a zebra, which turned out to have been a white pony on which a con man had painted black stripes.

He'd done it all and he was only twenty-eight. They'd assigned him to be my medic because he was the only one in the unit who spoke Italian. The American Army felt I was worthy of special attention.

I was his first-ever patient, in addition to the other firsts.

The unit hadn't been large to start with. Twenty men. For the time being, as I must have figured out for myself by simply looking around, a large percentage of them were in these beds, in varying degrees of injuries and recoveries, as a result of having met up with some Germans. The rest of the army wasn't near this part of the country yet.

This unit was an advance group. Ground reconnaissance. Pioneers, you could say.

Long ago in America, *pioneers* were the people who left their homes in the East and in the middle, and traveled across enormous stretches of wild, hostile land, meeting peril at every turn—blizzards, Indians, wolves, tornadoes, accidents, bandits, diseases. Whatever you could think of going wrong, it did. The ones who stayed alive built houses and set up farms on land they didn't have to pay for. Then many of them died of starvation, waiting for the crops to come in. Compared to that, Germans with heavy guns was a minor inconvenience. It was always good to put things in perspective.

I was not to apologize for all the vomiting. The tricky part about head injuries was that so many of the symptoms took a while to kick in.

I probably hadn't broken anything. It seemed to him that all my bones were in one piece. If my skull had been fractured, even with a crack the width of a hair, it was a pretty good bet I would not be just a little while away from holding up my part of a conversation with him. Which he felt certain I was.

Heads were pretty good with self-repair. Faces, too. Also jaws. And eyes especially. Eye bruises always looked worse than they were. The reason why injuries to the head should cause vomiting, he didn't know, but probably, actual physicians didn't know, either.

Sorry he couldn't offer me morphine, but it said in the medical kit directions, "Do not administer to head injuries." The *codeine sulfate* seemed to have had an effect. I seemed to be a little more relaxed, now that it was in my system. He was hoping it would stay there. If I didn't manage to keep it down, I'd be faced with the reality that all they had left to kill pain with was nothing.

Could I try to stay awake? He wasn't calling what was wrong with my head a *concussion,* but just in case, it said in the handbook that if one was suspected, the patient was required to stay alert. Sleeping before the danger had passed could result in a sleep that would never be all the way awakened from. In other words, a coma.

It was a shame they couldn't allow civilian visitors. But this was a military place. Regulations were regulations. Wherever they'd taken my friends—well, don't worry, they'd be safe.

Sorry there weren't screens to separate the cots. Sorry there weren't any interior walls, just this one huge room. But at least we had a roof. Well, most of one. Good thing it wasn't raining.

It was terrific I hadn't been cut up. No abrasions, no broken skin. Ice would be the perfect thing. Too bad there wasn't an icebox in this *dump.*

It had looked so spectacular from the outside. His first *palazzo*—that is, his first one to go inside. It must have been abandoned around the time when there were still Roman emperors. Italy was his first foreign country not counting Canada, next door to his home state. Five minutes after he'd stepped foot on Italian soil, which was about two weeks ago, he got sick of saying the word "old" to describe things. That also went for "ancient."

I could rely on him, honest. His medical background was road-and-wheels first aid, but it came in handy. He'd had a lot of experience with pulling over to help accident victims. When you're out on the road, one thing you could count on was that someone was always smashing into something.

One time when he was hauling oranges across a California desert, he happened on a guy hauling water. The guy had fallen asleep at the wheel and crashed into a cactus the size of a *redwood.* All the water in his tank leaked out and evaporated. He wouldn't have died of thirst, though. He'd have died from not having anyone apply first aid to his face and head wounds, plus tell him to *stay awake.* Now, that had been a fractured skull. The guy never drove again.

A redwood was a big American tree, so tall it was unimaginable to an Italian. Did I know about a desert personally? He was asking because he thought he detected a response. Sorry if he was wrong about that. What would an Adriatic Italian know about deserts?

They were the worst place to drive. Nightmares. All that sand. Sand was such a *killer*! Don't even get him going about sand.

The reason he knew Italian was that his second stepfather—there'd been four—had emigrated from somewhere in Umbria.

A stonecutter. He'd worked on American churches, not just Catholic ones, then he ended up in the concrete business, sidewalks and house foundations; a nice guy, never learned a word of understandable English except swears. Even though his mom broke off with him, Frank kept in touch. The other three stepfathers as well as his mother's first husband—that is, the guy who wasn't a step—weren't worth talking about. Sometimes Frank told people that his actual father was the Italian.

You could get away with that sort of thing in America. His mom was in the trucking business, too. In the office end of it. It used to be that he vowed to himself, his whole childhood and adolescence, that no matter what happened in his life he'd get married one time, and that would be that, but unfortunately, or very luckily, depending on how you looked at it, God had given him a disposition that was favorable for the ladies. He wasn't trying to be a braggart, but people often told him he resembled the great American actor Spencer Tracy.

Did I know who that was? In Hollywood he was a king. The greatest thing about him was that he proved you don't have to be suave or even handsome to have women adore you.

Personally, the business with the self-vowing had not worked out. The number of wives he'd had already was two. He didn't have anything lined up for sure for when he got home, but there was a girl in Nevada—another desert state—who'd told him to stop by, to find out if she was still available.

Linda was her name. He'd met her about a year ago at a roadside diner in the *middle of nowhere*. She had hair the color of honey. She was a waitress. There'd been letters back and forth. She could actually be waiting for him. You never knew.

It might be all right to settle down in a place like Nevada, not Reno or Las Vegas, which were cities people usually thought of when you mentioned the state, but maybe one of the lesser-known ones, like Crystal Bay, Silver City, Armagosa, Blue Rock.

He was thinking about it. He'd done some research before he'd shipped out. He'd memorized some names of Nevada places. There was also a town called *Last Chance.* He'd been getting sick of the coast as a base of operations. As a whole, the state of Washington was pretty fucking wet. It rained about three hundred days a year.

Did I know that American word, *fucking*? It came from *fuck.* He only mentioned it because he felt I needed to have a sense of it, considering the company I was in. It was the most popular word in the army, and the most useful word in the English language. Just the other day, a *pal* of his who used to be a college boy came up with the insight that you can use it as a noun, an adjective, an adverb, and every other thing there is. A great, great word. He felt I must have heard it a thousand times since they'd brought me in.

It was impossible to say the *middle of nowhere* regarding a geographic location in Italy, because everywhere was somewhere. But Americans said it all the time. If he had a *nickel* for every hour on the road he'd gone nearly out of his mind from having nothing to look at, because nothing was there, just road and dirt and maybe some trees now and then, or cacti, he'd be rich. A nickel was a coin. It was the second-smallest-in-value portion of an American dollar, after *penny.*

Was it unbelievably difficult for me not to talk, seeing as how I was Italian? Soon it would be all right. He and I could have a fine, two-way conversation at some close future point. For the moment, absolute stillness was required. The bones of my facial structure would benefit from the inactivity. The cloths on my face had the need to be aligned, unmoving. He'd do everything in his power to keep them cool and damp for me.

That nun's outfit was bound to be around somewhere. He'd try to find it, but it was in pretty bad shape. He wasn't planning to ask me questions about my reason for having worn it. You don't go into someone else's country in a war without learning that it's impolite to intrude on personal affairs. Had I lost the *wimple* somewhere? He wasn't Catholic, but he'd heard that wimple was what you called a nun's veil. It was obvious I wasn't a nun because my hair was too long for it, and anyway, he knew about my son.

Most Americans called what I did *throwing up.* I looked nice in khaki. The shirt and trousers didn't fit too badly. Sorry they couldn't give me any, you know, underwear.

Sorry there weren't any women soldiers to have borrowed a proper outfit from. Or nurses. The name of the female branch of the army was Women's Army Corps. *WACs,* for short, like *cera,* the wax of a candle, but not like *wacky,* which meant *nuts in the head.* They were very responsible. American military women were the best in the world.

And those gals in Intelligence! Classy and brainy, every one of them. But I must have an inkling of how terrific they were, from having spent some time getting to know, he'd heard, a girl by the name of Malone.

Mallo was her nickname, he'd been told, like the candy.

Did I know what that was, a *Mallo Cup*? It was a round little chocolate bar with marshmallow cream in the center. It came in a bright yellow wrapper. *Marshmallow* was gooey white stuff, highly sweet. You called it a cup, *tazza,* because it was made in *cupcake* pans—yes, cake, *torta.* To call a pretty girl a cupcake or a *torta della tazza* was an act of affection and admiration.

But as I was likely to have discovered myself, a word like that might not be a *big hit* with a girl like Mallo.

He'd heard she was tough. Too bad she'd disappeared. Too bad she wasn't trying to get inside to pay me a visit, see how I was. The army couldn't stop her like they stopped the civilians. She was army herself. Well, Intelligence.

Was I having some uncomfortable feelings of annoyance and even anger toward that American acquaintance of mine? I might want to say a few things about that later. Army Intelligence people were always up to things they didn't always remember to tell other army people they were up to.

Mallo must have made an impression on me, seeing as how she was a lady player of golf. Some guys had been mentioning that. She was a golfer and she was also a girl with a criminal record. Sure, she'd got off the charges against her by getting recruited into Intelligence—did I know that? Did I know what he was talking about? Did I know I'd been associating with an American criminal?

That subject would probably come up again. Were my clothes satisfactory? It was a uniform of the smallest guy in the unit. That was him over there, Peewee Wilkins, in the bed by the curtained-off operating area.

He came from Kentucky. Besides being a GI, he was a *jockey*—well, he'd hoped to become one before the war interrupted his life. So far, all he'd done was shovel a lot of manure and do training runs.

Did I know what a jockey was? It was the person who sat on the horse in a race. Peewee's home state was half in the South and half in the North. This division had been established in the Civil War, which no American would ever attempt to explain to a European. It was just too emotional. The state of Washington, way up in its private corner, had not existed in Civil War days. So Frank had no personal connections to that conflict.

Peewee had never said what side of Kentucky he was from. He didn't need his shirt and trousers. He wasn't going anywhere soon, having met up the other day with German fire.

He was not looking good. It might happen that he'd never need his clothes back. That was all he wanted to say about Peewee. A good man. Maybe there'd be racetracks in heaven.

Sorry my friends weren't allowed in to see me. Sorry I'd been separated from them. Was that older woman who screamed at the sergeant a relative? I could fill him in on that later. And what about that guy who tried to get in, on the basis that America owed him a favor plus a new furniture factory? Not my husband, obviously. I wasn't wearing a wedding band. I was a widow, right?

Was the furniture guy an admirer? I must have had hordes of them.

He himself had never been to an opera but he knew a truck driver who went through New York City sometime around the war before this one, around 1917. It was his first time there. He'd left his truck at a depot. He went to Central Park to see what it was like—this guy was from the West. He'd never been in a big eastern park before. And what did he happen upon?

He happened upon an outdoor show with one of the most famous, most legendary Italians there ever was, not counting Christopher Columbus: Enrico Caruso. It was Caruso himself, up on a stage, singing the song by George M. Cohan that every American knew by heart—well, at least the chorus. "Over There," it was called. It was a fighting song, patriotic.

"Over there, over there," went the chorus. "Send the word, over there, that the Yanks are coming, the Yanks are coming."

"Over there" was Europe, which was now, for him, here.

Yank was a word I'd probably heard before, with a general meaning, for all Americans, although there were many Americans who found it insulting. It was not the same as a *Yankee,* which was a baseball team.

Maybe after the war, baseball would come to Italy. All the partisans could form teams with their *buddies,* having learned a few things about teamwork. His Umbrian father used to say that the basic nature of an Italian is anarchy. But that was before partisans.

Poor Italy. Did I know that Mussolini was on the cover of the most famous magazine in America, *Life*? This was maybe five or six years ago. Lots of Americans had thought he was *fabulous.*

The Umbrian had sent Frank a long letter when he'd heard about the orders to head for Italy. He'd taken it personally.

In the letter, he quoted from something Mussolini wrote. It was called "The Doctrine of Fascism," and Frank remembered some of the quotes because the Umbrian had written them in big capital letters, with much underlining, and a note on the side that said "Memorize this!" *In rejecting democracy, Fascism rejects the silly untruth of political equality. Liberalism spells individualism, and Fascism, thank God, curtails harmful liberties.*

The Umbrian, not that he could vote, because he was in America illegally, was a *Democrat* in his sensibilities, and a man with a conscience. It really burned him up that Mussolini made such a big show of how his dictatorship was based on God. *I, Benito Mussolini, acknowledge myself as the most spiritual man of this country! That's how I got to be a dictator! What people love best is authority!*

"Son," the Umbrian had written, "going to the bar and throwing darts at Mussolini's face on the wall isn't giving me the satisfaction I had hoped for, so please, while you're in my country, go and put a bullet through his stupid, dangerous heart."

Sorry to get a little carried away. Maybe he was, himself, in his interior, besides speaking the language, Italian, if I could imagine someone inheriting something from someone who wasn't their actual parent.

One day, when the Umbrian was still married to his mother—he was a gardener—he called Frank outdoors to look at his tomatoes, which were spectacular. He'd taken a fat, juicy red one off the vine. He broke off the stem at that *belly button* spot a tomato always has, the *ombelico.* He held up the tomato for the purpose of being sniffed. He said, "This is what my soul smells like, and now, so does yours."

That was what you'd call spiritual. That was what you'd call the opposite of Mussolini.

Sorry about the surroundings. He didn't have the words to apologize enough for this place. He just couldn't understand why the officers of his unit picked the worst-off *palazzo* in Italy.

Nice floor, though. Nice tiles. Someone had said that this area was famous for mosaics. In America you'd never see a floor full of artwork like this. It was really something. Julius Caesar–type guys in togas and sandals, ladies with big round eyes, very classical. Boats, plants, trees, dogs, all kinds of things. Imagine walking on the art! Only in Italy.

Perhaps later on I could talk to him about outstanding Italian artists. He was willing to open himself up to an educational experience. All those painters to find out about! Michelangelo, for example, who decorated the Vatican. And the guy who painted that world-famous lady, Mona Lisa. Did my son like paintings? He already knew that his name was Giuseppe, in honor of that revered and famous patriot, Garibaldi, whose footsteps, it appeared, he was following.

Probably, there were so many Italians named for Garibaldi through the years, you'd never be able to count them. There was nothing special in parents wanting to endow their babies with an extra edge. But all those other Giuseppes had not gone out of their way to be heroes.

I must be proud of him. Did any operas have mothers of heroes as the leading lady? If so, when I got myself back to my career, I'd play them with gusto, with an extra layer of emotion from my war experience.

He never imagined he'd say this in his life, but *geez,* he wished he knew about opera. Someone had told him I'd appeared ten times on the stage of that top-notch pinnacle of theatrical places, La Scala.

Was that in Rome? He was hoping he'd get to Rome. Did I ever hear of the movie *Roman Scandals*? It was American. He'd seen it six times. Three evenings and three matinees. It was playing in some town he'd got stuck in—not in Nevada—for most of a week, in a flood that had washed out the road; it was always something. A swell film, though. It was about a decent, ordinary teenage boy—this was very complex, so never mind the details—who traveled backward in time to ancient Rome, and ended up in an emperor's court, very lavish, with fancy costumes and dancing and singing, not all of it awful.

The boy lived in a town called Rome, but it was in Oklahoma. It was unbelievable how many small American places were named for European big ones. Paris, Berlin, Poland, you name it, it was on the American map. Oklahoma was a state in the West—*hey!* What was that? Was I trying to nod my head? Did I know about Oklahoma? It would be amazing if I did. Maybe tourists from that state, or maybe fans of mine, before the war, had told me about it?

Or maybe I'd heard about that particular American state from my son. He'd heard I didn't know where Giuseppe was, but then, there were an awful lot of mothers in the world right now of whom one could say the same thing, not that it was any consolation. His own mother had decided to take up with a lady back home who told people's fortunes and claimed she did mental telepathy. Like talking to someone on the telephone without the telephone.

It wasn't, so far, effective. By now his *mom* could have been well into the process of getting herself another marriage. "Make sure you come home from the war in one piece so you can find out who my husband is, in case I don't reach you through brainwaves," she had said, which was a pretty good reason to put effort into staying alive. He was hoping she'd go back to the Umbrian. He was planning to pull some strings with her on that.

Mother-and-son emotional blackmail, you could call it. Anyone who was ever a son, or a mother of one, if they loved each other, would know exactly what that meant. It didn't need an explanation. He had the idea that I was pretty fond of Giuseppe, that we confided in each other all the time.

Surely I knew that, back in my hometown, my son had blown up four German artillery trucks, a tank, and a bunker, before going into hiding. Everyone was talking about it.

In fact, when Frank first heard of it, from the sergeant, the name he'd heard was *Baldi*. The way it had been put was, "A hotheaded partisan named Baldi, for Garibaldi, is causing a lot of trouble, and who the hell is Garibaldi?"

Imagine not knowing about that fearless giant of nineteenth-century Italy, who probably had a statue to his memory in every *piazza* in the kingdom!

He wasn't giving away any military secrets here, and he wasn't worried about being eavesdropped on, as that was a benefit of speaking a different language, but he felt it was only fair to let me know, friendly like, that the American Army had some anxieties about Italians with guns and explosives, even though everyone was on the same side now.

You could see the rationale. You could imagine a bunch of generals sitting around in some other *palazzo,* nicer than this one, newer, asking questions like, "Hey, how are we supposed to know the locals won't start aiming those weapons of theirs at us?"

There'd been *copycat* demolitions by partisans all over the place. A German car in Rimini, a tank near Cattolica, a munitions hut by the sea—it added up.

Copycat was when someone followed the example of someone. It was American slang. Copying. It didn't have anything to do with a cat, like the expression *letting the cat out of the bag,* which meant telling secrets you were supposed to keep to yourself, and which he'd sort of done by telling me about the nervousness of the army regarding partisans.

It was only the up-ups who were wary of locals. With the GIs it was a different story. A GI was at the bottom of the ranks, like himself. GIs were of the opinion that they could use all the help they could get.

Guiseppe had a brigade, right? All trained sharpshooters, right? And ex–Italian Army, right? Experienced Adriatic fishermen, some of them, right? Fishermen who knew a few things about *harpoons,* right? A harpoon was what you killed a whale with, or any large fish.

He would enjoy it if, when I was able to talk, I'd talk about my son. He was hoping to hear everything about him! It would break up the tedium. It would appease the depression of looking around and seeing so many of his friends knocked out of commission.

Wasn't it astonishing that American officers would get all

worked up about armed, non-uniformed Italians, when they were all pointing guns at the exact same target? It made you wonder. He personally would especially be delighted to hear about how Giuseppe was getting his guns.

Probably what they had for guns were Berettas. That was his guess. There was probably a storehouse somewhere. Someone's cellar? Barn? One of those fishermen's huts near the beach? Under cover of darkness, the partisans would make their way there, carrying well-concealed objects to add to the stock of their arsenal. Well-concealed objects from where, one wondered.

Did they have a *clubhouse,* the brigade? A place where they met, spent some time, privately? A sort of headquarters, in other words.

Clubhouse was the word Mallo Malone might have used for it. Did she ever visit it? She was pretty tall, right? She must have stuck out like a sore thumb.

Here. Time to take the cloths off. Wasn't that better? Already the bruising appeared to be healing, as minimal as it was. There was nothing to be anguished about. The swelling was almost gone. There was nothing a little makeup wouldn't artfully conceal.

Hold on a minute. Who was that, coming over here? An unfamiliar person. It must have been all right, though, or he'd never have made it past the guards.

Oh, an orderly. A GI, as he'd said, was at the bottom rank, but an orderly was even lower. This was probably that new one. They didn't usually hire Italians, but he'd heard they'd picked one up on a country road, poor kid. They'd said he was desperate for work.

Confidentially, the kid was maybe the same age as himself, but you had to call him a kid because it seemed he was deficient when it came to mental capabilities. In America you called someone like that *retarded*. Or you said, *he's not playing with a full deck*, like a deck of cards.

"*Ciao*, Orderly, with your mop and your bucket! *Parlo italiano*, as you can see," said Frank, pronouncing each word slowly. "Be careful not to bother this injured lady. She's very important. She's an opera star. I'm your superior, but you can call me Francesco. What's your name?"

A shuffling, a few grunts. A spilling of astringent, soapy water onto the floor.

"I . . . am . . . *Li*," said Lido Linari.

"Li? That's it? Just Li? Like an Oriental? I never heard of an Italian called Li. I'm not trying to give you a hard time. I'm just a soldier, trying to be friendly here."

A big grin. Yes, just Li. Friendly, yes.

My God. The effort to withhold my amazement took a lot. The brightest, loveliest, liveliest of the waiters was standing there with a mop, staring at the handle as if it were golden, as if it enchanted him.

It was a shame there hadn't been music for his entrance. Something light. Something warm. Something wonderful. Strains of Puccini came into my head. *Bohème*. Nothing specific, just some background, vaguely. Puccini never composed a piece called "A Pleasant, Sunny Little Tune To Be Rescued By," but that was what it sounded like.

Funny how everything changed when there was a song.

12

THERE WAS NO SIGN of the Lido whose girlfriends called the restaurant so often, Beppi would answer the phone with, "This is Aldo's, but if you're looking for Lido Linari, you've got a wrong number."

He was a thoroughly Puccini waiter. *La Bohème* was his favorite. He was always begging me to sing as much of it as one program allowed, but he'd settle now and then for the Rodolfo and Marcello in the opening scene, lamenting their stove in a grim Paris winter.

He'd imagine that France was as cold as the Arctic, and only Puccini knew how to warm it. *Love is like a fireplace that wastes too much, too quickly, where a man is the bundle of kindling, and a woman is the spark. One gets burned in an instant, but meanwhile, my friend, we're standing here freezing.* In honor of Lido, and to shut him up, I'd sing Puccini on non-Puccini evenings as a warm-up.

He was not allowed to handle tables where an attractive wife was with an unattractive husband, because everyone knew what would happen. A note slipped discreetly, a whispered word. "At least we'll make it hard for him," Nizarro would say, putting Lido with patrons who were elderly, or Fascists, or tourist groups leaving Italy right after the meal, and also large families, where the wife would look too exhausted, or too fed up with men to notice him.

He had turned himself into an idiot. The perfect village idiot.

How had he managed that look on his face, all loose and slackened? His skin was like a sail that's been emptied of wind and just hangs there. He was messily grizzled with beard, which he picked at, as if looking absentmindedly for lice; his eyes were as darkly inanimate as two round pieces of charcoal. Drool was in a corner of his mouth, and his thick, curly hair, which hadn't been trimmed in quite a while, looked like it had never been washed, brushed, or attended to in any way.

Those curls in real life had a soft, corkscrew-like intensity. "If I could scalp him like an American Indian chief, without killing him, I would do it," Beppi used to say, when he'd started balding.

"I'm going out for a smoke, but I'll be back in a couple of minutes, so make sure you do a good cleanup job, Li," said Frank.

Lido bobbed his head energetically, with an odd scrunching up of one eye, as if he suffered from nervous tics. I wouldn't mention this to him, but he was overdoing it.

"Signora Fantini, when I come back, I'll be anticipating the sound of your voice, even though all you'll be doing with me is talking. We'll have a terrific conversation! As I'm sure I'll repeat to you later, I'd give a lot to hear you sing. Who knows? Maybe one day I will!"

Frank's big toothy smile was genuine. He did have a certain charm.

Into the bucket went Lido's mop. He was waiting until Frank was well out of earshot before he spoke to me. Into my head came a tune from not Puccini, but Mozart.

Bino. His nickname at the restaurant was Bino, for the

lusty, exuberant, woman-besotted, unsoldierly soldier of *Figaro,* Cherubino.

I sang his famous *"Voi che sapete che cosa e' amor, donne, vedete s'io l'ho nel cor"* not only on Mozart nights but whenever I felt the need for something simple and lovely and clear, and so honestly moving it could melt a block of ice. "You, ladies, who know what love is, see if I have it in my heart."

It fit Lido perfectly. He'd only started hating the nickname when he found out one night at the restaurant, probably from Beppi—no one ever owned up to it—that almost always the role is sung by a woman in a young man's clothes.

Lido had been so shocked he froze, then started trembling. On his next trip to the kitchen, where he was supposed to get *antipasti* for one of his tables, he inadvertently picked up an enormous tray of boiled crabs. Back in the dining room, realizing his mistake, he went to pieces completely and the tray flew out of his hands.

The crabs soared off in all directions. Someone was hit on the shoulder, someone else caught one in the air, refused to give it back, and started breaking it apart to eat it, even though he hadn't ordered it and wouldn't pay for it, and Nizarro started yelling, and Beppi yelled louder, and the waiters fumbled about and didn't know what to do, while trying their best not to look like they were enjoying it. The cooks came out to see what had happened, and people jumped up as if the things were alive, were crawling all over their feet, were trying to bite them. To top it off, a well-known Fascist, an officer, a real, high-ranked bastard, was sitting at a table close to Lido. A crab landed on his thigh, in his lap, almost, and he was getting the feeling it might have been done on purpose.

It was a madhouse, with sinister overtones. I wasn't supposed to go on for another half hour, but I decided not to wait. It was a Verdi night, so everyone settled down quickly.

"You saved me," Lido said to me later. "I was worried that Beppi or that Fascist might rip me apart. If anyone calls me that horrible nickname again, I'll take the biggest crab that ever came out of a net, and I will jam it, alive and kicking, down his throat."

No one ever called him Bino again, to his face.

And here he was, mopping the floor around my cot. "Lucia, *ciao,*" he whispered. "You're smiling at me. That's a good sign. How am I doing?"

"You could be on the stage."

"Thanks. There's going to be a diversion. I'm getting you out of here. The American golfer is outside with some friends of hers. She's got a car. Did they drug you?"

"I think it was only aspirin, although they called it a fancy name. They told me I'm bleeding in the brain."

"Brains don't bleed unless you're dead or dying, which you're not. Can you walk?"

"I can do anything."

"There hasn't been news of Beppi. No one knows anything, but as Nizarro said, he's got to be somewhere, and when we find him we'll know exactly where he is, and that's all we should say about it or we'll go crazy. Nizarro went and looked at your house. No one bombed it."

"Are Germans there?"

"He didn't say."

"You're fibbing."

"All right. A few. Let's not talk about that. Did you figure out that this guy who's been talking to you is no ordinary soldier, and he's up to no good, or should I explain a few things about his tricks, about the type of information he wants to get from you?"

"I'm going to pretend," I said, "that the only reason you asked me that question is that you're still very young."

"I apologize. I just wanted to make sure you know he doesn't like partisans."

"I know that, Lido. Where's Marcellina?"

"I don't know."

"What about Etto Renzetti of San Guarino?"

"I don't know where anyone else is except Nizarro, who's looking for Beppi along the coast, in case he's hiding in a fisherman's shack—which Nizarro can manage, because he knows where the mines are—and also Geppo and Roncuzzi. I slept in a hayloft with them last night. It just occurred to me, this is the first time I ever did anything with a mop that didn't belong to the restaurant."

"Lido, listen to me. These soldiers think Beppi blew up half the German Army. They think he's the new Garibaldi. They're worried. They want to control him. Now he'll have to hide from the Americans, too."

"I know. Rumors, gossip, you know how it is. Nizarro says this always happens in a war. Let's hope no one else invades us. Beppi's got enough people after him as it is."

"Are we waiting for the diversion?"

"We are."

"What is it?"

"A surprise. How are you feeling?"

"I don't feel like I'm bleeding anywhere, but how do I look? I haven't seen myself in a mirror."

"You look a little pale. They didn't tell me you're dressed like an American soldier. I never saw you in trousers before. I think they call what you're wearing *fatigues.*"

"They belong to a horse racer. What's going on at the Pattuellis' village? The church was bombed."

"I heard about it, but I don't know any other news."

"What about Carmen and Mauro's children?"

"I don't know anything about them, but they're probably making trouble somewhere."

"Is Annmarie all right?"

"She's *jolly well bloody good.* One of her friends is English, and he says that about everything. You know how we thought these Americans were so organized? They're not. The left hand doesn't know what the right one's doing. I think some of them became just like Italian politicians as soon as they got here."

"You seem to be enjoying yourself, Lido."

"I'm just doing my job!"

"I don't know who we can trust."

"I do," said Lido confidently. "Annmarie's commander has different ideas from these guys in the unit that captured you, not that anyone knew at the time that it was a capture. They must have been feeling that, if this were a chess game, they'd got the queen. Look at this floor! Now that I'm cleaning up the mess here, the mosaics are showing. Romagnan Roman! These tiles should be in a museum, if we've got some that haven't been bombed. I think I'll mention this to Beppi and Nizarro. Wouldn't they look *topping* in the restaurant? That's the other word I just picked up. I'll have to remember where this place is."

"Never mind all that, Lido. Tell me about the plan for getting out of here."

"I already did."

"You didn't, not in detail."

"Well, for one thing, we'll make our escape out that window just over there. The one that's got a blanket covering it. We're on the ground floor, so there won't be any jumping—the sill's not very high. You'll see a row of olive trees to the right, as you're facing them. Behind them is an old stone farmhouse, not bombed, just decrepit. Behind that is the car. Oh, I almost forgot to tell you about Nomad. I *do* know where more of us are. Being an idiot must have affected me. Nomad's gone to help the American Army liberate Ravenna. It's packed with Nazis. They needed a translator. He took the Batarra brothers with him, because Nizarro said, after what Beppi did, he's putting an end to individual action. He said no one except himself can do anything alone, and the Batarras know the city. Remember, the two of them used to live in Ravenna? They had side-by-side shops, tobacco and a pharmacy, just like what they ended up with in Mengo. The Americans in Ravenna are *good guys*. Annmarie said so. One of them is her *fidanzato*! He sent her a message. She didn't know he was here. He's Italo-American. Tomasino? Is that his name? I wasn't clear about it. He's an officer, a genuine army big shot. They don't all want us unarmed like babies. The proof of that is the fact that he's arranging to get us guns called *Brownings*. They're rifles. I think your smuggling days may be over. What's the matter? Why are you getting upset? Am I doing badly with the floor? Are you scared of going out the window?"

"I'm not upset."

Suddenly there was an immensely loud pop just outside the front of the building. It wasn't anything like the booming of thunder-like bombs out of airplanes—but something sharper and crackly, like a firecracker. Gunshots. In rapid succession there were more of them, then a chaotic jumble of what could only be explosions.

It was like listening to an orchestra in which the only musicians who'd shown up to play were the percussionists. The room filled with shouting, with a frenzy of commotion, and Lido threw down the mop to lean toward me, grabbing my arms, tugging at me. A look of pure naked terror was on his face.

"That's not the diversion," he whispered hoarsely, breathing hard. "I think it sounds like Germans. Come *on.*"

I felt strangely unafraid. Perhaps I was beginning to consider myself an old hand at attacks, even though this was only my second one. And I was furious—*furious*—not at the attackers, whoever they were, but at that officer big shot, a stranger to me, heard of and never seen but looming largely, unexpectedly, in my mind: Tullio Tomasini. What was he doing in Italy? Had he come to be married to his *fidanzata* and spoil my hopes? Why was he involving himself with guns and partisans? Did he imagine himself a hero in a Hollywood movie, an Italo-American Spencer Tracy?

I had spotted a pair of boots below the end of the cot, on the other side of the room, where the jockey soldier Peewee lay absolutely still, covered to his chin by a blanket.

That shape was like a small teenage boy's. I wondered if his compatriots had made fun of him. Maybe, somewhere in the state of Kentucky, his mother walked around in her American life trying hard to not imagine that he was in the situation he was in. Maybe she kept staying close to horses in his honor. Was it night in America? Was everyone sleeping? Maybe Peewee had a wife or a girlfriend, dreaming of him.

Well, mother, wife or girlfriend, and sisters, too, if he had some, couldn't hold it against me for wanting his boots, especially since I already had his clothes. And the reason I was barefoot in the first place was that I'd been *bombed by an American.*

I'd lost two Berettas because of that American, besides my shoes. My feet were as raw and aching as if I'd walked on broken glass, which, quite possibly, I had done.

There weren't any pistols lying around for me to seize and make off with, but those boots were just sitting there. They were made of good brown leather, ankle-high, in excellent condition, with thick black soles. They looked like my size.

I saw I had a chance. In the noise and confusion, I might not be noticed in a dash toward that cot across the room. It was close to the surgical area, where makeshift curtains of tent canvas had been strung up on ropes. They'd collapsed, along with part of the outside wall.

Mortars, I guessed. Sunlight appeared in places that five minutes ago were solid stone. The surgical area consisted of a high old marble-topped table, probably from the *palazzo*'s dining room. The canvas had toppled on most of it, like a soiled old tablecloth at the end of a meal, as if whoever cleared away the plates and glasses and silver had forgotten it.

But it didn't fully cover the body of a man along its length. A soldier. A big one. His rigidity contained the look of someone who had died. His shirt had been torn open. Blood was everywhere, slowly being absorbed into the canvas.

"Lucia! Come! We're going into the cellar!"

Lido pointed to a back door. He couldn't understand why I wasn't in a hurry to go. He'd never been under fire before. I shook him off me. I could get to safety on my own.

"Go, go," I said. "I'll be right behind you."

"You have to go first."

"I'm older than you, so do as I say. Go on."

I hadn't needed to mention my age. I was the widow of his first boss and the mother of his second, but who was the one who'd kept everything going all those years? Did people pour into Aldo's for the food? The location? There were a dozen better restaurants on the coast!

He had no choice but to obey me, and anyway, I couldn't bring myself to ask him to get the boots for me, or even to mention them. He hadn't looked over at that part of the room since the shooting had started. He didn't know about the soldier on the table. He hadn't seen anyone dead from a war yet.

Off he went. I lowered my head, as if caught in a storm, and made a beeline for the boots. I was able to shut away everything else—all movement, all noise. I was good at it. It was the same thing that went on at Aldo's, when it was *time to go on, Lucia,* and I'd make my way to the front, to the spotlight-spot, through obstacles of tables, chairs, diners, waiters, outstretched arms and legs, those crabs off Lido's tray that night, and sometimes babies, crawling about underfoot, or a kitten or puppy some patron had smuggled in, undetected by the staff until it jumped out from its hiding place and I'd manage, just in time, not to step on it.

Did the clatter from the kitchen bother me when I was singing? Did a patron, in a fit of coughing? Or cars going noisily by in the road? Or Fascists, taking out guns and laying them alongside their plates?

I squatted down to get the boots, leather shiny and newly cleaned. I clutched them to my chest, as I'd held on to my purse long ago last night in the Saint's Grove, lying on the seat of what used to be Ugo's car.

Oh, no, I thought, my purse.

Where was it? There weren't any candy boxes full of bullets in it—Annmarie had taken them for the Lugers. If the Americans had it, they'd have searched it. Had it been with me when I walked in the moonlight with Etto? I couldn't remember. What about when I'd thrown myself into his arms? Was it hanging on my shoulder when I kissed him?

What was I going to do about Etto?

He was certain to be out there somewhere, waiting for me, watching for me, troubled and frightened and upset and possibly in shock all over again, if it had worn off the first time. How could I undo kissing him, embracing him?

"It was the moonlight," I might say. "Etto, the moonlight made me a little crazy." My purse was nowhere to be seen. Etto would take it badly. He'd gone to so much trouble to find it for me. "I'm sorry to disappoint you," I could say, and really mean it.

I did not look at the jockey soldier, but I knew that he had died. I could feel the presence of death without looking, like a change in the temperature.

A dead American was on the cot just behind me, and a dead American was on the marble table just above me. You have to learn in a war to pretend to be wearing a blindfold. I'd only just thought of this, but I said it to myself as if they were words of wisdom, handed down to me by someone who knew what they were talking about.

Perhaps those words belonged in a song: *A blindfold in a war, a blindfold! Pretend to be wearing a blindfold!*

Gunfire was still going on. I could pick out the different sounds of pistols, rifles, shells.

I knew there was a cellar to go to because Lido had said so. I didn't know what town this was. I didn't know where I was. I'd have to remember to tell Frank that there are *middles of nowhere* in Italy after all.

There was no sign of him. Outdoors for a smoke. The Umbrian's stepson.

The boots felt all right. A bit heavy, but all right. I'd have to forget about my purse. I'd have to start making a list of the things that had been lost: the black market flour, my purse, my good wool coat, my own clothes, my shoes, the Berettas, the habit, Ugo's medical bag, Ugo's car, Etto's factory.

Beppi couldn't be on it. *We're going to find him, you know.* The list was for things I knew I'd never see again. Beppi was somewhere. When I found him, I'd know exactly where he was.

"Grazie, americano," I said to the jockey soldier from Kentucky, without looking at him. "I'm grateful for the *fatigues* and the boots. May you rest in peace forever, to make up for the hell you have died in. If I believed in a thing like heaven, I'd hope—like the Umbrian's stepson, wherever he is—they have horse races, and you enter them all, and win all of them, amen."

Tito Roncuzzi, the butcher, was one of those staunch, stout Mengo men who were called by their surnames, like Nizarro. He was old enough to be Lido's father; it seemed he'd decided to make the most of it. "You're in trouble, Lido."

With his solemn, chubby face, and the pale dome of his head, and the half-moon of tidy, gray-black hair around the back, in a perfect crescent, exactly from the top of one ear to the other, Roncuzzi carried a weight of authority. His high forehead was multi-wrinkled, like a sideways swatch of corduroy. His deep-set eyes held the gleam of someone who is self-possessed, confident, and irreproachable: a world unto himself.

He looked like a painting of a medieval monk in a shadowy cell of a room, in any city in Italy—a monk whose age you could measure in centuries, who looked out at the world with an expression full of character: thoughtful but not bookish, *simpatico* but highly judgmental, shrewd but not narrow-minded, decent but not sanctimonious, openhearted but discreet, and involved one hundred percent in all things of the senses which life had to offer, as if, behind him, blocked from view, there was a happy, large-bosomed woman, by a table laid with brandies, wine, all sorts of delicacies, and naturally, platters of excellent meat.

His father, also named Tito, had been a butcher. Both his grandfathers had been butchers. His wife, originally from Mirandola, was the daughter of one. The elder of their two daughters had married one, and she'd gone to Mirandola with her husband when he took over the shop of his grandfather-in-law, at his death.

But the other daughter, Valentina, seventeen, was an independent-minded girl who refused to eat anything that had once been alive. She had plans to go into office work, perhaps in accounting—she was good with numbers. The war had halted her schooling. She didn't want to work for her father; she never went into his shop. She liked to think she'd landed in that family by mistake.

Roncuzzi didn't come to the restaurant unless it involved deals; he liked to eat at a *trattoria* that only served seafood. But his family used to turn up often. His wife and daughters had the right to request songs.

Only Valentina ever had, and it was always the same thing, *La Bohème*—the stove, the freezing apartment, Paris, and Rodolfo, Rodolfo, Rodolfo, Rodolfo. Eventually, we realized she'd set her sights, as Beppi had put it, on Cherubino.

"Mama, don't encourage her." He couldn't bear the thought of losing Roncuzzi; a lovesick, underage daughter of a principal supplier, he didn't need.

He wouldn't let Lido near Valentina's table. He told him he'd have the cooks cut off his beautiful hair if he so much as looked at her; he'd be cranially skinned, like a rabbit. "Mama, if that girl wants a seducer, go to an extreme and give her *Don Giovanni*. It's the one thing Mozart did well, like an Italian. Set it up nicely, then give her the floor as it opens at the end, and he drops feet first, shrieking and howling, to his infernal, everlasting reward."

I knew from Marcellina that, one night at the restaurant, Valentina composed a note to Lido, and gave it to the waiter at her table to be passed along. The waiter was Nomad, one of the youngest; if it weren't for Lido, he would have been the handsomest. He must have seemed, in Valentina's eyes, sophisticated and bohemian, from his experience living abroad, even though it was England, not France.

Naturally, Nomad read the note before tearing it up and dropping the pieces in the kitchen fire. It contained the directions to a private little stream behind the villa of a friend of hers, where Valentina spent weekend afternoons. "How I love that bubbly water! How I look forward to talking together! How lonely I am!" Then the takeover had happened.

Roncuzzi couldn't have known about any of that, or he wouldn't have talked to Lido so amiably.

"You were lucky," he was saying. "But remember, in the future, the next time you go into an unfriendly building, especially if you're trying to rescue someone, you'll have planned what to do if your first plan fails, which, I promise you, nine times out of ten, will happen, war or not."

Lido nodded at him self-righteously. He was bursting with the desire to defend himself. Until now, he'd been quiet.

With all respect, he felt he'd done nothing wrong. He could swear he'd never said "cellar" in the way I thought he had meant it. When the attack had begun, he came to the conclusion that it was not a good idea to stick around, so he'd said, in a general way, something like, "Lucia, come on, there's a cellar." It was fully nonspecific.

He'd simply assumed that the *palazzo* taken over by the Americans had a cellar.

Who wouldn't have thought the same? Attack, cellar! The two things went together like rain and umbrellas. *Palazzi,* including run-down, abandoned old ones, were all the same. You had a roof, you had walls, you had floors, you had mosaics, you had a cellar.

It was common sense. He hadn't lost control of himself when the Germans turned up for a battle. He hadn't panicked. If the other partisans suspected he was out of his depth as a partisan, they were wrong. Did anyone care that he was the only man in that battle who didn't have a gun?

He didn't have a gun! He was supposed to get a Luger from my run. It was his turn! Why did he have to be the last one to get a gun, which he never got? Even Galto Saponi had a gun, and he was *old,* and all he'd ever done was fish. What kind of a squad let old people on it? Every other one had young men only. Half this squad was middle-aged! Didn't anyone think that was weird? It was weird! If someone came to Italy and took photographs of squads and put them together in a scrapbook, all the other squads would look *youthful.* One squad alone would look like it had guys who'd gone back to their old school for a reunion!

"Roncuzzi, are you going to let him get away with that?" said Geppo.

"Yes, because he's guilty and he knows it, and he's letting off steam."

He wasn't just letting off steam! He felt that I had no right to be so mad at him. When he said at the *palazzo* hospital—when the attack had begun—that we were going to hide in the cellar, he was speaking hypothetically! He'd never said he *knew* there was a cellar, or where it was, or how to get there.

In fairness, he deserved some credit! That tipped-on-its-side American truck in the *palazzo* yard had offered plenty of protection. He was a fully competent partisan! He'd done stupendously well with his impersonation of an idiot! Why was everyone picking on him?

His plan had been, hide in the cellar, then, as soon as possible, get to the golfer and her friends. Right here. This was the meeting place. Honestly, no one would have predicted that the golfer and her friends would not have been waiting as promised.

He wasn't saying that the golfer was a cowardly runner-away, or a driver-away, since the car was gone, too. He didn't want to insult her. He knew she'd been helpful to partisans, and to me—this wasn't personal. But still, an empty space where someone's supposed to be waiting for you was a really, really empty space. One naturally felt a little suspicious.

He was willing, though, to say he was sorry for not having planned ahead of time where to go, specifically, in case of an attack, or if the original plan fell apart. But how was he to have known that? This was his first war!

It had turned out well! The escape had been accomplished! And it didn't matter that Roncuzzi and Geppo had been looking for Beppi, not us, when they found us.

A satisfactory outcome! The Germans had retreated! The American Army held on to the *palazzo,* not that it did partisans any good, since that entire unit was *antipartigiani.*

And if there'd been a cellar to hide in, we never would have been rescued. Geppo was all right with tight, dark spaces, but Roncuzzi, absolutely, would have had none of it, and they never would have separated. It was a blessing there hadn't been a cellar! Why were we talking about fear and mistakes, instead of the joy when we were found accidentally?

All right, so there'd been a bit of a fright when I'd run out of the *palazzo* and felt confused, without a cellar I'd thought was there. It was only a couple of seconds!

Roncuzzi was claustrophobic. He was worse than Beppi

about it. Once, in his apprentice days, he'd been stuck in a meat locker for four hours. He didn't want to talk about it, but he never wanted to experience anything like it again. That was the reason why most of the walls of his shop in Mengo were glass.

"It's true, Lucia," said Roncuzzi. "I'm not taking Lido's side, but if you don't count Beppi, I believe I'm the most claustrophobic human being there ever was."

"I didn't know that," said Geppo. "Are you feeling that way now?"

"No, this place is all right. Depressing, but all right."

The stone farmhouse—a hut, actually, consisting of one room—must have once been part of the *palazzo*'s estate. The four of us were seated at a rough old table in front of a fireplace that looked and smelled as if it hadn't been used for a long time. We sat on upside-down wooden barrels that smelled like apples. There were six. No chairs. It seemed no one had lived here for years.

There was one small window, with closed shutters. Boards had been nailed in crossbars on top of it. There was no plumbing, no water, no sink, not even a basin. The only other furniture was a narrow bed made out of logs. The mattress was flattened straw. No blankets, no sheets, no anything. But people were living here: the four old women and two old men who'd let us in. Their average age was probably eighty. There hadn't been room inside for us all.

Only one of them spoke to us: a soft-faced, gap-toothed woman who appeared to be the oldest. She was the one with the most wrinkles and seemed to be their leader. She didn't look Romagnan—although the others did—but she spoke in dialect, which Roncuzzi translated for me. I'd never got the feel of it.

"We'll let you hide here for one hour and then you leave."

The two waiters and Roncuzzi had questioned them but got nowhere. Why are you here? Where did you come from? Where are your families? Are you related? Are any of you married to each other? Are you wounded? Are you sick? Are you lost? Do you know who this famous lady is, in her American-uniform disguise? Why aren't you answering us? You're safe with us, for Christ sake, we're partisans.

No response whatsoever. "Stubborn beyond words, and twice as tough," Roncuzzi had said. "If they were cattle, they'd never end up on anyone's plate. The knife does not exist that would allow me to section them."

The *anziani* had crammed themselves together on a pew-like bench just outside. The low doorway was very small. The door was open; dusk was falling. It seemed as if they'd stepped outdoors to enjoy the sunset.

Maybe they'd come from one of the boardinghouses near the shore. They wore too-tight coats, all strangely bulky. They must have been wearing layers, perhaps of all the clothes they owned. One of the men was completely toothless. The woman who'd spoken to us wore a green-and-gold kerchief around her head, tied in the back. It was hard to make out the design of the cloth; it was filthy. It was possible that some of those stains were bloodstains.

They had no belongings, nothing.

It was chilly and damp. My fatigues did little to hold back the cold. Roncuzzi offered to give me his jacket, but I didn't accept it. He'd been away from Mengo for quite some time, but still, it smelled like a butcher's shop. I wondered if his daughter Valentina made him take a bath when he went home at night, before she'd kiss him to say *ciao.*

I knew I should try to eat. The two waiters and Roncuzzi

looked at me gently, hopefully. The pain in my face had started up again, worse than ever. It was centered around my forehead and eyes. The tightness of my skin made me know that there was swelling.

"What do I look like?" I said, and they rushed in with all the ways they could think of to say fine, fine, perfectly normal, same as always, a little under the weather, sure, but only from exhaustion and the war, and nothing time itself won't cure.

"Do I have black eyes?"

They looked shocked that I would imagine such a thing.

"Do I have bruises?"

They were even more shocked.

It didn't matter what I looked like. How many soldiers had I counted, dead or dying on the ground, in the time it took me to go with Lido from the back door of the *palazzo* to that bombed-to-its-side truck?

The color of the truck was dull green. *Army drab,* Lido had called it. He'd enjoyed the symmetry of the two of us finding shelter in the same type of vehicle Beppi had exploded. Same vehicle, different army. We'd been lucky.

I hadn't had time to count bodies. Many.

What about along the way to the hut where *Annmarie wasn't waiting*?

Many more. I'd kept my eyes looking nowhere but straight ahead. No details. Not all the bodies had been lying flat. I'd noticed shapes. Some of them had appeared to be kneeling. Some of them had been curled up, with knees bent high, and hands covering faces, and chins nearly touching the knees, as if the people who'd lived inside the bodies had tried to make themselves tiny.

Don't think about Annmarie. Don't try to guess where she was.

"Lido, face it, you had a mission, which you screwed up by having a Plan A, and not a Plan B, at least, not a Plan B that was based on actuality," said Roncuzzi. "Please never do that again. Please expect bombs and guns all the time. But you and Lucia came out of it all right. You made a good idiot back there with the Americans, and we're proud of you. That was something you did in an exemplary way."

"Thanks. Am I off the hook?"

"For now," said Geppo.

Roncuzzi bit into a piece of *piadina,* which looked far from fresh. He'd taken it out of his pocket. He chewed it carefully, in a ruminating way. "Is it true some Americans are afraid of us?"

Lido bobbed his head. "Terrified. They think we should work for them. They think if we have guns, and we're not in their control, we might feel like shooting GIs along with Nazis."

"It's a reasonable speculation," said Roncuzzi. "Immature, but reasonable, considering what they've been doing to us. What was the diversion outside the *palazzo* supposed to be?"

"An American Army friend of Annmarie's, a lieutenant, had one of those horns they call a *bugle,*" Lido answered. "He was supposed to play a song in the courtyard, a song which, apparently, makes Americans drop what they're doing and start singing, or at least pay careful attention. I don't know what the song is. Maybe it's patriotic. If Lucia and I hadn't made it out the window by the time it was over, the horn player was going to take requests."

Roncuzzi gaped at him. "A horn player? And they turned their tails and left you as soon as the Germans attacked? And you're interested in not saying that was cowardly?"

"I'm just trying to not be depressed," said Lido.

"I roasted these chestnuts myself, Lucia," said Geppo. "At a charcoal fire near a goat pen, where there wasn't a fence. The wood had been taken for fuel and it was all used up. The boy who was minding the goats—of which he only had a few, and they didn't look good—gave them to me in exchange for a voucher for a free lunch every day, back-to-back, for one month, starting from the first day we reopen. I didn't have anything to write the voucher on, and I didn't have anything to write with, but he said he would trust us. He's the skinniest boy I ever saw. I looked at his ribs through his shirt, every one of them. His whole life, he's been wishing he could go to Aldo's. He wants to eat veal."

"But we only open for lunch four days a week, and they're not back to back," said Lido.

"Beppi said when we're open again, we're never closing. Lunch, dinner, every day."

"That's good news," said Roncuzzi. "The orders will pour in."

His shop was shut down at around the same time as Aldo's takeover. His wife and Valentina had gone to the other daughter's house in Mirandola. We didn't talk about this, but it was common knowledge that Roncuzzi's son-in-law got along well with Fascists. "Blackshirt-friendly." That shop of his was still in business, was prospering.

I wondered what Valentina Roncuzzi was eating there. I wondered what feelings had come over her when she learned that her father would join a squad of mostly waiters from Aldo's, including Lido Linari. A girlish lightness? A woman's smile curving slowly, privately?

Had the Americans bombed Mirandola? Was Valentina all right? Was she hoping her father was close to Lido, keeping him safe for her? Was she alone in a room, looking out a window right now—if it wasn't boarded up—at the last orange haze of this sunset? Was she waiting to see the moon come out? Was she pining for Lido? Did she touch her mouth with the tips of her fingers, imagining kissing him, imagining making love with him, in spite of the war?

And I wondered where Etto Renzetti was. The Umbrian's stepson had said he'd tried vigorously to get into the *palazzo* to see me. With Marcellina.

I didn't want anyone to know I had no memory of how I'd got there. I'd kissed Etto. I'd listened to a Pattuelli talking of black eyes, then I'd dressed as a nun without a veil, in that moonlit, half-bombed house. Then I was in an American bed—an army cot—in different clothes. Mosaics on the floor.

I tried to picture Etto and Marcellina at the guarded *palazzo* front door. I wondered what their reactions would be concerning my outfit. Marcellina would accuse me of conspiring with the bombers; she'd scream at me to change; she'd tell me I'd be better off naked if there was nothing else to put on. "The pants are very becoming, but I thought you were much more attractive in the habit, not that, when I held you in my arms, I felt that I was kissing a soon-to-be nun," Etto might say.

When I kissed Etto, I felt young. As young as a girl like Valentina.

"Lucia, it's getting darker. Those *anziani* are looking at us uncomfortably. We'll have to give up on our American friend with the car. I'm not saying she won't show up for you, but we'll have to leave soon. First, you have to eat something," said Geppo.

"As moderately well as you look, Lucia, you might do well by having a doctor examine you," said Roncuzzi. "I wonder where Ugo Fantini is."

"I wonder where everyone is who's not us," said Lido. "I wonder if we have to go through the rest of the war like this, walking around looking for everyone who, you don't know where they are."

"Pincelli went with Galto to the Pattuellis' village to see what happened to the church the Americans blew up," said Roncuzzi. "Poor Galto was going out of his mind, worrying about his daughter and Mauro and his grandchildren. Ugo might be there, too. Nizarro's looking for Beppi, like we are. It's not as bad as it could be. I'm trying to keep up my spirits."

"Nomad went with the Batarras to Ravenna," said Lido helpfully.

"Do you know where anyone is, Lucia?" said Roncuzzi.

I'd decided to follow the example of the silent *anziani*. I thought, "I know where Aldo is. Inside the earth. Put there from natural causes."

Some of those shapes in the *palazzo* yard did not appear to have been part of nature in any way. Heaps of clothing. Mineral-hard helmets. One body on top of another, two, three.

I wondered if Valentina Roncuzzi was being successful at getting food—vegetables, cheese, eggs, macaroni, bread, nuts, fruit—through the Fascist connections of her brother-in-law. I wished I could send her a message, even though I'd never spoken to her before. I felt bad that I'd never sung her requests. I wished I hadn't listened to Beppi, telling me not to encourage her.

"Stay alive, Valentina. Puccini! Rodolfo! Surviving is worth the effort. Go home at the end of the war and throw yourself at Lido Linari, as wrong for you as he is, and in spite of the trouble it will cause. If you already feel, ahead of time, the romance between you will last only one hour, don't be stupid about it. *Have* it."

"Lucia, here." Geppo had peeled three or four chestnuts, which he'd broken apart into very small pieces. He held them out in the palm of his hand, like someone feeding pigeons in a *piazza.*

What possessed me to slap him, I didn't know—Geppo Ravaglia, of all people, the most even-tempered man who'd ever drawn a salary from Aldo's.

He was younger than Beppi by several years, but he'd always seemed much older. I'd never heard of him quarreling with anyone, and that included Mariano in the kitchen. Mariano would interrupt himself in the middle of a demented-sounding shouting fit, directed at one of the cooks, if Geppo happened to appear. "*Ciao,* Geppo, how are things going? Is there anything you need?" Then he'd go back to yelling at the cook.

Aldo used to say that the reason he'd hired him, having stolen him from a wealthy family in San Marino, where he'd been some sort of butler, was that it couldn't hurt business to have someone around who was a genuine amateur intellectual and a perfectionist, as maddening as that could sometimes be. No one set a table half as well as he did. No one folded napkins as perfectly.

"The Etruscan," he was called. He'd come from a town north of Rome. Viterbo. He'd grown up in a house near the museum there.

He was obsessed with Etruscans. He'd talk to customers about the subject as if talking about his present-day neighbors and friends: their coins, their sophistication, their clothes, their sublime, astonishing tombs, their intelligence, their meals, their pottery, their elegant, extremely admirable stone faces.

"Today, we are the Etruscans, and the *fascisti* are those old-time Roman homicidal bastards. But because we know our history, we know we don't have to be doomed," he'd say to customers who weren't Fascists. "You should order the lobster tonight, for solidarity with creatures who have excellent systems of self-defense." He was equally at home with people with educations and people without.

No one held it against him that he'd had almost no formal schooling. He was unable to add up a bill, and had to have Beppi do it. A customer would order spaghetti with squid and he'd say, "Good choice, that's just what an Etruscan would do. Did you know our Roman ancestors began the process of exterminating them by smashing tablets on which their language was written? They cut off the hands of every Etruscan caught writing. Then they took over their irrigation system. And finally, they stopped being so subtle, and just slaughtered them. I recommend the roast pork for your next course, with a side of peas, do you agree with me? An Etruscan would answer yes to that, by the way."

He called himself "a private ancient historian and archaeologist who earns a living as a waiter." He'd come to Romagna to look for burial sites. He wanted to create a new museum, perhaps near Aldo's, not that he'd found anything to put in it. He didn't have a building yet, either.

He'd been waiting out fascism, even when things kept getting worse. The Fascists hadn't wanted him to dig. "No digging." He was probably being watched, but he dug anyway, late, late at night, feeling his way into the past. He was never assigned lunch shifts because that was when he slept. He had married, not long ago. Younger than Beppi and married.

His wife was a Mengo girl, someone's sister. A cook's? Yes, Fausto Fabbi's sister, blond like he was. There was one child, an infant, a boy.

All these things, these facts, presented themselves in a vivid way in my mind, crowding each other, as if striking Geppo were a stone thrown into a pond, and these were the ripples.

I threw water at Etto, I remembered.

Throw water on one man in moonlight and the next day, by light of the setting sun, take a swing at another. There seemed to be something rational about this. Something consistent. I wasn't sorry I'd hit Geppo. What was happening to me? It wasn't that I'd merely swatted him away. I'd discovered a hidden reserve of energy, and with a long, wide thrust of my arm, I hit him hard. I hadn't realized my hand had been fisted.

"I'm not hurt. It's not a problem. Don't apologize. Don't even think about it. Larth hits me harder than that all the time, in far more sensitive areas," Geppo was saying to me.

I didn't know who Larth was.

"My baby," said Geppo. "The name is Etruscan."

"Remember what Beppi said about it?" said Lido. He was trying to hide his relief. He was glad I'd swung at Geppo, not him. "He said it's awful. He said it's like the sound of a fart. He wanted you to change it."

"Well, I didn't," said Geppo.

The pieces of chestnuts went all over, mostly on the floor, like the time Lido dropped crabs off his tray because Beppi had compared him to a girl.

Who would have thought the toothless old man on that bench could come inside so quickly to pick them up? He looked as if he hadn't moved fast in fifty years.

Roncuzzi leaped up from his chair. The old man was on his hands and knees next to it, feeling for crumbs below the table.

"He's the oldest man I ever laid eyes on, and he's starving!" Lido cried.

Roncuzzi had just finished eating the last of his bread. His hand went to his chest, just above his ample belly, as if he'd felt a terrible urge to protect the bit of food inside him: a guilty look came over him. The lines of his face wavered in sad confusion.

"We didn't even ask these people if they were hungry," said

Geppo. "We're Italians, for Christ sake. We're Italians and we haven't got food. You know what I think about the parable of Christ on the hill with the loaves and fishes? I think it's bullshit. I think there won't be a Catholic left in Italy when this is all over."

Roncuzzi took hold of the old man's elbow and pulled him up to his feet, which looked as easy as if he'd picked up empty clothes.

The bench outside emptied all at once, like at a soccer match. Maybe the *anziani* thought Roncuzzi meant harm to their friend. But it became apparent that they had lost what self-control they'd had. They came crowding inside, letting out strange hissing noises, and little yelps and muted groans.

They wanted the few chestnuts on the table that hadn't been peeled yet, and the shells Roncuzzi and the waiters had tossed into the fireplace, as if they hadn't been picked completely clean.

Lido and Geppo had bread in their hands, but the two of them were quick to put it in their pockets. Lido got the rest of the chestnuts before anyone else did.

The press of people around me made me gasp for breath. My throat went dry; my heart was pounding hard. How could I be more afraid of these people than of *nazifascisti*? My legs felt as rigid as wood. I could only smile weakly at Roncuzzi and Geppo, by way of saying thank you, for helping me get out of there.

They lifted me, between them, one at each side. Lido went outside ahead of us and lifted his foot to that bench and kicked it over.

"It's going to be all right. I'm sure someone's looking for us," Geppo said quietly.

"I'm positive about it," said Roncuzzi.

"There might even be someone close by. I haven't given up on the golfer," Geppo added.

"We're turning into dogs!" cried Lido.

We hurried away. The outside air was cold, damp, biting. This time I didn't object when Roncuzzi offered his jacket.

It was night. Up ahead, the *palazzo* windows were shrouded. There was not a trace of light in any one of them.

There was a plan.

The plan was to walk two miles or so to the next village. It was manageable. It was a good idea to stay off the roads. Two miles or so. One step at a time. There weren't any planes in the sky. The moon hadn't risen.

Geppo was good at walking in the dark. He'd negotiated a great many miles in darkness in his life so far, first in his youth, in villages so small they weren't on maps, then here.

His interest in staying alive was keen. He was happy to describe his feelings concerning survival. He was really committed to it. A million times by now, he'd dreamed about himself as the founder of a museum; he was convinced it was going to happen. Plus, there was his son and his wife to be considered. His wife was going to be the general manager. His son was going to inherit it, having grown up in it. There was going to be an alcove inside, or a outdoor terrace, or both, where refreshments and snacks could be bought. He didn't want his waiter's experience to go to waste. There'd be an authentic all-Etruscan menu.

The trick of it was, you had to believe in the future. You had to imagine a future, and then you had to believe in it.

"No one's turning into dogs, Lido," said Roncuzzi. "We're all staying human. I promise."

I couldn't stop thinking about the fact that I could not remember changing from Annmarie's habit to the uniform.

I wasn't wearing underwear. Where was my bra? My underpants? More lost items. My lost memory: one more. How was I supposed to get used to knowing that my brain wasn't functioning right? There seemed to have been a partial shutdown.

"There's never been anything more graceful than the carvings on Etruscan tombs," Geppo was saying. "I don't just mean the technicalities. It came from their souls. Everything they made was full of grace."

"Etruscans were pagans," said Lido. "How can you be a pagan and have grace? I thought you had to be a Catholic."

"You have to be a Catholic to be a Fascist," said Roncuzzi.

"A Fascist can't have grace," said Geppo. "You have to have a soul to act as the container for it. No one can argue that point."

Always when Geppo was around, an intellectual discussion. People were always willing to talk about Etruscans as the opening move of a conversation. You never knew where it would lead.

"You can be a Catholic and not have grace," said Roncuzzi.

"I agree," said Lido. "But maybe when you're talking about a pagan, you should call it something else."

"Such as what?" said Geppo. "I'm open to suggestions."

"I don't know. Pagan grace," said Lido.

"Lucia," said Roncuzzi. "Is there such a thing as an opera about Etruscans?"

They weren't giving up on trying to get me to join their chatter. Persistence was a good quality in a partisan. But I wished they'd stop talking.

"It's a blot on our culture that there isn't," said Geppo. "I've told myself a hundred times, I should find someone to write one."

"I wish Puccini wasn't dead. He could do the music," said Lido.

Roncuzzi let out a weary sigh. "If I wrote an opera, it would have to be about butchers. But no one would pay money to see it."

"I would write one about us," said Lido.

Everywhere one went, one heard about Italians wanting to create new operas. Aldo had wanted his pirate giant, Etto wanted his crazy, love-thwarted Orlando, and now this. It was good to know that it was something the war hadn't changed.

In the fields, on the paths, going away from the grounds of the *palazzo,* it was easy walking. They wanted to carry me. Take turns with it, or figure out a way to make some sort of stretcher, or something.

I held my ground. As long as I wore a soldier's clothes and boots, I felt, I should try to march like one. I wasn't sure how it was done. The only marching soldiers I'd ever seen were Fascists.

Maybe the boots would know on their own what to do. I'd put my faith in the boots, I decided.

Pick up one foot, put it down, pick up the other one, put it down. How long did it take to go two miles or so? Half an hour. Forty minutes. Forty-five at the most. Less than the length of a program in the spotlight at Aldo's, including encores.

I was aware that I had reached a threshold of pain: a limit to what I could bear. I knew I was walking a line between being able to bear it, and not. I couldn't imagine what the "not" might involve. I felt like a *pioneer.* Which village were we heading to?

We were going inland. The reason I knew the moon wasn't up yet was that there wasn't any moonlight. I tried to tip back my head to look up at the sky, then gave up on it and decided not to try again.

Looking straight ahead was all right. I didn't need to see the sky. If stars were up there, they were up there, and if they weren't, they weren't.

If it had happened after the bombing that things were shifted in the constellations, and nothing was where it should be, or if huge tracts of stars had gone missing, it would be better, I felt, to find out about it later.

My eyes were used to the dark. I could see in the dark. I wouldn't let anyone hold on to me, but they were close by, matching their pace to mine. Geppo was at my right, Lido was at my left, and Roncuzzi was just behind me.

It was Geppo who said, quietly, gently, "Lucia, please, when I give you a signal to close your eyes, will you do it, without questions, please? Close your eyes and keep walking? I swear, I won't let anything happen to you. You won't fall, or even stumble."

"Tell her what the signal is," said Roncuzzi.

"Tell me, too," said Lido. "I'm already not looking in the same direction you are."

"A little cough," said Geppo.

Almost immediately, I heard the sound of Geppo letting out a cough. I shut my eyes and kept moving. I let myself be steered. March, march, march, march. The absoluteness of the darkness felt strangely comforting. I barely knew what my feet were walking on—dirt, pebbles, dry grass, twisted vegetation. Small slopes now and then to be worked out carefully. Waves of earth.

"I'll go off for a minute," I heard Roncuzzi say, "and see if we know them."

There was no slowing down of the pace. When Lido reached over to take hold of my hand, I didn't push him away. His chilly fingers closed hard around mine. I didn't have warmth to give him; my hands were colder than his. But I didn't pull away from him.

"We don't know them," Roncuzzi called out softly. "You know what I think? I think I hear a car. We're not that far from a road. I think it's a non-Fascist one. Fascist engines don't sound so noisy."

My eyes still closed, I strained my ears to hear it. But there were only some echoes of faraway guns, too soft to be thunder, rolling gently through all that silence. Pick up a foot, put it down, pick up the next one, put it down. Trust the boots.

When Roncuzzi was back in place behind me, Lido said, "Did you go and look at someone who's not alive?"

"A few of them."

"Are they Italians?"

"They're Germans," said Roncuzzi. I knew from his tone he was lying, but Lido seemed to accept his word.

"Good," said Lido. "Now we don't have to remember this spot, to come back and get them buried."

"You can open your eyes now," said Geppo. Lido slipped his hand away from mine.

Shapes of trees. Shadowy outlines of bushes, stone walls. Not counting Roncuzzi's jacket, I was only wearing two articles of clothing. I realized I had never been out in the world before without underwear.

And this was my first pair of pants. "I've got pants on, like a man," I said to myself. "I'm wearing *pants.*"

"Roncuzzi? What's the matter?" said Geppo, looking back over his shoulder. Roncuzzi had trailed behind. I pretended not to notice the sounds he was making.

"Nothing, nothing. I'm all right," he finally answered. His voice was hoarse, choked, like someone who'd been shouting for a very long time.

"Remember when you trained those dogs to piss on the boots of the Fascists, Roncuzzi?" said Geppo. "I just want to tell you, I admired it. I thought it was brilliant of you for thinking of it."

Roncuzzi caught up with us again. He couldn't let a subject like that go by without talking about it. "I was the one with the shop where the dogs always congregated, so that was how it happened. It wasn't difficult. You can pretty much always get them to do what you want, if you're a butcher. I was the only human in Mengo they respected. But it wasn't brilliant. It was stupid. That's on my conscience, by the way. The dogs were a hundred times smarter than I was."

"How many of them got shot?" said Geppo. "I forget."

"Four," said Roncuzzi. "It took me a week to teach them the trick. But it took me a month to untrain them."

"How many had learned it?" said Geppo.

"Ten, maybe eleven."

"That's six or seven not shot," Geppo said.

"In case you think it makes me feel better, it doesn't."

Now the ground was fairly level. Nothing dangerous. Nothing to require the lifting of a foot any higher than I was doing already. It wasn't much different from singing. One knew the point at which one's voice might break, like a glass.

"Honest to God, were the dead guys Germans, Roncuzzi?" said Lido.

"I wouldn't lie to you."

"Then why did you puke?"

"It must have been something I ate."

"Plus, you were upset about the old folks," said Geppo.

I thought about the way I used to talk to my voice. "Don't let this be the day you leave me." As if my voice were a living thing. As if I were praying to it.

Please. Don't leave me. I wondered if I was getting feverish. Was that something the limit would allow, a fever?

Don't think about any more problems. Think of something else. Did American soldiers have marching songs? Too bad the boots couldn't transmit one: the memory of a song stitched into the leather, traveling up my legs as mysteriously as a telegraph message.

But just because it couldn't was no reason to lose faith in the boots. "Keep trusting the boots," I said to myself, as an order. It had a nice rhythm: da *da* da da *dum,* even though it didn't sound march-like.

The rhythm started tapping itself in my head. It didn't hurt.

Keep trusting the boots,
Da da da, da da dum.
Keep trusting the boots, da da dum.
This is my first pair of pants in my life!
Da da da, da da da, da da dum.

"Lucia, here. I made you a sandwich."

Between the time he'd snatched the chestnuts off the table and now, Lido had managed to peel them. He'd broken them into bits, as Geppo had done before, but he'd gone further. He had pressed the bits into the bread. The small piece of *piadina* contained them neatly.

"If you don't eat this, my heart will break," he said.

I didn't want to break his heart. I could eat on the move. I could force myself to swallow. Keep trusting the boots, da da da, da da dum, keep trusting the boots, da da dum.

14

Folcore was before us: a tightly packed, walled medieval town of stone, towers, alleys, and narrow streets, with outlying farms and groves. It stood on a plain between the sea and the Apennines, beyond a wide, gently rounded hill. At the top of the hill was a small peach orchard. There weren't any peaches. Geppo, Roncuzzi, and Lido had searched every tree; they'd scoured the ground as well.

Moonlight was everywhere, but this time it was hard and thin and cold, as though it came from something covered with ice. There were stars to be seen without trying. As far as I could tell, nothing had shifted. Nothing appeared to be missing.

No smoke, no fog. No planes.

The sky was all right. I could generalize about it from the slice I could see. It was empty and black where it was supposed to be. It was starry where it should have been. The constellations were in the right places, and all across the sky, around its giant, wide belly, the belt of the zodiac was intact, not having been loosened, tightened, altered in any way, or taken off. How many notches were in the belt?

"Aquarius," I said to myself. "Pisces, Aries, Taurus."

I didn't know how many there were. I didn't know any more names.

I'd found a fairly wide trunk to lean against: a substitute backbone. I'd been running out of strength. The bark was smooth, cool. A net of delicate leaves was around me: pretty leaves, not bombed, still attached to their twigs. As dark as it was, I knew their color was green, like it was supposed to be.

I tried to remember names of shapes, particularly regarding peach leaves. Oblong. Oval. Almond-shaped. Pepper-shaped.

A strange sensation was in my feet. Wetness. Had I stepped in a puddle without knowing it? I trusted the boots not to leak at the soles, but water might have seeped in from the tops.

"It's only from a deep puddle," I said to myself, because certainly, if one were bleeding, one would be aware of it.

When we looked down at Folcore from the top of the hill, we saw that it was filled with Germans.

"I used to come here all the time. There was an elderly man in the post office with a drawer of Etruscan pottery shards. He was cataloging them. He'd been at it for thirty years. He was an amateur expert," said Geppo.

"Maybe he can help us," said Lido.

"Fascists tried to get him to be an equipment manager for one of their brigades," said Geppo. "He sneaked away. I don't know where he went. I don't know if he took his drawer. I hope so."

"I used to know the two butchers here," said Roncuzzi. "They had rival shops and they hated each other's guts. The only subject they agreed on was me. They had it in common that they hated me equally, because every time their rivalry got out of hand, which was often, the townspeople here, plus a few commercial proprietors, to avoid the antagonizing, came to

Mengo for whatever they needed. I was always glad to help out. Last I heard, they'd closed up, having had nothing to sell. They joined a new partisan group, somewhere north. I wonder how they're doing."

"We don't know anyone here?" said Lido. "Is that what you're saying?"

"Lucia, do you know anyone in Folcore?" said Geppo.

I didn't know. I didn't think so. I couldn't even remember how far Folcore was from Mengo, or from the sea, or from anywhere.

"The name Folcore, heart of Folco, comes from the illegitimate son of the thirteenth-century duke who used to live here," explained Geppo. "The duke had locked him up in a tower to hide him from his jealous wife. Folco had everything he needed, because the duke was not a sadist. He wouldn't have killed a child. He was waiting, so he could do what he considered an honorable thing, and kill his son as a grown man. In the tower, Folco had his own staff. He had servants and tutors, whom the duke believed he could trust. He had books, amusements, excellent food, all the sorts of things that rich people had. Then one day, around the time of his fourteenth birthday, when the duke went up to see him, as he regularly did, for he actually felt some affection for him, Folco wasn't there."

"He jumped out?" said Lido.

Geppo shook his head. "There were bars on the windows, which anyway were just slits. On his writing desk was a bloody heart. The note beside it said, 'Papa, this was mine, and now it's yours. It was removed with my own two hands. You'll never find the rest of my body because, by the time you read this, it will have been left too long in the mountains, for the birds.' "

"It seems to me he had help from the servants," said Lido.

"The servants loved him," said Geppo. "The duke didn't dare touch the heart. He believed he could see it still beating. He fell to pieces and underwent a religious conversion. To everyone's amazement, he put on sackcloth and went to a dozen different priests to confess to the murder of Folco's mother, a gentle yellow-haired girl from the north, who'd been a maid in his castle. He moved his whole household to a *casale* on the grounds of a monastery. He took vows of celibacy and poverty and his wife ran away with their daughters, never to be seen again. But his legitimate sons stayed with him. After his death, they came back, armed to the teeth, to take possession of their town. Folco was waiting for them, and he was *strong,* as if living all those years in a tower had turned him into one. For every weapon the other sons had, he had three. He killed them all. And you know, later on, when he became the duke, he kept his bedroom in the very same tower."

"I bet it was a sheep's heart on the desk, not a human one," said Roncuzzi. "I bet he had help with that from a butcher."

"Maybe so. I wish he were with us. This would be a good time to have him around," said Geppo.

There were sentries at the walls, at all the large buildings.

"Two tanks," counted Lido. "All sorts of trucks. Big ones, too, bigger than in Mengo. Black cars and motorcycles, all German. Heavy guns on piles of sandbags in the *piazza,* soldiers napping behind them, but of course at the slightest sound they'll wake up. Nazi flags and banners streaming from balconies, not that they could hurt us, but they make me nervous. Two flags, eight banners. All brand-new, by the way. Mounted guns on a few flat rooftops, five of them. No Folco, I'm sorry to say. I'm telling you, we cannot, *cannot,* go down there."

"Nizarro told us before that the Germans would set up a barrier along the mountains to block off this whole part of the country," said Roncuzzi. "This must be a stronghold for them. A command post. A lot of those cars belong to officers."

"We've been lucky so far," said Geppo. "It might hold."

"We're not going down there," said Lido.

"Keep your voice down," said Geppo calmly. "See that tower over there, the highest one? That's Folco's. There's a song about him. A troubadour sort of song, very old. It sounds best with guitars, although originally, it was probably played with lutes. Lucia, do you know that one? It's called 'Folco's Day' and it's beautiful. You never heard of it? I'll give you the gist. Folco gets out of bed before dawn and looks out the eastern side of his tower to watch the sun come up on the Adriatic, with the sea spread out like a mirror, on which thousands of white jewels are glittering. When the sunrise is over, he turns slowly, very slowly, like the hour hand on a clock. It takes him a whole day to get his back to the east and his face to the west. Then he watches the sun, in a blaze, go down behind the Apennines, the most perfect range of mountains that ever rose up from the deep and formed the backbone of a country."

"You're idealistic, Geppo," said Lido. "Maybe it comes from studying your Etruscans. You're not on good terms with reality."

"That's because reality is something that gets in the way of what you want to be doing," said Geppo.

"What's in the way right now, excuse me for reminding you, is a substantial portion of the German Army," Lido said. His voice was shaky; he couldn't conceal his nervousness.

"They're all asleep," said Geppo.

Then he had a question for me. "Do you remember my wedding day, Lucia? I will never forget what it was like when you sang. Everything was so solemn. It was all Palestrina. Two motets, a madrigal, a Magnificat. Everyone there felt the same way about it. The guests, the other waiters, the cooks, Adalgisa, and I—well, to put it succinctly, we could have listened to double as many songs, easily, without shifting one inch in our chairs, and all along, barely remembering to draw breath. Remember how Enzo broke the rules and said Mass for us in the restaurant?"

"He could have been excommunicated," pointed out Lido. "Before the Mass, the sacraments were in the kitchen on a counter, next to *antipasti* platters. It was unorthodox, but then, as everyone says, the Vatican's a long way from everything else in Italy."

Adalgisa had to be the name of Geppo's wife. Just a name. It came to me with no information.

"Don't you have to say 'hymn' for that man Palestrina, Lucia?" said Roncuzzi. "I mean, it's all very churchy. I don't know anything about opera, I admit it, but when it comes to holy music, remember, my father's only brother, who wasn't a butcher, was an organist. The only time I ever heard that stuff outside a church was at Geppo's wedding, not that I'm saying it was disrespectful to have chosen it. That wedding was unforgettable. Shivers go down my spine when I recall it."

"You can say 'song' for Palestrina," said Geppo. "It can be holy and be a song."

"You got married a week after Aldo's funeral," said Lido. "The restaurant closed for a funeral, and then it opened again for a wedding, which was the best, if strangest, I ever went to, especially since everyone except the bride wore black."

"Not Lucia," said Geppo. "Lucia, do you remember? You wore a gray gown, which Adalgisa admired. She said that when a woman wears silk the color of iron, she's really saying something about her basic character."

Lido let out a little gasp and made a noise as if rebuking himself. "I'm sorry, I just realized, is it all right to mention Aldo? Did I put my foot in my mouth?"

"It's all right, isn't it, Lucia?" said Geppo. "You don't seem to be looking at us like you think it's taboo."

"No one who ever knew Aldo would think he'd want anyone not to mention him. He'd want everyone to have nothing else on their minds," said Roncuzzi. "I loved him like a brother. Even when we weren't on speaking terms over business transactions, and even when I wanted to never see that face of his again, I loved him. I miss him every day. I knew he was someone you don't see the likes of very often."

"Well, there's always Beppi," said Geppo.

Roncuzzi agreed. "You're right, but Beppi doesn't fight with me, and he's better at paying the bills."

"He fights with me all the time," said Lido. "Once, he told me if he had one of those tomahawks like an Indian, he would scalp me."

I didn't remember Geppo's wedding. I didn't care if they talked about Aldo or not. I didn't remember singing Palestrina.

"Lucia?" said Roncuzzi. "I respect you for being so quiet. I'm not asking you to converse with us, or hum, or sing. I'm not asking about memories of days gone by, either. But I'm going to ask you something. We can't put off talking about this, as much as we've been trying to."

It was sad to think that peach leaves couldn't be eaten. Roncuzzi had been right to insist that everyone would stay human. Leaves weren't food. Only a human being with a mind and a memory would know this.

Yes, peach leaves were pepper-shaped. It was an accurate observation. They reminded me of the long conical peppers Mariano Minzoni grilled whole, then dipped into oil and served with squid. I remembered smells in the kitchen at Aldo's. That was something.

"I don't have a full-blown case of amnesia," I said. "I can tell you're all worried about that. Was that going to be your question?"

Roncuzzi was quick to answer. "It was, although we wouldn't have said it so bluntly. What kind of shape do you think you're in, exactly? I only ask because of what needs to be done here. We're certain that no one came this far to look for Beppi. Here we are, and you see the conditions. We don't think he was captured, never mind by this regiment, but all the same, we're going down there. Maybe all of us, maybe not."

"You want to leave me behind?"

"Your mind is fine!" said Lido. "You just proved it!"

"It's not because we think you'd be in the way, or we think you're a bad partisan," said Geppo. "It's because we'd rather have you wait for us."

There wasn't a fruity smell among the trees, not at all. It seemed impossible that peaches had ever grown here, had ripened, had dangled on bending branches, sun-sweet and firm and delicious. I'd always liked peaches.

"Captured," I said to myself. It wasn't like "Adalgisa." It wasn't only a word.

"We just need to check," said Geppo. "I'm sure we'll find someone who's willing to help partisans by way of information. This town is small. If the Germans have prisoners, everyone will know. There's nothing to worry about. We want you to go back down this hill the same way we came up. There's a hollow and plenty of bushes. You'll be safer there."

"Come daybreak, even a sparrow wouldn't be protected in these trees," said Roncuzzi. "But no doubt we'll be back to you before daybreak."

"No doubt!" said Geppo.

It seemed that the plan had been formed already, without me.

"We'll leave Lido with you," said Roncuzzi. His jacket was wool. He'd given it to me. The sleeves were much longer than my arms. Just because I couldn't see my hands didn't mean they weren't there.

"I'll protect you," said Lido. His sigh of relief was so enormous, it seemed to stir some low-hanging leaves, like a breeze.

Prisoner. That wasn't just a word, either. I pushed myself away from the peach tree. I tried to not feel dizzy, like I was seasick. I tried to feel strong, like Folco.

"I'm a tower," I said to myself.

"But you might want Lido with us, as three of us will be better than two, down there," said Geppo. "One of us can cause a distraction, if necessary, and the other two can start looking around."

"You could benefit from the experience," Roncuzzi said to Lido.

Lido stamped his foot and put his hand on his hip, petulantly, like a little boy. "I've had experience! I was already involved in a distraction!"

"No, you weren't. It didn't come to fruition," said Geppo.

Poor Lido. The shape of his arm, with his elbow poking out from his body, was called a triangle. It was a basic geometric form. "Mama, men who have restaurants don't have to study geometry. Why do you make me? Why do you torture me like this?"

Other forms were called square, circle, and rectangle.

The zodiac was a circle.

The sky was a rectangle, more or less. Or maybe one should call it a cube.

It wasn't as if I weren't able to keep my mind occupied with important things. If I insisted they bring me with them, they'd let me come; I knew that. But I'd never be able to keep up with them.

"Tell us what to do, Lucia," said Geppo. "We think you can make it down the hill, as wounded as you are, or we wouldn't have suggested it."

"Aquarius," I said to myself. "Pisces, Aries, Taurus, Gemini, Cancer, Leo, Virgo, Libra, Scorpio, Sagittarius, Capricorn. There are twelve. Just like the months of the year."

My own sign was Pisces. Aldo was a Scorpio. Aldo, that son of a bitch, where was he? I would have appreciated his help. Maybe there was a good reason why he wasn't available. Maybe he was with Beppi. Maybe he had his hands full, protecting our son. Not even a ghost could be in two places at once.

Wasn't there a song about the zodiac? Somewhere far back in my mind, a few notes of a tune started up, lightly, not played by an instrument but hummed by a man's voice. Whispery.

Aries was the Ram. Beppi was an Aries. "Mama, change my birthday. I want to be a Scorpion like Papa."

Three of them looking for him would be better than two. I didn't need protection.

"Take Lido with you," I said. "I'll be fine."

I didn't look at his face in the moonlight. This was no time to feel the fear of another person. If Beppi was down there, Lido might be the one to find him! It would give him confidence.

I didn't tell them that I couldn't remember the way we'd come up the hill. What hollow?

"Good luck," I said. "I'll be waiting."

I hadn't forgotten what I wore. I was military. I knew how to give myself orders. I could talk to myself like a commander. "Don't worry! Don't feel wobbly, don't feel sick, don't *throw up,* as there's been quite enough of that already. The zodiac is still there, holding everything together, same as always. No one shot it apart, and tonight, this is true, the stars are on your side. The whole zodiac is on your side. You have allies. Just because you can't see them doesn't mean they're not there!"

I'd been asleep. It had been a strange one, as if I'd thudded into it, like walking into a wall. No dreams.

My eyes were open. Looking up. I wasn't surprised to find myself outdoors.

"*Salve,* Signora Fantini. Or perhaps I should say *buongiorno,* as we're well on the way to dawn. I've heard a lot about you," said Enrico Caruso.

His head was high, against a brightening sky. He had come to a stop in front of me with a long-handled, two-wheeled cart. It was the type of cart that was usually attached to a bicycle.

Odd to see it pulled by a person. Especially that one.

"I've heard a lot about you, too, naturally. I recognized you right away," I answered.

"Is that so? Did she show you a photograph?"

I nodded, although I'd no idea what he meant by "she." Who wouldn't have recognized him? His face was marvelously large and expressive, and his eyebrows were very distinctive—they were longer than most men's, reaching all the way to the bottom of each eye. Also, there was that unmistakable cleft in the chin. I'd read somewhere that it was said to be the thumbprint of the God of Tenors, put there at the great Caruso's birth.

It was obvious, by the way he was dressed, that he was on his way to, or coming from, a performance, not in a recording studio but onstage. I recognized the costume: homespun, loose-fitting white shirt, with the top buttons undone to reveal a glimpse of his chest. Over it was a long, dark, wool vest. He wore high-topped boots, with trousers tucked into them tightly, showing off a pair of strong thighs.

Cavalleria rusticana. He was the hot-blooded Sicilian, Turiddu, and what was Turiddu's mother's name? Lucia. The coincidence was stunning.

He said, "May I offer you a ride to the home of some people you can trust? They're new friends of mine, the Galimberti family, and they're not far off. I hope you're not getting agitated about the name, as you'll be calling to mind the fact that, the last time you saw a few of the boys, they were attempting to rob your family's restaurant, unfortunately while you were singing, for which I'm sure they'll offer their apologies. They told me all about it. I know your son was distressed that they managed to disentangle themselves from his grasp, make a getaway, and remain at liberty. In their favor, they came away empty-handed, and they had quite enjoyed your voice."

I didn't remember anything about thieves at Aldo's, or anyone called Galimberti.

"I fell," I said. "I was coming down the hill, and I fell. That's why I'm on the ground like this."

"We saw you."

"I was looking for peaches."

"With your friends. We know. May I ask you to go easy on the Galimberti boys? I only mention it because, as you'll find out yourself, they're not in good shape. When those Germans on the other side of the hill passed through this area, they found it necessary to act like roughnecks. The Galimbertis put up a good defense. They're good boys, in spite of their criminal tendencies."

"I'd like somewhere to rest, if you don't mind. I'm very tired."

"I'm going to help you."

"I feel lucky you found me," I said.

"So do I!"

He beamed at me in the moonlight—moonlight combined with almost-sunlight. What was it Puccini had said when Caruso had shown up to sing to him one day? Someone, some enterprising voice broker, had arranged an audition. It must have been around 1900. At the sound of Caruso's voice—young, then, and raw and pure and astonishing—Puccini had dramatically gone through the motions of someone who'd been knocked on the head by a thunderbolt. He'd made a big show of falling off his chair, and he'd cried out, crouching on the floor, "I understand too well who it was who sent you to me! It was God Himself!"

Poor Caruso. He must have been terrified, going before Puccini like that. He was barely educated. He was a boy of Naples, impoverished, the son of a drunkard. A hick. How had he worked up the nerve?

I felt I now shared something important with Puccini. But I wouldn't say it was God who'd sent Caruso to me. I'd say it was my *lucky stars.* I'd say it was the whole zodiac.

A song. I felt myself reaching for it. I was certain I hadn't learned it when I was young. It wasn't Sicilian. What was it?

The spot at the bottom of the hill where I'd landed was some sort of trench, like a canal without water. The ground was hard-packed, cold, bare. I had managed to arrange my body so that my head was resting against the slope. One leg was tucked under me and the other was at an angle, poking up from the trench. I didn't recall having fallen. I'd only said so because I was sure I hadn't chosen this position consciously.

Caruso reached into a pocket of his trousers and took something out. A tube, like an ointment container.

"Look what I have," he said quietly. "From the Galimbertis, who found it in an American parachute drop. It's no compensation for all the bombs, I know, but it's useful."

I didn't care what he had. I wanted to tell him about the song. I was trying so hard to remember it.

The belt that holds the belly of the sky.

Aquarius, Pisces, Aries. Beppi. Something to do with Beppi.

"It's called, in English, a *syrette,*" said Caruso.

Oh, the tube. A syrette. He must have picked up the word when he was in America. He'd been there for so many years. It was nice to know he hadn't picked up an accent. He didn't sound American. Aldo used to say it was shocking to listen to Italians who'd been there—been there and then returned. Their vowels became corrupted, and worse, the music went out of their words, which was something to watch out for, like New York thieves, traffic, bad shoes, all sorts of vulgarities.

He had wanted so much to live in America. The Metropolitan Opera House, he had felt, would become our second home. American audiences would throw American flowers at me. They would love me as they loved Caruso.

How many recordings of Caruso's did I own? I didn't know. Beppi counted them once. A high number. How many were duplicates? How many were Italian-made? How many had Aldo bought by mail from New York? I used to know all those numbers.

"When I was younger, I almost went to America to sing," I said.

"I would have gone out of my way to hear you, if you had,

although Italy would have suffered from your loss. Look, a small needle comes with this. For the injection. It's clever, don't you think?"

Maybe I'd have sung the zodiac song in New York. A man was in it. A hero, larger than life-size, striding through the night sky, all night long, with some sort of weapon in his hand. Moon, sun. Folco's hill.

A mosaic. On the floor. Old. The part of my mind that was my memory kept delivering things—pieces of things—that needed to be put together. I was just like the old-time mosaic makers. It was an art. On the floor, Roman faces, clothes, a fish. What floor?

"Is this place Folcore?" I said.

"We're outside of it," Caruso answered. "You've been injured, and now you'll have to trust me, *va bene*?"

He fiddled with the tube, never taking his eyes off me.

"I think you're supposed to do this on a bare upper arm, but I'm sure you wouldn't want me to ask you to take off this jacket and roll up your sleeve for me. Am I right about that?"

What was he talking about now? "Are you cold?" I said, concerned. "Do you want my jacket?"

"No, no, although it might fit me. It's a man's, yes?"

"I don't know."

"This may pinch."

He crouched down and leaned toward me. He took hold of my wrist and pushed up my sleeve—both sleeves, of the jacket as well as my shirt—so a bit of skin was exposed. He might have been attempting to put a bracelet on me, as if he'd brought me a gift of jewelry.

The pinch was only that: a little prick, like touching a thorn on a rose. It didn't hurt. A gift. A long, melodious whistle was issued from Caruso's throat, followed by two shorter ones.

"That sounded beautiful," I said.

"Thanks. I was sending a signal. I was letting my friends know you're all right, relatively speaking. This medicine shouldn't take long to start working. Don't worry."

Folcore. Named for Folco. Everyone knew the story of Folco. It was one of those legends so ingrained in one's mind, you didn't know where you'd heard it first. A tower that was also a prison. The sky out the tower windows. Great strength, great courage. Vanquisher of enemies! But he wasn't the hero of the song.

Heart of the Scorpion, scales of the Fishes, mane of the Lion, horns of the Bull. The Scorpion's heart was red. A song I'd sung to Beppi? I must have learned it in Mengo. A Romagnan song.

I couldn't quite get it. It was like reaching for something on a shelf that was too far over my head. There wasn't a stool to step up on. There was no pole, or broomstick, to knock it down with. There was no one taller to do it for me.

Dawn was coming. It was the kind of sky where the sun was coming up one side while the moon, at the same time, at the opposite edge, was descending. Beppi used to believe that if you went outdoors and stood between them, you'd have a lucky day.

There'd been a picture of the sky on the wall behind Beppi's bed, a long time ago. Stars. What picture? It seemed important. Did it have something to do with the zodiac? Yes.

"Are you all right?"

"I am, Enrico. May I call you Enrico?"

"You may call me whatever you like. I'll try to make your ride in this cart as comfortable as possible. It'll be a little bumpy, but I doubt very much you'll be aware of it."

Caruso had stood up. The sky at the back of his head looked purple, like a bruise.

Soft. Everything felt soft. Myself, the ground, the whole world.

"Enrico, there's a song . . ." I couldn't understand why my voice came out sounding as if I'd whispered. I hadn't whispered. I tried again. "A song . . ."

It's raining gold coins in Palermo. Thank you, Beppino Strepponi. That wasn't it.

Where was Aldo? Why was he always talking about composing things that only remained in his head?

"I'm here, Lucia."

"I thought you were at the restaurant."

"They don't need me. Beppi's safe, you know."

"I was so worried about him."

"He's fine, he's fine. Look, I've got the new song. It's done, finally. It's all about stars. Lucky ones. I was inspired by the picture over his bed."

There it was, revealing itself to me. A sort of tapestry, about half the size of a blanket. A dark background. Black, like the night sky. A gold circle, or wheel, on it. A gold belt. Signs, pictures, all recognizable: a ram with spectacular horns, a scorpion with shiny eyes and a dark red dot for a heart. Beppi's picture. It was the last thing he looked at every night before he slept.

"The zodiac song?" I said.

Aldo murmured yes. He was proud of himself.

"I've been trying for ages to remember it. Did you write down the words, Aldo?"

"I did. Beppino Strepponi, I'm happy to tell you, is about to step into the sky. He's going to commit robberies on a much grander scale."

Aldo reached into his pocket. He took out a piece of paper, which was covered with his handwriting. I couldn't make out the words, although he held the paper close to my eyes. "I'll read you the lines, so you can learn them," he said. "It starts where it's supposed to. The horns of the ram are lethal weapons, by the way."

I pictured myself at the restaurant, ready for the spotlight. It wasn't a Verdi night, or a Puccini, or a Rossini, or anything I had a color-coded dress for. So I'd borrowed my husband's clothes. A pair of pants, a shirt, a jacket. No necktie. Nothing fancy, just old clothes Aldo wore around the house. His shoes, too. Why did Aldo's shoes fit me when his feet were so much bigger?

I asked him about that.

"It's magic," he said. "Remember, Beppino's incredibly strong, and he is also Sicilian. He might get banged up now and then, but he can never die, so don't worry. Up in the sky, he has chores to do, like Hercules."

I pictured the whole zodiac. I pictured Aldo's hero with a face that was just like Beppi's. A club was in his hand. He was walking across the sky.

I knew the words. The spotlight had never felt as bright, as warm. I'd been so very cold, and it was warming me thoroughly.

"What about the tune?"

"Oh, make it up as you're going along," said Aldo.

"I'm not a composer!"

"It can't be all that hard. What did I do all those years ago when I was singing the song about raining gold coins to our baby? I just thought of a note, then another, and another, and so on, just like drops of water. One thing leads to another. A critical mass is achieved, at a certain height, and before you know it, what have you got? You've got a waterfall, Lucia, plain and simple."

"What's the first note?"

"Anything at all, but I suggest that you imagine you're

Rossini's Rosina. Unsweet and somewhat dry, so you can feel all the edges. Fizzy, light, and *buoyant*!"

The waiters had stopped working. They'd gathered by the kitchen door—Lido, Geppo, Cenzo, all of them—and there were the cooks, taking off their aprons—Fausto, Gigi, Romano, Rico, and Mariano Minzoni, the tyrant, who grinned at me and held up a fist with his thumb sticking out, pointing behind him. I knew what the signal meant. "Wait till you see what I cooked for you for after the performance, Lucia. I hope your mouth is *watering*."

Enzo was at his private table with Marcellina. Beppi was sitting in his usual place, looking up at me. Ugo was beside him, in his brown suit, looking down at the floor. "I'm all ears for you, Lucia," he was implying. No Eliana. She must have been with her parents, up on their cliff.

Over by the windows, trying to make himself unnoticed, like a bashful young man at a dance, was Enrico Caruso.

"God Almighty, that man is Caruso," Aldo said. "Magnificent! I thought he was in America! Caruso himself!"

I was thrilled to see him, but I didn't let it make me nervous. The air smelled of food, same as always. I could make out the scents of garlic, onions, rosemary.

Aldo said, "Do you need something to hold in your hand? Shall I get you a salt cellar?"

"I'll just hold on to the air."

No panic. No sand. No Fascists, no Germans. I welled up my breath to sing. It was the story of Beppino Strepponi. It really was.

First, I had to sing to the sky, then I had to sing to Beppino. Joy rose inside me. I held back my head, looking up to the light.

Zodiac!
Aquarius Pisces Aries Taurus Gemini Cancer!
Leo Virgo Libra Scorpio!
Sagittarius Capricorn!
Watch out! Here comes Beppino Strepponi!
Look how he's walking through the stars! Beppino!
Kill the water-bearer Aquarius before he bombs you! He has bombs!
Bring home the fishes of Pisces for dinner!
Cut the horns off the ram of Aries! Arm yourself with them!
Kill the Nazi bull before he gores you!
Kill the Gemini twins! They're Fascists!
Kill the crab! Kill the lion! They're also Fascists!
Bring home the Virgo woman! Marry her!
Get that scale of Libra! It's solid gold! We'll trade it for guns!
Embrace the fire-hearted scorpion! He makes you strong!
Kill the Nazi Sagittarius archer!
Kill the Nazi Capricorn goat, before he kicks you where it hurts!

Suddenly another voice was in my ears.

"I know you can hear me! Lucia! Don't pretend you can't hear me!"

Shrill, raucous, a crow's voice. Go away.

The spotlight went out. A terrible desolation hit me, like a punch.

"Lucia!"

Was this a dream? I was on my back. I was warm.

"Lucia Fantini! I can't begin to tell you what I've been through! I forgive the Galimbertis for trying to steal from the restaurant! They've been good to us! Two of their boys were shot, but they're not dead, and neither are you! Etto went to look for Annmarie! Etto Renzetti! With Tullio and some Americans! They wouldn't let me in their *palazzo* to see you! Or Etto, either! Tullio from America! The *fidanzato* of Annmarie! The one who saved you! He gave you morphine! But it's all worn off now! There's no more, so don't get your hopes up! There's a nice bean soup here! We have to eat! Then we have to go back to finding Beppi! Tullio says the Germans haven't got him! Tullio's an officer! Very high up! Intelligence! Secret missions! You saw how he's in disguise! He borrowed clothes from the Galimbertis! He thinks the Germans have Annmarie! If anything happens to her, he'll go insane! I'm sick and tired of how all we ever do is look for people! I told Etto to stay here! The Americans have maps! They didn't need him for a guide! They should find their own way around! Etto wants to be a hero! He's over fifty! He'll have a heart attack like Aldo! I just know it! Where is Cherubino? Where is the butcher? Where is the Etruscan? You were supposed to be with them! Now every Galimberti who wasn't shot is out looking for them! Not counting the old auntie! She's the one who made the soup! I have questions for you! Open your eyes, or I'll pry up your eyelids myself, with my own fingers! Wake up!"

"SIGNORA FANTINI, please, weak as you are, excuse me for seeming as rough as my two great-nephews, who are bandits, I'm not denying it," said the Galimberti *anziana*.

She said "bandits" the way a relative of priests would say "priests." She smelled like garlic and rosemary. Her face was paper-white and so was her hair, a mound of it, bundled up with pins so extremely untidily, with loose ends everywhere, frizzing and spraying outward, she looked like one of those pictures you used to see all the time, when electricity was new, of what would happen if you stuck your finger in a socket.

She was a very small woman; the heap of her hair looked twice as large as her face. In spite of her words, she didn't look capable of roughness. She looked as soft as a dumpling.

What room was this? Hers. The old woman's air was proprietary. Her bedroom, her bed.

Candlelight, soft and muted. The little windows had been covered with black cloths. It was the type of cloth used in churches to shroud statues during Lent.

What name had the old woman introduced herself with? It began with an A, and suggested an important feast of Mary. The Assumption into heaven? Was her name Assunta, like Cenzo

Ballardini's wife who raised chickens and was the mother of a deaf girl? What was the deaf girl's name?

Pia, that was it. Pia the deaf-mute. Aldo had been fond of her. A sweet girl, small-framed, slim, pretty, flower-like. Fizzy hair, curls all around her face. Glowing, healthy skin. Younger than Beppi, but not by much.

"There's a certain magnificent quality about silence." I'd overheard Aldo saying that to Cenzo. Maybe he'd been trying to offer consolation. He hadn't sounded convincing.

Cenzo was Beppi's favorite waiter.

Now a memory was somewhere close by, trying to make itself known to me. Cenzo's wife and daughter at the restaurant? The girl, Pia, paying us a visit, with all that silence inside her head? I might have looked at her with envy, in a way. If I woke up one morning as a deaf-mute, I'd never sing again. Would that have been something I'd have hoped for? It was possible, on a bad day.

On a good day, what I had was a gift. On a bad day, it was a curse. "If I were deaf like Pia Ballardini, I wouldn't have to work." I couldn't remember a moment when I'd said those words, but I believed I might have.

Three Ballardinis. Cenzo, Assunta, Pia. Pia an only child, like Beppi.

Assunta bringing eggs. And Beppi was there, yes, excited and happy, as if a party were taking place. Pia Ballardini hadn't seemed to be someone he felt sorry for.

"Mama, you should let her put her hands on your throat when you sing."

Wake up.

Smells. Good ones. Annunziata, that was it. Annunziata Galimberti. The Feast of the Annunciation, not the Assumption.

Bean soup. Rosemary, garlic. Rosemary in bean soup? In the

restaurant kitchen they would have been shocked, disgusted. They'd call her a madwoman. The cooks. Prisoners of war in their own kitchen. *Captured.*

Rosemary was for meats. Sometimes with chicken, but only in a stew. Mariano Minzoni would say that the flavor of rosemary in beans was a sin.

An independent soul, Annunziata. Her house, her room. Those black window shrouds probably had been stolen.

No religiousness, in spite of her name. The candles weren't like vigil lights. No Mary, no Jesus, no crucifix, no pictures of Popes. Unusual. Marcellina's room at home was like a shrine: saints everywhere, prayer cards in frames, the Holy Family on the bureau, a porcelain infant Christ on the night table, standing there with a gilt scepter, wearing a silk nightgown, which was regularly removed and washed. You felt you had to genuflect, just glancing in that doorway.

These walls were a soft shade of green, like the Adriatic horizon on a calm spring morning. For furniture, besides the bed, there was a small table between the windows, and nothing else. The candles were on the table, a half dozen of them, flickering warmly in little bronze cups.

It was not a small room. It was not austere. The absence of decoration did not suggest a lack of worldly goods.

If the walls could talk, they'd be saying, "The owner of this room can afford the luxury of open space and a great deal of clarity." The spareness was like the beauty of a stage on which only a few simple things have been set, for the type of drama you don't go to for the designs but for the people, for what they're thinking and saying and doing. And maybe singing.

I felt myself basking in some sort of glow, as if I'd want to start singing. Maybe it was only the unexpected comfort. I became aware of an unfamiliar pressure on my feet. Bandages?

I was pleased to see that I still wore my American uniform. This wasn't like waking up in the *palazzo.* This was all right. Where were my boots? Maybe they were outside; they must have been filthy.

The bed was in the center of the room. It did not seem ungainly that those windows were covered. It seemed perfect.

"I've heard you sing at least thirty times, through the years, so believe me when I tell you I respect you with my heart as well as my ears, which are sensitive as well as highly discriminating, but this is my house, and this is my room, and I want your maid to keep quiet now," Annunziata Galimberti was saying, in a gentle, soothing voice. "I promise that, if one more sound escapes her, I will knock out her brain with this pan, and when I'm finished with her, I'll put the mess into a bag, go over the hill to Folcore, and feed it to the dogs of the Germans. When you're fully awake, by the way, I'll feed you, and then you can sing to me, seeing as how you're here."

An iron frying pan was in the old woman's hands. She'd heard me sing. I'd never seen her before. She must have listened from out in the yard. It seemed correct to assume that the only time a Galimberti would enter a place like Aldo's would be to rob it.

She wanted a song. I was curious. Which one?

"I'm not her maid!" cried Marcellina. "She can't sing to you! She's on strike! Plus, look at the shape she's in!"

I sat up. It was a narrow bed, sturdy, with a good thick mattress. The pillow was filled with feathers. The linens were just-washed clean. The quilt had a satin lining. It was wonderful to touch it.

"I never make threats, only promises," said Annunziata. Up went the frying pan a few inches. No menacing look, no glowering. Just an ordinary, routine thing.

"Marcellina, for the love of God, be quiet and sit down beside me."

Marcellina was beet-red in the face, as if she'd been boiled. She needed a bath. She smelled terribly, dankly sweaty, and a little pissy, too.

"Some soup would be nice," I said. "Would you like a song my husband, Aldo, wrote about the stars and Beppino Strepponi?"

"I know who Aldo is—I mean, who he was, may his soul rest in peace," said Annunziata. "But I was thinking about a song from that incomparable man who is the *sommo* of all, Gioacchino Rossini, son of the Adriatic, who stopped composing anything interesting before he was forty, though he lived to be seventy-six. I can't begin to describe to you my dismay to know that he squandered his genius, choosing to be a fat old man, lolling about for years, as lazy as a slug, but of course it was the fault of his parents, having started him far too early. He was only fourteen when he entered Bologna Academy. Poor Bologna! They say there are now more Nazis in the streets than Italians! The best city in Italy, overrun as though by rats! In case you're wondering, the particular Rossini I'd like to hear is the song about Lambrusco, the one people say you fashioned from Rosina's genius of an aria, about how she'll sting like a viper if she doesn't get her own way, from of course the most excellent opera ever composed, *The Barber of Seville.*"

Marcellina's expression was a combination of worry and bewilderment. She dared to speak, but she was crafty about it.

"With all respect, Signora Galimberti, that aria, with its excellent opening line, *una voce poco fa,* is absolutely the most perfect song ever written, not only by an Italian but by anyone. I salute your aesthetic taste. Let me ask you something. Do you know a woman named Brunella Vizioli? The mother of the waiter at Aldo's, the one who's called Zoli?"

"I don't," said Annunziata, "socialize."

"Well, if you ever meet her, please run the other way," said Marcellina. "I have reason to know that she's a horrible woman. She is not to be trusted under any circumstances whatsoever. One has to know who one's friends are, after all."

Oh, God, I thought, look what she's up to. Marcellina had bowed her head deeply, so that her chin was touching the top of her chest. This was her way of projecting an air of humility, along with a temporary, necessary submission—an old tactic of hers. The flattery was, as always, like frosting on a cake. It was irresistible. Annunziata looked at Marcellina with new eyes.

"Lucia!" cried Marcellina, back to her old self. "Are you going insane? What star song? You must have meant the song about the rain of coins in Palermo. Aldo only wrote one song."

What a strange thing for Marcellina to say. Well, she was old. She was tired.

"Is it an aria?" said Annunziata.

"It's a lullaby. It's about a robber, and it's beautiful," Marcellina answered. "I think something's wrong with Lucia's mind, I really do. Her poor dead husband had pined to write an operetta. May he rest in peace. He was a giant of a man in many ways, but frankly, between the two of us, he had as much talent as my big toe, not counting that one song."

"How does it go?" said Annunziata.

Where was the soup? Was I supposed to leap out of bed and find the kitchen on my own? With bandages on my feet?

"Once upon a time there was a heroic Sicilian giant of a bandit, with the heart of a saint," began Marcellina.

"Excuse me, where is the soup, please, and who put these dressings on my feet?"

"I did," said Annunziata. "Don't ask me to describe what they looked like when you got here. You don't want to know."

"I wonder if her head was injured, too, which would explain her dementia," put in Marcellina, as chatty as if she and Annunziata had known each other their whole lives. "She was buried alive in the San Guarino bombing, did you know that?"

"I didn't, but I heard that her son blew up half a dozen Nazi tanks in your hometown, and now he's in hiding."

"He's a hero, but he's a pain in the ass," said Marcellina.

Annunziata nodded knowingly, as if to say, aren't they all? "What kind of bandit was this Sicilian?"

"A successful one," said Marcellina.

"We could have two songs," Annunziata said. "First, the Lambrusco."

"If I don't have something to eat, I'll become unconscious again, if anyone is interested," I said.

Just then came a commotion at the doorway. The bedroom door was open. The faces of the two old women turned instantly pale. Fearful.

Heavy footsteps, male voices. Familiar.

The head of a man appeared, peering in tentatively. Annunziata was about to rethink her frying pan as a weapon, but Marcellina cried, "We know him! Teo! Teo Batarra, the Mengo pharmacist! Teo! You're supposed to be in Ravenna! Where's Nomad? Where's your brother?"

Teo was trying to look cheerful. He wasn't doing a good job of it. "They're right here," he answered. "We couldn't get near Ravenna. Germans were everywhere. We've got Nizarro with us. I warn you, things are not good. Are you Signora Galimberti? Sorry to barge in like this. If you don't mind, is there another bed in this house?"

Annunziata gave a shrug. "Not counting the two mattresses in the next room, which are occupied, this is the only bed in one piece. We were bombed, in case you didn't notice. Why my own special part of the house was spared, God knows, but I don't feel guilty about it. At least we've still got a kitchen."

"Half of one, in fact," said Teo. "*Ciao,* Lucia, we heard you were here. It's good to see you. If you're not very badly injured, do you think you could get up? Turn it over to Nizarro? We already sent a message to the doctor."

"Ugo Fantini?" cried Marcellina. "Is Ugo coming here?"

"Yes. He'll soon arrive," said Teo.

And a moment later, the two Batarras and Nomad entered the room, supporting Nizarro among them: a nearly inert Nizarro, his arms around Nomad's and Teo's shoulders, shuffling his feet forward, walking without bending his knees. One eye was purplish-red, swollen shut.

That was all I saw, before looking away.

Barrel-chested Nizarro, boss of the waiters, as strong as a force of nature! Everyone said he looked so much like Beppi, they could be taken for father and son, but there wasn't an actual resemblance, just physical dimensions, like two American football players who tackle their opponents to the ground. Who had said that? "Nizarro is bigger than your son. If Nizarro tackled you, you might die."

Annmarie, whom I'd thought of as my potential daughter-in-law and mother of my future grandchildren—many of them, as many as the Pattuellis, all of them strong and smart and lovely, playing golf with their mother in a mowed-down field, or out in back of the restaurant, and then they'd all come inside and we'd sing.

A dream. Just a daydream. Marcellina had said her boyfriend was here. There was a boyfriend and he was here. Looking for her. Where was she? *Prisoner.* Don't think about that.

I remembered I wore the clothes of a dead man. That soldier, at the hospital-*palazzo.*

I remembered Frank the truck driver. He hadn't been a true medic. I'd been his first patient. I had liked the sound of his voice.

Don't think about that, either. Get up. Stand up. Ugo was coming? This house had been bombed? Nizarro had been shot? That wasn't just sweat all over his jersey? It was a brown wool jersey. What was on it was blood. And the others, Teo, not wearing his white coat of the pharmacy, and his brother Emilio of the tobacco shop, and Nomad Calderoni, who'd gone away to London and then came back—if they had jumped from a roof onto a cobblestone pavement, they would not have looked more bruised. Don't look!

I didn't know the Batarras well. I'd never been in their shops. Hadn't Teo been in Beppi's year at school? Yes, at the top of the class always. When he was a boy, he'd been pale in an unusually chronic way. He became a pharmacist, Beppi had said, because his skin was as white as a pill.

And Emilio, a little older. A little stouter. He sold cigarettes to the waiters and cooks at a discount. When he came to the restaurant to eat, they charged him half price. Once, he asked me if I ever sang Wagner. When I said no, he looked so unhappy, I considered learning something from the *Ring*. Somewhere, someone must have translated the whole thing into Italian. It might have been marvelous—but then, there was the takeover, the invasion. Germans *verboten*.

Annunziata and Marcellina rushed to the men, all business, seized with urgency. Looking past them into the shadows beyond the doorway, I saw what Teo had meant about the kitchen. There really was only half of one.

Another bombed house. Dust in the air with the sunlight. White dust from plaster, tan dust from shattered wood, pink-red dust from roof tiles.

Too much sunlight. The kind of sunlight that comes into a house when the roof and walls aren't all there. Ugo was coming?

I forced myself to make it across the room. I felt I'd be all right if I positioned myself at the wall by the table.

A voice was calling out weakly, not here, not in this room. The next room. There was a room next to this one. From the reverberations, I could tell it was intact.

"That's my great-nephew Pippo," said Annunziata. "I thought he was still knocked out. He and his brother Giorgio ran into some trouble with Germans. God bless them, they're keeping themselves alive, with the help of American morphine. That's my sitting room they're in. It's a luxury, I know, to have two rooms to oneself, but this is a big house, or it was, before they bombed it. I always felt I deserve the extra space."

"Who is here? What is happening?" The voice on the other side of the wall was as faint as if it came from the bottom of a well.

Prisoners in cells must sound this way, communicating with each other when the guards had wandered away. Was Beppi in a jail cell? Was Annmarie?

"I'll come to you in a minute," called out Annunziata. "Partisans are here. They're worse off than you. But a doctor is coming."

I wanted to stand by the candles. I wanted to be close to something that was the opposite of cold and dark. I realized that I was moving exactly like Nizarro. I knew he was on the bed; it had let out a creaking. Or maybe it was Nizarro himself, creaking with pain.

"Marcellina?"

"Don't talk to me, I'm too busy. I'll be damned if Nizarro dies on us. Nizarro! You're not dying! If you don't put some effort into breathing, I'll send for Enzo instead of Ugo! Those candles will come in handy for your Last Rites!"

"Marcellina, I want to know where everyone is."

"Don't talk to me!"

"The bullet isn't still in him," said Teo Batarra. "It went out the other side."

"That's always good," said Annunziata.

"I'll kill you if you die!" cried Marcellina.

"I'm breathing, I'm breathing, shut up," came the voice of Nizarro.

"Lucia, why are you dressed like a soldier?" said Nomad.

I put my hands on my ears. No explaining. No talking.

It was no good trying to stay upright. I let myself sink down. When was the last time I sat on a floor? I didn't know. It wasn't uncomfortable. I couldn't ask for a pillow because Nizarro deserved it more than I did. The bed had only one pillow. Annunziata Galimberti slept alone. So did I.

Nomad's real name was Franco. Blood was on both legs of his pants, in splatters, as if he'd been messily painting something. He told us once about something interesting he'd learned when he lived in England. He said that the English believe the only way to get a good night's sleep is to have a bed to yourself. He said they bragged about how intelligent they were when it came to the hygiene of sleep. Everyone had separate beds, including married couples, not like in Mengo, where sleeping alone was like sleeping in your coffin ahead of time.

I pressed my hands more tightly against my ears. Nizarro was moaning, moaning. There was a lot to be said in favor of silence.

Pia. Pia Ballardini, with her mother, visiting the restaurant. Assunta. The other Mary feast. Assunta named for the

Assumption. "I've brought you some eggs from my ladies, Signora Fantini, not for the restaurant, but for your home."

The girl was beside her. Peaceful. The most peaceful-looking human being I had ever laid eyes on. Big, wide eyes, but of course you'd expect that. Certainly, deaf people possessed acutely developed other senses.

Maybe Pia saw things other people didn't see. She didn't look imbecilic. She looked thoughtful. She looked serene. "Mama, let her put her hands on your throat and hear you sing."

Beppi happy.

Why had I refused? What danger could those small hands bring, touching my throat for vibrations? Well, it was barely afternoon when that visit had taken place. A Sunday, yes. I'd just arrived at the restaurant for the afternoon program. I'd come early. Beppi was still in school, and there'd been something requiring study, some book to be read. I'd planned to hole up with him in Aldo's office.

It wasn't singing time. You don't let a stranger put their hands around your throat.

Quiet Beppi. Sad Beppi. Peaceful Beppi, standing there beside the deaf girl, a strange stillness all around him, as if it came from deep inside him, as if he'd caught it from Pia. The one person who had no ears to hear me.

Then softly, sadly: "It's all right, Mama. Maybe Pia will come back another time."

There'd been no other time.

The Ballardinis. They had a cottage not far from the Mengo church, on a back road heading to Rimini. Trees, flower gardens, chickens all over the place. I'd driven by there with Aldo. He always slowed down. Assunta's chickens enjoyed strolling about in the road.

A little stone house was in the back, a proper-looking, squat, one-story house, with a peaked roof and windows, as if it were for people. Assunta the Chicken Lady. Aldo always said the same thing when we rode by. "Why can't that woman do something normal, like keep her poultry in a regular coop?"

The air near their home smelled like feathers and chicken shit. It was awful, even with the car windows closed.

Suddenly I knew where my son was.

It just came to me naturally, like a shell being placed on the beach by a wave. "Cenzo Ballardini, you son of a bitch," I said to myself. "I was with you in San Guarino, drinking your wine. I remember that. You never said a word. You son of a bitch, you could have told me."

Where were my boots? Where were my *boots*?

They were drying in the not-bombed part of the kitchen, that was where. By the not-bombed stove.

Unsteadily, but full of resolve, I made my way into the kitchen. The boots had been cleaned and polished, and had a waxy, ebullient shine. I welcomed them like old friends.

What about the bandages? Thin white strips of cloth had been wrapped around my feet, and tied securely in well-made knots. There wasn't any blood. The cloths hadn't come loose. They were on me as tightly as stockings.

Stockings they'd have to be. I stepped into the boots. Anyone was capable of anything, I felt, as long as one's feet weren't bleeding.

It was difficult to breathe in the gritty, bombed air, but it was better than having a throat packed with sand. My throat was clear, empty.

I found the pot of soup. The stove had survived without a dent. There was warmth. It was impossible to tell what bits of debris had fallen into that pot. Sprigs of rosemary lay here and there on the top, like festive decorations. A white bean soup. Milky-looking broth, not too thick. There wasn't a table or a chair. I couldn't find a ladle, or a bowl, or a spoon.

It didn't seem that anyone noticed I'd left Annunziata's room. An argument had started up. Marcellina and Annunziata were like two old bullying nurses in a ward, dividing up the chores. Six injured men in their care.

"I'm not lying down on that bed beside Nizarro," came a man's voice. Not Nomad. A Batarra.

Then Marcellina, casually. "What do you dislike more, Signora Galimberti, blood, or open sores?"

"Open sores."

"What do you think they need first, a bath or some sleep?"

"We haven't got water."

"Sleep, then. Could we put the two head wounds back there with your boys?"

"We could. But check to see if they have lice."

"Good idea."

I stood there and listened to what it was like to be forgotten.

"Auntie, Auntie, come quickly, I was spitting on the floor and it wasn't just spit. The color, I swear to God, is crimson."

"Hold your horses! I have only two hands!"

"Get your hands off my head, Marcellina. We haven't got bugs."

"You might not be able to feel them. You're all in shock. Nizarro, move over so the druggist can share the mattress. Even though your ribs are all broken, you can move."

"I'd rather lie down on the floor. He stinks like an outhouse."

"Auntie, Auntie, where is the doctor?"

"He's coming! He's coming!"

"Before they shot him, did they beat him?" That was Marcellina again.

Nomad replied, "Can't you tell? The bullet was the least of it. He played dead, and then he got up and ran like hell."

"Germans did this?" said Marcellina.

"Who else? Hardly any *fascisti* are left. They fled like spiders, cowards that they are, as soon as the Americans started bombing."

"Signora Galeffi," said Annunziata, "do you think you'd recognize gangrene if you saw it?"

"That's not gangrene," said a Batarra. "That's stain from moss. I slept in moss last night."

"That's not moss," said Marcellina.

"Now that I'm looking closer, I think it's just pus," said Annunziata.

"Blood, pus, shit, sores, bugs," said Marcellina. "I bet anything, when people write about this war for the history books, they won't put any of that into it. Nizarro! Keep breathing!"

"It hurts."

"Stop complaining like a little baby," ordered Marcellina. "Dead will hurt more, because I know what you're like, and you won't be going to heaven."

I'd finished lacing up the boots. I pictured Nizarro running like an American, in the type of football that wasn't soccer—the type where you carry the ball with your hands. That was the difference between what the Americans did and what everyone else did, besides tackling. A useful fact. Americans use their hands.

I faced the big pot as if I intended to tackle it. I wasn't sure I'd have the strength to lift it, but I did. I only needed to hoist it a few inches to be able to tip it. I'd never drunk from the rim of a pot before.

It occurred to me that I should leave before Ugo's arrival. He was coming. They'd said so.

He'd take one look at me and that would be that. I didn't

need a mirror to know I looked alarming. But I was sure I looked worse than I was, the way a bruised, discolored piece of fruit is all right beneath the skin.

I set down the pot to rest my arms, then picked it up again and drank more. I licked my lips. They tasted like rosemary.

It would not be all right if Marcellina, along with Nomad and Nizarro and the Batarras, regardless of their physical condition, had the chance to observe Ugo anywhere near me in these circumstances. They'd drop their jaws, asking themselves, "My God, are they in love? Are they? Are they? Are they?"

That was why, as I quietly made my way to a person-size hole in the wall of the Galimbertis' kitchen, and stepped outside into silence and shadowy afternoon light, I said to myself, "The only reason I'm slipping away like this is to protect poor Ugo from prying eyes."

It did not feel abnormal to make an exit through a wall. It felt sensible, as if the bombers had done it on purpose, to help me.

17

I FELT AS SAFE as if I'd put myself under a spell, rendering my body invisible. And I felt rested—a credit to that marvelous room. It was amazing what a difference a good sleep made. Perhaps I'd write Annunziata a letter, praising her. "Thank you for everything. I hope that one day I have the chance to sing to you—stars, Rossini, whatever you want. Your soup was delicious. Remind me to ask how you prepared it."

I stopped to use a stand of little pine trees as a toilet, marveling at my ease with the pants, the business of squatting, using leaves as wipes. Ahead of me were four, maybe five hours of daylight. The sun was going west, in its same old downward trajectory. No planes.

All I needed was a song. There was a marching song. Boots. A boot song, a boot song. I couldn't remember it.

There would have to be another, something lively and invigorating, propelling me to Mengo, to that chicken house, to my boy. It was almost like being at home, planning a program. But the song that came into my head, completely inappropriately, was "Last Night I Made Love With A Blackshirt."

There was no getting rid of it. It was hugely popular; everyone at home knew it. It was a tavern sort of thing, for late, sad nights, in smoke-filled air. I'd never sung it in public, but the waiters often asked for it on nights when there weren't any Fascists at the tables. It was a favorite of theirs; a waiter was in it.

Waiter, bring me a coffee.
Are you allowed to sit and talk?
Last night I made love with a Blackshirt.
I did, I really did.

It took me a moment to realize that I was singing, in a small, whispery way.

Waiter, he's no brute with me. His body is fully a joy.
I hate Fascists. I'm miserable about it.
My three brothers are brand-new partisans.

Were those voices coming from the Galimberti house, calling my name, faintly? Certainly by now they'd have discovered I was missing.

It might have been only one voice. Maybe it was mine, echoing strangely, as if my ears had lost the ability to take my voice for granted, and had to learn it all over again.

Waiter, give me my bill.
It's nearly dusk. I must go now.
If you want to stop me, you'll have to shoot me,
Unless I take care of it myself,
With the little black pistol he gave me, a gift,
Wrapped up with a pretty, red bow.

I'm thinking about it.
But first, I want one more night in his arms.

Maybe a proper marching song would present itself later. As the saying went, beggars couldn't be choosers. I had something to sing. It didn't matter what it was. I was singing, and my feet weren't bleeding.

All was well. I surveyed the look of the land. There was a patch of woods up ahead. Through the trees, I saw the edge of a field, yellow-brown and stubbly from mowing. There was sure to be an old wagon road beyond it, which would lead to another, and another, in an intricate, trustworthy system of Italian byways, webbing steadily to the east, away from the sun, toward the sea, toward Mengo. I reasoned that there'd be plenty of trees and bushes for cover if I had to hide quickly.

"Waiter, bring me a coffee," I sang softly.

After a while, I was able to put some bounce into it. "La la la, la la la, I hate Fascists, la la la, la la la. I'm a partisan, and so is my son, la la la, la la la, la la *la*."

"Stop! Stop! Signora! I beg you! Stop at once!"

I halted at the sound of the voice—an old man's voice, behind me, raspy and unfamiliar, but not hostile, and not threatening in any way. I thought he might be a farmer.

He wasn't issuing a command. He seemed to express a genuine, impassioned concern, and I expected to see some terrible danger up ahead, like a tank with its gun barrel pointed at me, or a bull in a corner of the field, ready to rush and attack me. A real bull, not Taurus in the sky.

Nothing was in sight to harm me. I whirled about, and found myself facing—well, looking down on, as he was shorter than me—the stumpy-legged, hoary-faced, odd little fisherman known at home as the Octopus Man.

Polpo, he was called, as if he were one of those creatures himself. He was the reason why Aldo's, unlike every other restaurant on the coast, did not have octopus on its menu.

He'd made converts of Aldo and Beppi. He was just like a missionary. Octopuses were sacred; they were smarter than people; they were glorious in every way; if one of their arms broke off, it grew back, no problem. They changed colors at will. They were composed purely of mind, without bones. They were mysterious; they were solitary; they shimmered with radiant beauty; they were perfect. Yet every day they were captured, slaughtered, crammed into tins, fried in oil, boiled, grilled, laid cold on platters—all sorts of things—as if they'd been, in life, as mindless as onions and peppers.

To cook and eat an octopus in the well-known opinion of Polpo was to cook and eat an angel.

One day there'd been a diving expedition—this was long before Aldo's first heart attack—Aldo, Beppi, Polpo. Down in the sea they were embraced by long, thin, soft arms. Not tentacles. Arms.

That was how they'd described it. Beppi had ended up sick in bed with ear infections. Aldo had nearly drowned, having spotted a glittery object stuck up against an underwater cliff; he'd tried to retrieve it, thinking it was treasure off a wreck. It was just a piece of junk.

But they'd come home from the dive as glowing and dazzled as if they'd fallen in love, the two of them. Everything was octopus, octopus, octopus, and it didn't wear off. They fell in love with Polpo, too, for giving them the opportunity to be enraptured. And so the menu was changed forever.

Mariano had tried raising his voice as head of the kitchen, after Aldo died, to go back to what used to be one of his specialties: spaghetti in garlic and oil, with basil, a little lemon juice, and chopped-up, slightly sautéed *polpo,* but Beppi had held his ground. If customers wanted octopus, they'd get squid. No one in Mengo had ever stepped forward to defend and protect the lives of squid.

And here was Polpo, coming up beside me, talking almost as fast as Marcellina, almost breathlessly. "Please, excuse me if you think I've sneaked up on you. It's as lovely as ever to hear you singing, Signora Fantini, and I hated to stop you, but I don't think it's a good idea for you to walk across that field up ahead, unless you wish to be blown to pieces, seeing as how it's been mined by the Germans—who, as it happens, until a few days ago, were living at that farm, which it seems you're headed for."

"Mined?" I said, feeling stupid. A mined farm field?

"Those Germans felt that, if anyone wanted to call on them, the hospitable thing would be, have them step on explosives. Mines are their idea of welcome mats. You seem surprised to see me."

"I thought you never left Mengo except to go into the sea."

"I had no choice, or I wouldn't have."

He grinned at me, exuding a sense of ruddy good health. In his worn wool jacket and heavy fisherman's knitted vest, he appeared to be composed of nothing but muscle. His fingers were pale, as if he suffered from a lack of proper blood circulation, and they were a bit too long for his short, blunt hands, which were rough with blisters and calluses.

It was not preposterous to think of Adriatic octopuses swimming up to Polpo and touching his fingers with the belief that, if one fell off, it would grow right back. I was sure they didn't perceive him as human.

"The truth is," he was saying, "I stand beside you only because my sweetheart sent me to follow you."

Sweetheart? That word didn't seem to fit Annunziata Galimberti.

"She's your *sweetheart*?"

"Yes. Now you know. She finds it comical that you might have thought she didn't notice you fleeing that house. She has eyes in the back of her head, which I'm sure you've found out about. I'm curious, though. At my age, one knows a few things about impulsive, suicidal tendencies. You've been through a lot, as I've heard. Have you come to the end of your rope? Do you wish to be blown to pieces?"

I decided to behave as if it weren't bizarre to, first, encounter him here, and, second, to consider that old woman in his arms, in her airy, splendid room.

"I've gone to a great deal of trouble in the last few days to keep myself alive," I answered. "I haven't got a rope, but if I did, I would not be at the end of it."

"I'm content in my heart to know that. Stand absolutely still. By the way, the reason you're only just now meeting me, after all these years, is that she keeps me all to herself. I'm a man on a leash, and it's only about this long, believe me."

Polpo held up a thumb and index finger spaced about two inches apart. What was he talking about, "after all these years"? I'd only just met Annunziata. What years? An old man's confusion?

"She gives the impression that she's very nice," I said, trying to be helpful.

What I wanted to do was get rid of him, but he'd dug in his heels, growing more and more animated.

"Nice? You think she's nice? Ha! It's only when she wants something. We can be honest with each other, you and I. She's ten times more jealous than the devil himself, but that's another thing you'd know," he said, as he bent down to pick up a stone. "However, I love her. What else can I say? You have no idea how I suffer. I do what she tells me. Ignazio, go here, do this, do that, go somewhere else, get out of the way, go and make yourself scarce. Ten minutes ago, it was, 'Ignazio, go and follow Lucia and bring her back, and if anything happens to her, I will cut off'—excuse me for the crassness, but I'm only repeating her words—'those little apples between your legs, or what's left of them, you old man.' As if she were twenty herself! As if she weren't five years older than me! I ask you. Did you ever blow up a German mine? No? Here, I'll show you what it's like. You might be wondering what I wanted this rock for."

Ignazio. The name might have suited him if he weren't already Polpo.

The stone was about the size of his hand. He pulled back his arm and threw it hard, like a child throwing rocks at the windows of an abandoned building, prepared to be elated by the results. The stone landed in a patch of hay stubble, and nothing happened.

"I'll try it again," said Polpo. "This is just like fishing. You throw out your line, you never know what's what, or what's where. It always takes a few tries. Did you know, Signora Fantini, that when an octopus mother gives birth, she holes up in a cave with her babies to protect them until they're big enough to go out, not eating the whole time, and then, when they're old enough to risk life on their own, she dies?"

"I didn't know that."

"There are benefits to being a person. I'm sometimes willing to admit that. I suppose you want to ask me why I never married her. Go ahead, ask me."

"I'm in a hurry. There's somewhere I must absolutely get to."

"I'll take that as your question. I never married her because she wouldn't let me. 'Go to hell,' she tells me, every time I bring it up."

I didn't let on that I was startled to hear that—the same thing I'd said to Aldo in Sicily, a lifetime ago, a world away. All those times. Go to hell, Aldo. Then one day I heard myself say, "Yes." As if that was what one said when one was sick of saying "hell."

It was an interesting coincidence, but I didn't mention it. I didn't want to set him up for any more confidences; we might have stood there chatting forever.

"Oh," he said, "she likes all the sneaking around. She truly *likes* it. I'm not complaining. But now that she's sent me to follow you, everything's out in the open. I had the devil of a time finding her in the first place, let me tell you. But I didn't doubt myself. If she were a needle in a haystack, I would find her. If she were one grain of sand on the beach, the same thing."

He'd found another stone, a larger one. "Do you know that a rock is the preferred method of bashing an octopus by Italian murderers of octopuses?"

"I didn't know that."

"Cephalopod. That's the scientific name, for your information. It's very dreary. I don't like it. But it's useful to know. All right. This one will be the rock that hits a mine. You can't understand the danger of mines until you've seen one erupt. It's like a volcano, in a way, without the lava. Get ready, Signora."

He threw with all his might, glancing at me to make sure I admired his strength. The stone flew to the middle of the field and dropped like a shot-at bird, and again nothing happened. It came to me that he might have been lying.

I eyed him warily. "Did Annunziata tell you to tell me there are mines in that field to scare me, so I'd go back to her house with you? I bet Germans were never there!"

"Who is Annunziata?" said Polpo. He gave me a look that meant only one thing. He didn't know who I was talking about.

Fog-head! I'd been doing so well with thinking clearly!

I didn't know what to say to him. Marcellina told me I'd had morphine—the real reason I'd slept so well. It wasn't just Annunziata Galimberti's good room. Which Polpo had never been in? The morphine must have been acting on my system all over again, with an effect of befuddlement.

"I have to go now," I said. "I have a fairly long distance to cover, to get to where I need to be, and there's not much daylight left. So if you don't mind I'll be on my way now. Goodbye, Ignazio. What's your last name?"

"My real one, or the one I go by?"

"Whichever you prefer."

"Galeffi is the one I go by privately. I don't see why I should conceal that from you, now that we're on intimate terms, conversation-wise."

Galeffi was Marcellina's name. An old Mengo name. She had no relatives I didn't know about; everyone knew all the Galeffis. There'd never been a fisherman in her family.

Maybe I'd heard it wrong. It didn't matter. Should I cross that field and take my chances that the mines were fabrications, or should I skirt it for the longer route? What did you call it when people put guns in their mouths, when one bullet was in the chamber, which might or might not go into you when you pulled the trigger?

Russian roulette. That was it. My mind was fine, once more. I tried to picture myself sitting at a table in a bar, shadowy, smoky, the sort of place where they'd sing the I-made-love-to-a-Blackshirt song. In my hand, a pistol, with one bullet, and what would I have done with it?

Put it down on the table, that was what. I was a mother. Who had to *get to her son.* "As I was saying, goodbye, Ignazio, ah—what's your actual last name?"

"Innamorato," he said. A lover, in love.

"No, I mean, really."

"That's really it. My initials are like the number eleven or the Roman number two, depending on how you like to write a capital I. And now, please forgive me for what I'm about to do, which is, grabbing hold of you."

He clutched me by a hand, with his long white fingers squeezing in, as tightly and neatly as if he'd caught me with a hook. It was no use trying to break free of him.

"I really am very sorry, Signora Fantini."

"Tell me if there are mines."

He shook his head. "The farm's been abandoned, but there really were Germans. They all went to Folcore, because they'd run out of food."

He relaxed his grip as he spoke, but not by much. Maybe he'd come with me to Mengo. Maybe I'd be able to talk him into it. "Let's go visit Cenzo Ballardini's wife and daughter," should I say? Something like that.

What about offering him money—well, to be paid later on, after the war—for escorting me? Surely he'd appreciate cash. Enough for a new boat. Fishermen always wanted new boats. What did a boat cost?

"Let's go back to that house you came out of," Polpo said gently.

"I want to go to Mengo."

"So do I. Perhaps we will, tomorrow."

Tears shot into my eyes, hot and stinging. I turned my head because I didn't want him to see me cry.

"Come," he said, tugging me. "I feel rotten about the mines. You know, when I followed you, I could have fully observed you when you were taking care of some business in those pine trees, but I did not, and excuse me for mentioning it. Anyone who knows me will tell you I'm an honorable man. I swear, the only time I tell a lie is when she asks me to, since I deny her nothing. Plus, when she makes threats to me, I believe them."

"Let go of me."

"That I cannot do. I said to her, 'Marcellina, sweetheart, I'll be back in five minutes with your Signora, and look, it's been much more than that already."

Marcellina?

The shock made the tears stop immediately. He'd been talking about Marcellina all along? The deviousness! The cunning! The secrecy! All these years!

Marcellina and the Octopus Man of Mengo! How had she managed it? Under my nose! And this was how I found out about it! Was I supposed to congratulate him for not watching me go to the bathroom? And lying about mines, and tossing those stones? The fakery! The two of them! Marcellina and this man! Years and years!

And a voice cried out, far back, in the direction of the Galimbertis' house, clear and ringing in the air. "Lucia! It's me! Roncuzzi! We came out of Folcore! Beppi's not there! The Galimbertis rescued us! I see you're still wearing my jacket! Polpo, is that you? *Ciao,* but what are you doing here? Come and tell me, but later! Come at once! We're going to the Galimbertis' cellar! We're in danger! It's about to be bad! The Americans will bomb Folcore! In a minute! We just saw some soldiers who told us! This time, they've given us warning! We're in the line of attack! I have to rush back now, to help with the wounded boys! Nizarro's got to be carried, and you know what he weighs! Come! Run! Hurry!"

Roncuzzi turned away before finishing; the last of his words trailed after him, thrown over his shoulder.

And Polpo—bless him, bless him after all—let go of me. He hadn't been able to resist the urge to wave both arms in the air at Roncuzzi. "I'll help, too!" he cried. "I'll be there in a jiffy!" He was palpitating with eagerness. When he set off, in a hurry, he didn't pause to consider the possibility that I might not be behind him.

I seized my chance. I commanded my feet to give me no pain. "Feet! No hurting!" Maybe there were further stores of morphine inside me, dormant, waiting to be called into play.

I turned and set off running, not into the field, but along it, where there was tree cover.

Run! I'd done it before; I could do it again. This time there wasn't a hill to be coped with. The ground was flat. I lowered my head and hunched my shoulders, imagining myself running with a ball in American football.

I knew what to do, keep going, la la la, la la la. Run to the goal, run to Mengo.

"I hate Fascists," I sang to myself, so that the beat would keep pounding in my head, like the beat of an engine. "La la la, la la la. It's a good thing I don't have a pistol, or I'd be shooting my no-good, lying servant, la la la, la la la. Waiter, bring me my bill. I'm a partisan, and so is my son, la la la, la la la, la la *la*."

When I glanced back, I saw that Polpo still rushed in the opposite direction, like a boat getting smaller and smaller, far away at the rim of the sea.

I felt as stealthy as a fox. I felt invincible.

"Waiter, I must go now, and don't try to stop me. I don't care about bombs. I don't care about this stupid, rotten war. I'm going to rescue my Beppi, la la la, la la la, *from that horrible house, with those horrible chickens,* la la la, la la la, la la la."

18

THEY COULDN'T TAKE ME to Mengo. They were only going as far as Cassaromilia. Yes, that was its name. Just because I'd never heard of it didn't mean it didn't exist.

Cas-sa-ro-mil-ya. A small place up ahead on the plain: stone houses with tiled roofs and gardens. A village of people who before the war went east every day to work along the shore, not as fishermen, not in boats, but in businesses, hotels, restaurants, private enterprises.

Stone houses and the Church of San Stefano.

Unfortunate things had gone on there. Very bad. Hadn't I heard? It was incredible that I wasn't familiar with that church. It had been built in the year after Christ 1 or 2. That was how it was always described. It was probably an exaggeration, though. It was probably more like the year 10.

Very old indeed, a parish of several original martyrs. Mosaics all over the walls, the floor, the altar. And quite a few drawings on stone, which someone found a long time ago near some cave and hauled in; they'd been placed with the Stations of the Cross. They were not only pre-Jesus but pre-Roman. Very much the work of cave dwellers: animals, stars, sea monsters. Beautiful to behold, in a way.

Also, because in places like this, there was always a tower, there was a tower, poor thing, which leaned. Not like Pisa. This one tilted backward, like it was tired and wanted very much to lie down, as though it hoped a bed were waiting just behind it.

The Weary Tower, people called it, the home of a famous, heavy bell, a *basso profundo* of a thing, completely masculine. It was said that the sound really carried, all the way to the sea. I'd probably heard it often, without knowing what it was.

A lift was being offered. I couldn't just stand there on the side of the road as if waiting for a taxi, and I didn't have to introduce myself, for Christ sake. Just because they were farmers didn't mean they didn't know who I was, even bruised like this and dressed like this, which surely had a story behind it, but there wasn't a need for me to summon the breath to explain.

I'd find that no one was interested in asking me personal questions. They'd been through hell already with Fascists and Germans and Americans, and everything was about to get worse, but if a diva of the Adriatic, not currently at the top of her form, felt disposed to walk around by herself in a GI uniform, and a man's civilian jacket on top of it, and also a pair of boots, the likes of which, it was safe to say, had never been worn before on the feet of an Italian matron—well, that was the business of the diva.

Plus, everyone knew I was Beppi Fantini's mother.

Did I know of a musician in Rimini—well, not in it at the moment, as he was actually below it, hiding in a cellar? I didn't? His instrument was the guitar. They'd heard he was writing a song in Beppi's honor. The title was "Five Hundred Bullets In My Pockets."

I hadn't heard about that? The point of view was that of a partisan who had no prior experience with guns. It was somewhat bawdy, but only to people who knew the folk song it was based on.

"Five Million Seeds In My Apples," it was called. It was Sardinian, a shepherd's song, about a big lusty boy, just coming of age and a virgin. All his life, he's been up on a hill with sheep, and now he's getting ready, with some nervousness, to go into town and make love with as many girls as possible, perhaps ten, all in one night, he imagines. He plans to rest the next day, then move on to another town, and on and on, no more sheep.

I have five million seeds, five million seeds, five million seeds in my apples. The shepherd's nervousness is expressed in the lines "If on my first few tries I miss my target, I won't fret, I'll try again, I've got plenty of ammunition to spare."

Those lines would be reproduced in the new song, which Sardinians were going to love. They were always saying no one in Italy ever thought about them at all, never mind appropriated something from their culture. The tune would be reminiscent of a *tarantella,* very fast, very lively, very much something that anyone with two feet and a beating heart would respond to.

Wasn't that excellent? I should make an effort one of these days to contact the guitarist and learn it. Anyone in Rimini who wasn't a Fascist or a German should know which cellar he was in. Proud mother!

Did I know why the roads were so empty? Not an invader in sight. Two occupying armies, not to mention what was left of the local Blackshirt brigade, and look: a condition of absolute safety.

This was because everyone was saying the Americans would bomb Folcore. But did I understand that when you don't expect bombs, there they are, and when you expect them, there they are not?

Look at that fog rolling in. Light at the moment, yes, but bet you anything, it's a whole lot thicker to the south, where the planes were. This fog was coming up from the south. There was also fog developing in the usual places east. Anyone with a little knowledge of natural phenomena could make a forecast of heavy fog and be correct.

American pilots weren't ignorant about certain things. Sure, they were bastards; look what they'd done already, in just a couple of weeks. One wondered if they looked out their cockpits to see what they were aiming at, or if they ever aimed at all. One wondered if they closed their eyes in prayer and begged their American God to forgive them.

Lots of them were probably Catholics. They must have consciences. Sure, they were treating this country like it was Nazi Germany; it was all the same to them. But they must have learned a couple of things about Italian fog. They'd know to climb back in their bedrolls when they saw it close the sky like a big, heavy, white lid.

No need to worry.

Was I astonished that someone had gasoline? They had gasoline. American, British, Canadian. Well, they had enough at the moment to get where they were going. It was nice how it didn't take long to be adept at stealing it. It was purely a matter of knowing where to go and when—and how not to let any of it into one's lungs in the process of sucking a tube.

So, Signora Fantini, it's an honor to have encountered you. You're our first-ever diva. It does not appear you've got a choice here. You can't be wandering around. When the fog starts getting down to business, you won't be able to see your own hand in front of your face. You look a little dazed, to be honest.

All right, climb up in the back, there's room. Everyone's packed like spaghetti in a box already. One more won't make a difference.

"Diva," I said to myself.

The truck was a dark Fiat pickup, battered and rusty and dusty, with a grille in the shape of a heraldic shield and two high headlamps, like the eyes of an oversized insect. Farmers were in it, all farmers, men and teenage boys, in field clothes, and in much the same condition as their vehicle. But they looked at me with gentle, friendly expressions.

In the cab with the driver, taking up all the space of the seat, and on the floor as well, were piles of what seemed to be newly washed laundry, all linens, all white: bedsheets, big towels, small towels, cotton blankets, curtains, tablecloths. The linen on the floor had been wrapped in brown paper, but most of it had fallen off. I had the idea that this was a delivery errand. I wondered if their wives, at home on the farms, might be laundresses-for-hire in their spare time.

It seemed so. I would have liked to have made myself small enough to fit in the seat, but not an inch of extra room was available.

Were the trains running? Was there a station in Cassaromilia? Was there a bus?

There was a church, San Stefano—did the priest have a car? He might want a change of scenery. He might offer me a lift. Maybe he knew who I was. Maybe he had connections in Mengo. Maybe he knew Assunta Ballardini and her daughter. Maybe he'd consider it an act of charity to go out of his own jurisdiction to see a deaf girl, offer some prayers. Maybe they'd give him a chicken. Maybe he'd cure the deafness! Maybe he was beatific. His first miracle, maybe.

If the girl weren't deaf, would it be all right for her to be with Beppi, if things with Annmarie didn't go as I wanted? There was the problem of that *fidanzato* of hers. I wasn't forgetting that.

The undeaf daughter of a waiter and a chicken lady?

Why was I even asking myself the question? I didn't believe in miracles. I was letting my imagination run wild.

Why had I thought to use the words "be with"? Pia *with* Beppi. There were biblical-type connotations there. The daughter and her mother were only hiding him, surely. They might have bewitched him.

The farmers helped me up to the back of the truck as if I were a bale of hay or a sack of potatoes or a vagrant, prodigal member of a livestock collection.

The truck gave a lurch and started moving. There was no room to sit. Like everyone else, I was upright, arms at my sides: a woman in a tight crowd, enclosed, safe. Earth smells, men smells. It felt good to be riding while standing and not be alarmed I'd fall out.

The driver's name was Adriano Venturoli. His wife was seven months pregnant. Their first child. She'd been suffering from terrible pain in her lower back, and spent most of her time lying down. He was nervous about it. The only reason they were letting him drive was that this was his truck.

Everyone else was a Venturoli, too. Or they were a Cardella, a Perilli, a Meneghini, a Baraldi, a Braccini, a Muzzioli, a Farinazzo, or a Fusi.

On their farms were hay, corn, wheat. Pigs, cows. Artichokes, tomatoes, onions, beans, eggplant, squashes, peas, five hundred kinds of peppers. Chestnut trees, apples, lemons, oranges, figs, apricots. Melons, berries. Rabbits in hutches, ducks in a pond, you name it.

Now, to admit to reality, there wasn't much. They hadn't stopped working; they still had chores by the hundreds, but things weren't looking good. In fact, if this were the Old Testament, they'd be Job.

A respectful veneer of privacy all around. Their first diva.

No one had ever called me that before. I'd noticed that some of them had what looked like guns in their hands. Stens and rifles, I'd thought, held close to their bodies, like splints.

But those things weren't guns. They were shovels. Small ones, long-handled ones, and here and there, trowels the size of pistols. They must have been going to help someone plant a field, not that any of them looked hopeful in any way.

Damp air was on my face, sweet, soothing. I had never been in a truck before, except once, when we didn't have a car. Aldo and I had stayed at the restaurant so late one night—no, not the restaurant, the first *trattoria*—we hitched a ride home on the back of a milk wagon, our legs dangling over the edge, all that milk at our backs, and sunrise just beginning.

That had been a happy time, holding hands, my head against Aldo's shoulder. "You sang well last evening," he must have said. "In my head, your voice is still echoing, and I want it never to stop, until the next time you sing, Lucia." If he hadn't said so, it wouldn't have been a good time. But he nearly always said so.

Naturally, when we got home, out came Beppi, throwing a coat over his pajamas, rushing at us—how could it have happened that he'd been born to parents who'd ride with the milkman without him? How could we do this to him? Where was God and where were the angels when he needed them? Always a conspiracy against him! He was doomed. He climbed up to the seat of the wagon, with a cheerful *ciao* to the milkman, prepared to spend the rest of his life there. It took forever to drag him away; he had to go to school.

"Mama, why don't you want me to be happy?" I could hear him now. "Mama, why didn't you let Pia Ballardini put her hands on you to feel the vibrations when you sing? Do you think she's a bad person? Did you think she smells badly because of the chickens? Did you think she would strangle you, with those small, soft, pretty hands?"

The truck wheels had met up with resistance from ruts. This was a country road, bumpy, deeply grooved. The engine groaned but kept going.

"Adriano!" called out a farmer, up near the cab. "Put your pedal to the floor! You're driving like a little girl!"

"If we stall, we're done for," said another man. "You know how low the juice is."

"We should have taken your mules," said another.

"They've hardly eaten for three days. They wouldn't have the strength to pull one piece of grass, in their condition. Anyway, they're pissed off. They're on strike until I come up with something to feed them. To make it worse, I think they've been looking at me like I'm their next meal."

The young man at my right—I was crammed in a corner, near the tailgate—was being careful to not let his shovel bump against me. It was a short one; the blade rested on his feet. "I don't want to impinge upon your person," he whispered to me. "I wouldn't be able to bear it if I caused you bruises, on top of the ones you have already, which bother me unspeakably."

I gave him a little nod by way of thanking him for his consideration.

"Once, several years ago, when the Fascists weren't fully devils yet, just apprentices at it," he said, "I went to Aldo's, to the yard. I'd been visiting my mother's family near Bellaria. They had a small hotel there, bombed now. I welcome the pleasure, Signora Fantini, to tell you that the windows were open, on a fine spring evening, and I heard you sing—"

He was cut off abruptly. The truck gave a jolt.

Someone cried, "Keep going! Adriano! Keep going!"

"Cardella, you're crazy. Adriano, stop! We have to cut them down!"

"No, no, no, keep going!"

"Stop! I know them! All three of them! The partisans from Bologna! The ones my wife gave rice to last week!"

"Adriano, go faster! I'm your father, do as I say! Look at those ropes, look at those trees, they're booby-trapped. German booby traps!"

"What is it? What is it? I can't make it out, I want to see!" cried the voice of a boy.

"Shut up! Keep your head down! Shut your eyes! Adriano, faster!"

That rough voice belonged to the man just behind me. Adriano's father. I could feel his breath on my neck. I had tipped back my head, although it hurt to. My eyes were looking up at a pale blue bit of the sky, rectangular like a doorway. The clouds above it, and the wispy layer of fog beneath it, seemed to only be there to make the blue more attractive.

"Blue," I said to myself.

Far away in the driver's seat, the man called Adriano had not made up his mind. The truck speeded up, slowed down, speeded up, slowed down.

At last it shot forward in a burst; it seemed to have decided on its own to start racing. I was pushed back, along with the farmers, without actually moving, as if a huge wind were blowing against us, with a whistling. The tailgate had been well secured and did not spring open.

Blue was for Mozart.

"I heard you sing, as I was saying," came the voice of the young farmer. "I don't know what it was. It was beautiful. It was the most beautiful thing I ever heard. After you had finished, long after, I found myself still there, as if under a spell, and a man came outside to me, a big guy, who looked something like a thug. I thought he'd order me away for trespassing, but he had brought me a plate of spaghetti and a napkin and a fork. He said to me, 'Here, we had this left over. Don't be alarmed. You're not the first person this ever happened to. She's pretty good, don't you think?' His name was Nizarro, first name Vito, which I remember because I asked him. In his person, he reminded me of a Galimberti. As everyone knows, that family's composed of thugs."

"They're partisans now," said a farmer. "I heard two of the boys have German bullets inside them."

"But all their lives, they've been Fascists," said another.

"That's only because of youth camp, which brainwashed them, like a million others. I haven't got anything against the Galimbertis. They don't rob farmers."

"How was the spaghetti fixed?"

"With clams. As many clams as noodles, I swear."

"Out of the shell or in?"

"In. I had to sit down on the ground to manage it."

"They didn't give you a glass of wine?"

"I wouldn't have drunk it if they had. I was feeling intoxicated already."

"What was the sauce?"

"Clam juice, oil. Seasonings, I don't know what. Garlic, a few chopped-up tomatoes, hardly even stewed. Very fancy."

"It doesn't sound it."

"That's because you didn't taste it."

"My wife's sister went to an opera once in Milan," said a farmer who hadn't said anything yet. His voice was shaky. He seemed to be making the effort to speak the way a man in a fistfight would get back on his feet, reeling and hurting, from having been knocked to the ground. Back in the fight.

"She went to La Scala," he was saying. "She also had a tour of the premises. She said it was interesting, but everything was moldy and she went home sneezing. It wasn't a famous opera, and no one famous was in it, but she had a good time."

"I didn't see any booby traps. Where were they?" said a boy.

"Everywhere," said Adriano's father. "Especially in the branches the ropes were tied to."

"They didn't have their shoes on," said another boy. "They might have been dead already, before they were strung."

"Adriano!" shouted his father. His voice reverberated in my ears. "I know you've got the window down, because you're sick to your stomach when it's not, so answer me!"

There was a moment of stillness while everyone waited for the driver's voice, coming back to us on the wind, the fog, disembodied.

"Adriano!"

"Papa, I heard you! What was the question? How can I answer a question you didn't ask?"

"Never mind! Keep driving!"

The truck had resumed a more regular speed. "You're a good boy, Adriano," called out his father.

"Stop talking to me! Don't distract me!"

"He's right, Venturoli. Leave him alone," someone said. "He's got problems enough. Who's going to be the one to convince Marianna that Mussolini's been killed, so she can go ahead and feel all right about having her baby?"

"Probably me," said Adriano's father.

"What are you talking about?" said an older farmer.

"Oh, you never know what's going on," said another. "Marianna thought everything would be all right when our fucking Duce went down and the Americans came, but when we heard he was saved by the Nazis, she made a vow to God she'd not deliver. Not until he's down for real, for good, in the ground."

"Well, she's got a point."

"Fusi, don't be an imbecile. You've got half a dozen kids. A baby comes out when it wants to."

"You know, after my wife gave those partisans that rice, they said they were on their way to Folcore."

"The Americans will probably bomb it tomorrow," said a farmer from somewhere in the middle.

Their voices went on calmly, as if they were gathered together at someone's barn, taking a break between chores.

"Maybe they'll bomb it tonight, if the fog rolls off after sunset," said the farmer called Fusi.

"They bomb at night?" said one of the young ones.

"Sure, those planes are like bats."

"Who knows how to take apart booby traps?"

"Well, all of us."

"So why didn't we stop, back there?"

"Because they're not the kind of traps you catch a fox with, and we promised Cassaromilia we'd be there before dusk," said Adriano's father.

"One thing at a time, you mean."

"Yes. Like always."

"I'd like to go to an opera myself, one day," said Fusi. "Not in Milan, but in Ravenna, closer to home."

"You'd have to lose some inches off your belly first. You'd have to wear the suit you got married in."

"I think you can rent them. I think there's a shop, closed at the moment, where you can even get a rented handkerchief to put in your pocket."

"Are we nearly there?" said a boy. "I'm sick of this. Every muscle I own, it's cramped. I'm barely able to breathe back here."

"A few more miles. When we get there, you'll wish you were back on the road."

"I doubt it."

"Wait till we get there, then see for yourself."

"Signora Fantini?" said another young farmer. "Why don't you tell us about some of the operas you've been to, in theaters here as well as Sicily? We know you're Sicilian. Even hearing of one place would be a pleasure."

I'd stopped looking up. Not much of the blue was left in all the whiteness. The fog was feeling watery, was tasting salty.

Nizarro. I'd been thinking about Nizarro. Nizarro handing a farmer some dinner, in the darkness, outside the restaurant. Nizarro on Annunziata's bed, creaking. Nizarro, shot. The other Beppi, but bigger. Beppi's other Beppi.

Don't think about Nizarro.

"White," I said to myself. White was for Verdi.

"Signora Fantini? Are you all right?"

I felt I'd placed myself behind a door, against which someone was knocking, someone who would not go away. What was "all right"? I didn't know what that meant, not anymore.

"Adriano!" called his father. "Don't forget to turn left when you come to the crossroad. Is that smoke in the sky up ahead, or more fog? I can't tell. You can't, either? Here comes the turn! Turn the wheel!"

The truck veered off so sharply, it seemed to be taking the turn on two wheels, like a little trick car in a circus. But it didn't tip over.

"He's showing off," said Adriano's father. "I hate it when he does that."

I pictured a drawing Aldo had bought in a shop in Bologna; he'd had it framed. It was Verdi's Lady Macbeth—not the character herself but a print of a mannequin in a costume, with a crown on the head. Where was it now? In a drawer somewhere. Aldo had wanted me to sing the role.

I'd never learned it, not even one song. I couldn't remember why. I must have had a good reason. All that killing. All that blood. Was there blood on the necks of the Bologna partisans hanging from the trees? Did one bleed when one was hanged?

"Signora Fantini? Please speak, because this silence is scaring me, worse than I'm scared already, which I don't mind admitting. Will you speak, please?"

"Nico, leave her alone," said a farmer softly.

Nico. The one who'd gone out of his way to hear me sing. He'd stood under a spell. He'd sat on the ground, opening clams from the kitchen, twirling spaghetti with one of Aldo's forks. As many clams as noodles. He'd felt intoxicated.

I couldn't ignore him, now that I knew his name. "Don't be afraid," I said. "By the way, to answer another question, I've never been to an opera."

"You're fooling with us, am I right?" said the farmer whose wife gave rice to the partisans. I was getting the hang of whose voice belonged to whom.

"I don't fool."

"Then you might be dodging the question because you feel, I imagine, with all respect, that this is not the time for descriptions of luxuries, seeing as how the theaters are shut, and also considering what was hanging in those trees back there, not to mention what we're headed for," said the farmer who'd called Fusi an imbecile.

"Opera," I said, "with all respect to you as well, is a necessity, not a luxury."

"You might not say so, Signora, if you had to sell a pig, which you had needed to eat, in order to buy a ticket," said one of the teenagers, and Nico said quickly, "Braccini here is a Communist. But he's really saying that because he only likes American jazz."

"If communism weren't good for us, the Pope wouldn't be against it," Braccini shot back. "Lolo, agree with me."

"I agree," said the boy called Lolo.

"How can it be you've never seen an opera?" said Nico.

I could feel him staring at me—not judging me, just staring at me, puzzled.

"If you want to know the truth, I have a problem with crowds," I said.

"Excuse me, but as it happens, you're in one. We're a crowd," said the farmer called Fusi.

"I don't have a problem with you."

"It's kind of you to say so."

"Is it claustrophobia, or is it general nervousness?" said Nico. "I'm not trying to pry. I'm curious."

"It's both," I said.

"It's nothing to be ashamed of," said the farmer whose wife gave rice to the partisans. "Me, I can't go near horses. I see a horse even half a mile away, I break out in a skin rash, I get palpitations, I start sweating cold sweat. Cows, I'm all right with. Mules, oxen, anything, just not horses. My whole life it was like this. It's irrational, but, there it is. By the way, I'm a Communist, too."

"Communists don't like any kind of music at all," called out someone near the cab, impatiently, as if he'd been waiting his turn to speak for a very long time. "They've all got tin ears. They only want to talk, talk, talk."

"Pardon me for changing the subject, which I always do

when it's politics," said a farmer somewhat closer to me. "I'm wondering how that song will go about your son, Signora. I hope the composer is through with it soon. I admire the title with all my heart. 'Twenty-nine Grenades For Thirty Of My Enemies.' "

"No, no, Toto, it's the other way around with the numbers. The whole point is having an extra one, not being one short. Thirty for twenty-nine."

"I was making a joke. I was making fun of it for not being realistic."

"You'd have to expect one's a dud," said Fusi. "Like with clams. You'd never get thirty cooked clams with every one of them opening the way they should."

"At the restaurant that night, every clam on my plate was perfect, and there were a lot, as I told you," said Nico.

"They threw out the bad ones," said the farmer whose wife gave rice to the partisans, and there was a murmur of agreement.

"Communists like music!" cried Braccini. "Communists don't put partisan necks into ropes off a tree branch! How are we supposed to sleep tonight? You think any of us won't be dreaming about that? About how we left them there? Like they'd think we didn't give a goddamn?" Now he sounded like a little boy, trying to not cry.

"Let's go back and cut them down," said the boy called Lolo.

"Shut up!" said Adriano's father. "There's Cassaromilia! Adriano! Put your foot on the brake! Slow down!"

The truck came to a stop in the middle of the road and the engine shuddered and went off, with an expulsion of dirty exhaust smoke that made a few of the farmers start coughing, including Braccini, who might have done so to cover up whatever sobbing he'd not been able to hold back. He sounded almost feminine about it, like Verdi's Violetta, stricken with tuberculosis, dying extravagantly, unrealistically, gorgeously.

I remembered a magazine article from Rome about a famous soprano—I couldn't recall who it was—who coughed seventeen times in six lines. The audience, the article said, loved it. The singer was called out for so many curtain calls, she finally shouted, "Let me go home, I beg you! I'm so tired!" As if they were holding her captive. Dramatic flair, it was called.

I'd *never* make a sound that wasn't singing in an aria. If I coughed while singing Violetta, or Mimi, or any other dying heroine, the waiters would come with lozenges, a glass of water, aspirin; someone would look for Ugo, who'd come running, a big mistake; Beppi would jump from his nearby chair with his arms out, ready to catch me, as he'd assume I would faint, fall, crack my skull.

Chaos, it would be, with one tiny cough.

"I have thirty grenades in my arms for twenty-nine invaders," I said to myself. I wondered what the next line would be. I wondered if putting it the other way around would be more useful—as if being realistic had a use.

I wondered how the farmers would feel if I explained that the gossip about Beppi was outlandish, that he'd only blown up one truck. "Oh, we knew that all along," they'd probably say. "But the reality wouldn't make a good song."

Funny I hadn't lied about describing operas. "I've never been to an opera." I hadn't planned to say it. A lack of energy, I decided. I didn't have it in me to come up with the deceptions I'd used in the past, at the restaurant, anywhere, when someone asked the same thing. Oh, back in Sicily before I married Aldo, you know, I went here, I went there, I had pre-performance suppers with such-and-such, and here on the mainland, every prominent house, I've been there, I've seen this, I've seen that, all inspiring, and if I had the time, I'd tell you all about it.

It felt good not to be moving. I waited for Adriano to get the engine going again. The pause was like a brief intermission.

Thirty grenades, twenty-nine enemies in my neighborhood. The tune would have to be lively, like my own squad's song. Back home, they'd often sung it a bit too merrily, sometimes clapping their hands and stomping, as if it were written to commemorate something pleasant. *Oh you ask me why I closed up my shop, brought up my boat to dry land, walked away from that restaurant.*

I could hear myself singing it, the only soprano among all those male voices.

Do you want me to say I went into the hills with guns
Because of love in my heart for liberty,
With the fight in my blood for the freedom of my country?
I will tell you, please, put your fancy explanations up your ass.
I went into the hills with guns . . .

"What's happening? Have we stalled?" said the farmer called Toto.

We hadn't stalled. Adriano had shut off the truck on purpose, because of the obstacle just ahead in the road. What obstacle? Animals? Had they let out their sheep?

No, not animals. Remember that grain warehouse, about four hundred years old, four villages had used it? A great deal of what it used to be was in the road. Stones. Many. A little mountain.

"Fuck," said Adriano's father. "Fuck, fuck, fuck. Fucking Americans. Fucking *bombs.*" Still, as the tailgate was lowered, and I was helped to solid ground, I had no idea that in just a few minutes, I'd be calling to mind what Etto Renzetti had said about Dante, long ago on the night I kissed him in San Guarino, in that moonlight—kissed Etto Renzetti, and felt so young! Right now I was too busy stretching myself, stomping my feet to get my muscles working again, and singing in my head, all the while, the rest of my partisans' song.

19

CASSAROMILIA.

Dante Alighieri had problems, but he was never bombed. It's not a metaphor if you've been bombed. Perhaps now, in my arms, you'd like to discuss my hickness—that is, if you're not wishing I was Ugo Fantini. But if you are, I don't mind, as it's the greatest joy of my life to be holding you, under any circumstances at all.

Was that how Etto had put it, exactly? In my arms.

Grenades for my enemies, in my arms. Thirty for twenty-nine.

"Signor Venturoli," I said to Adriano's father, "what are those shovels for?"

"Call me Berto."

"Berto, what are those shovels for?"

"A chore."

"What are those linens for? Your son's arms are full of them, and also the arms of the young man called Nico, and two others whose names I didn't learn."

"Those are Venturolis. My brother's sons."

"I had the idea that it's laundry."

"Well, at one point, it was, so you're not mistaken."

If only that mountain of rubble in the road were higher! If one more wall had been blown this way, my view would have been blocked.

People. Impossible to know how many exactly. Enough to fill the window-side tables at the restaurant. They looked like an audience.

They stood near one of the bombed houses—no, not a house. A church. In the midst of the rubble was a section of pews, undamaged, and a baptismal font, with part of the bowl missing, leaning sideways against what appeared to be part of the altar rail.

The Church of Saint Someone. Weary Tower. Like it thought it had a bed behind it, waiting. Stefano, that was it. San Stefano. Bombed. That was what they'd been talking about in the truck.

"What are those people doing?"

"Praying," said Adriano's father.

"All I've been trying to do is go to Mengo."

"Listen to me. I don't feel right about a woman being left on her own. But this is no place for you. Wait for us down here in the truck. We'll take you where you want to go, later on."

"I couldn't ask you to do that."

"You didn't ask. I offered. Will you do that, wait here?"

"For how long?"

"Until we're finished."

He spoke with farmer bluntness, and with a sad, heavy weariness. Just beyond him, I spotted a footpath, like a way out of a maze. It seemed that a signpost was there, with my name on it, saying "Path to Home."

"Your advice is excellent," I said. "Thank you for helping me."

Then looking back to Cassaromilia, watching him walking

away—I didn't want to make my escape until he was out of sight—I saw them.

I hadn't known. I had always called the Pattuellis' village "the Pattuellis' village." Everyone did. Mauro himself had called it "our village" or "the place we moved to when we got thrown out of San Guarino for not working at Etto's factory, and also for having too many children who, let's face it, are a little unconventional."

All of them. I took inventory and realized that this felt normal: the counting up of familiar faces, looking for absences. It was the same way Aldo, then Beppi, counted the silver and small objects that could have been put into pockets, after an event with guests who weren't personally known to the restaurant. All the spoons are here, all the forks are here, all the knives are here, Mauro, Carmella, Marco, Francesca, the first twins, Rudino, Antonella, the second twins, and Beppina, squirming in Carmella's arms, looking cross. She must have felt she was too old to be held like a baby. Beppi was the same way, at that age.

And Carmella's father was there, Galto Saponi the fisherman, standing rigidly, with his head bowed low, so that it seemed his body had formed a question mark, and who was that beside him? Ferro Pincelli, older brother of the apprentice cook, pimply little Rico?

Yes, Ferro, there he was, as lean and fit as ever, wearing a dark cap pulled down on his forehead, all the way to his eyes. He always wore caps when he was out in the world among strangers; he didn't like being looked at strangely, for the color of his hair. His father was Apulian, from the toe of Italy, but his mother was as much a Scot as Robert Burns, whose poetry she had translated.

Ferro used to ask me to sing poems called "Red, Red Rose,"

"My Heart's In The Highlands," and "The Jolly Beggar." But no one had been able to find sheet music for them, although his mother had said music existed, and then the war came. I didn't do recitations.

I remembered that Ferro had been a soldier. The Italian Army was where he'd learned waitering. He'd been a valet to a general. Before that, there'd been boyhood Fascist camp and weekend drills—he'd been a star. He'd been decorated. He'd once shaken hands with Mussolini.

He was obsessed with physical fitness. He used to slip outdoors between customers in the middle of his shift to do calisthenics; he kept barbells in the wine cellar.

Once in the parking lot, late, some staggering-drunk officers started singing anthems, and poor Ferro, washing a table, moved his lips with the words from the instant they burst into *"Giovanezza,"* that Mussolini favorite. When he realized what he was doing, he was so upset that he cried out, "I thought I'd unmemorized those goddamn words! I nearly killed myself unmemorizing them!" He picked up the bucket of water he'd been dipping his sponge in, poured it out on his head, threw himself down to the floor, and began performing push-ups, frenetically, with one hand behind his back. They couldn't get him to stop, until Beppi refilled the bucket and emptied it on him.

Well, they all said later, goddamn that song—it's been cemented in all of our brains.

Ferro had a wife and four children, all dark-haired. Why had his Scottish mother come to Italy in the first place? It seemed sad not to know.

A pleasant lady. Whenever there'd been tourists from Scotland, she'd show up at the restaurant to talk about Robert Burns. She lived with Ferro and his family. The Apulian had died around the same time Aldo had his first heart attack. Poor man, his death hadn't received much attention, with everyone going crazy over Aldo.

What were those lines? Ferro used to quote from them, in English: *bonny, lassie, sire, lads, auld lang syne.*

I was alone, leaning against the truck. I should have learned some of those poems, such as the one about the red, red rose. *"Rosa,"* I said to myself. I tried to remember what a red rose looked like, smelled like. I tried some words like the opening of a song. *"Rosa rossa rossa . . ."*

It wasn't a song. The graveyard next to the church had been bombed. Bombed and bombed and bombed.

The little cemetery was like a field that had just been tilled, ready for planting. The bones could have been old bulbs, or forgotten potatoes, or bits of objects with archaeological significance—medieval tools, Roman statuary, prehistoric creatures whose skeletons had fossilized. The coffins seemed to have bobbed to the surface as if they'd been stuck at the bottom of the sea, and whatever had bound them down there had come loose. They'd risen up with a current and, meeting air, they fell apart.

It seemed that more bombs had fallen here than on San Guarino and the Galimbertis' house combined.

How much simpler those were! All that wreckage: Etto's factory, all those houses, the train station, which I'd been part of. And openings in walls that were big enough to walk through. And the stuff of people's lives catapulted haphazardly outdoors, all strewn and shattered.

Simpler, yes. This was different. You wouldn't think tombs would yield their contents.

I realized I had a connection to people who had been buried, and now were not. I felt I could speak to them. "I was buried myself, in a bombing, not far from here, in San Guarino."

Here and there, as if someone looped rags to dry on a clothesline, and a wind had whipped them off, I saw cloths from wrappings, all tattered, and filigreed with rips and holes. Pine boards were everywhere, like wrecks of boats on a shore. The ground was heavily cratered, as if an extraordinary storm of rocks had pummeled the earth, as if an evil-minded giant of a god had been at work here, hurling boulders with his massive arms, turning this place into a hell.

Not all the houses had been destroyed. Maybe one of the all-right ones belonged to the Pattuellis, who hadn't noticed me. They weren't looking in my direction.

On the ground, between the people who were standing there praying, and the ruins of what used to be their church, there were bodies laid out in a row, still uncovered, being looked at. A dozen? No, more than a dozen, many more.

The fog had thickened, just above what few trees had been left standing. Bombed trees. Nightmare trees, under a cover of hard-looking fog, unmoving, not descending, not swirling. There must have been fires. The trees still rooted in the ground had few branches left, if any.

Maybe a great deal of the ash lying everywhere had been leaves. Maybe some of it had been clothes: dresses, suits, socks. Maybe some of it had been hair.

An eerie light. White-gray. Not quite twilight. Not sunlight. Beppina Pattuelli slipped out of her mother's arms and took hold of her grandfather's hand, looking up at him.

Those children should not have been looking at what they were looking at. The older ones were like sleepwalkers who'd paused for a moment: stillness, blankness, terror. The younger ones looked droopy and tense and ferocious, like children who've stayed up past their bedtime and plan never to sleep again.

The farmers had reached them. Two of the teenagers, lagging behind, had pulled up their shirts to cover their mouths. The group opened to receive them, and there, I saw, was the Triumvirate.

So this was what they'd been talking about in the Saint's Grove in San Guarino. This was where they'd rushed off to, with Ugo. And the children had found their way here. Of those bodies on the ground, waiting to be covered, waiting for burials, some were very small. Their school friends. Their playmates.

Ugo had been here. He'd been on his way to the Galimbertis' mostly wrecked house from here. Our paths had crossed again. I understood why he'd not been needed here. No one needed a doctor in Cassaromilia.

"On the same day, I suppose, you and I came up from having been under the ground," I said. I was back to talking to the old dead.

The old dead had no skin. I had skin. I hadn't really been under the ground, only the blown-apart stones of the San Guarino station. I realized the difference. It seemed like a very small one.

The Triumvirate's faces came fully out of obscurity: white-haired Cesare, round-faced Zoli, and that son of a bitch Cenzo Ballardini, the one man in Italy I most wanted to speak to, not counting Beppi. He looked tired. He looked grimy. He looked bewildered. He looked angry. He looked stunned.

A farmer with two shovels handed one to Zoli. He gazed at it as if he couldn't remember what it was or how it worked. The only thing a waiter ever did with a shovel was ply it on the compost pile far out behind the restaurant, a job usually handled by little Rico. Sometimes Beppi went out there to do it himself, to work off steam from some argument, but he'd never do much. He'd just make a good posture about it. He couldn't stand the smell: clamshells, eggshells, fishbones, vegetable peels, stalks of things that couldn't be eaten.

At tilling time, a Mengo farmer who grew most of the restaurant's produce came over with a wagon to take it away. It was Zoli who'd made the fence to enclose it to keep out dogs, cats, vermin: a good fence, high, steel mesh, chicken wire. Cenzo had helped him.

A smell like that compost was everywhere, with no escape vent, not with that fog. The fog was just like a closed trapdoor.

The prayers were over. There was no priest in sight, leading them.

Back at the Galimbertis, were they all in the cellar, waiting for the sounds of the Folcore bombing? There was a cellar. The fog might not have reached them, not yet. Maybe Annunziata had brought her bean soup down there, in case the house was bombed again. Was Marcellina in Polpo's arms, terrified, praying, waiting for the not-thunder thunder, boom boom boom boom and that would be that, and they'd all climb out in silence, to return to what was left of the world, if anything was left?

"Stay in that cellar," I said, as if my words could escape, compressing the distance from here to there. "Stay, so I know where you are."

There was another significant movement among the living. Cesare Morigi stepped forward and walked over to what must have been the front door of the church. He stepped carefully, picking up his feet in what looked like exaggerated, too-slow motions, the way a mime might act out climbing up a staircase.

He was going to sing. What song would he choose?

He raised his arms a little, as if shrugging in apology. I saw him make grimace-like motions. I knew he was nervously exercising his jaw.

Poor Cesare, that baritone, that lion of a man, a real Leo, singer at weddings and funerals, frozen with stage fright the one time he'd had the chance to sing at the restaurant. I'd gone to his house to comfort him. For him I had broken my rule of never visiting waiters.

He would have to sing something religious. Something from Palestrina? Something out of a requiem? Or the Mass? Something Latin? A Romagna hymn? Something especially for the children?

The children. They made me think of what Beppi was like when he used to wake up with a nightmare.

We'd rush to him. I'd turn on the lights, take him in my arms, kiss him, soothe him, swear to him that whatever he'd seen, it wasn't real. Beppi, look, here's Mama, here's Papa, here's Marcellina too, in that frilly, ridiculous nightgown of hers. Here we are, and everything's all right.

He wouldn't believe us. He'd tremble with anxiety, open-eyed but still asleep, still in the dream; it took a long time to get through to him. On his face was terror and the blank, soft mask of sleep. Aldo, in a fit of distress, would take on the expression himself. He couldn't bear it, his boy, something had to be done, but what? Were we supposed to forbid sleep? Were we supposed to get a prescription from Ugo? Put some sort of medication into a child, which could result in permanent damage, which Beppi would never let us live down?

That was why Marcellina hung the zodiac on his wall. I remembered that. Marcellina had felt he could be trained to wake himself up and turn his eyes to it and be calm, or at least be distracted enough to snap back to real life: everything important in the universe, right there, all his.

"Look at your stars, Beppi, and hurry up about it; I want to go back to my bed," she'd tell him gently—yes, Marcellina talking gently. Then came the zodiac song. Was that accurate? It must have been, or why would I recall it?

A good memory? Singing Beppi back to sleep with Aldo's star song, blanketing his whole world with my voice? All those constellations. I couldn't remember how it went.

The fog was descending, or another wave of fog had come in, from a different front. Two invading armies from two different countries, two invading fogs; it made sense. Soon everyone would look like ghosts, like Aldo.

No sound came from Cesare. He looked smaller and farther away. Again, he held up his arms. He closed his mouth tightly, then bowed his head, and gave up trying.

Thirty grenades in my arms.

The farmers were giving their piles of linens to some women of the village. Which sheets or towels would be used to wrap the new dead? Which were for the old? Were there enough to go around?

For twenty-nine.

I had no comfort this time for Cesare. This was no place for me. Berto Venturoli had been right. "Fucking Americans," he had said.

It had been nice of the farmers not to ask questions about the way I was dressed. Too bad there wasn't a spare set of clothes in the truck—overalls, a shirt, anything that wasn't American. I'd have given a lot to be able to change. I'd hang on to Roncuzzi's jacket, though. He'd want it back. I turned toward the footpath. What if it didn't go to Mengo, wherever it was? I didn't know where Mengo was.

I didn't know! How could I not know that? I didn't even know what direction to face, in order to be certain I faced home!

Stay calm! Don't be helpless like Cesare! Keep making plans! Think of the boots! Trust the boots! Mengo was somewhere! I'd get there! What should I do with the boots when I got to Mengo?

Throw them into a compost pile, that was what. Assunta Ballardini was sure to have one. American leather would rot eventually, like the outer leaves of a cabbage. Or maybe I'd toss them onto a beach, or into some field, where it looked like mines had been placed, and really look forward to the explosion.

20

OLIVE TREES, these were olive trees, just a few, gnarled and barren, miraculously recognizable, not bombed, and I imagined Aldo beside me, in a piss of a mood, complaining.

Why had so many things gone wrong? Why didn't we plant olive trees at home? Why did we only have nut trees? It would have been a pleasure to pick olives, fill a basket, bring them inside, dump them out on the table. His own olives, a peaceful activity. A small press to make oil, for home use exclusively. His own private brand. He'd really missed out on that. Ugo had been after him for years to take up an interesting, calming hobby, remember? Something to counteract the stresses of the restaurant, the Fascists, the daily tensions involved in being a non-Blackshirt boss. If he'd grown his own olives, he wouldn't have had all those heart attacks. It was the fault of poor planning and not listening to the right advice.

He'd always been nervous in fog. This one was exceedingly low and thick, with mists that clung tightly to branches, leaves, and even rocks, as if glued there.

It was perfectly still, and denser than the worst of the steam in the restaurant kitchen, when pasta was cooking in three or four pots, and crabs were being boiled, and clams were being steamed, and dishes were being washed, and the cooks would refuse to open a window; they hated fresh air. Aldo would wander in cordially, innocently—as he'd put it—just to see what was what, just merely to say hello, and he'd feel blinded and overwhelmed. His clothes would curdle with dampness; his eyes would water; his hair would get moist, which drove him crazy. A cook would hand him a towel to pat it dry, and the towel would be wet, on purpose, to torment him, or it would be freshly stained with meat juice, to torment him further.

He'd never learned. He was always going into the kitchen when they didn't want him, which was moderately stupid of him, but there was no comparison, he felt, with what I'd done.

Christ Almighty. It was an indescribably, unspeakably stupid thing, setting off on an unfamiliar byway alone, when I'd seen it was foggy already.

I should have known it could only get thicker. Look how bad it was: I could open my mouth with the sense I could drink it, which would be wonderful, since I was thirsty, and hungry, too—he could hear my stomach make those rumbles, like on performance evenings, and he'd stand there begging God to silence my belly, especially during that important moment when everything became hushed, expectant.

One doesn't want an audience to be aware of the singer's stomach. Yet I'd rarely eaten a meal before singing. How many times had Ugo told me to have supper before going to work? If not supper, at least lunch?

Stupid beyond belief! Had I considered what might be floating around in the fog? It was getting dark; I couldn't see the danger. I might have been breathing tiny fragments of poison, metal, plaster, wood, stone, glass, tiles, the Weary Tower, the *basso* church bell, and worse things as well, things from inside the ground.

Cassaromilia was behind me. So was San Guarino. So was Folcore. It could only get better. At least I'd known enough to sit down and take a rest. For that he would have to congratulate me, begrudgingly.

He never gave me credit for making sensible decisions, not counting the one I'd made to marry him, then the one to go home with him to Romagna. No regrets there. I was Mengo's first singer and first Sicilian. He knew I enjoyed the distinctions.

But remember when I wouldn't go to America when he wanted to go to America? The Fascists had marched on Rome. Italy was filling up with Blackshirts; it was a nation of sheep being herded by one demented dog, this psychotic little dog—originally the runt of his litter—and suddenly he was armed, his skull was coated with metal, he was lining up all the dogs that barked back at him, bared their teeth at him, were bigger than him, were smarter than him, and look what had happened.

Well, that was Italy.

Why hadn't we gone to New York, even though it would have meant the misery of first, being Italian in America when Mussolini was climbing into bed with Hitler, and second, being Italian in America when America was bombing Italians?

Did I remember what I'd said to that? Beppi didn't want to go. He was too dug in where he was. He was already rooted.

Beppi didn't want to! Beppi was too dug in! Beppi was rooted! Did I think our son was some kind of tree—an Italian nut tree, or an olive tree—that couldn't be transplanted?

He could have been transplanted! People grow olives and nuts in America! I loved Beppi more than him! Admit it: he came second in my affections. Or third, if you counted singing. Or fourth, if I cared to delve into the subject of Ugo.

Which I did not. But what about that coach? Remember

when he wanted to hire that theatrical coach from Milan who'd been willing to guarantee, *guarantee,* that if I put myself in his hands for one month, he'd have me strolling out from the wings, one hundred percent confidently, onto any stage in the world? And I wouldn't need a prop in my hands for reassurance. And I'd be able to sit in audiences of other singers' performances, without feeling that the next breath I drew would be my last. And walk into any theater as comfortably as if I owned it.

Did I honestly believe it was *all his fault* that I only sang to diners and the help and the locals and tourists who gathered outside for free?

I was the one who'd turned down the offer. I was the one who didn't believe in coaches.

But I was also the one who'd wanted so badly to go onto the stage, the genuine operatic stage. Did I remember I had a husband who would have turned himself inside out to see me established in the places I'd had the talent to be, the highest places, no expense spared, no matter how much debt he went into? He was going into debt all the time anyway. He didn't give a damn about it. He could always find financing. He was a genius at getting people to bankroll him.

But no, I had to cling to my old ways: if I couldn't do something on my own, all right then, forget it.

You can't always do everything on your own. Think of Beppi! Had I made Beppi by myself?

I should have listened to him about that coach. He would have treated the recurrence of sand in my throat like a good physician—like Ugo, for example, getting rid of a blood clot or an ulcer, or a good physician's impressive wife, such as Eliana, with her herbs and prayers and wisdom, getting rid of people's allergies, warts, stutters, nervous tics, psychological disorders, all kinds of phobias—so many, in fact, it would take two hours to list them, not that we didn't have the time for it, as it appeared—what an *idiot*—that I'd marooned myself.

I should do the sensible thing and look around for some shelter, get something over my head. Was I prepared to accept that I might be stuck here all night, alone, on the side of a path that appeared to be as treacherous as the edge of a cliff, and taking one more step meant walking off it? Did I remember that somewhere on an airfield, American planes were tanked up and ready, waiting for an opening in the fog to come and drop some more bombs? Also, had I considered the proximity of Germans?

A battalion could have set up camp nearby. Those shapes in the distance could be tents, tanks, cannons. Those pine trees across the path could be soldiers.

Did I remember the time Ugo was out in a fog like this one, but even worse, as it was closer to the sea? He hadn't taken his car for whatever patient's house he'd been called to. It had seemed a nice night for walking. On his way home, having believed he'd gone the right way, he found himself off-course, on his ass, in a pit some Fascists had dug for a pig. They'd planned to roast it the next day, which was Mussolini's birthday.

Had I honestly believed I was following a path to Mengo? Where was it anyway, this path? It seemed to have ended. It was swallowed up in fog.

I'd been walking on something that was all swallowed up. And I didn't know where I was to begin with. Would I be able to draw a map of this area, if I had anything to write with? Could I sum up the number of miles I'd traveled since leaving Mengo on that train?

Don't bother answering those questions! As my husband, it

was his duty to point out the truth. My situation was obvious. I was lost.

Actually, he felt it was understandable that I had not gone into Cassaromilia. He wasn't calling me a coward. The only reason I didn't step forward to help Cesare was that I'd gone on strike against singing in front of an audience.

All the same, it would have been nice if I'd offered those people a song. Cesare might have found a way to join in. Think of it, a duet, soprano and baritone, which would have been appreciated doubly, since the people of Cassaromilia had been forced to say their prayers without a priest—and for God's sake don't be wondering what had happened to the priest, inside that church with his parishioners, all of them thinking they were safe and then . . .

Naturally, my thoughts had gone to my outfit. Any Italian in my position would have wanted to change their clothes, too. A normal reaction. Admirable, even. It was only the strike that had caused me to not go up there and sing.

Yes, surely it was only that. It wasn't that I suffered from heartlessness. It wasn't a lack of human feeling. I still had plenty of human feeling, right? I'd only acquired a sort of clinical detachment about tragedies and suffering, right? Like Ugo's doctorly professionalism?

"Aldo," I said. "All you talk about is Ugo. You're annoying me. Go away."

But wouldn't I like to know his idea of what I could have sung for the new and old dead of Cassaromilia? And the people without a priest? And those children?

Why, Verdi, of course.

My Desdemona was famous in our part of the world. When I sang from *Otello,* in a white dress, or a silver one, the waiters had to wait at least ten minutes before venturing back to the tables. The cooks had to keep everything on warming plates. The restaurant became transformed. The whole place would seem temporarily paralyzed.

Oh, it didn't matter that I didn't like the character, that I felt there was something abnormal in a woman who didn't spit in the eye of a husband who made false accusations against her: spit in his eye and walk out, not wring her hands in anguish and doom, and stand around waiting to be smothered.

You couldn't blame Verdi for that. You had to blame Shakespeare, who was probably only concerned with the drama. A heroine in a murder scene would fill more seats than a heroine who used her own wits and felt she'd do anything to stay alive.

Think of it: me and Verdi, and Cesare backing me up, a baritone echo, as deep as the bell that would never ring again from the Weary Tower.

Did I feel a little guilty about not singing to Cassaromilia? Did I feel a little selfish? Did I feel a little Fascist?

"Aldo, shut up. From now on, when I want you to talk to me, I'll invite you."

"I'm trying to help."

"Don't. You make everything worse."

"Very well. I surrender to your decision. You've hurt my feelings, but I'll be off now. *Ciao,* Lucia."

It was as if he were at home, ready to set off for the restaurant. Looking at himself in the vestibule mirror, checking his hair, his tie, brushing dandruff or lint off the shoulders or collar of one of his beautiful suits.

"*Ciao,* Aldo. Go to Beppi now. Tell him I'll be coming very soon."

Beppi always went in before his father to oversee deliveries and supervise whatever cleaning was going on. Someone in the kitchen would be laying out flour on a smooth wood counter for pasta. Someone would be starting soup from yesterday's bones. Someone would be taking the bones out of fishes, for fillets. Someone would be chopping onions or bulbs of fennel, with flesh that was whiter than fog, whiter than bones, whiter than my dresses.

The fog contained its own silence, the way a volcano contains its own noise. It settled down on me with a surprising comfort. I told myself that I'd only sat down in the shelter of the olive trees out of weariness.

"Ave Maria," I said to myself. "Hail Mary, full of grace."

Verdi's prayer in *Otello*'s fourth act. An invocation—quiet, coming up from a depth that ordinary church hymns could never reach, would never attempt—well, that was Verdi: Hail Mary, full of grace, show your pity. Pray for those whose heads are bowed by affronts and spiteful destiny.

They were only words. I had no music in that silence. They were only some words to which my mind was indifferent, as if I'd remembered a few lines from an advertisement in a magazine. It was only exhaustion, I felt, that bowed my head.

It was shadowy and getting darker. My senses were in a state of over-alertness, so that I thought I heard many different types of sounds, all frightening and sinister: breathing, groaning, footsteps, boot steps, distant thunder, the chugging of heavy trucks on roads built for carts, the drone of planes, echoes of explosions—a world of war sounds dredged up to mock me, as if my ears had memories of their own. All the noise of war I'd ever heard seemed to gather together into one mass, then shatter into hundreds of fragments, amplified and terrible, riding the back of the now-lifting fog.

In that moment, I allowed myself to acknowledge the dead soldiers.

My eyes became eyes that had lost the power to blink. I couldn't fool myself any longer into imagining that those shapes were anything but what they were: four, maybe five, maybe half a dozen, just several yards away, sprawled on the ground below a couple of trees that were unusually close together, with trunks that nearly touched and crowns so intertwined they appeared to be sharing branches. The soldiers were American. Their boots were the same as mine. I maneuvered myself to my hands and knees and crept closer.

They looked as if they'd been there for a while. They must have gone into the olive trees for shelter from the fog. My hands grazed the side of a boot, not being worn: big, a big man's boot. All the feet were big. All men. Not a woman among them, a tall woman, slender, short-haired, American, a golfer.

They hadn't died from a bombing. It was too dark to see bullet wounds, but I knew they'd been shot.

A patrol. Germans had found them here. One of the small objects on the ground was a belt buckle, damaged, discarded: my fingers probed it. When I realized what it was, I pulled away, as if it might contaminate me. I'd seen those things often enough. Luftwaffe, an officer's. Metal. Ornately decorated, with the shape of an eagle in the center, within a wreath.

Perhaps the Germans who killed them were the same ones who'd done what they did to the Bologna partisans. It made sense; it wasn't that far away.

I got down to business. There were pieces of equipment all over the ground: belongings, a rucksack, a bedroll, helmets. They'd taken off their helmets. I didn't notice any guns. I noticed a tin can, another, and another, on their sides, open. Paper-wrapped packets.

A calmness came over me, unlike anything I'd felt before, except perhaps at the end of a performance. My hand closed around a packet. I thought it might be some sort of thick, square, hard biscuit. The paper had been torn back about an inch or so, but it was all there. It had not been partially eaten, or bitten into. I sniffed it. Chocolate. Something like baking chocolate, in the shape of a small brick.

I managed to get hold of two open cans that weren't empty. Some type of thick stew. Meat, potatoes. Maybe bits of vegetables that once had been green.

I found several other cans that were sealed. I didn't take them, although I paused for a moment, feeling about on the ground for a can opener. And a spoon or a fork. I didn't find any of those things.

"Excuse me," whispered the voice of my husband. "I've come back again because I forgot to tell you something."

I pictured him turning on the walkway at home in a snappy little pirouette, charming and delightful, especially for a man of his size: elegant Aldo. There'd always been moments when he knew how to carry his weight.

I imagined myself in my own doorway. He came near me, his face furrowed with worry.

"Lucia, where's Marcellina?"

"Oh," I said, "never mind about her."

"I don't want to never mind about her. You know how she is. She must be wondering why you're not with her. Why aren't you with her? She must be—"

"Stop telling me what to do."

"I will, except for one more thing. The rims of those cans are very sharp, very pointy. Be careful not to cut yourself. I wouldn't be able to bear it."

"I won't cut myself," I promised.

Why did Aldo have to bring up Marcellina? Her face seemed to loom up in the fog, as if she were haunting me, too. Did I have to go back and get her, and take her with me, and probably her boyfriend as well? Did I *have* to? Or at least go back and let her see I was all right? She always said that when someone goes off somewhere without a *ciao* to people who love them, they are committing a sin. If they go off without a word of their whereabouts, causing all sorts of frantic worrying, they are commiting another one, worse.

I put the chocolate into my pocket. In each of my hands was a can. It wasn't stealing. When I got myself back up on my feet, I was careful not to rush away like a thief. I took my time, moving slowly back onto the footpath, seeking the shelter of another tree, a good distance away, to sit beneath for a while, and eat my supper in peace.

21

If the American boyfriend who looked like a young Caruso had not played *baseball* in his youth, with a specialty in a position called *shortstop,* and if he hadn't walked into what was left of the Galimberti kitchen from the side, from Annunziata's room—which he'd only done because he was hungry, he'd smelled food, and he wanted to find out what the women were cooking—and, most importantly, if he hadn't been successful at liberating Annmarie—he and Etto, who'd been a big help—he would not have been there, in the right place, in exactly the right set of circumstances, to have intercepted, like an *infield pop fly,* the onion Marcellina had flung at my head, the instant I appeared in the hole in the wall, the same one I'd left from, which everyone was using as a doorway because the real door was fully blocked up now, from the second bombardment, the Folcore one, which had not gone as planned.

Bombs had fallen profusely, all around this area, but they had not destroyed Folcore. The old main tower had gone down, but that was all.

Good old Folcore. The Germans were evacuating, were going west.

Down here, there'd been hits. Many fields had new craters,

which, on the bright side, might one day serve as ponds for irrigation. It had been possible to gather root vegetables without having to dig for them, thanks to the disturbances of the land. Several farm buildings had been lost, several barns.

Marcellina was not sorry about the onion, which she'd been about to chop up for soup. The only reason she'd thrown it was that she'd needed a substitute for her voice. She had a rotten, potentially fatal head cold, no doubt from hiding from the bombs in the Galimbertis' damp, awful cellar, and while her throat wasn't sore, it was filled, it felt, with little rocks, and she was suffering from a case of laryngitis, which Ugo refused to pay attention to.

It was true he had his hands full out there in the tents with what seemed like half of Italy, including refugees from Folcore and San Guarino; Etto, who was sleeping, and who planned to sleep straight through for a couple of days, which he deserved; farmers whose houses had been destroyed; and half a dozen Galimbertis.

But still. Busy as he was, Ugo could have acknowledged her ailments as a direct result of the war. He could have taken the time to confirm what she'd figured out for herself: that a head cold in wartime for someone her age was likely to become pneumonia. She could drop dead any minute, and she probably would, as soon as the soup was hot, like poor Aldo. In fact, she was shocked she was still alive, considering what I'd put her through, *running away from poor Polpo without a word, like a sinner.*

The tents were American. The Galimbertis had raided one of their encampments while they were all out on a mission. It had taken forever to get them set up. They'd been all rolled up, without a set of directions, which anyway would have been in English, so it didn't matter.

The boyfriend—the *fidanzato*—had turned up just in time to

offer advice. Sometimes things worked out all right. Not often, but sometimes. The news about Beppi was the same. The news from Cassaromilia was so bad, it was better not to discuss it. But now that I *had come back from God knew where,* when everyone had been *insanely frantic* about me, things were getting better, not counting certain things.

Everyone knew where every squad member was, excluding Beppi. The partisans who'd been here before were still here, taking up room in the tents with the rest of the occupants: Nizarro, Nomad, the butcher, the Etruscan, Cherubino, the Batarras.

Everyone else was in Cassaromilia: Mauro, the Triumvirate, Ferro, old Galto. Even Enzo and Eliana Fantini were accounted for; there'd been a message. They'd gone to Eliana's mountain. Her home village had been bombed. Her family was alive, but their priest was badly wounded. Another fallen priest! They'd heard what happened to the priest in Cassaromilia! Americans were going out of their way to bomb priests! Enzo should have disguised himself!

The laryngitis was not preventing Marcellina from communicating her feelings. I noticed the way she wasn't saying anything about the secret she'd kept from me all those years.

I wasn't going to bring it up. She'd probably find something else to throw at me.

They were composing the soup out of root vegetables: carrots, potatoes, and so on. They were cooking three at once. Three was the number of pots they had, counting the one from before, which had held Annunziata's delicious beans, which could not have been called soup, as intended, because *a certain person greedily drank up all the broth.*

Three pots, but they were basically all the same soup. Yes, one lucky result of the bombing was that, when nearby fields were hit, the disturbed ground had yielded these very vegetables, unexpectedly.

"Welcome back, Signora Fantini," spoke up Annunziata, barely turning around from her stove.

Annunziata had a cold as well but she was tougher; she was already halfway recovered. She didn't have a throat full of stones that made her voice sound like a crow's.

"I'd offer you a glass of water," she said, "but we haven't got glasses, and the water we had, given to us in bottles by Americans, has all gone into the soup. It's your own business if you don't want to tell us where you've been. You owe me a song or two, but I'm willing to forget that. You don't look so good, but cheer up. You're fortunate that my friend Marcellina chose the onion, and not the knife she was holding. It's very sharp, so be glad doubly. I'm not sure the American would have stuck out his hand for it."

I tried to remember what the words "cheer up" could possibly mean.

Morning. Cold, pale.

A long night behind me. A daze. Backtracking along that path slowly, carefully, with the feeling I was walking on a tightrope.

Finding my way to the truck. Waiting for the farmers. Not looking at Cassaromilia. Not looking anywhere.

Pretending that the sound in the distance was thunder, and not doing a good job of it, because I knew what direction the blasts were coming from. Saying to myself, "I remember when the only thing to worry about dropping out of the sky was bird shit."

The farmers had been grim, dirty, exhausted, dazed, beyond words. Some of them had stayed behind. The burial work was far from completed, but there were still morning chores to go home to. Chores, and checking to see what damage had been done to their homes and fields, so near to Folcore.

Not talking about bombs. Not talking about new or old dead. Not talking, period, except to tell them—Adriano's father in particular—that I had changed my mind about my destination. Would they take me to the Galimbertis' house? They knew where it was. They asked no questions.

Stopping on the way only once, by the trees of the partisans from Bologna. Not there. On the ground, the discarded ropes, like skins from which snakes had crawled out.

Wondering where the Germans had acquired ropes for hangings. Maybe they'd been brought from Germany in a box labeled "Ropes for Good Nazis to Hang Bad Italians."

Wondering who cut the partisans down. And where the bodies were taken. Don't ask. No one felt like talking.

With the ropes, booby traps: glass shards, pieces of metal with corrugated edges, like teeth. Neatly piled up, as if swept in a housecleaning. The branches of the trees were just branches, ordinary, unmarked. No signs of what had been done there. No scars.

The truck proceeding with an air of invigoration.

Riding in the cab where the shrouds had been.

Getting out of the truck at the end of the lane that led to the Galimbertis' house. Waving goodbye to the farmers.

Tents, an encampment. Don't look for Ugo.

"That was a great *pop fly*! I'm still good! I've still got it!"

"If you don't give back our onion, a frying pan may come in contact with the side of your big, thick skull, and then you won't get anything to eat."

"My dear Signora Galimberti, baseball players don't keep the balls they catch. They have to throw to a *baseman* for an *out*. When there aren't any runners, they have to throw to the *pitcher*."

Handing back the onion. Caruso. It was kind of him not to mention the other night, the cart, picking me up from the bottom of the Folcore hill. But everything else he wasn't saying was much more significant than that. My own part was minor.

I couldn't remember his name. He was American, he'd grown up in America, but no one could have looked more Italian, not even Caruso himself. He was freshly shaven. Hair slicked back. A crisp, clean shirt, unbuttoned at the neck, no jacket. Clean, new-looking trousers. *Khaki.*

Turning his gaze to me. Sad, tired, gentle, polite. Determined to put up a strong front. "Wonderful to see you again, Signora Fantini. I'd forgotten you were dressed as one of my compatriots. Isn't it a good thing we're all on the same side? Tell you what. You don't seem to be busy right now, so why don't you follow me in there?"

"In there" was the same as before. The room of Annunziata.

Cooking smells in the background, eradicating the oppression of stifling dust, dirt, post-bomb air clutter. A type of fortification. If something was cooking, everything was not as bad as it could have been. Maybe it wouldn't be bad.

Getting down to business. A touch of the American's hand on my arm as I paused in the doorway.

I didn't want to go in.

His voice was low. Visit-a-patient low. "Look, we've got chairs. We borrowed them from some neighbors. Marcellina and Annunziata sat with her last night. It's good you arrived when you did. We've got a car on the way, to take her to a hospital. Romagnan, but one of ours. South of here. Secure. A spot where it's clear now."

Secure. Clear. Think about those two words as words containing a dependable reality.

"How does she look?" I asked.

"Don't worry. She's been medicated. Your relative the doctor gave her a sedative. She won't know you're here. It took an American general and a trade with the Germans to get her back. They had her, you see. We gave them eight Nazis from a camp of ours near Naples."

He sounded like a black market trader. What was the worth of a life? Was one life of more value than another?

I looked inside. The shutters were open. No warmth was in the air. The light had turned paler, as if it weren't the sun up there but some other, weaker, farther-off star, barely adequate for anything alive. As if the real sun was gone forever, bombed.

"Mama," Beppi used to say, looking up at the zodiac on his wall. "What's the biggest, strongest thing outside of the earth? And don't say God, like Marcellina does."

"The sun," I'd answer.

"Is it holding everything together?"

"It is."

"Can it break?"

"It's gas. Gas can't be broken."

"How do you know?"

"Because I'm your mother, and I say so."

Beppi's head on his pillow, past terror. His eyes closing gently, safely. Another nightmare abated. Try to think about that: being present in a state of peace. Try to remember what it was like.

Try to think this was only a nightmare.

In Folcore the big tower had fallen. Folco's tower. Folco the boy had kept his eyes on the sky, watching the arc of the light in his long-ago century. He had problems, but he never had to worry about someone up there in a plane, blowing up the sun.

22

IT WAS A DIFFERENT ROOM from before, although the only things that had changed were the addition of two chairs at the side of the bed and the bed's occupant. The chairs looked homemade, with matted straw seats and high backs, which gave them an air of formality. They hadn't come from Etto's factory.

Annmarie. *Annamaria.*

"She was a nun when I met her," I said quietly. "Her hair was covered."

"It was a perfect disguise," said the American. "The opposite of her personality, and her life as well. I mean, the way she lived her life before the war. I don't know if she told you, but she used to raise hell, pretty much everywhere she went. In America they have a word for it. *Hellion.* On the golf course and off."

"Hellion," I said, trying it out.

It took a lot of effort to make the sound of the letter H. A ridiculous American noise. A wasted breath, pushed too hard.

A weariness had come over me. It wasn't just from being so tired. I couldn't remember the last time I'd felt so heavy in my own body. Maybe when I was pregnant, all those years ago. Maybe never.

A whole new level of heaviness, unexpected. I said, "She told me she went to a convent school."

"She was a hellion there, too. I didn't have the chance to see her in the habit. I would have enjoyed that."

"It was gray," I said.

"I wonder what happened to it."

"It got lost," I said.

Her head was covered now, but this time by a swaddling of bandages, which fit her like an odd white cap, with a missing top, exposing a patch of that sand-colored hair. One ear was partially covered, the other fully. No marks on her face, no bruises.

She lay on her back, eyes closed, with Annunziata's linen sheet pulled up to her chin. Her skin was as pallid as the light.

I heard them arguing in that half-bombed kitchen. Something to do with the soup. Marcellina really did sound like a hoarse old crow.

Soon more voices joined them—masculine, saying my name insistently, Lucia, Lucia, Lucia. Like diners at Aldo's after a performance, when I'd slipped away to the kitchen or back into the office. Wanting something—a conversation, an autograph, a souvenir, a handshake, or even a kiss. I never knew what they wanted.

"Let's never mind about the rest of this household," the American said, closing the bedroom door. Latching it. I hadn't noticed the lock when I was here before.

Just the two of us. Just the three of us. At least this wasn't pitch-darkness. At least I could see the chairs, the door. Everywhere one went, one found oneself sitting down on something that hadn't come from Etto's factory, in a place one did not wish to be.

There would never be more of Etto's chairs. Or his tables,

bureaus, cabinets, whatever else they'd made. I didn't know what else.

Trouble.

"She told me," I said to the American, "she joined your military because of trouble. Something she'd got into. She never told me what it was. I'd like to know, please."

"She needed to stay out of a certain litigation in court."

"She broke the law?"

"Is that what you really wanted to ask me about?"

"It's secondary."

"You want to know what they did to her. I'll tell you. They wanted information."

"Don't tell me you're worried she gave any away."

He seemed to cheer up at that. "She did! Did you know about a certain book she had, a sort of diary?"

"My son was the one who found it. With the song about the *surrey*."

"The very one. I hadn't been told of the connection. They'd got hold of it. She told them the song was an American code. She claimed that the words represented—oh, I don't know, troop movements or something. But the thing was really only lyrics of a song. I found out a few days ago that a pilot of ours has a girlfriend who's the understudy to the lead character in the play it's from. The girl writes songs in her letters to him. He'd copied the surrey song into his journal, which was a gift he'd only just received, also from the girlfriend. He was trying to memorize the lines because it made him feel a little better about things in general."

"I know that feeling. I know the name of the play, too. It's like the name of one of your states. In the West. Okla-*ho*-ma," I said, resenting another H.

"That's right."

"So she gave them this information, and they concluded they didn't need to hurt her any worse than they had already?"

"No. It didn't happen like that. They wanted more information than one code."

"It was bad?"

"Yes."

"How bad?"

"For one thing, the head wounds are fairly superficial. For another, both her arms were injured. They're in splints and bandages, waiting to be properly set, which isn't possible here, without the right materials."

"By injured do you mean bones?"

"Both her arms are broken. They'd found out she was a golfer."

Stay calm. Surely in the history of golfing in America, there'd been golfers sidelined with arm injuries. With the right methods of treatment and recuperation, they'd all have the chance to get up and go forth, sore but intact, swinging their clubs, devoting themselves to a little white ball. I imagined an army of Americans with clubs in their hands instead of guns.

"A hospital," I said.

"Yes. At a base of ours. For a while. For however long it takes. Then home."

"To Con-eh-tah-kit?"

A little chuckle of approval at my pronunciation. "Her family's there. But she also has a house in a place called—"

"Ar-ee-zo-na."

"Yes."

"The desert. In the West."

"Exactly. That's where she'll want to go. She confided in you, I can see that."

"South of here," I said. "A base. A hospital that's a tent?"

"It's a building. By the sea. It's a small hotel that the army was able to borrow. To adapt. I'm told it's comfortable."

"And she'll be there for however long it takes for what? To set the arms? To find a way home to America?"

A pause. "Her house in Arizona is near one of the most famous places to play golf in the United States. Did she tell you she's a champion?"

I turned so I was facing the American. I couldn't think of a way to ask him what his name was. "She told me, champion, yes. Do people tell you all the time you look like Caruso?"

"All my life. Even when I was a baby. My parents had high hopes for me. But as it turned out, I can't sing."

"I've often wished I wasn't able to," I said.

"That's impossible."

"It's true. We don't have to speak of that. Do people tell you all the time your Italian is very good, without an American accent?"

"It's always nice to hear that. Thank you."

"You're welcome. Under the covers, if I were to pull them back and look at her, would I find myself getting distraught?"

"Let's not pull back her covers."

"All right. If that's what you wish. You're going with her, when they come for her?"

"I'm not able to. I'm being reassigned to—well, reassigned. I can't say where, I'm sorry."

"I understand. You came to Italy to be with her."

A face appeared at the window: Roncuzzi, pale and looking exhausted, smiling at me, averting his eyes from the woman on the bed. That was all right. He wasn't ignoring Annmarie. I could tell he was being respectful, in the belief that an unconscious foreigner deserved privacy.

"*Ciao,* Lucia. They told me in the kitchen not to bother you.

But here I am, and here you are, still wearing my jacket. I'm happy to know that. Nizarro, who used to be one heartbeat away from dead, and is now his same old pain-in-the-rear self, sends you a *ciao* also, and so do the rest of them. We are living like Gypsies, but at least we're alive."

Coming up beside Roncuzzi was Etto Renzetti. He didn't exactly give the butcher a sideways shove, but he came close to it, as if intending to displace him absolutely. For a long moment he gazed at me, his head tilted a bit to one side, then the other, as if a camera were in his hands and he wanted the picture to be perfect, and couldn't decide on an angle.

"You're still in one piece," he said.

"I am, I am." I found it impossible to let him know that I wasn't unhappy to see him. That I wasn't forgetting San Guarino, the moonlight, the way he'd watched out for me, that house, the way he'd held me.

I knew he was looking at me with the eyes of a man who's looking at a woman he has kissed, has embraced, has played the part of a lover to. I really was glad to see him. But it wasn't the same "glad" as the one I knew he wanted.

"They told me you helped a lot in the rescue, Etto," I said.

A shy scoffing, a shrug. "I was a temporary American aide. It worked out. How is she doing?"

"No change," said the American.

"Lucia," said Roncuzzi, shouldering himself back into my line of sight. "If Etto here joins the squad, which he's thinking about, there'll be five non-waiters, which is one more than before. I think you should encourage him."

"There are four?" said Etto. "You and the two Batarras, I know. Who's the other one?"

"Saponi the fisherman," said Roncuzzi. "He's old, but he didn't want to be left out. If you bring along some of your carpenters, we might have an equal number of normal people, instead of an overwhelming majority of waiters. I'd enjoy that."

"What's the matter with waiters?" said the American.

Roncuzzi let out a chuckle. "Did you ever eat in an Italian restaurant?"

"When I got here, they were pretty much all closed, except for the Fascist ones."

"There's nothing the matter with them," said Roncuzzi, "if you don't count an air of superiority. They are, to put it bluntly, the whole lot of them, snobs. I'm interested in balance."

"I started making a squad before, but now I don't know where my carpenters are," said Etto. "There's just me."

"I encourage you to join, Etto," I said.

I couldn't bear his tender, hopeful look. I went over to the window. "I'm going to have to close the shutters," I told them. "It's getting cooler. And I think it will be better for Annmarie to have it darker in here. And quieter."

Roncuzzi backed away from the window at once; Etto took a little longer. Again that look at me. But level this time, steady. Asking a question without putting it into words.

The question, I got.

"*Ciao,* Etto," I said.

"Wait. I want to know . . ." He furrowed up with indecision, turned away, turned back, then said, "How is it going with finding your son?"

"It's going all right."

"He'll be turning up soon, I am sure of it. Do you still remember when he was a little boy and you lost him at my place? And he was sleeping in the bushes?"

"I remember."

"Good. I just wanted to make sure you do. It's important to

remember things. Things that are, you know, important. Things in the past. *Everything.*"

"I won't forget. I promise."

"*Ciao,* Lucia."

He gave me the courtesy of hurrying away, so that I didn't have to close the window, literally, in his face, which I probably wouldn't have done. It could have been awkward. I tried to picture him getting along with everyone, fitting in, catching up on things he'd missed out on. I tried to picture him with a gun, taking it apart to clean it, loading it, feeling the heft of it in his palm.

Maybe. Everything in his life had been lost. Not just his factory. His house, too. His bed. He'd told me that. Me? Did he count me as one of his losses? Maybe he'd really be all right on the squad.

"It's not getting cooler," said the American. "And it wasn't all that bright to begin with."

"I had the feeling that those two wouldn't be the only ones to show up to talk to me."

"Do you mean someone's around? Someone you choose to avoid? For personal reasons?"

I returned to my place on the chair beside him, taking my time to answer that question. "Excuse me for being blunt like Roncuzzi," I said, "but if I felt that way, it wouldn't be something I'd tell you."

"Sorry. I was out of line. I was being American. It's my job to ask questions, usually about something that's not obvious on the surface."

Those last seven words lingered in the air like the last phrase of a song—the type of song that keeps going, with echoes creating more echoes. Ugo was under my surface, I realized. I'd never thought of him in quite that way before.

The shutters didn't completely block out daylight from that weak, pale sun. They were old, disjoined, worn. Annunziata's bedroom took on the other-world atmosphere of a small church with darkly painted windows. The feeble light began taking on a luster, an importance.

The American had come to Italy to be with her. That was the last thing we talked about before the interruption. "You came to Italy to be with her," I repeated.

"I did."

"But you're not going to the base hospital by the sea. Because of the reassignment."

"It's not my decision. Now that they've got me here, whatever I do, or don't do, it's not from making my own choices."

"The same thing's been happening with me."

"You understand me, then. Things in Italy aren't going well. Mistakes have been made."

"Things are going well in other parts of this war? Mistakes aren't made in other places?"

"I don't care about other parts and places. In case you haven't thought about this lately, Mussolini is still very much alive. The Fascist imagines himself a full-blown Nazi now. Do you know what it's like? It's like the bully in a schoolyard being finally forced out, and then he goes and joins a criminal gang, just to save his own skin, and since he's stupid he never figures out that the gang considers him an incompetent, undependable, laughable, slow-witted failure."

"If you grew up here," I said, "your political analysis might be a little more complicated. A bully in a schoolyard doesn't have his own army, plus the adulation of most of the school, plus enormous amounts of money to do what he likes with—which would be, in part, to find the means to get rid of anyone who disagrees with him. And a lot of his money, let me point out to you, came from America in the first place."

I sounded like Ugo! The American looked taken aback. He hadn't counted on being corrected.

"I'm not disagreeing with you," he said.

"Fascists are as criminal as Nazis."

"They're not."

"They are."

"All I'm saying is, they are failures at a different type of evil. It's not complicated at all. But what I'm trying to say is that, what I care about is right here. Everything I care about is right here, in front of my eyes."

I felt aware that there was still something he wasn't saying. Behind his words was a silence. I was determined to pay careful attention to it, the same way I listened to the different silences of an audience, before and after singing.

There were so many: the hush of expectation, in the moment the spotlight went on; the silence that filled my ears when I paused for breath; the astonishing quiet at the end of a song, when it was still too soon for applause. And the Verdi silence, a special one, serene and a little awesome. And the Mozart silence, which was even more special because the only thing it ever was, was beautiful.

And the silence of the cooks and waiters and Aldo, after a certain type of performance, when it was not a good night, when I was not at my best.

And other silences, too, new ones, newly learned. Counting them up, I listened to them all, sitting there.

The silence after a bombing.

The partisans from Bologna in the trees.

The Americans whose food I ate.

The hungry *anziani* at the farmhouse.

The farmers in the truck, returning home after their night among the dead.

The *basso* bell of the Weary Tower.

Etto's factory.

The new and old dead of Cassaromilia.

Cesare not singing.

Normal life in a war.

Annmarie Malone, who had helped me.

"Are you unwell?" the American said. "Would you like to go out, get some air?"

"I'm all right."

"You must be so terribly anxious about your son. Forgive me for not saying so earlier."

"You have other things on your mind. I was just thinking, I owe her a debt. You know, in your football, what happens when someone grabs hold of someone else, on the opposite team, to knock them down to the ground?"

"*Tackling,* it's called."

"Yes. She more or less did that to me. On a train. Well, getting off it. If she hadn't done that, I believe I would not be here. I have a suspicion that the train we were on was destroyed in the bombing. It's just a guess, but it's a reasonable one."

"She saved your life?"

"It's possible. And before that, she managed to keep me away from some Germans who were looking for me. Tell me where she was when they caught her, please."

"I'm not sure."

"She was in a car," I said. "With others. Americans, an Englishman. What happened to them?"

"I believe the men who were with her didn't make it."

"I see. The car she was in was outside an American place where I was. A *palazzo.* There was an attack."

"I know about that. We lost some men there."

"She was waiting for me. To take me away. When I came outside, she wasn't there. She was there, and then she wasn't."

"It's not your fault. Was that going to be the next thing you'd say?"

"The next thing," I said, "is for you to tell me, the base hotel hospital for however long it takes for what, please?"

"May I point out to you the interesting fact that, if I ask you a personal question, you tell me it's none of my business, and yet, you don't extend that feeling to me? It seems to me you have a double standard going on here."

"It's my right. I'm older than you. And I'm only asking you for the finishing touches on information I have already. Or should I say, intelligence, seeing as that's your actual position, Mr. Intelligence Officer. The hospital for however long it takes for what?"

He was a soldier through and through. If I hadn't known he was military, I would have been able to tell. Only a slight twitching of his nose and lips, like the involuntary gesture of someone who was about to sneeze, but then didn't, betrayed the reality of his feelings. He loved her.

"They were rough on her," he said slowly, with great formality. "The possibility exists that, during the time they imprisoned her—more specifically, during the time they interrogated her—they caused it to happen that she conceived."

It took me a moment to understand what he meant.

"It's not a good idea to wait till she gets to America to . . . to undo something like that," he was saying. "To have, you know, the necessary medical procedure. It can be taken care of in this country. It'll be easier on her. She's not fit for a long journey."

His voice wasn't bitter or angry. Just low, flattened.

Another kind of silence. The silence of the absence of tones.

"Easier," he said. "I take that back. Nothing is ever going to be easy again in any way. But the hospital was chosen especially. They're ready for her. She's not the first one this has happened to."

Why did I close those shutters? Why hadn't I wanted anyone else to come looking for me? This would have been the perfect time for another interruption.

Where was Geppo, where was Lido? Why weren't they bothering me the way Roncuzzi had? Anyone! The yard out there was crowded! Ugo!

Why wasn't he at that window, or at the bedroom door? He'd have got past the women at the stove. He knew what the American was telling me. He was the one who'd given Annmarie whatever he'd given her to keep her so still. He was the one to have bandaged her. He was also the one—the only one—who might have taken one look at me and figured out, instantly, something to say, or something to do, to make this heaviness of mine go away, this whole new degree of heaviness, in my bones, my heart, the voice inside me, all of me. "Ugo," I wanted to say. "Appear. Do something. Say something. Make me lighter."

With all my will, I focused my thoughts on that closed, bolted door, commanding the sound of his knock, his voice, here I am, here I am.

I gave myself a little shake.

"They raped her," I said, after a long moment. "They raped her and you think she might be pregnant. There. I've said it. Things will have to go on. Things will have to be done. I'd like to tell you what I'm wondering. I'm wondering, what was the trouble she made, to have, as you put it, litigation?"

The American looked at me with a shock of amazement. His jaw dropped; his expression made me almost giggle. "This isn't the time—"

"It is, Mr. Intelligence Officer. I want to know. Make me intelligent."

A quick, genuine smile. He was willing to make a small act of surrender.

"She was in a golf tournament," he said, and some tone began creeping back into his voice. "She was the only woman competing. This was—oh, three years ago. We were engaged—"

"You were married to someone else, before," I broke in.

"I can't believe she told you that!"

"We were stuck together for quite a while."

"I was married. Legally, I still am. It doesn't have anything to do with what you want to know. Do you know what the Fourth of July is?"

"An American holiday. Yankee Doodle Dandy. A song that Caruso sang—"

"In a famous American concert. It was one of the first songs he ever recorded. Did you know he always wore a pearl stickpin in his tie when he made a recording? When I was old enough to start wearing ties, my parents gave me one for a birthday gift, hoping it would perform a miracle on my vocal cords. They wanted to be the parents of a tenor very badly. Actually, I disappointed them in many ways. The fact that I became an officer compensated for some of it."

"Your wife was Italian?"

"She was. She is. A fresh immigrant, when we were introduced."

"Your parents, they liked her?"

"I thought I was telling you about the Fourth of July."

"Continue."

"On that day, a certain golf club—this was in Arizona but not her home club, which had hired her years before—put on a tournament. Her club is near a city called *Phoenix* and this one was farther south. It doesn't matter where it was. The Fourth of July Four-Ball, it was called. Golfers lined up and shot four balls and whoever hit the farthest won a trophy. It was a very big deal. They'd never let a woman play before, and I don't remember how they let her in, but she got in. I was in Washington then and I went out to watch. She was terrific. I wish you could have seen her."

"Did she wear brightly colored clothes, for free from American designers?"

"She told you about her golf clothes?"

"We're women. Women talk about clothes."

"She only wore bright colors in exhibitions, which are—"

"I know what they are. When you show off."

"Exactly. For competing she always wore—oh, tans, whites."

"I'm trying to picture it."

"Tan skirt, white blouse. Her skin was so brown, she looked like an Indian. And her hair was bleached out by all that sun. A beautiful Indian with pale yellow hair. She was taller than most of the men."

"She's taller than you, too."

"I kind of know that."

"Don't tell me she didn't hit the best ball."

"Oh, she did. On her last try. Her first three were great, but the fourth, her own Fourth Fourth, as she called it, went up in the air, I swear to you, like a rocket, in the most beautiful arc I ever saw, and believe me, I've seen a lot of golf. The spot where they were hitting the balls was down in a little sort of trench, and you couldn't see where it landed. They had distance markers set up. They had club officials out there to record whose balls were whose, which wasn't difficult, as the balls had been marked with the golfers' initials. A.M. were her letters. As it happened, a man by the name of Merrigrew, Philip Merrigrew, had his turn just before hers. I think she underestimated the resentment some of those guys felt toward her. Or their level of corruption. They ended up saying the initials were the same. That her fourth ball was actually his."

"But what letter does Philip start with?"

"It starts with a P, actually. And here's the interesting thing. His nickname was *Ace.* It's an American word that means, when you use it for a person, someone who's good at something, who's the best."

"He was the best golfer, besides her?"

"No, he was the worst. He was fairly competent, but not good, with *long drives,* which this was. With everything else, he was terrible. It was an ironic name for him."

"We do that in Italy all the time," I said. "I understand. Sometimes it comes out of affection."

"Not in this case. This guy hated being called Ace, but he put up a good show about it. He wanted everyone to like him, but he only gave people reasons not to. He used to be a member of Annmarie's own club, so she knew him pretty well. A real *jerk.* He never used his nickname. See, golfers put their own initials on their balls, and he never would have put an A. They only used nicknames for golfers who had matching initials and there wasn't any other P.M., so he definitely would have put a P. It could never be proven, since all the balls that said P.M. had mysteriously disappeared."

"So they told her she lost?"

"They did. She was sometimes all right controlling her temper, but this wasn't one of those times. No one from the club took her side. She was an outsider there anyway. She'd only gone into the tournament because her home club didn't have one as big. Also, more importantly, she'd wanted to stick up for a principle. She was sick and tired of their no-women policy. They were one of those clubs, like most, that refused to call a woman golfer a professional, regardless of how good she was, or how much money she made, or how many trophies she had. She refused to call herself an amateur."

"I understand. She told me that in your home state they didn't let Catholics near their clubs."

"Would you call that Fascist?"

"No. It can only be Fascist if they arrest you and maybe kill you, not just discriminate against you. A different evil, yes?"

"You've got me there. But she was arrested. For assault."

"What did she do to this man called Ace?"

"It wasn't him. Although in my opinion, it should have been. He knew he hadn't hit that ball. And he was standing there, this cheap little cheat of a man, with this look on his face, this look of joy, and he was saying, over and over, 'I won! I won! I won!' Like he was talking himself into it. The guy she went after was the club official in charge of measuring those distances. The one who decided it wasn't her ball. To her credit, when she went at him, she remembered to put down her club. It could have been worse. He was a big guy, not much older than she was. Did she tell you that at her convent school they taught boxing in their athletics program? They had a gymnasium. Boxing for girls. The nuns were keen on rowing, you see. The school was near a river and they competed for all sorts of boat prizes with other schools. They were always interested in building upper-body strength. Of course, with Annmarie, it all went into golf, not oars. She hates the water."

"She didn't tell me that," I said.

"The man she punched, and it was only one punch—no, it was two; it was one to one side of the head and then a second, to the other side—was taken to a hospital in an ambulance. It didn't look good, with all that blood, but nosebleeds often look worse than they are. We'll never know if she knocked him out, or if he was shamming about that. He claimed later she had broken his nose and made him partially blind in one eye. Also, that she had injured his spine. A knob in his spine was displaced, he claimed. He swore when he went down, he'd landed on a rock, extremely hard, and everyone believed him. No one stopped to think that the last thing you'd find on a *putting green,* which was where the ball landed, was a big rock. A putting green by its very definition is the smoothest surface on the course. It's the place where the little hole in the ground is, where the ball's supposed to go, in the end."

"Did she go to jail?"

"No. Her club hired a whole pack of lawyers. A sort of squad, you might say. But the thing was on its way to trial. There would have been headlines, none of them in her favor. A lady golfer slugging an innocent clubman out of fury at finding herself a loser, on the Fourth of July. The other club was dying to get her into court. Eventually, the United States Army got wind of it. They put two and two together, and they took a look at her, and asked all kinds of people who knew her all kinds of questions, and then they found out she speaks Italian. And that was that. The army had her arrest record wiped clean."

"You're a good storyteller," I said, getting the feeling he'd come to the end.

"Only when I'm telling the truth."

"You made me think of her as a fighter. Strong."

"I wanted to be able to marry her before she went into training. It didn't work out. Would you like to know how many years it's been since I began to try getting divorced? Fifteen, give or take a few months. My own day in court, I've been waiting for, for fifteen years."

"Your wife doesn't believe in divorce?"

"She believes in waiting for me to not want one anymore. But that's not part of the story. We couldn't marry, and then she shipped out."

"And here we are."

"Yes."

"After the hospital, she'll go home."

"Yes."

"Maybe to Arizona."

"Yes. It's sunny there. The desert. She can rest."

"Maybe one day she'll go back to the golf place where they cheated her."

"She can't."

"Broken arms heal."

"That's not it. They banned her. If she puts one foot on their property ever again, the police will turn up and believe me, a scene will be made. I almost forgot to tell you the part where, after she threw her punches, she found it essential to pick up her golf club and go over to the table where the trophy was, the winner's trophy. She swung the club against it before anyone could stop her. Did I tell you it was made of glass?"

"You left out the glass."

"It was a glass flagpole about two feet high on a wooden pedestal. The pole in fact was a golf club. Attached to it was a glass American flag. Extremely fine glass, very thin, very expensive, with all the right colors and stars and stripes of the actual flag."

"Well, it was your Yankee Doodle Dandy."

"It most definitely was. It's against the law in America to do anything violent to a flag."

All along, I kept glancing toward that figure on the bed, watching for movement, any type of movement at all, a fluttering of the eyelids, a turn of the head or a leg beneath the covers, or a change in that slow, light breathing. She didn't stir.

Even though one ear was covered, she wasn't deaf. Maybe she was listening. Maybe her ears were storing everything up. Everything that was said here might come back to her later like a recording on a phonograph record. "They kept talking about me," she might say to herself. "They talked about me like I wasn't there."

Another silence. The silence after a long story.

"Thank you for not letting that onion hit me," I said.

"You're welcome."

"I just remembered something else. Thank you for giving me morphine. It made a big difference. I had a good night's sleep. Thank you for rescuing me from the bottom of that hill."

"You're welcome. She was the reason I was in the area. They had her in Folcore, had I mentioned that?"

"No."

"I don't know what I would have done if she'd been in that town when they bombed it."

"She's alive. Isn't that the only thing that counts? Everyone is either dead or alive."

"Now you're the one who's not acknowledging complications. There are complications."

"For the living, I suppose. I must tell you, I don't recall your name. I'm sorry. I should have told you when I first came in. But I didn't."

"That's all right. In America I was called *Tom Tully.*"

"Yes. I remember. She told me that."

"If you like, you can call me Enrico. Honestly, I don't mind."

"May I confide in you, something personal?"

"Finally. Please."

"I would have liked to have been her mother-in-law. I had thought about that. You might call it a daydream. I had pictured her in my family. Is that upsetting to you?"

"I can only answer that I wish my own mother would feel the same way."

"Perhaps I should adopt you."

"I'm too old."

"Tullio," I said. "Tullio Tomasini. That's it. You worked at a golf place. What's the name of it?"

"Hatfield. The Hatfield Country Club, in Hatfield, Connecticut."

Another H. I didn't feel like wasting the breath to try pronouncing it. I said, "You told them you were a Protestant. Irish, but a Protestant. Looking like what you look like, you got away with that?"

"I was younger then. I was better at being able to function within rules set up by someone else, even rules that were wrong. I did what I felt I had to. It's hard to be an immigrant in America. I worked in the office. I was good at my job. They wanted to keep me."

"You met her there. She told me that."

"I did. She was only fifteen. She used to sneak in to play, early in the morning. Very early. In the dark, sometimes. She lived near the course. Her school was near it, too. A born golfer. Did she tell you where she got her first set of clubs? No? From her nuns."

"Did she ask for them?"

"No. She had wanted to take up archery. She wanted a bow and arrow, and she begged them to make it a school sport, like boxing. She put up a good argument, Greek goddesses and things. But they thought, given her personality, it might not be a good idea to arm her. So they thought, oh, let's try golf. She was the only girl who took it up, but there were a couple of nuns who knew a few things about it."

"They were unusual? Or are all American Sisters like that?"

"They were unusual. They never knew about . . . us. No one did. We never . . . she and I . . . I never said a word to her, personally, until after she graduated. Until after she got the offer at the club in Arizona. I waited. She was so young. I was married. I married at eighteen. My wife—it was an arranged marriage. A business deal between our fathers. I was just a kid. It was . . . it was . . . you can't imagine what it's like to be in love when you're not supposed to be."

I sat still. I imagined my face as a mask with no expression. Another silence.

"Even in winter, Annmarie would be out on the course," he said. "Always secretly. I'd get there early and pretend I didn't know. Pretend that every move she made, I wasn't watching. She knew I was watching. She used to dip golf balls in cans of paint so she could see them in the snow. Eventually, the people who ran the club realized the talent she had, and let her play there whenever she wanted. In fact, she was given free lessons. But they never let her have member privileges. She couldn't go inside any of the buildings, not even to use the bathroom."

"She resented that, I imagine," I said.

"She didn't complain. She just wanted to be a golfer. Were you told that when Folcore was bombed, the only place they hit was the tower?"

"I was told, yes. You were there when Marcellina mentioned it. That tower has an interesting history, by the way."

He didn't care about that. "The tower," he said, "was where they made her a prisoner. They raped her. There. I've said it, too."

One more silence. I sensed the tension, all through him, of

holding back. A big force. A terrible, enormous containment, volcano-like: the silence of a volcano that was not erupting, but should have been.

"Signora Fantini!" came a voice from the other side of the door. Annunziata. "Signora Fantini and Tulli! Both of you! Come! We have lunch! Hurry before the partisans and my family devour everything!"

23

I FOUND HIM ALONE, away from the house and the tents, on the other side of a high pile of post-bombardment debris. The Galimbertis had been cleaning up. Possessions of theirs had been carefully, admirably stacked—ruined chairs, bed frames, cabinets, mattresses, boards, rugs, all sorts of things—like a bonfire waiting to be lit.

Everywhere one went in Italy, debris.

He was sitting on a rock near something that appeared to be another piece of junk. But as I went closer, I recognized it: the long-handled cart I'd had a ride in from the bottom of the Folcore hill. The Galimbertis must have decided to save it. It was upside down, with one wheel missing and one all right. A chunk of the base was gone. One end was badly splintered, in a strange, ragged way.

Going out to him from the house was like switching in a program from one opera to another. Even as the echoes of the song I'd just sung resounded in my head, I'd bear in on the next one, changing roles, tones, moods, in a way that seemed, to other people, effortless. At the start of every song, in the spotlight, it was necessary to believe no others had gone before.

No others. There he was, like the song at the end of the show, the best one, the one I'd been saving. The one I'd feared I'd never manage to get to.

No one was present to watch us. He could look at me. He didn't have to tell me he was pleased and relieved that I'd come. I could see it.

He was a changed man. It seemed that his normal process of aging had speeded up, turning his hair grayer. The eyebrows Beppi used to call caterpillars looked as if they'd thinned out considerably; the familiar black-and-gray tweed was still there, but not in the same measure. There, too, gray was winning. New wrinkles had come into his forehead and around his eyes. He wasn't wearing his jacket, but he'd not changed his clothes since San Guarino.

He sat with his shoulders hunched: a smaller Ugo, a new sight.

He was rumpled, soiled, a mess. His shirtsleeves were rolled up to the elbows, and little blotches of dry, faded blood were here and there on both forearms, blended into his skin, like an old man's brown age spots. It wasn't his own blood—just stains.

"Will you look at that wagon?" I said, as if I'd never seen it before. "It looks like a shark came all the way here, somehow, and took a bite from it."

"Maybe one did. I wouldn't be surprised if there are sharks in the Adriatic now. They're probably as hungry as I was. If the ladies hadn't given me a meal, I might have started eating that wood myself."

"How are you, Ugo?"

"It doesn't matter how I am."

He looked up at the sky, scanning it carefully, as if to assure himself that there weren't any planes. There was no sound, but he might have feared that a new, silent type of bomber was up there. Why couldn't I read his thoughts? Why couldn't people do that, with certain people?

The cart didn't give way when I sat down at the edge. I was grateful for that. I had never been alone with Ugo before.

He said, "Did you eat?"

"In the kitchen. There's only one bowl. People are taking turns with it."

"I had mine in a tin cup in the tent."

"It was good."

"It was delicious. I was worried about you, Lucia."

"I was worried about you, too. Isn't it strange that we're here at the house of gangsters? Did you know that a couple of Galimbertis tried to rob the restaurant?"

"Better to be a gangster than a Fascist. I trust them. They're all partisans now. The boys who were shot aren't doing very well. But they'll pull through. They're fantasizing about the places they're going to steal from when the war is over. It keeps them going. Aldo's is off-limits to them, now that they know us. They swore it."

"That's good to hear. So you're living like a bachelor these days. They told me Eliana went home to her mountain to see what damage there is, with all those houses on the side of a cliff."

"They're probably not there any longer. She's with Enzo. They want me to join them. I was just trying to decide what to do."

"Deciding between what?"

"A long list. They want me in Folcore. Here, they want me to stay. I've got plenty to handle in those tents. And some Americans showed up a little while ago and asked me to go with them to Forli to take a look at some GIs in bad shape. They haven't got a medic, and they can't find anyone else, and that's the place I'm inclined to choose. It's not far, and I'll be able to get supplies there. Some, I was able to acquire in Cassaromilia. I plundered the one physician's office. Do you know what happened there?"

I didn't want to talk about Cassaromilia. "Poor Forli," I said. "For the rest of time, all it will ever be is Mussolini's hometown."

"Maybe not. People will pretend they've forgotten all about him."

"What's happening, Ugo? I haven't had any news."

"Mussolini's being protected by Germans. No one is dead yet whom we would like to be dead. Remember how everyone thought, after the Americans landed, it would be only a matter of a couple of weeks, or a couple of months at most, that this war would keep going?"

"That seems like a long time ago."

"It's going to be a long time more. No one had stopped to consider just how badly the Germans in this country want this country. And more of them are coming all the time."

I didn't want to talk about the war. I wanted him to stop talking to me with this detachment, this aloofness. There was nothing coming from him that was personal in any way, not even the kind of personal that should have been there as Aldo's cousin, the only family Aldo had, not counting me and Beppi and Marcellina. Aldo and Ugo, like brothers, the two of them the only children of parents who had died. No one else, just Ugo. All those years.

And no questions from him—not, where have you been, how are you coping with your anxiety about Beppi, how is the pain from your bruises, why are you dressed as you are, how do you like wearing pants?

Just, did you eat? The one thing Italians ask each other all the time. As commonplace as breathing.

"Ugo," I said. "Something has happened to me. There's no song in my head."

"I thought you went on strike."

"Not inside. I kept singing to myself, sometimes out loud. But now there's nothing. I've run out of songs. When I try to listen to myself, inside, all I hear is silence."

I wondered if I sounded like a patient, describing symptoms.

"The songs will come back. I don't know when," he said.

"I was in the house with the Americans. Tullio and Annamaria. I know everything."

"She's had a hard time of it."

He had shut himself away. He could have been speaking to a colleague, a partisan, a Galimberti, anyone who'd happened by, Polpo, a farmer.

"Are you very worried about Beppi?" I said.

"Of course I am."

I thought, should I tell him what I know—the deaf girl, Assunta of the eggs, the chicken house, how I'd thought of it, how I'd been trying and trying to get there? I was on the verge of spilling out everything, but then I stopped myself.

I was too far from Ugo to touch him by simply reaching out an arm. I wanted to take hold of his shoulders and get rid of that slump of his. I wanted to put my hands on his face. I wanted to touch those new wrinkles and make them go away. And the wrinkles of his clothes, as well.

I felt warmed, steadied. It wasn't just the vegetable soup in my belly. I wanted to take him by the hand and say, oh, all the choices you have of where to go, don't be concerned about them, I'll make everything simple for you.

I wanted to do the same thing I'd done when I'd been here at the Galimbertis' before—the same thing with two differences. This time, Ugo would be with me, hurrying away furtively, and no one would know about it. Just stealing away, feeling sure of ourselves. Feeling youthful, even.

Oh—there would have to be another difference. I wouldn't choose the same route.

There'd be a new one, not near Cassaromilia, and, in fact, not anywhere near Mengo. Couldn't Beppi wait a little longer for me? In spite of a possible female Ballardini enchantment, wasn't he safe and not sitting in a corner alone, miserably, stinking of poultry, begging God to send his mother to him? He wasn't in danger! He wasn't a little boy!

There came rising up in my mind a picture of the map of Italy, which I could scrutinize as if planning an ordinary excursion, as if this were an unexpected holiday—a free day, no problems, no responsibilities, no danger, where shall we go?

The map held no starting point, since I didn't know my exact location. I thought only of the future. To Venice? South, down the coast, San Marino, Ancona? Tuscany? Florence? Arezzo? All the way down to Siena?

South was safer. North was *nazifascisti*. What about Umbria, tucked in the center? As if war were not everywhere. As if we could set out on foot and discover a waiting car, loaded with gas, key in the ignition. Not Ugo's car. It had been bombed in San Guarino. I remembered that.

"The car's coming, Lucia," Ugo said.

I'd been so carried away by my fantasy—imagining myself beside him, driving away, the window rolled down, fresh air pouring in, my head against his shoulder, no one else on the road, no tanks, no trucks, no roadblocks, no soldiers, neither dead nor alive, nothing in the trees but leaves and branches—it made sense to me that Ugo must have entered into it, must have known what I was thinking.

What he'd meant by a car was an ambulance. The one for Annmarie.

It was American, dusty, drab green, boxy, with an escort of a small squadron of jeeps coming up behind it, as slowly as a line of turtles, spitting exhaust smoke, one at a time in the narrow lane: four of them. A convoy. They were friendly, but it felt like an invasion.

"I don't suppose the American intelligence officer told you that Annamaria, as you call her, is important," said Ugo quietly, as if it were difficult for him to take me into his confidence, and he feared he might be eavesdropped on. As if the rock beneath him had ears. "Or, more specifically," he continued, "she has connections in high places. A general, here in Italy. It seems she taught him to play golf, some time ago, somewhere in the American desert."

His voice had fallen to almost a whisper. He seemed afraid.

Why, he's been injured, too, I thought. Dear God, he's not just exhausted. He's not just shutting himself away from me. He's been injured in his nerves, in his self, in his soul.

The war had got inside him. He'd never planned on being a war doctor.

"Ugo," I said. "You need . . . you need . . ."

"What, Lucia?" he said. "What is it?"

I didn't answer. I didn't know how to say what he needed. "Me," I wanted to say.

A change took place in his expression, softening the lines of his face. He was the old Ugo, restored in a flash, coming toward me, remembering everything. It was joy that lit up his eyes when he held out his arms to me.

Yes, joy. All it would have taken was one step to be in those arms.

A commotion rose from the tents and the house—a big welcome for the rescue party. I sprang to my feet and let out a gasping little cry. I felt as if I were ready to leap through the air, from the edge of a roof, or the top of a tree, or a cliff, like Eliana's family's house. Eliana! Eliana would have said I'd go to hell for loving Ugo. And so would he, for loving me back. But there was no Eliana. There wasn't any Aldo, either. There wasn't anyone else in all the world.

A shout! It came from behind Ugo, beyond the huge pile of debris, that bonfire-like stack, sitting there waiting for a match.

"Mama! Mama! Are you here? Where are you? Mama!"

Beppi burst into view like a wholly different kind of explosion.

Oh.

Nothing was wrong with him. He looked fit, glowing, in clothes I'd never seen before, a green wool vest, a plaid shirt opened jauntily at the neck. He was freshly shaven but his hair was long, too long, a little messy. He'd put on weight around his middle. How could anyone put on weight in this war? He looked as if he'd been very well fed. He looked as if he'd been eating a great deal of chicken.

Not a mark on him, not a bruise.

"Here I am! I got a ride in a jeep! With Americans! They let me drive it part of the way! Ugo! Mama! *Ciao!* Mama! Isn't that Roncuzzi's jacket? What are you doing back here?"

"Talking," said Ugo. "Talking!"

"I found you! Here I am!"

Throwing out his arms he took in both of us. He was big enough to do that.

"Don't cry, Mama. I knew it. I knew you would cry. Are you mad at me? You are! I knew it!"

24

MILK IN A COCONUT.

Sap in a tree.

A turtle.

A clam, a mussel.

Snails.

Life in wartime.

Like a song. A song called "List Of Things With Hard Exteriors." Try to keep adding to it. Try to make substitutes for singing.

"List Of Things With Hard Exteriors For Me To Think I Am Like."

In the hospital the whole world was the hospital. Days went by without distinction—a week, two, more, blending into each other in a shadowy way, without edges, all the same.

At first it felt strange to be outside of measured time. There wasn't a calendar in the room. I made an effort, for as long as I could, to keep myself aware of things like Sundays and Mondays and Tuesdays and all the rest, but I soon lost interest.

Somewhere the sun was rising, setting. An article of faith: dawns and dusks. The light in the hospital was pretty much always the same. Almost-twilight, all the time. There wasn't a clock.

It occurred to me a few times to try to find out what town I was in. I didn't know how to. Soon, it didn't matter. I'd never been this far south of Mengo, in this part of Romagna, but it was still Romagna and it was still the Adriatic, turquoise and shiny, with its same old shimmering horizon and languid waves.

On the outside, it was winter. Inside was more important than out.

I rarely left the room. It did not look out on the sea, which was just as well. The view was a war one. The beach was a graveyard of bombed boat hulls, all types of boats—sailboats, fishing boats, rowboats, big, small, medium, tiny, enormous—and past them, in a pretty little bowl of a harbor, with only half a pier still standing, were the remains of boats at anchor, bombed, not yet sunk, swaying gently.

I saw these things on the day I arrived. Along the shore, fish carcasses, dead crabs, dead birds. The smell was horrible, but the hospital didn't let it in. The hospital had a smell of its own.

The room was in the low-rate side of the hotel this used to be. Two beds, old and musty. A small table between them, a shelf on the wall, a closet of a bathroom. The only window looked out at the eyesore of a building next door, not bombed: a training school from the twenties, a four-story brick lump, a real monstrosity, like all the rest of them along the coast, like the very face of Mussolini.

No Fascists were in occupation, but it wasn't empty. Ropes were strung up for drying laundry; smoke from little braziers floated out from slightly raised windows.

Families were in there, all sorts of people, refugees from their own neighborhoods, bombed. Now and then a face would appear—a child, an old man, a teenage girl—all with sad, baffled eyes, waiting, watching. And yet the war did not end, did not end, did not end.

Better to keep the curtain closed. At least I knew the name of the hotel. Jewel of the Sea. There was nothing special about it. An artificial jewel, I decided, which the owners, whoever they were, had felt pretentious about. No hotel staff, naturally.

"I'm at the Jewel." It sounded nice. The sign had been taken down but the name was inscribed in tiles by the front door. It must have happened that visiting Fascist officers, on tours of school inspections, had stayed here. It seemed like that kind of place.

It was American territory now. Not like before, when I'd been the patient, at the *palazzo,* which had felt, in spite of all the soldiers, so Italian, with the soldier named Frank speaking my language.

One minute talking, and the next, not. One minute walking out of a doorway, and the next, not ever coming back. "I'm just going out for a smoke."

Frank *Agnello,* lamb, like what's born from a sheep. An Umbrian's stepson. I remembered him. So many ghosts.

He had said that Annmarie's nickname was *Mallo,* like a particular type of American candy. I tried it out, softly, gently, an Italian sort of word.

"Mallo? Explain how I can make you comfortable. Mallo? Will you speak to me?" No response. No recognition. Maybe she hated that nickname?

"Annamaria? Would you like to have me describe how Beppi found me? You would not believe what was happening to me when he appeared. Shall I tell you about it? Would you like to know where he'd been? Would you believe me if I told you there might be a wedding, when this shitty war is over? Not that I'm saying I'm fully thrilled about the choice for the bride, not that it matters to Beppi. You met him yourself, if briefly. You know what he's like, a real pighead, and I say that with complete objectivity."

Nothing, for so many days. Annmarie was too far away. There, right there, and far away. Even when she opened her eyes.

Near and far. Those two conditions could exist simultaneously. It was easy, like being outside of time.

"Mama, what are you doing?" Beppi had said, back at the Galimbertis' house.

He was dumbstruck with confusion. He knew I'd been fixated on finding him. "I just got here," he said, "and you're getting in that ambulance and *leaving*?"

I stayed calm. I had not had a choice. "I don't have a choice," I told him.

"Are you all right, Mama?"

"I am now. Because you are. But you should have told me about that truck."

"I'm *sorry*. Do you want me to say it a thousand times?"

"It would take you too long. Can't you see they're waiting for me?"

"If I told you ahead of time, you would have tried to stop me."

"Perhaps."

"You wouldn't have believed I'd pull it off."

"I'd believe it!"

"You wouldn't. You'd think I'd get everything wrong, and end up exploding nothing except myself."

"Well, it was your first time. Papa would have been proud of you."

"Oh, I know."

I held him in my arms. My boy. My cheek was pressed against his. I was nuzzling him, and filling myself with the old familiar smell of him, the feel of him. I had this. I truly did. That sweet, strong, wonderful thing, unbombed, unwrecked, unchanged: the thing of being a mother. To know he was all right was like the difference between a tree that's been torn from the ground, and whirls madly about in a windstorm, and a tree standing still, rooted as deeply as roots can go.

My roots, I thought. Then I pushed him away from me. "Are you going to tell me where you've been?"

"Hiding."

"Hiding where?"

A sigh. A droopy, woebegone look, then an earnest attempt to change the subject.

"I noticed Polpo," he said, as if this were the most important thing in the world. "I was wondering, why is he here?"

"Ask Marcellina. Were you with a girl, Beppi?"

"I don't want to answer that."

"It's answer enough. All of a sudden, you're mysterious? You were never any good at keeping secrets. Your whole life, you were just like a spaghetti strainer. You could never keep a thing to yourself, and suddenly, you're different? Do you expect me to think it's normal you don't tell me things?"

"Don't be mad at me."

"This girl you were with, do I know her?"

"You might. Maybe. A little bit. How can I know if you know someone, or you don't? How can I answer that question?"

"You just did. You were in Mengo all this time?"

His eyes went wide with surprise.

"Mama! You thought I was in Mengo, when they were looking for me in every corner? Every rock, they turned over. Honestly, did you think that? Where exactly? At someone's house, did you think? You reached a conclusion, I can tell. I'm willing to bet almost anything on that. Whose house? The house of a girl I might marry? A girl you think is unsuitable, but if you think so, there's a very good chance I don't agree with you?"

"Unsuitable for what reason?" I said.

"Unsuitable for no reason at all, as far as I'm concerned, Mama. Unsuitable if the only person who thinks so is yourself."

I looked at the way his cheeks were flushing up. That pinkness told me everything. What was it going to look like to other people, a son of a singer with a deaf wife?

Assunta and Cenzo Ballardini, I reminded myself, had normal ears. It didn't seem to be an inherited condition.

"This girl you're being so forthcoming about," I said, "would she happen to have someone in her immediate family who's a waiter?"

"Maybe."

"Would he know about you and this girl?"

"No. I mean, the waiters haven't been home in a long while, Mama. They're all too busy being partisans."

Well, I couldn't be mad at Cenzo Ballardini. I felt bad that I'd thought of him as a son of a bitch. I said, "This girl, do I know her mother?"

"Maybe."

"They took care of you?"

"You can tell that with your own eyes."

"Are you going to go back there soon?"

"I don't know. I'm back in the war now. Pia feels that—"

He'd blurted out the name without wanting to, as though it wouldn't behave itself, wouldn't stay tucked away. It seemed to have come out of him like a bubble, iridescent and sparkly and lovely: Pia!

How did they communicate with each other anyway?

Beppi recomposed himself. Now a new topic. "Germans

were at our house, Mama. They may be there still. First the restaurant, then the house. We're exiles."

"We're alive."

"The American girl, is she going to die?"

"Ugo says no."

"She doesn't look good."

"No one looks good. Only you do. Are you in love, Beppi? Are you *engaged*?"

"Do I have to tell you everything? I can't tell you everything! Not now! I'll tell you everything when I'm ready and I'm not ready! You've got to leave! I can't believe you'd leave when I just arrived! They're waiting for you! You've got to get into the ambulance!"

Then I was kissing him, his cheeks, his forehead as he bowed his head to me, blessing-like.

And I was caught in a rush of last-minute instructions, like bubbles of my own, but not about love, not about deafness, not about anything there was to wait for, to postpone, to talk about later. It was all about the present, practicalities, listen to me, Beppi, go and have a good talk with Marcellina. Try to get along with Cherubino. Try *hard*. Welcome Etto Renzetti to the squad. You know he always liked you. Remember he once called you Jesus? Make sure you keep the squad together in one place, because everyone goes crazy when they don't know where everyone is. Go out of your way to pay a visit to Carmella and the children. Be careful with guns. Don't go off on your own to blow up things. Once was enough! Don't let Nizarro get up until he's fully recovered. If he tells you his injuries are minor, don't believe him.

He trotted after the ambulance for a while, waving. But he quickly ran out of breath. He hadn't yet discovered that everyone was talking about him, that a *tarantella*-like song was being made for him, that he had entered the realm of a legend—good Christ, I thought, I'll never hear the end of it, not for all the rest of my life: Mama, Mama, I'm a hero, I'm a legend, I'm a hero, I'm a legend, and I'm in love with a girl with a chicken house and there's a *song* about me, and I don't give a damn that she'll never be able to hear it, and neither should you, so *there.*

And here I was. Soft inside, hard outside.

Was staying still and holding on a very different thing from marching all those miles, with my feet in such bad condition?

It was a very different thing indeed. It was harder.

Ugo. "Don't become hard inside. I will come to you. Don't let this war inside you, now that you've excised it from me. The moment I held out my hands to you, before Beppi interrupted us, you excised it. It was that simple. And now you're leaving so quickly. Goodbye, but only for now. She's still my patient. I have an interest, professionally. I'm wanted there by those Americans. You know they're short on help. I can help. After Forli, after finishing here in the tents, after a very short trip to Eliana's mountain. My list of things to do, in that order. I was never in a hotel converted to a hospital before. I'm interested in how they've managed it. Of course, I'm not sure I can trust anyone else to do, you know, the procedure."

"Procedure," I'd repeated, like a stupid echo.

"Yes. If there needs to be one, I'd prefer to take care of it myself. She deserves that. You look surprised. Lucia, I'm a doctor. Did you forget that? Do you think there haven't been women in need of procedures? I will come, no matter what. Eliana will be staying where she is. Until the war ends. I'm certain of that. I don't think she's lost her faith, and it's not because a priest is with her, to keep it shored up. She's more religious than Enzo anyway. Her family took a terrible beating, but I don't think she's ready to give up on God. Not like us."

"Maybe she'll enter a convent, Ugo. A cloistered one."

"This isn't a time to be joking."

"I wasn't."

People were watching. Galimbertis, Marcellina, Beppi, partisans poking their heads out of the tents, farmers, a big crowd. Don't let the truth show. Be careful. Talk softly. No kiss goodbye, not even a family-style kiss in his role as cousin-in-law of the widow.

"I will come to you." A decision, hard. Said in a whisper, but hard. "No one will know, not even Beppi. Everyone on the squad is still mad at him, but it won't last. If he doesn't want to talk about where he's been, that's all right with me. I think we should leave him alone about that. But I'm sure he'll tell his friends. I'm sure he'll be bragging his head off."

An excision. He felt I'd gone inside him. As simple as that. He would have thought so before if he'd ever looked at me. It shouldn't have taken so long.

As if I were his surgeon. Until the war ends. Was I supposed to hope it never would, to be with him?

Hard inside was Fascist. Harder than bone, harder than rock, harder than shells, harder than metal. That was always their secret. As if their souls had been fossilized.

"Don't become a fossil," said Ugo. "Do that for me."

Hold on for now. Think of things.

Things to be like. It wasn't a song, not really. Just another list.

A scallop.

A lobster.

A crab.

A head in a helmet.

Arms in plaster.

Sand in a bucket.

A cushion in a car.

Food in a can.

Winter.

A declaration of love in a war.

"My reward," I said to myself, about Ugo. "My reward for staying alive." I couldn't go to hell for loving him because there wasn't a hell to go to, not outside of this world.

Inevitably, I spoke to my husband.

"Aldo, I'm at the Jewel," I said. "Isn't that a nice name? It's an Italian hotel, but American now. In a way, it seems I got to America after all. America in our country. What do you think of that? Your old dream. It's not how you meant it, but still."

For a while I talked to him often, avoiding the subject of Ugo. I imagined Aldo in a melodramatic way: sulking, hurt, growling, furious, aligning himself with Eliana. "Aldo, give me some credit. I never betrayed you when you were alive."

He wouldn't want me to be lonely. He must have been placing his bets on Etto. Were the chairs at home in our kitchen, including his own, made at Etto's factory? What about the table? I couldn't remember. Probably.

"Aldo, a long time ago, I made up a song about Eliana and her basket of herbs. I feel bad about that now. If you want to know if I feel guilty, I do, but only about that. Only that little song. I enjoyed it very much when I composed it, though."

I couldn't blame Aldo for his soft spot toward Eliana and her rugged ways, her faith in God, her hair coiled up at the back of her head, her quietness, her goodness, her lack of bitterness because things had not worked out the way she wanted, because her womb had let her down, because she couldn't bear a child.

Don't say "child." Don't say "bear." It's not the same thing, what they did to her.

"Aldo, everyone says Ugo's the best physician in Italy. Did you know that in the past he performed a certain procedure on some of his women patients? You probably knew that. He probably confided things like that to you."

Aldo would have hated it here. There wasn't much to be impressed with in this hotel-hospital America. Green, khaki. A land without color. Green and khaki weren't colors. The walls were neuter, a sort of dirty white. The blankets, which had belonged to the hotel, not the army, were light brown. The floor tiles were dirty-white and gray. The bricks of the building next door were the same as dried-up shit.

Annmarie's in-bed attire was white sheets, plaster, pale skin. The bluish tinge of bruises didn't count. Neither did the areas where dressings and bandages were regularly applied. Those weren't colors. They were aberrations.

Some progress was made. It wasn't necessary to despair. She started talking. Whispers, what is happening to me, I don't feel well, why are you fussing with me, why are you making me eat, why are you giving me juice? I don't want it, it hurts, I'm going back to sleep now, leave me alone, go away.

She only spoke English in her sleep. Dream murmurings. Nightmare murmurings. Awake, she spoke Italian. She knew where she was. That was something.

"Go with her," the American had said, unexpectedly.

Enrico. Mr. Intelligence Officer. Mr. Intelligence Officer, *sir.* The soldiers who'd turned up at the Galimbertis' with the ambulance had called him sir. He had touched me on the shoulder, like a comrade.

An offer. A deal. "Stay with her. I know you care about her. She can trust you. I know you brokered guns for that squad of yours, which you can't do any longer, since even the black market's not functioning. I'll give them all the guns they want.

You're not required in that particular department. I beg you. It's not as if I'm asking you to cancel singing engagements. You see how it is. Things are not looking good for her. We're worried about internal injuries, besides the one I already told you about. I have access to many resources. Let's make a deal. Tell me what you want."

Tom Tully. It felt better to think of him with his American name.

So sure of himself. Everything held inside, in check. A volcano not erupting. Maybe he'd learned to be that way in America, at the golf club. Maybe his officer's training had only refined it. Would she ever play golf again? Win more championships? Throw more punches at cheaters? Would she? Would she? Would she?

"Tell me what I can do," he said, looking at me directly, unblinkingly. "I'll arrange anything you want, to express my gratitude to you. It's a lot I'm asking for. Leave your son, your squad. Or tell me how to pay this debt, if that's how you want to think of it."

"Let me remind you, the debt is mine to pay. To her."

"All the same, tell me what you want."

I didn't have to look for Beppi anymore. That didn't need to be the thing. "Find Mussolini and get rid of him" didn't need to be it, either. Someone was probably already going about that. "Fill my plate at every meal, and put everything you blew up back together again" was what a child would have said. "Make Eliana leave Ugo, as if God had instructed her to do so" was not a possibility. "Cure the chicken girl's deafness before she has my grandchildren, just to make sure" could not be it, either. "Make me want to sing" was out of the question. How could he take the silence out of my head?

"Exterminate my restaurant," I said. "When that's been accomplished, exterminate my house."

He knew what I meant. "That's a big order. There's an awfully big infestation. It might take a while."

"I've got a while."

"You're a courageous woman. It's an honor to know you."

"I'm tired. I'm empty. I'm falling apart. I'm in pieces. I feel I'm inside a shell, which may be smashed apart at any moment."

"You're mistaken. Cowards don't have shells."

Then a handshake, firm, hard. He thought I was *brave*?

Maybe I could pretend, like Aldo saying there was money in our bank account when there wasn't. Bluff like Aldo! Remember how, when the first *trattoria* was getting by just fine, he'd got those plans for a new one, twice its size, into his head. And then a huge leap of faith, and much more bluffing, from the second *trattoria* to the restaurant. A restaurant with as many seats as a midsize theater. For me.

Always, graciousness. I hadn't lost that.

I was able to put up a good show for the doctors, all American, coming and going, mostly incomprehensibly. The arms, set. Plaster from top to bottom, including the wrists, right up to the knuckles, both hands. A terrible paleness in the fingers and thumbs.

Worry about circulation, among other things. The blood was not flowing well, not only in the arms. The legs, too. Like a plumbing problem. We're fixing that. We're trying and we won't give up.

Gestures. A lot can be said without words. Weary military doctors, needing baths, not getting them. Keep her still.

"Aldo?"

Sometimes when I closed my eyes to picture him, all I saw

was just that, a picture, like a photo of him I'd happened upon, faded and crumpled, at the bottom of a box.

"Aldo, Beppi wouldn't come right out and tell me where he was. Oh, sooner or later, he will, but he's mad at me for figuring it out. Did you think, before, I was crazy to tell myself he was in that chicken house? Granted, I was wrong about my feeling that they were holding him there against his will. I admit that."

It began to happen that when I tried to remember the sound of Aldo's voice, it wasn't there. It was like coming to the end of a record, with the phonograph needle scratching and scratching on a soundless disc.

Then at last, his silence felt like something normal. An empty record, going around and around. I was thankful for that.

The ordinary, necessary silence of the dead.

And then a suitcase. Brought in by a young American soldier in *khaki*. He hadn't spoken. He'd only made gestures to let me know I was the one it was meant for.

The suitcase contained three wool skirts—a brown one, a gray one, and a black-and-brown plaid. And four blouses, all white, and underwear, including a bra that was exactly my size; four pairs of wool stockings, all gray; a thickly knitted brown cardigan sweater, and two vests, one gray, one tan. Everything fit. They were definitely not Italian clothes.

On my feet, the boots.

Soon I was picking up more English. New phrases. One of them was *vee-eye-pee,* which was written in three letters of the alphabet, V, I, P.

There'd been a woman soldier who sat for a while at the side of the bed, looking at Annmarie. No, not just a soldier—some kind of counselor. Wanting to have a discussion. She was about

Annmarie's age. She patted the plaster arm casts as if the skin beneath could feel it.

Unlike all the Americans in this place, that woman soldier knew a bit of Italian. *"Non bene. Molto non bene."* A smile for me, a hopeful look. She wanted so much to talk. Probably no one had told her that the patient was being kept sedated. Soon would come the medical procedure.

VIP. She'd squatted down to the floor, writing the letters in the talcum powder a nurse had spilled—an unfamiliar nurse, very young, new to war. It had been time for fresh dressings and a bed bath, which had not immediately happened. She dropped everything she'd carried in, poor girl. All dry things, though. Powder, lotion, fresh bandages, a hairbrush, a sponge. When she picked up those fallen things, her hands had been badly shaking. I had already pulled back the bedsheet, had already removed last night's wrappings, and thus had exposed the whole of Annmarie's body.

Maybe in American nursing schools they didn't prepare girls for this sort of thing. Or maybe there wasn't a chart, filled out in detail, to be looked at ahead of time. The hospital was a busy place, packed, understaffed. Or maybe American nurses were only instructed about injuries to men. An educational insight. Women get hurt in war, too.

Really look.

That long, long body, white, soft and hard, still an athlete's. The bed was just long enough so that her feet didn't dangle off the end. The breasts had been beaten, the belly, the thighs, the shoulders. The areas requiring dressings were those where the skin had been compromised, had been transformed to sores, near the hips, at the top and the side of one breast, and just above one knee. They weren't burns. They were lashings.

Both knees were badly swollen. One knee was no longer like a knee at all: just a strangely smooth thing without bones, somewhat octopus-like; the similarity was striking. In the first week, they came and took her to surgery. Surgery, not procedure. Two different things.

Now there were scars on both sides of that knee where stitches had been. It still looked as if it belonged deep down in the sea, but the size was considerably smaller. At the ankles, there were more sores, but those had already started scabbing.

No damage had been done to the other side of her. Just the front. Just.

There weren't bedsores, and there weren't going to be. She was turned to one side or the other as part of the daily regimen. A tricky thing with the arm casts, but manageable.

Bedpans, cleanings. Massaging the fingers. It was always good to rub lotion on the back, the buttocks, the backs of the legs, unhurt.

Her hair had grown longer. It was easier to brush it, now that the head bruises had healed, but sometimes there were tangles, which needed to be undone carefully. Little burr-like knots would form at the back of her head from a particular version of nighttime tossing and turning.

In the next bed, I was awakened not only by the regular mutterings of Annmarie's English sleep talk but also by a humming-like moaning. I'd look over and see her turning her head on the pillow from side to side, side to side, side to side. And up and down, up and down, up and down.

Sometimes it only took a minute or so to make the motions cease: my hands on either side of Annmarie's face, palms flat. Sometimes it took a lot longer.

"Beppi had nightmares all his childhood," I told her. "I never knew what he saw in those dreams, because he never remembered. But with you, I know. You're imagining yourself on your golf course, aren't you, Annamaria? In the American desert? In your exhibitions? In your colorful clothes?"

As if turning her head from side to side was saying "no" to a bad shot, and up and down was saying "yes" to a good one.

The talcum powder was American, not masculine, not military: a scent of something vaguely flowery. Annmarie liked to have it patted on her back and her face, places it didn't hurt to be patted. And sprinkled inside the casts. It must have reminded her of home, of something familiar.

It was fortunate that she didn't know about the spill on the floor. The waste would have upset her. I'd meant to clean it up. There hadn't been an opportunity. In came the woman soldier. There'd been just time to dart between her and the bed to pull the sheet up, with the arms on the outside.

The letters in the powder were like letters in beach sand. The woman soldier pointed to them, then to Annmarie. "*Molto importante persona,* vee-eye-pee. In America. *Golf-o.*"

"Golf," I said. I didn't bother with trying to find a way to explain that *golfo* was a gulf.

Another pointing, this time to the skirt and blouse and vest and cardigan and two pairs of stockings I was wearing. Then pointing to the suitcase, then the rest of my new wardrobe, folded up on the one shelf.

"From Ireland," said the woman soldier. "Irish. *Da*—oh, hell, what's the word for it?—*Irlandesi. Isole verde.* Leprechauns! See, Americans were in *Irlandesi.* They had orders to come here. *Vieni qui.* Airmen. *Pi-lot-o. Air-o-plane-o. Il gen-er-al-o* arranged these clothes for you. Special! *Da Irlandesi!* Her friend the general. *Il gen-er-al-o essere molto molto buono amico di golf-o. Capisce-me? Essere bizarr-o, molto strange-o, Irlandesi, capisce?*"

I nodded as energetically as I could. But I didn't care where the clothes had come from—Ireland, or the moon.

"Vee-eye-pee," I said.

"Bambino!" she said, pointing now to Annmarie. "Poor, poor lady. Now *bambino,* but soon, *non bambino.* Germans! *Crim-in-al-i!* Evil!" She covered her face with her hands, started sobbing, and rushed away, slipping on that powder and nearly falling.

When the new nurse returned, tight-lipped, with a broom, I explained with gestures that I'd made a decision. Just because I'd had no training didn't mean I couldn't do nursing. From now on I'd take care of the bathing and the dressings myself. Seeing as how I was here anyway.

Suddenly in the doorway one morning there appeared a stranger: an Italian-speaking American. A boy in a naval uniform, blue. A red badge was on his sleeve. He couldn't have been more than eighteen. Dark, long-nosed, big eyes like dark marbles, flecked with gold, like tiny bits of sunlight. His smooth young face was pink—ruddy from outside, from the cold.

Unfortunately he only had a minute. He had to rush back to his ship. "Are you Signora Fantini?"

"I am."

"Merry Christmas, even though it was four days ago. And best wishes for the coming New Year, with the hope, in spite of the odds against it, the new will be better than this one."

I hadn't known it was Christmas, or that the year was about to change. It didn't feel strange to be indifferent to those things.

What felt strange was that my eyes were looking at colors. Red, blue, pink, bits of sun. Colors!

"I have a message for you," he said.

First a gift, pulled out from behind his back. He'd been standing there with his hands behind his back. In one hand, his cap, white. In the other, a bottle. It took me a moment to decide if I ought to accept it. Lambrusco.

"This is from whom?"

"He said to tell you, from Tullio. He said to tell you, your cousin the doctor is on his way. He said to tell you, your squad is doing fine. He said to tell you, he'll be arriving himself in about a week. He said to tell you, he doesn't think you should worry any longer about the problem of the infestation of your property."

Before turning crisply to hurry away, he put on his cap and saluted me, sharply.

Try to feel normal.

Try to feel the way one should, upon receiving good news.

Try to believe that the coldness inside was only normal winter cold.

Try to believe that instead of sand in my throat, there was only a touch of frost, no different from the stuff that filigreed every window in Italy, including the one in this room, with lacy, pretty white swirls. I didn't have to raise the curtain to know that there was more frost on that window than glass.

Lucia, time to go on. You look so beautiful tonight. I could hear them—Beppi, Nizarro, Geppo, Lido, Zoli, Nomad, all of them, and the cooks, too, gathered by the kitchen door, growling at each other, arguing over the best spots. On would come the spotlight like a star. Inside me, a voice.

Don't let this be the day you leave me.

Always a talk with it. Always in a tone of supplication. Was that true?

Had I been wrong about that, like being wrong about the deaf girl and her mother, holding Beppi against his will? He'd gone there of his own free will, all right.

Do *not* let this be the day you leave me.

Maybe it had never been a prayerful sort of thing. Maybe it had never been weak of me. Funny how I'd always thought so. Maybe it had been more of a command, all along.

"Annamaria, good morning," I'm saying, leaning down to her.

I can do this. The regular routine, the right motions, like putting on the right dress, like walking the right way to the place at the front of restaurant all eyes would turn to.

"Soon you'll be going home. Ar-ee-zo-na! Do I pronounce it correctly?" Stroking her hair. Not the time now to look for snarls.

The eyelids slowly open. It's still a shock to watch those eyes try gamely to make sense of what they're looking at, then give up, like Cesare trying to sing to the people still alive in Cassaromilia.

"Annamaria, look, it's me, Lucia. Look at me. Here I am, same as always."

"I want to go back to sleep."

"You will, later on. Keep your eyes open. If you shut them, I'll pry them open myself, with my own fingers!"

"Don't yell at me."

"I won't, if you do as I say. Now your washing-up and some powder. Soon they'll give you something for a good, sweet sleep, and then you'll wake up again. Waking up won't be hard. You'll see. Ugo, do you remember Ugo? Of course you do. Soon he'll be here. He's going to take care of you, and then we'll have a celebration. We have some very nice wine. Do you see that bottle on the shelf, with my clothes from Ireland? From Ireland, isn't that *bizarr-o*? That bottle's for us. It's just a little procedure. You won't feel a thing, and then we'll have a nice talk about how it will feel for you to go home and win more trophies. Win! Isn't that a good word? You can tell me all about your golf. Tell me what it's like to hit the little white ball into the hole. Everything's going to be all right. All the news is good. Listen to me. After Ugo comes, your sweetheart will come also. *Tom.* Without his wife. There's no wife! Isn't that something to look forward to? Where I'm standing right now is where he'll be. That's a promise. I know what I'm talking about! A voice in my heart explains everything! Would you like a song? As it happens, I know one about this very type of wine. Shall I sing it to you? I'm a little out of practice, but I'll try."

A NOTE ABOUT THE AUTHOR

Ellen Cooney is the author of six previous novels. Her short fiction has appeared in *The New Yorker, The Literary Review, Glimmer Train,* and many other publications. The recipient of fellowships from the Massachusetts Artists Foundation and the National Endowment for the Arts, she taught creative writing at Boston College, MIT, Harvard, and the University of Maine. She was a lifelong resident of Massachusetts and now lives in midcoast Maine.

A NOTE ON THE TYPE

This book was set in Monotype Dante, a typeface designed by Giovanni Mardersteig (1892–1977). Conceived as a private type for the Officina Bodoni in Verona, Italy, Dante was originally cut only for hand composition by Charles Malin, the famous Parisian punch cutter, between 1946 and 1952. Its first use was in an edition of Boccaccio's *Trattatello in laude di Dante* that appeared in 1954. The Monotype Corporation's version of Dante followed in 1957. Although modeled on the Aldine type used for Pietro Cardinal Bembo's treatise *De Aetna* in 1495, Dante is a thoroughly modern interpretation of the venerable face.

Composed by Creative Graphics,
Allentown, Pennsylvania
Printed and bound by R. R. Donnelley,
Harrisonburg, Virginia
Designed by Virginia Tan